Ripping

Ripping Publishing
PO Box 286
Epsom, Surrey,
England KT19 9YG

Published by Ripping Publishing

First Edition Printed 1996

ISBN 1 899884 02 5

Printed by Cox & Wyman Ltd, Reading

THE AUTHOR

Warren James Palmer was born in Solihull, England in 1965. A place he describes as *'Suburbia at it's least desirable, particularly the multi-complex cinema and plastic pubs'*. He grew up with an obsession for flying, photography and an allergy to punks and heavy metal. At the age of eighteen he fled to London to seek fame and fortune in the traditional manner. For the past ten years he has worked as a photographer and designer for no particular reason other than it seemed like a good idea at the time.

Minds of the Empire was his first self-published novel which confounded everybody by making to the top of the Forbidden Planet SF charts in August 95. His second book was a non-fiction title called the *'Battle of Britain Memorial Flight'*. This book was surrounded by controversy when the commanding officer of the RAF Memorial Flight was quoted as having said a few words more than he should have. For a period Warren was paranoid that the book would be banned by the Ministry of Defence and remembers the launch party as, 'The most bizarre evening of his life.'

Dominator is his second novel and writing it was the most fun Warren had in a very long time.

Warren lives in Surrey with his girlfriend, who like himself is an obsessive glider pilot. When asked about the future he again replied 'I'd rather be flying.'

ACKNOWLEDGEMENTS

Thanks to all those readers who sent me letters of congratulation! There's nothing more heartening than getting a bit of fan mail in the same post as a depressing letter from the bank! Please keep the letters rolling in!

Heart felt thanks to the Roy, Louise and Jane who made sure that Moss and the gang kept true to their characters.

Thanks also to everyone at MDL.

A WORD IN YOUR OTHER EAR

Well here it is! I know a lot of you have been waiting for the sequel for a long time—soz about that—but I finished it eventually! Following the tradition of *Minds of the Empire* this book is once more nothing but pure adventure, a 'Ripping Yarn'. If you take it more seriously than that then I can recommend a good doctor.

Thanks to everyone for supporting *Minds of the Empire*; there's nothing better than receiving letters of appreciation. They're far more preferable than all those red bills I usually get on my doormat! Please keep sending me your thoughts. In fact, I'm keen to expand the number of adventures Moss and his gang get up to, so if anyone has some thoughts on what the team should doing in the future, I'd love to hear them.

I've done my best to spoll clock this book as I know *Minds of the Empire* had a lot of miscakes—no promises that you won't find more though. But hey! What's a few cockk-upps between friends? If you're into dotting the I's and crossing the T's, you have my sympathies.

At the bottom of this page is my E-mail address for anybody who wants to hurl abuse in my general direction. It would be nice to get some feedback from you, the reader. Ripping publishing in its first year has become more than just a book production line. It represents anyone who believes life is too short *not* to fill it to the brim with adventure! Exactly what Ripping evolves into in the future is down to you—I'm just the helmsman. So let me know where *you* want us to steer!

Grab a beer, put your feet up and enjoy another Ripping story.

Cheers

Warren James Palmer

100612.3072@compuserve.com.uk

FOR LOUISE — IT WAS STILL WORTH IT!

FOR MY FLYING CHUMS AT LASHAM
— FARMER PALMER DOES IT AGAIN!

FOR ANYBODY WHO STILL CAN'T ANSWER
THAT ONE QUESTION — WHY?

DOMINATOR

BOOK TWO

UNITED NATIONS/WORLD DEFENCE FORCE

By the year 2020 the United Nations World Defence Force was the single largest armed force on the planet Earth. The spread of multinational corporations and the removal of all trading barriers across the planet had led to a period of economic and political stability. The wars of the 20th century which were largely a result of disputes over political boundaries and the distribution of raw materials, were a thing of the past.

This world wide political stability was reinforced by the WDF network of orbital laser defence platforms. These defence platforms were able to track and destroy tanks, aircraft and missiles anywhere on the planet regardless of weather. It was this orbital defence network that finally put an end to territorial disputes.

Unfortunately the laser platforms were no defence to the Dyason invasion of March 15th 2025.

IMPERIAL DYASON INVASION OF EARTH

In a blitzkrieg attack the 'Dome' ships of the Imperial navy destroyed all the WDF space platforms in the first few minutes of the war along with all military communication and navigation satellites.

Within a few short weeks the United Nations were forced to capitulate. Given complete control of the 'high ground' that was space, the Dyason dropped asteroids on the cities of Earth, pulverising them and killing millions. The United Nations leader Jean Paul Ricard officially surrendered and ordered the disbandment of the WDF on April 3rd 2025.

However, as the Dyason occupation forces set about enslaving humanity not all the members of the WDF were happy to hand over their weapons and spend the rest of their lives in prison camps.

Resistance units were formed across the planet and began hit and run operations against the Dyason occupation forces. One of these units was run by ex-WDF pilot Paul Jenson.

Together with his sidekick Han Sandpiper, Squadron Leader Jenson set about unifying the various factions of the resistance under one command. However, it wasn't until nearly two years after the invasion that the resistance became an effective fighting force.

IMPERIAL DOME CRUISERS

Built from very heavy armoured plating, the vessels used in the invasion of Earth by the Imperial Navy did not possess hyperspace drive. They relied on the worm-hole in the space time continuum for passage from Dyason to Earth. The worm-hole that connected the two star-systems allowed passage between the Dyason home-world and Earth in a reasonable period of time.

When the worm-hole became unstable in 2027 the Imperial Navy attempted to use human telepaths to artificially open up new worm-holes. The results of these experiments were catastrophic.

The Dome vessels were crude but efficient in construction. Their method of propulsion was unique if hazardous. Small pellets of radioactive material were released in thermonuclear explosions beneath the massive base plates of the cruisers which resulted in gargantuan thrust.

The Imperial fleet was largely destroyed in the final conflict with Excalibur in the battle for liberation.

GULAG

The cloned son of the Emperor Nimue, Gulag was a mentally unstable psychopath. He was responsible for building the fortified wall around the city of London and for the genocide within that city's ghetto's.

Gulag was the only known example of a Dyason telepath at that time. He was killed in a mental battle with Moss Pendragon onboard Excalibur during the battle of liberation.

MOSS PENDRAGON

Born Moss Paterson in London in 2011 his family were killed during the occupation by Security Leader Gulag. Moss survived in the ghetto's of London by using his emerging Paranormal talents to steal food and supplies from the Dyason occupied West End of London.

He became a member of the resistance and was instrumental in resurrecting Excalibur from caverns buried deep below the ancient monument of Stonehenge. His actions during the occupation and the battle of liberation made him a worldwide hero.

EXCALIBUR

Discovered in caverns below Stonehenge, the starship Excalibur was built by an unknown ancient race several millennia before humans walked across the surface of the Earth.

Excalibur was restored to space-worthiness by Moss, Sqn Ldr Jenson, Flt lt Sandpiper, Myrddin and the Brabazon twins. The ship was then launched against the Imperial fleet during the battle for liberation.

The data-banks onboard Excalibur later allowed the WDF to develop hyperspace drive and immediately advanced human technology by several hundred years.

MYRDDIN

Born several centuries before Christ, Myrddin has been known by many names during his lifetime. Merlin is the most common of these names. His little understood Paranormal powers stop him from ageing and he has been instrumental in the development of many human civilisations.

Moss Pendragon is believed to have been a direct-line descendent of Myrddin, although there is no proof of this. He was responsible for leading the young Moss to the caverns below Stonehenge.

NIMUE

The twin sister of Myrddin. Nimue was forced into another space-time continuum by Myrddin after the battle that killed King Arthur in ancient England. She later emerged on the planet Dyason and set about creating an empire under the puppet king Alorne. Nimue kept her identity secret from the people of Dyason. The Imperial invasion of Earth was her revenge for being expelled from her home-world by Myrddin.

Given the title Envoy, Nimue created Gulag from an experimental cloning technique.

LUKE AND JOSH BRABAZON

Telepathic twins and scientists. Luke Brabazon was forced to work on the Dyason experiments into artificially creating worm-holes by telepathic means. Josh Brabazon was instrumental in making Excalibur space-worthy.

Luke Brabazon was killed by Gulag during the battle of liberation.

JENNIFER HAMILTON-SMITH

Later to become the consort of Moss Pendragon, Jennifer was rescued by him from a slave-labour factory building prototype Imperial space cruisers. A competent telepath she fought with the resistance in the battle of liberation and later joined the World Defence Force.

CHAPTER ONE

The heat shimmered in waves over the desert making the image in the binoculars swim in and out of focus. She shifted her position so that she lay more comfortably behind the rocks, pulling the hood of her robe over the crown of her hairless scalp to protect it from the blazing sun. The floor of the desert was made up of millions of minute glass beads that mercilessly reflected and magnified the heat. The glass and the bleached ruins she now hid behind were all that were left of a once green and prosperous land after it had been nuked a few times.

With the patience of a wasteland nomad she resigned herself to being uncomfortable, ignored the open sores on her mutated skin and concentrated on the strange machine sitting on the dried lake bed below her.

Over recent months she had spent many hours in this uncomfortable spot, ever since the troops had arrived to re-open the old launch site. There had been several of these strange machines brought to this place, all of them the same shape. Each was about one hundred metres long and thirty at its widest point. The somewhat box-like body tapered to a heavily glazed nose, while the large rear stabilisers bled into stub wings that supported two large pods and intakes at their tips. The black diamond and red circle of the Imperial forces were emblazoned across the wing surfaces.

Two of these machines had blown apart in a blaze of spectacular pyrotechnics in recent weeks, but this third prototype so far had remained intact, at least until now. Today there was a lot of activity around the field, activity that led her to believe they were going make another attempt at launching the contraption. Neehmad clicked on the image recorder built into the binoculars, and taped the activity.

A crew bus drove up to the vessel, carefully avoiding the connected umbilical cables, and stopped just in front of the glazed needle nose. Eight men climbed out of the bus, moving awkwardly under the weight of their pressure suits, walked to the small boarding ladder and climbed aboard. Once aboard one of the masked and suited groundcrew closed and sealed the hatch, then the umbilical support cables were removed and stowed away. The groundcrew boarded the bus with its large low pressure desert wheels, and drove to the safety of concrete bunkers sited half a klick away.

Neehmad crouched lower behind the ruins. Although the research centre was more than a klick away, she had nearly been hit by the flying debris of the two previous crafts' disintegration, and had no wish to be the target of shrapnel again. However, it was her duty to record the movements of the Imperial Navy, so she made sure that the vid-binoculars were trained on the latest machine.

For several minutes nothing happened at all. Then, almost imperceptibly at first, came the sound of a low-pitched whine, increasing in volume and pitch, like the sound of an aircraft's turbine spooling up The whine became louder and higher in pitch until it reached an ear-piercing crescendo. But externally nothing had altered. The vehicle remained unmoving on the desert floor, no smoke or jet exhaust emanated from the wing mounted pods. There was just the incredibly loud whining. Neehmad kept the binoculars trained and the recorder running, despite an almost overwhelming desire to clamp her hands against her ears to shut out the terrible noise. It was at this point in the proceedings that the previous test vehicles had self destructed and she expected the same to happen to this one as well.

However, it did not explode. Instead it gently rocked on its skids, then to her amazement it slowly rose off the ground. At first there was only a thin shaft of light beneath the undercarriage, but this grew until the machine hung some twenty metres above the desert floor. It paused at this height, motionless, for several minutes, whilst the whinning reverberated off the nearby cliff and rock faces. Then the nose lifted upwards and it began to move forward, slowly at first, then as it gained acceleration, faster and faster until it was screaming almost vertically upwards. Neehmad increased the magnification and followed the disappearing vessel for as long as possible, but it was only a matter of seconds before it vanished into the upper atmosphere and silence returned to the desert.

She lowered the binoculars, but kept looking towards the heavens, straining her eyes against the glare of the blazing sun. For several minutes she lay there unmoving, but eventually when nothing else happened she decided it was time to return to the encampment.

The adrenaline surged through the veins of Flight Commander Polzine. By all expectations he should be dead by now. The other test pilots had died on the launch pad before the prototype 'Destroyers' had even got off the ground. Although he'd said nothing to the other two crew, he'd been expecting the same to happen to them. Instead everything had gone as per the simulations. The status fields that contained the artificial singularity had wound up and the Destroyer had pitched towards the heavens and accelerated towards the stars. Inside the cockpit there was no sensation of acceleration, no g-force crushing them into their seats as with a conventional rocket-propelled craft. In fact once they left the ground the only visual clue to the speed of the ascent was the darkening sky and emerging stars.

'Altitude 80,000 klicks and climbing,' said the co-pilot Delante in a breathless voice.

'Status field stable, thrust 100 percent,' monotoned Moritzon, the flight engineer. Moritzon was unflappable in any situation, and was here at the insistence of Polzine. He was a good counterbalance to Delante who although a born flyer, was sometimes a little too excitable.

'Roger that,' he replied, 'Keep monitoring those fields. If anything goes wrong, the voice recorder will be as important to the technicians as the data transmissions. God, what a ship!'

'Altitude 100,000 klicks. We're at the very edge of the atmosphere now. Velocity 23,000 kph and still accelerating,' Delante read off the instruments. Polzine didn't bother to reply, he was too busy scanning the controls himself. His left hand rested lightly on the small joystick. The craft was being flown by the computer but he was ready to take over at any moment. The damn thing failed as often as it worked. His eyes constantly scanned the numerous control panels and warning lights with an eye honed from hours of simulated flights. Anybody entering the cockpit for the first time would be overwhelmed by the sheer number of dials, lights and knobs but Polzine knew just where to look, which dials and instruments would first indicate trouble, which to give credit to the designers was exactly what they did.

Thirteen minutes and twenty-four seconds into the flight a small almost innocuous light winked on the powerplant control panel. 'Power fluctuation light panel two!' he called out.

'Got that,' replied Moritzon from his position at the rear of the cockpit. 'We've got a minor power surge in engine two. I'm damping it down now, should have it back within parameters any second...oh shit!' The control board lit up like a Christmas tree, lights flashed and warning klaxons reverberated through the hull. Polzine only had the chance to feel a brief moment of regret that they had come so near to escaping the boundaries of the atmosphere before the prototype Destroyer became an expanding ball of plasma that for a brief second was hotter than the core of the sun.

As Neehmad turned to pick up her small ragged bag containing food and water the sky lit up with a flash that was many times brighter than the blazing sun. Instinctively she dived to the ground hands over her head waiting for the searing heat and deadly winds of a nuclear explosion, but there was nothing. A warm breeze blew across her body for a few seconds then died. The flesh melting heat never came.

Eventually she rose to her feet, a bemused look creasing her mutant face. Once again she raised her head to stare at the point where the strange craft had disappeared into the heavens. It didn't take much to figure it had something to do with the explosion. So intent was she on trying to pinpoint the source of the explosion her instincts failed to notice the Imperial desert troops creeping up behind her. Only the air moving in front of the descending rifle stock warned her of the attack, but by then it was too late. The impact on the side of her cranium sent her into unconciousness.

There were so many wires attached to the subject it was difficult to know where the machine ended and flesh and bones began. From his position on the circular viewing gallery above the operating theatre Zhevosky checked that everybody and everything was in place for the experiment. The numerous generals and admirals stood against the railings, their faces pressed against the large windows in eager anticipation, staring with morbid fascination at the poor bastard strapped to the operating table.

Zhevosky leant over the intercom and ordered the start of the experiment.

A low humming noise transmitted through the glass panes heralded the start as the experiment began to draw on huge quantities of power. In fact this particular experiment needed such vast amounts of energy that a fast breeding reactor had had to be built near to the site of the secret laboratory just for this specific purpose.

'As you can see gentlemen,' Zhevosky began, 'the subject's brain patterns are rapidly increasing in activity as it absorbs both the electrical current and the chemical stimulant. The video monitors above you show this.' The generals and admirals looked up and briefly watched the numerous graphics mapping the subject's brain activity. They soon became bored with this and returned to staring down at the object of the experiment as it moaned incoherently and writhed against the restraining straps.

'How do we know when the creature is nearing the fourth dimension? These graphs and gadgets mean nothing to us doctor,' asked a particularly fat admiral weighed down with gold braid and military decorations.

'The monitor on the far right,' the doctor replied, silently cursing the scientific naiveté of the military high command, 'shows the input and output levels of the subject's brain. For most of the time the output level, that is the extra-sensory transmission, is greater than the level of electrical power fed into the frontal brain areas. However, as the creature nears the fourth dimension, these levels will gradually match. This is because the force needed to continue ESP transmissions as the subject nears the dimensional barrier becomes ever greater. In real terms we see this as a drop in the total output. The problem until now has been that eventually the power input combined with the chemical stimulant hasn't been sufficient to force the subject beyond the fourth dimensional barrier.

When the previous subjects have hit the barrier the brain output has tailed off dramatically, usually resulting in the creature's death. Today, however, we are confident that we have solved these problems. The subject wired up has a genetically altered, cloned brain, being fed a molecularly altered chemical stimulant. These modifications, we are confident, will enable us to break through the fourth dimensional barrier. Hence the reason for your visit.'

In the operating room, medics carefully watched over the huge machines supplying the power source, whilst others carefully monitored the flow of stimulant along numerous tubes that fed directly into the blood stream. The creature arched its back as spasms coursed through its body repeatedly, forcing its limbs to convulse violently against the restraining straps. It clenched its hands so tight blood seeped out from wounds caused by its finger nails digging into the soft flesh of its palms. A constant scream of agony slipped past the gag in its mouth. Zhevosky looked up at the monitors—good, the subject was nearing the barrier. The brain output levels were tailing off and the power levels were nearly at maximum. The creature was also showing the signs of physical distress that went with the last moments before encountering the barrier.

'Gentlemen, as you can see,' Zhevosky announced to the audience, 'the subject's ESP output is beginning to tail off and the creature is showing signs of physical distress. However, there is nothing to be alarmed at—we have made sure that it is securely restrained. Now, in the past it has been this point at which the subjects of the experiment have failed to break through the fourth dimensional barrier and have died. Today we shall witness the beginning of a new era as the extra input of power and stimulant, forces the subject finally through the barrier. We shall penetrate the impenetrable. Please watch closely.'

The generals and admirals surged closer to the barrier to get a better look as Zhevosky leant towards the intercom and gave the order to proceed. Down on the operating floor a medic turned a large heavy-duty dial, the humming intensified and the lights flickered as a huge surge of power was fed into the creatures body. Simultaneously another medic opened a valve and stimulant poured into its blood stream. The creature howled and screamed even louder for a brief moment then collapsed immobile on the operating table. There was a sigh of disappointment from the collected assembly and Zhevosky cursed. Damn it—he was sure that this time they would break through. What had gone wrong? He turned to face his audience, whom he knew would take failure badly, but when he looked up they were still staring transfixed at the body on the table. Zhevosky looked back at the subject and froze in astonishment.

Although the body was still inert, there was some sort of metamorphosis taking place. Beneath the numerous probes and tubes the flesh of the creature was becoming translucent, as if something were broiling underneath the skin. As he watched with unbelieving eyes the skin turned black. No, black was a colour, this thing had no colour. It was as if the very light was being absorbed from around the operating theatre. The spot lights above the table dimmed and died and small pinpoints of light flashed across the creature's skin. The flashes became more and more numerous, as if, for want of a better description, a star cluster was being formed inside the dead body of the subject. The flashing lights became more and more intense and began to whirl round and round like a vortex. The vortex grew until it spread throughout the creature's body and then to Zhevosky's disbelief it sprang out of the body and into the operating room. Medics screamed and ran as the vortex swept through the theatre swallowing everything in its path. Lights, machinery, people, everything was swept into and swallowed by the black vortex and its flashing lights. Realising the danger they were in Zhevosky turned and ran for the exit, the generals and admirals of the military command close on his heels. They were too late, with a crash of breaking glass the windows collapsed and the bodies in the viewing gallery were swept into the vortex. Zhevosky could only wonder briefly about what he had done before his life was snuffed out.

On the mountainside a shepherd watched over his undernourished and bleating flock. When the ground began to shake he calmly lay down in a shielded dip and waited for the quake to pass. In his seventy odd years he'd weathered many a disturbance. The rumbling and shaking carried on for several minutes and when it finally subsided he wearily rose and finding himself still in one piece went to find his scattered flock. Yet when he climbed out of the dip he was surprised to find his flock still together and all staring across to the next mountain. When the shepherd looked up to follow their gaze, surprise turned to disbelief. Where only a few minutes ago stood the Peak of Shallat which rose forever into the mountains, was—nothing, just a huge circular basin that dropped several hundred feet into the ground. Thousands of tons of rock and stone, a complete massive mountain had disappeared, just like that. There was nothing there except for a few wisps of smoke that for a fleeting moment seemed to flash with small pinpoints of light.

From what little he could see from the shuttle's tiny viewing port, Hurzon's first impression was that is was big, very big, but also very ugly. The main hull was rounded at the prow but elsewhere was largely squat and fat. Gun blisters, carrying the latest fast recycling laser cannon rose from the welded steel skin like a bad attack of acne. Huge powerplants hung below the main hull on squat stub wings and even from this distance he could make out the bright flashes of welding guns as numerous work parties swarmed around the incomplete vessel. The Imperial Navy's newest battle-cruiser may be the fastest most heavily armed ship in the star system, but it was still bloody ugly.

It was the first time Hurzon had seen the orbital construction site. The project was top secret and although it was generally known that the navy was working on a new dreadnought, details were sketchy and photos non existent. The work gangs that came up to work on the vessel were to stay there until the monster was finished ensuring watertight security. He looked around the shuttle bay at the rest of the group straining for their first glimpse of their new home. One of the shuttle crew peered out of the cockpit into the hold and shouted 'Docking in five minutes. Strap yourselves back into the acceleration couches.'

Somewhat reluctantly, Hurzon and the others drifted back from the viewing ports and strapped themselves into the well-worn acceleration couches bolted to the floor of the military shuttle. For the hundredth time he checked that the pocket of his flight suit still contained the small package. Satisfied that the familiar bulge was still there he lay back and forced himself to look relaxed, even though his heart was pounding.

The firing of the manoeuvre thrusters pushed him gently back into the couch and he soon felt a jolt as the shuttle finally docked. As he moved to undo the straps, the first thing he noticed was gravity. Instead of floating above the seat with nothing but the straps to stop him from floating away, he was now being firmly forced into the seat cushions. The 'Dominator' was the first battle-cruiser to use artificial gravity and as the shuttle neared the docking port, it had gradually came under the influence of the Dominator's gravity field. Although the field produced less than half normal gravity, it was still sufficient to keep everyone firmly glued to the decks. He had no idea how the field worked but was impressed all the same.

The shuttle hatch opened from the inside and a heavily muscled military policeman stepped in and snapped, 'Right you worthless pieces of scum! Collect your kitbags and follow me to the crew processing centre!' Hurzon and the rest of the new workcrew undid their straps, took their kitbags out of the overhead lockers and dutifully followed the MP. The shuttle was connected to the crew processing area of the Dominator by a small enclosed corridor and Hurzon found he had to be careful not to leap down it in huge strides in the low gravity. Once inside the crew processing area, a poorly lit compartment packed with security scanners, the workers lined up behind a desk where they showed more MPs their ID cards. Then they went to one of four areas where more officers strip searched the workers and went through their kitbags.

An officer beckoned to Hurzon and he moved over to one such desk and handed him his kitbag. For one brief second the MP stared directly into Hurzon's eyes before taking everything out of the bag. Hurzon avoided his gaze and stripped off his flight suit. A few minutes later his kit was handed back to him, and when he put the suit back on the small package was still in the pocket. Without a second glance he picked up his belongings and followed the rest of the new workers to the briefing room. From the shadows of a hatchway, the eyes of the chief of intelligence followed his every movement.

Hurzon waited over three weeks before making his move. He waited until he knew the innards of the Dominator like the back of his hand. His job as an electrical engineer responsible for wiring up the numerous control stations to the central computer bank, meant he was free to move around the whole vessel unlike many of his work-mates. His security rating also gave him a legitimate reason for intimately examining the wiring diagrams and blueprints for the whole of the Dominator. It took time and patience, but eventually he found what he was looking for, the Achilles heel, the one weak spot that would lead to the destruction of the Imperial Navy's newest and most deadly battle-cruiser.

He lay on the top bunk staring at the grey walls of the dormitory. He'd just finished another ten-hour shift and was physically exhausted, but his mind would not rest. He kept wondering when the "sympathisers" would get in touch with him. His mind kept going over the scenario time and time again. Once he had been given the go-ahead he would place the small detonator against an internal conduit in work-station five on the engineering deck. The conduit supplied power to the main computer controlling the status fields of the main powerplants. These status fields kept the artificial singularities in a stable state. These singularites, a result of quantum mechanics, were the very heart of the propulsion system. If the conduit was cut the computer would fail and as the backup computers were not yet on line, the status field would collapse leading to a catastrophic failure of the singularities and a chain reaction that once started would be impossible to contain. Within minutes the Dominator would be turned into space dust and he would be on his way back to the planet surface in an escape pod. The plan was good. It was simple and effective. So why was he scared shitless? He tried shutting his eyes and going to sleep, but his senses were too alert. He was painfully aware of the snoring and whispered conversations of the other workers in the claustrophobic dormitory, of the stench of unwashed bodies and constant background noise of the ship.

There was a commotion from the other end of the dormitory. Hurzon got up onto one elbow and saw with alarm a security officer and a group of troopers marching towards his bunk pushing the other workers out the way, ignoring their protests. The officer halted in front of his bunk and demanded, 'You, worker, get off that mattress and stand in front of me.' Before he could comply, two troopers grabbed him by the arm and literally pulled him onto the deck. He collapsed in a heap in front of the officer and dragged himself to his feet. As Hurzon rose off the metal grating of the deck floor he very nearly lost control of his bowels when he realised who the security officer was. It was the same officer who searched him the day he arrived on the Dominator.

What was going on? This man was supposed to be one of the sympathisers. He was supposed to be on his side. So why was he here? Had Hurzon been betrayed? A thousand thoughts flashed through his mind.

'You three,' the officer snapped, 'strip his bedding and search his locker, leave nothing unturned. I want the stuff found.' Three troopers began pulling Hurzon's few belongings apart. He stared hard at Hurzon, his thin lips curled up into a sneer. 'Strip,' he demanded. Hurzon undid his jump-suit and stepped out of it. Another trooper picked it up from the deck and handed it to the officer. Hurzon stood there naked, shivering despite the heat of the dormitory while his clothing was searched. A few minutes later one of the squad came up and whispered into the security officer's ear. 'What do you mean you've found nothing? You've searched everywhere?'

'Yes sir!' the trooper replied with a note of desperation.

'And you've found absolutely nothing?'

'Nothing sir!' The officer cursed and threw the jump-suit back at Hurzon. 'Right, this time you're lucky Hurzon! But just remember I've got my eye on you! One false move and I'll personally shove your fat arse through the air lock myself! The penalty for bringing liquor onboard is a view of the star system without an environment suit! Just you remember that!' With a click of his fingers he turned and marched out of the dormitory followed by his squad of troopers.

Shakily Hurzon picked up his clothing and put it back on. His hand automatically reached for the top pocket. Relief swept over him. The small container was still there but there was also a small slip of paper. With shaking hands he opened the slip and read the single line; 'Tomorrow 14.00hours'. So that was what the little charade was about! Quickly Hurzon popped the paper into his mouth and swallowed it. His stomach turned. Frantically he ran for the head at the other end of the dormitory but didn't quite make it. The dormitory stank even more.

The console was a remote operating unit on the systems operations deck that mirrored the controls in the engine room and acted as a backup in the event that the area became contaminated and had to be evacuated. It was linked to the ships main computer and the separate engine management computer and it was the data and power conduits that Hurzon was now working on. He had the access panels off the back of the console and a pile of cables spread over the deck floor like the intestines of some butchered animal. Occasionally he would peer up to check the blue prints spread over the top of the console then disappear inside the unit itself, torch in one hand, multi-tool in the other. The time was 13.45hours. Hurzon had been working in this section of the ship for the past eight days, wiring up the numerous control and display units. His supervisor had long since given up trying to decipher the thousands of wiring diagrams for this part of the Dominator only too happy to let Hurzon do it all for him. Which suited Hurzon just fine.

Very carefully Hurzon took out the small package from the top pocket of his jump-suit. It was a small cylinder about the size of a cigar case with a screw cap on the top. Slowly he rotated the top until he heard a faint 'click'. Then he pulled at the top until the cylinder extended to twice its original size. A small digital clock began to count down from thirteen minutes. Crude, but effective, the small incendiary device would ignite at exactly 14.00 hours and cause an intense electrical fire at the same time that it blew through the main computer power conduit. This would cause a power surge that would corrupt the engine management computer and disconnect the main computer. Main engine meltdown would irrevocably occur about four minutes later. Hurzon placed the device behind the conduit and secured it there with electrical tape. Satisfied the device was armed he extracted himself from the back of the unit.

With a contrived sigh he stood upright, stretched his back and hitched the torch and multi-tool back on his belt. With studied casualness he ambled towards the hatchway. 'Where do you think you're going?' demanded the ever-present security trooper.

Hurzon trying not to look like he was going to collapse in fright replied, 'I need the can. It's that crap they feed us on. Goes straight through you.'

The guard looked at him stonily for a moment before snapping, 'Make it quick then.'

Hurzon nodded glumly and squeezed through the hatch into the main corridor. Beads of sweat popped out on his brow. He had less than ten minutes to get to one of the escape pods and get away from the Dominator before the status fields went critical. He walked as quickly as he could without actually running, head bowed concentrating on the metal grating under his feet, trying to appear as inconspicuous as possible. He passed the small hatchway that lead to the toilets and kept going. He very nearly made it—just another couple of steps and he would have rounded the corner of the corridor and entered the ship's transporter, but it wasn't to be. A shout came from behind him. 'Oi you!' Hurzon turned and saw the same guard again. 'Where do you think you're going? You've gone past the shitter!'

Hurzon stopped dead in his tracks his heart frozen with fear. What was he going to do? There was no time to fob the guard off by going back and pretending to use the head. By the time he got rid of the suspicious guard the explosives would have detonated. There was only one thing for it; he ran.

'Oi stop! Stop or I fire!' yelled the guard pulling at his hand blaster. Too late Hurzon rounded the corner and bounded in the low gravity for all he was worth towards the elevator doors. When he got there he desperately punched the lift call button 'Come on, come on!' he muttered. Behind him he could hear the pounding boots of the guard pursuing him. Seven minutes. He was cutting it fine, too fine. The elevator arrived. 'Yes!' he cried in relief. There was still time. The doors opened and Hurzon's jaw dropped in surprise. He was looking straight into the eyes of the security officer who had searched his belongings the night before. Eyes that were bloodshot and sunken into a swollen face covered in bruising and lacerations. His uniform was torn and tattered and he hung limply between two burly troopers who held him by the armpits. 'What the?'

he briefly muttered before the rifle butt struck him on the back of the head...

'Is he awake? Good get him on his feet.' Hurzon's eyes slowly opened and he felt himself being dragged to his feet. An Imperial officer he'd never seen before swam into focus standing directly in front of him. He was tall and well built with a well-proportioned, but somehow evil face and very short dark hair. 'Ah Hurzon,' the officer began, 'I'm so glad you could join us. My name is security leader Gulag. The Dominator is my responsibility and I've got a few questions for you. Do you recognise this man?' He pointed to the other security officer lying in a pool of his own blood on the deck floor. Hurzon's mind was in a whirl. What time was it? Where was he? Had the charges failed to go off? How long had he been unconscious?

'I've never seen him before,' Hurzon muttered, stalling for time. He looked around ignoring the pain in his head. He was back on the engineering support deck. The console with the charge stood in the corner. A digital clock on one of the control panels said 13.56 hours. He'd been out only for a couple of minutes! The charges hadn't gone off yet! Desperately he struggled to get away from the troopers but their grip was too strong for him to break.

'Now, now Hurzon,' the officer named Gulag sneered. 'That's no way to behave. I already know that something is going to happen at 14.00 hours. Your friend there on the deck told me that, eventually. Unfortunately that appears to be all he knows. I was hoping you could furnish me with the rest of the details before the situation turned nasty.'

'I don't know what you're talking about,' Hurzon answered, but his eyes drifted back to the wired-up console. Three minutes left. It looked as though he was going to die along with everyone else. Without warning he felt an indescribable pain lance into his mind. It felt as if a red hot poker had been forced into his head and twisted around. He screamed out in agony.

Gulag smiled with pleasure. He always enjoyed the chance to exercise his skills in this manner. Raping another's mind was a crude but effective method of getting the information he needed. He'd brought in the security officer for questioning after he had been seen supposedly searching this wretch called Hurzon. Unfortunately the traitorous Imperial officer didn't know anything more than a name and a time, but now he had Hurzon he had the rest of the information he needed...the console. 14.00hours... the console would explode at 14.00hours cutting the computer from the engine room! Two minutes to go. Damn it! There wasn't enough time to find the device and make it safe. Hurzon collapsed on the deck next to the security officer his mind turned to jelly. Gulag turned and ran for the hatchway.

'Out, everybody out! Out now! Come on move! Leave those treacherous bastards where they are!' Gulag shouted as he ran. 'This whole deck is going up in flames in less than two minutes! Come on you dumb animals, move!'

The troopers didn't need any more encouragement. They dropped their weapons and followed Gulag down the corridor taking huge bounds in the low gravity. The elevator door was still open. Gulag bounded in and hit the door button. Two of the troopers made it through before the door closed, but the third wasn't so lucky. Gulag ignored his screams and hit the button for the main control room. The elevator began to move. Gulag then pounded on the intercom button.

'Control,' he snapped, 'this is Gulag. Power up the backup computers for the status fields! Do it now!'

'But sir,' a voice replied, 'we haven't finished de-bugging the software yet.'

'Don't argue!' Gulag screamed. 'Do it right this second or we're all going to die!'

'Yes sir!' the voice replied with a tremor.

Gulag grabbed hold of the support rail and clung on tight. Any second now... The elevator rocked in its cradle and the whole huge mass of the Dominator vibrated as the incendiary device ignited in the oxygen-rich atmosphere.

The last thought in Hurzon's mortally wounded mind was, 'Got the bastards!' then his body was incinerated.

CHAPTER TWO

Rain pounded incessantly against the third-floor windows. It was another miserable day in the Imperial capital just like the day before and the day before that. In fact the weather had been the same every day since the great patriotic war— rain, acid rain, rain that ate away at the flesh and bones of an unprotected body. Rain every day, all day.

Captain Hillmead, head of the homicide dept of the 35th precinct Imperial state police, stared out of the window down to street level. The citizens of Caranak barged their way past the numerous street vendors largely ignoring them and each other. His eyes fixed on one young lady wearing the latest in street fashion, a see-through environment suit and bright red breathing mask that had two thick glass apertures for her eyes to peer through. A 'Lobo', one of the underclass, wearing nothing but rags and no breathing mask leered at the girl from a doorway. Her male companion pulled a cosh from his environment suit and swung it at the 'Lobo'. It connected with his acid-eaten face ripping at what little flesh remained. Blood and gore stained the attackers environment suit but he ignored it and carried on down the street arm in arm with his girl. The 'Lobo' lay prone on the ground, his blood mingling with the filthy water that ran in the gutter. Within seconds other 'Lobos' pounced on the unfortunate and stripped him of anything vaguely useful. If he wasn't dead before, he was now. The other citizens of Caranak ignored the little incident and went about their business.

Hillmead sipped his lukewarm coffee and looked away; like the weather street life never changed. There was a knock at the door. 'Enter,' he called, stepping back to his battered desk and seating himself in his equally battered chair. His adjutant, a weasel-faced man sprouting a pencil moustache on his upper lip stuck his head around the door. 'You wanted to see me boss?' he said. Hillmead waved for the adjutant to step into the room and close the door. The familiar sound of a chaotic police precinct rose and fell as the door opened and shut. 'What do you know about this?' Hillmead asked, pointing to a written order sheet bearing the Imperial Military Command crest.

'Officially, nothing boss,' came the reply. 'Unofficially quite a lot, but I have to stress it is *unofficial.*' Hillmead knew that his adjutant, Pollowzki, constantly had his ear to the ground. He was the best source of 'unofficial' knowledge in the force. Where Pollowzki got his information from, Hillmead didn't know or care but he knew it was invariably accurate. 'Okay, spare me the disclaimer,' he replied. 'Just give me what you know.'

'Well boss,' started Pollowzki, collapsing into a chair on the opposite side of the desk and casually placing his feet on the desk. 'The word on the 'vine' is that somebody's been putting a spanner of the works in the Imperial Navy's latest toys. They've got a load of hush hush projects on the go that aren't going according to plan. There's been some explosions or something like that.'

'What's that got to do with me?' Hillmead asked casually, swiping the adjutant's legs off the desk as he always did. 'I don't see the connection.'

'That's easy boss,' Pollowzki continued unperturbed. 'The military believe that the Democracy Front are behind the sabotage.'

'What? That bunch of 'Lobos'? They're barely capable of a few terrorist bombs on the metro, let alone worming their way into the military!' Hillmead exclaimed in surprise. 'Regardless of that, all this is still a matter for military intelligence. What I want to know is why do they want to see me?'

Pollowzki got up out of the chair and sauntered over to the window. Casually he crushed a cockroach with his thumb and stared down at the street. 'That's easy boss. Even you should be able to answer that question.' He turned and looked long and hard at his immediate superior and closest friend. 'If the military has become infested with not only corruption but anti-Imperialists, they can't set their own people on the job of weeding out the activists. How would they know who to trust? No—they need someone honest, incorruptible and full of integrity. They need a poor bastard who holds the law above everything else. They need you!'

With that he left the office. Hillmead sat behind his desk and watched his friends disappearing back. As was so often the case Pollowzki had given him an invaluable insight into the bizarre logic of the Imperial government.

The Imperial guard waited for the palm prints to match with the main library files before letting the battered squad car through the main gates. Pollowzki gave a low whistle of appreciation as he drove around the parade ground towards the main entrance. The headquarters of the Imperial Forces were situated a few klicks outside the walls of Caranak in several hundred acres of once beautiful land. The years since the great patriotic war had ravaged the woods and gardens that surrounded the headquarters, but unlike most other buildings in Caranak, great effort had been made to maintain the centuries-old Imperial architecture from the incessant acid rain and vile pollution that spilled from the capital's factories.

'Frigging hell boss!' Pollowzki exclaimed. 'Can you believe this place? Just think how many million credits go into maintaining this place every year! No wonder our yearly budget wouldn't even pay for a pox-ridden whore. The combined Imperial budget is spent on this place!'

'Shut up Poll,' Hillmead answered from the back seat. 'This place is riddled with sensors and security systems. You can bet that there is sufficient hardware trained on us right this moment to turn us into our base components. Every word we say from now on will be recorded, so for the Lord's sake watch what you say.'

'Come on boss,' Pollowzki grinned back, 'you should know me better than that.'

'I do Poll. That's what worries me.'

The car pulled up outside the main entrance, Pollowzki leapt out and opened the rear door. Hillmead stepped out and turned to his adjutant. 'Listen Poll, you'd better not follow me in here. The orders just had my name on them. So go lose the car somewhere and have a sniff around. See if you can't find out something more about what the military are up to from some of the grunts here. OK?'

'No problem boss. Leave it to me.'

'Good man,' Hillmead finished before striding up the stone steps and entering the huge gothic edifice. Inside he was immediately met by an attractive young first lieutenant wearing the constricting skirt and blouse of the Imperial Women's Service Corp. With a stern look she marched across the marble floor to where Hillmead stood and said in clipped educated tones, 'Inspector Hillmead. You are expected. If you would be so good as to follow me.' With that she turned and marched towards the elevator. Hillmead remained where he was watching the swing of the lieutenant's hips. She was halfway across the lobby before she released Hillmead was still standing at the entrance. With a look of intense irritation the lieutenant marched back.

'Inspector,' she snapped, 'we must not keep them waiting! What is the problem?'

Hillmead stared the young lady straight in the eye and said in a flat monotone. 'I have no intention of going anywhere until someone tells me who I'm here to see and why. The military have no jurisdiction over the constabulary. I've co-operated so far, now I want some answers.'

A retort formed and died on her lips when she saw the look in his eye. Arrogance was replaced by mild panic.

'Please Inspector! The Envoy does not like to be kept waiting, nor does Group Leader Gulag! For both our sakes please follow me now!' she pleaded, ignoring the interested stares of the other military personnel that swam about the lobby.

'The Envoy?' Hillmead said in surprise. 'You mean the Envoy Nimue and that cloned bastard of hers, Gulag?'

The lieutenant took a sharp intake of breath and a flush rose up her cheeks. 'Inspector,' she whispered, 'I've told you more than I should. If any of the scanners are on us we're both in big trouble. Now please follow me before the situation gets out of hand.'

Hillmead looked at the woman thoughtfully for a moment, then nodded his head. Well this was certainly going to be interesting! This time he did follow the lieutenant across the lobby and into the elevator. She pressed the button for the ninth floor, resolutely avoided his gaze and carefully examined the walnut panelling. When the door opened the lieutenant took Hillmead to a small reception area where two Imperial troopers in formal dress frisked him with small body scanners. They took his small Hooch and Conner automatic and took the clip out before handing it back to him. The lieutenant tapped on a large ornate door and entered closing the door in Hillmead's face. Well that was quite enough of that, he thought to himself. Without knocking he turned the brass handle and stepped through the door.

The lieutenant took a step sideways in surprise and began to mutter, 'Just what in the fires of hell do you think...'

'That will do thank you lieutenant,' said a smooth but cold voice from the other end of the dark wood-panelled study. The young woman gave him a long dirty stare then left the room. Hillmead strode toward the large ornate desk placed at the end of the room and surrounded by dark wood shelves on which were placed numerous leather-bound books. The grey light spilling from the small leaded window fell upon the woman sitting behind the desk. Her age was difficult to ascertain, even for Hillmead's trained eye. He guessed she was somewhere between thirty and forty but with the body of a twenty year old. She wore the traditional uniform of the Imperial diplomatic corp, a tight double-breasted blouse with the epaulettes denoting her rank of Envoy. Her long dark hair was braided in a long pony tail that tumbled off her shoulders and down her back. She looked at Hillmead through beautiful but cold dark eyes. Without asking he took the seat in front of the desk and made himself comfortable.

'Inspector Hillmead,' the Envoy spoke in a low husky voice, 'this is a pleasure. Thank you for taking the time to come here. I know how busy the Caranak central precinct is.'

He returned her stare coolly. He knew all about the Envoy Nimue, he'd read her file, the unofficial file, the file that described her long association with the Emperor. The file that also described her mission to Earth, her role in the debacle that led to the loss of nearly all of the Imperial Dyason Fleet. However, there were large holes in the story before and after the return of the expeditionary force. There were rumours, plenty of rumours. It was generally well known that her current pet Gulag was a clone of the original Security Leader Gulag who was part of the fated Earth force. Cloning was something the genetic engineers had finally perfected after years of experimentation. Most of the poor mutated bastards that were created in the early experiments had died soon after creation. Gulag was supposed to be the first of a new breed; genetically perfect. He was in fact, not only a genetic replica of the original Gulag, he was supposed to be engineered to be the perfect physical specimen of a Dyason. He was also sitting on a couch behind the Envoy.

'Your thoughts betray you Inspector.' Gulag got up from the couch, moved out of the shadows and sat on the corner of the envoy's desk facing Hillmead. He wore the uniform of a Imperial Officer of the Space Fleet complete with highly polished knee length boots. The uniform itself was immaculately tailored and enhanced Gulag's well proportioned frame and chisel featured face. He looked like a recruitment artist's fantasy.

'If you can read my thoughts Group Leader then we can dispense with the pleasantries and get right down to business. What do the Imperial Military Forces want from a street cop?' replied Hillmead coolly and evenly, hiding his surprise. He'd heard rumours that Gulag had been genetically engineered to be a telepath, but he'd never really believed them.

Telepaths amongst the Dyason were literally unheard of. The only known operants were humans shipped here from Earth during the occupation.

'You're quite correct in surmising that there are no natural born Dyason telepaths and you may say that my talent is due to my genetically altered state,' said Gulag levelling a stare at Hillmead. 'You would be advised, however, not to encourage any further "rumours".'

Hillmead returned the stare. He would have to be very careful here and watch what he *thought* as well as what he said. At least until he was out of this office. 'I'm sure you didn't order me here just to throw abuse at me Group Leader,' he replied

'Please excuse the Group Leader, Inspector,' the Envoy Nimue interrupted giving the Group Leader a quick irritated stare before turning her charm on Hillmead. 'His manner can be a little aggressive at times.' She leant forward on her arms and looked him carefully up and down, a forced smile on her face. He tried to suppress the thought that it felt like being sized up by a hungry reptile.

'Obviously you are a man of action, a man who does not like to mince his words. I like that. It is an admirable trait befitting a true Dyason male of which you are one Inspector,' the Envoy continued. Hillmead cringed. Gulag went over to a shelf behind the desk, pulled out a folder and handed it to him. He glanced down at the cover noting the 'Top Secret' stamp and seal. It occurred to him that security at this place was so tight, the Envoy was happy to leave top secret documents sitting openly on her shelves, or at least that's what they wanted him to think. He saw the corners of Gulag's mouth turn up. So that was what he was supposed to think! Interesting.

'The folder you hold gives details on several current Imperial projects that are vital to the defence programme. Each project has suffered in the past weeks from a major setback. Some have obviously been the result of sabotage, others we suspect, but cannot prove treachery,' the Envoy explained. Hillmead broke the seal and opened the folder. On the top of the piles of papers and computer mini-disks were several photographs. He recognised one as an exterior view of the Dominator albeit with a piece missing. So far the Imperial Space Fleet's newest battle-cruiser was the planet's worst kept secret, more than likely due to some well placed leaks from the Imperial military itself. The other photographs showed projects he had no knowledge of. He put the photographs down and looked up at the Envoy.

'With respect Envoy Nimue,' he said with a frown on his face. 'What has this got to do with me? I'm a street cop not a member of the Military Detective Corp.'

The Envoy said nothing while Gulag answered. 'The MDC have been carrying out ongoing investigations into these and other acts of treason for the past eight months. Their efforts have revealed very little and to be frank we are no nearer knowing which group of individuals are set upon bringing down the Empire, or why.'

'Fine, so the MDC can't get its shit together. I'm sorry to hear that, but this still doesn't have anything to do with me. I'm a civilian cop who's good at cracking cases of fraud, vice and murder. The internal politics of the military are not my concern,' Hillmead fretted, unhappy at the direction the meeting was taking.

The Envoy opened a drawer and pulled out an envelope sealed with the Imperial Crest. She handed it to Hillmead across the desk, her eyes never leaving his. 'They are now Inspector,' she said quietly.

He took the envelope and broke the seal. Inside was a sheet of paper he recognised as written orders. Bugger it! Quickly he scanned the page, glanced at the hologramatic proof mark and his eyebrows shot up when he saw the signature at the bottom. He recognised it, it was simply that it had never appeared on any orders he'd received himself before. The scrawl was unmistakable and the name underneath was, of course, that of Alorne the Third, Emperor of Dyason. He was stuffed and he knew it.

'Looks like you bastards have me over a barrel,' he said with feeling, 'but why me? What more can I do than your own investigators?'

'As you can see from your orders Inspector, it is of the utmost importance to the security of Dyason that these traitors are exposed. The Emperor feels that a fresh look at the evidence is required and that an outside investigator would be able to bring in new ideas,' said the Envoy.

'That outside investigator is you Inspector. Your exemplary record leads us to believe that you can achieve the necessary break-through in the investigations that we so desperately need.' added Gulag.

Hillmead suppressed all the questions that flooded briefly through his mind. There would be time for that later. He didn't want to expose himself to the brain scans of the clone. Obviously there was more going on here than they were letting on, but this wasn't the time or the place. 'What about my current cases down at the precinct. Who's going to look after them? It'll take at least a couple of weeks to hand over the reins to somebody else,' he demanded.

'That has already been taken care of Inspector,' the Envoy said smoothly. 'There's no need to concern yourself with precinct matters any more. You are required to begin your new duties straight-away.'

Hillmead looked from the Envoy to Gulag. This was ridiculous, they couldn't do this, except that they had. For a brief moment he thought about telling them to go screw themselves, but once again he restrained his mind. 'No choice eh?' he said with venom.

Gulag nodded, 'That's right Hillmead. No choice.'

'Never mind Inspector,' the Envoy smiled sweetly. 'Consider this a career move. I'm sure I don't have to tell you that the successful completion of this assignment will bring with it great rewards.'

Hillmead said nothing.

'The lieutenant outside will furnish you with the rest of the information you require. From now on she will be your personal assistant and, of course, ease your route through the military channels; you will be given the rank of Colonel in the Military Detective Corp,' said Gulag.

'I already have an assistant,' Hillmead snapped. 'If I'm going to be press-ganged into the military at least let me bring along someone I can work with.'

The Envoy rested her chin on the tip of her hands. 'Ah yes, the small weasel-looking creature,' she said staring into the middle distance. 'I'm sorry Hillmead, but your orders are very clear. They make no mention of transferring any other personnel from the Caranak police force. I think that's going to be out of the question.'

The complete and utter bastards! Hillmead fumed. He realised that his only chance of getting out of his new military career was to find the poor sods they were looking for and hope they stuck to their word and gave him what he wanted.

'I guess that's it then. There's not much point in appealing is there?' he asked.

'None at all Inspector, or should I say Colonel?' the Envoy replied. 'Your shuttle flight to the Dominator leaves at 0800 hours tomorrow morning. Please make sure you are on it. Thank you for your time. Good day.' She turned to her computer monitor and began tapping on the keyboard. Gulag stared vacantly out of the window.

Dejectedly Hillmead lifted himself out of the chair, walked to the door and opened it. He looked back once more at the Envoy and the clone before stepping back into the reception area. Bastards! Angry and frustrated he stormed through the reception area and headed as fast as possible for the lifts. The young lieutenant, seeing him leave the study, stood up, straightened her skirt, cursed and marched after him.

'Well what do you think?' the Envoy asked the clone. 'He's very wilful and argumentative. Is he suitable for our purposes?'

'He's the best person for the job,' the cloned Gulag replied coolly. 'Not perfect, but very nearly so. He has a great sense of loyalty. For all his exterior facade, inside he is an idealist who still believes in the Empire.'

'Believing in the Empire is one thing, but being an idealist is dangerous. Can we be sure he will do as we tell him?' the Envoy said thoughtfully staring out of the window. In the courtyard below, Hillmead was climbing into his battered squad car, the weasel assistant of his at the wheel. The young officer Shalok stood on the steps, her pretty face contorted in anger. She stared at Hillmead for a moment then ran down and climbed into the squad car next to him.

The clone walked over and stood next to Nimue at the window. 'There are no certainties,' he said looking down as the squad car pulled away in a cloud of dust, 'but the presence of the young Lieutenant Shalok should keep him at least partially under control. Besides, if he becomes too much of a nuisance we can simply have him eliminated.'

The Envoy turned and faced the clone. 'Should we have told him the truth?' she asked, her eyes searching his.

'What? That we can't trust the MDC because we suspect that the traitors have infiltrated even as far as there?' he said. 'There's no point—he can figure that one out for himself.'

The Envoy pursed her lips and kissed the clone firmly on the mouth, her hands reaching down to his testicles. 'I'm sure you're right,' she murmured. 'That's enough of that—I want you to do it to me! Now!'

In an almost clinical manner the clone lay the Envoy on top of the desk and undid his trousers, his face stony and unreadable.

15.00HOURS GMT. JUNE 19TH 2031

The grey cratered landscape of the moon sped past the cockpit. The bright sunlight caused long shadows which highlighted the terrain and gave the moon an intense but cold beauty. Not that Moss was really paying too much attention to the scenery. His mind was concentrating on flying the small Flyship. Somewhere out there was his opponent flying a machine equal in performance to the one he was in and intent on firing first. He flexed his muscles and the Flyship rolled slightly in response. He willed the machine down and it sunk a little closer to the surface of the moon. Part of his mind watched over the craft's various control systems while another part absorbed all the information flooding in from the numerous sensors.

Damn it! There was no sign of the 'bogey', he'd lost track of the competition. They were obviously using their stealth capabilities as well as the moon's terrain to keep themselves hidden. Moss knew he was in trouble. He'd just broken the cardinal rule by losing contact and giving the bogey the opportunity of getting the upper hand.

There was a flash of light from the port side of the craft and Moss felt a sharp pang of pain in his left arm, which through the link up with the Flyship's sensors could mean just one thing—he'd been hit by laser fire.

Desperately he piled on the power and headed for the moon surface jinking wildly as he descended, trying to throw off his opponent's aim. There ahead of him— a tightly winding canyon just wide enough for the Flyship. Without even thinking about it Moss flew straight into the canyon wincing as once again he was hit by laser fire. Ouch!— that hurt! Well let the bugger follow him down here! Now they'd discover who had the biggest balls!

The Flyship whipped into the canyon, sheer walls of rock flashing scant metres past the stub wings. Moss guided the craft anticipating the bends and curves, adrenaline surging through his veins. God but this was really flying! He could feel his opponent still clinging onto his tail and he saw the occasional impact of laser fire against the walls of the canyon, but none hit the Flyship itself. The guy was good, Moss had to admit that, but not good enough. He was unable to get a clear shot in the confines of the winding canyon and so long as Moss remained there he was safe—except that the canyon was about to come to a sheer dead end. Balls! He flexed his hands and the Flyship reared up like a startled animal and shot towards the stars once more, the bogey close behind.

Okay he'd had enough of these games, now was the time to play his trump card. He just had to wait until the bogey was in just the right spot—right on his tail. He let the opponent close in right behind him, gave him exactly the firing position he was looking for, waiting until the bogey thought Moss was dead meat and then...full retro, everything into reverse...the Flyship decelerated rapidly, the g-forces making Moss grunt painfully as the straps dug into his flesh. He nearly blacked out, but not quite. With a grin of satisfaction he saw the bogey flash past his Flyship taken completely unawares by the manoeuvre. One, two, three, that was it, the perfect firing position. Moss willed the lasers to fire a full salvo and he saw the bogey take multiple impacts. Got the bugger!

The bogey slowed down to cruise speed and Moss heard in his head, *'Well you ballsed it up earlier kid, but I guess you made amends with that surprise manoeuvre at the end there. Well done, but remember, never, ever, lose track of your bogey. When the time comes, that will be what gets you killed—not your lack of flying ability.'*

Moss grimaced; he knew he'd made defeat look like success. The truth was, he may not be so lucky next time. *'Yeah boss,'* he thought back, *'I know that. I guess I lost my concentration for a moment back there. Sorry Paul.'*

'Sorry ain't gonna save your arse kid. Anyway that's enough for today. Formate and lets head back home. We can discuss this in de-brief.' With that

Paul Jenson turned his Flyship back towards Earth and rapidly left the moon behind. Moss closed up on the other machine and said nothing. He was suitably chastised and not particularly looking forward to the de-brief aboard Excalibur.

As they neared the huge ancient vessel Moss noticed a smaller ship docked onto one of Excalibur's ports. It was about the size of an Earth-side destroyer of the type that still sailed the world's oceans. Its flat delta shape was reminiscent of the early 'stealth' bombers, as was the dark black colour scheme. However, the similarities ended there. The scoop intakes and extended powerplant at the craft's stern identified her as one of the three scout ships built in a hurry after the capitulation.

Eventually Moss could read the serial number, just visible on the hull. His heart quickened and he suppressed the temptation to increase power. *'Heh kid, your girlfriends home!'* came the thought from Jenson's Flyship. *'That's the Observer docked there. They're back six weeks early. Something must be up.'*

'I know Paul. That's what's worrying me. Jennifer hasn't mind linked with me, like she usually does when she's on her way home,' Moss thought back at his friend and commanding officer.

'Calm down kid. The chances are that Jennifer is simply too busy or is under a security order. You know the two of you agreed not to telepath to each other if it constituted a security risk. You just concentrate on getting your Flyship safely back onboard.'

In close formation the pair of Flyship fighters entered the approach pattern for Excalibur. They gently added power to compensate for the starship's gravitational field and eased themselves onto the landing pads which then retracted down to the main hangar.

As soon as Moss shed his flying kit he headed for the briefing room. There he found a group of three men and two women still wearing their one-piece flying suits, deep in the middle of a mission de-brief. His heart missed a beat as he recognised the smaller of the two women. She was slim in build and her golden blonde hair was tied back in a business-like fashion. Her well proportioned face and full lips were unmistakable. The group looked up as he entered and Jennifer Hampton gave him a tired but warm smile.

'Ah you're back, excellent,' the intelligence officer said seeing Moss and Paul. 'I think the two of you should come over and hear this. This information is going to effect us all.'

Flight Lieutenant Moss Pendragon and Group Captain Paul Jenson joined the group and examined the holographic stills being displayed. Jennifer slipped her hand into Moss's and squeezed hard. The intelligence officer pretended not to notice.

23.44HOURS GMT. JUNE 19TH 2031
'LE PETITE OPPORTUNUN', RUE DE
ARRONDISE, PARIS, FRANCE

The limousine pulled up to the curb of the narrow cobbled street and the doors opened. Two agents conspicuously dressed in well cut business suits climbed out into the pouring rain and ran for the entrance to the 'Le Petite Opportunun', Paris's most famous jazz club. They flashed their passes at the doorman and stepped inside. Then they squeezed past tightly packed tables of Parisians and headed for the bar. On the stage a four-piece band were playing the kind of jazz that came from the 'golden era' of Paris in the 1950's.

They ordered two beers and turned to watch the band more closely. The sax player was taking his turn at a solo. He was good even to the ears of the two agents who had no interest in jazz whatsoever. The saxophonist was familiar to them. He was quite old with pure white hair, a heavily weathered face and incredibly piercing eyes. He wore a faded pair of blue jeans and a 'Bretagne' jumper under which could be discerned a lean trim body.

The agents leant against the bar and relaxed; there was time enough for them to wait until the end of the quartet's session. This jazz thing was something new to them, their idea of a cultured evening was a game of video bowls. Who knows? Maybe this strange music was something they could get into. They loosened their ties and enjoyed the ambience. The air was thick with scented smoke that diffused the light and made everything look like it had been shot through a soft focus filter. Most of the smoke was generated by a small machine beside the stage, but there were a few members of the audience drawing on cigarettes. Tobacco had undergone a resurgence of popularity since the war. It was one of the few pleasures still available in a consumer starved world.

The white haired saxophonist brought his solo piece to a dramatic climax then finished with a flourish. The audience stood and applauded loudly. After a lot more cheering and clapping, the quartet packed their instruments away and headed towards the bar. The old boy ordered a round of drinks for the other members of the band then joined a group of young Parisians at a table. A pretty young woman wearing an improbably short skirt kissed him on the check and parked herself in his lap. The two agents looked at each other, nodded and made their way towards the sax player's table. They wormed their way through the crowds and the taller one tapped the old boy on the shoulder. 'Senator Myrddin,' he began a little nervously, 'there has been an "incident" and you are required in Auckland as soon as possible.'

Myrddin turned and looked at the clean cut WDF officer. He'd noticed the pair as soon as they'd walked through the door—it was difficult not to. Business suits in a place like this was like wearing a space suit in the Ritz. 'What's the problem son? Can't the WDF wipe their arses without the help of an old man?' he replied with a mischievous grin. The officer's face went crimson with embarrassment. The girl in Myrddin's lap giggled.

'With respect sir,' the second WDF officer answered, 'we have our orders and I must insist that you accompany us. There is a plane waiting at De Gaul airport and you will be briefed in transit.'

Myrddin sighed deeply; it was always the same. He'd disappear for a few days' relaxation and the whole world would start to fall apart. Okay so a few days had turned into six months this time, but what was a few months compared to a few centuries? 'Okay kid,' he said, 'don't get your knickers in a twist. I'll come quietly, but at least let me finish my beer.'

The two officers looked at each other once more and nodded.

'Okay boys and girls move around the table and give the gentlemen a beer.' The agents sat down next to the other Parisians and the girl squirmed on Myrddin's lap once more. Usually Myrddin enjoyed the attentions of the young and beautiful, but the arrival of the WDF people had spoilt his fun. Sometimes he wondered if rejoining human society had been a good idea.

10.30HOURS LOCAL TIME. JUNE 21ST 2031. AUCKLAND NEW ZEALAND.

The New United Nations' President, James Gafton, sat on the couch in his study and looked once more at the photographs. They were a little grainy, which was hardly surprising considering the distance of the object from the camera, but clearly distinguishable. There was no mistaking the huge structure being built in space, and it was the realisation of his worst fears. He sighed, stood up and stepped out through the bay windows and into the presidential gardens. The morning sun was like a tonic soothing his tired face, thank the Lord for the therapeutic beauty of New Zealand.

During the occupation by the Dyason, New Zealand had been one of the few places on the planet largely untouched by the ravages of war. Gafton himself had used the Pacific islands to set up a huge resistance force and personally led the attack on the Dyason garrison in Australia. However, it was his ability as a politician after the war that had thrust him to the position of the New United Nations President and all the power and responsibility that went with the job. In a world devastated by years of war and occupation the task that befell the New United Nations seemed almost impossible at times, but much had been achieved in the three years since the final battle and Gafton liked to think that he'd played some part in the renaissance.

'So what's so bloody important that you have to drag me away from my vacation?' came a voice from behind. Gafton smiled and his spirits lifted; he recognised the voice, it could only belong to one person.

He turned, stepped back into the office and grabbed Myrddin's hand, pumping it warmly. 'Damn it's good to see you, you old renegade. I've missed your abuse at the senate.'

Myrddin returned the President's embrace. 'Ha, so you can't get on without me eh? Well I guess I've missed you too Gafton—sorry, I mean Mr President.' He smiled, and looked into taller man's eyes. 'So, as I say, what's so important that you have to drag me away from my vacation?'

'Myrddin. Most people take two weeks' vacation at one time. You've been gone six months when you said you were only going for a long weekend!' Gafton admonished.

Myrddin almost looked genuinely surprised. 'Has it been that long?' He stepped over to the long leather couch and made himself comfortable, his faded dungarees and denim shirt at odds in the more formal environment of the Presidential office—not that he seemed to notice. 'Well you know how it is. You lose track of the days as you get older and I guess I got a little side-tracked along the way.'

'So I hear.' said Gafton with a smile. Myrddin shrugged his shoulders. The President picked the folder up off his desk and handed it to his old friend. 'I've brought you here to take a look at these photographs. I suspect they confirm what we've been afraid of.'

Myrddin took the images out of the folder and examined them closely. They showed a planet not dissimilar from Earth half in sunlight, half in shadow. However, the planet wasn't what grabbed his attention. It was the large half-built structure in orbit that did that. It was shaped like a bulbous teardrop. A needle nose expanded into a broad body to which were attached three stub wings leading to large nacelles. Scoop intakes of some nature extended below the main body and these bled into what looked like exhaust outlets at what must be the rear of the craft. He flicked through the other photographs which showed the object in more detail. He could pick out what looked like gun emplacements built into the skin of the structure and what could only be small shuttle craft gave the whole thing a sense of scale. It was big, very big and also very ugly!

He looked up at the president and said simply. 'Well it was only to be expected. When did these shots arrive?'

'The scout ship arrived back in orbit three days ago. They came back early after they observed an explosion onboard that thing.' Gafton answered.

'An explosion?' said Myrddin thoughtfully. 'An accident perhaps?'

'Or possibly sabotage.'

'So, the Dyason are finally using the stolen technology and information to build a new battle-cruiser—which is what I said would happen, but is it possible that someone among their own ranks doesn't like it?'

'It looks that way, although we can't really be sure what the cause of the explosion was. However, it doesn't seem to have stopped construction. If it was sabotage, they didn't make a very good job of it, because externally at least, repairs have already been made,' said Gafton.

Myrddin tapped his fingers thoughtfully on the arm of the sofa. 'I take it your reason for suggesting sabotage comes from the interviews with the Dyason prisoners.' he asked.

'That's right,' came the reply. 'As you know we separated the prisoners into small groups and have slowly integrated them back into society working on projects to rebuild the chaos they caused. Only a very few have remained hard-liners, believing their fleet would be back for them. The rest have accepted that they will have to spend the rest of their lives here on Earth. What's been surprising is how many of them seem actively relieved to be stuck here.

'Life on Dyason obviously wasn't everything it was cracked up to be and if some of the prisoners are to be believed, there is the strong possibility that there is an anti-government movement on Dyason itself. It may be that these people are trying to halt the construction of the new battle-cruiser.'

Myrddin stood up and stepped through into the garden. The President followed him and the pair strolled across the lawn. 'So let me get this straight,' said Myrddin. 'The Dyason are apparently building a new fleet which if, as we suspect, they have in their possession the plans for Excalibur, may well have faster-than-light capability. The photographs you showed me are of the prototype vessel which is nearly complete, but has been set back by an explosion which may or may not be sabotage. Do we know any more about this battle-cruiser?'

Gafton shook his head. 'No not really Myrddin. The scout ship sits in high orbit over Dyason with full stealth protection. Its purpose is really to observe activity on the face of the planet and in orbit. The crew can also monitor radio traffic, but they can't move any closer to the planet for fear of detection. That means the only information we have is the photographs you saw and a name gleaned from radio transmissions.'

'Which is?'

'The Dominator.'

'A fairly typical Dyason name then. It's good to know their philosophy on life hasn't changed much,' Myrddin said, pausing to plant himself on a bench parked underneath an old tree. 'Seriously though, I've said all along that the Imperial forces would do something like this. The reports on the state of their planet's environment suggest that they only have a few years at most before the ecology collapses from total industrial overkill. The Dyason have abused their planet for centuries and in their minds they have no option but to find another planet or become extinct. The only other suitable planet they seem to have found so far is Earth, so inevitably they must come back at some stage.'

Gafton sat down next to Myrddin and sighed deeply. 'I know what you're trying to say old friend. I agree that we should have moved faster on building our own fleet, but you have to understand that the planet was completely devastated by the invasion. Resources are still scarce and simply rebuilding the tattered remains of our society had to take precedence over military spending. Besides we have the Excalibur.'

Myrddin turned and looked the President in the eye and said, 'Yes Mr President, we have Excalibur. We have placed all our faith in one ancient vessel and a handful of new, untried fighter craft. Now it looks like this will be all we have, to face a brand new Dyason fleet; a fleet based on the same technology as we have ourselves. Don't you think we just might be putting all our eggs in one basket?'

Gafton stared at the mountains in the distance for a moment before answering. 'Look Myrddin,' he eventually said, 'I understand your feelings and to an extent I agree with your sentiments. However, what we need to do now is find a way to solve the problem before it reaches our shores.'

Myrddin could see where this conversation was leading. He said nothing, simply raising an eyebrow.

'We need to find out if there really is an anti-Imperial movement on Dyason,' the President continued. 'If there is—then we need to nurture it a bit. If they were behind a bungled attempt at sabotage then we need to make sure they do a proper job next time. We need a group, a group that can work as a team, to land on the planet surface and try to make contact with the movement. We need—I need *you* to go there Myrddin.'

'Why me?'

'You know the reason why old friend. If she's returned there, then you are the only person who can face her.'

Myrddin sat and thought for a minute. Well, it was to be expected really. He realised that the final showdown had to happen sometime. Gafton preferred it to happen on Dyason rather than on Earth. God knows their own world had taken a beating from which she was only now recovering. Better that the next confrontation take place on the Dyason homeworld. If the Imperial Dynasty was to collapse at the same time—well that was all well and good. The President was right, he was the one to go, but not alone. He would need help.

'Okay,' he said finally, 'I'll do it, but I get to pick my own team, and you know who I'll want with me.'

The President nodded. 'I was counting on it.'

'Fine. What about Excalibur?'

Gafton shook his head sadly. 'I'm sorry Myrddin. Excalibur is our only real defence from another invasion. We can't risk sending her all the light-years to Dyason. If we lose her, we lose everything. One of the scout ships will be equipped with everything you need.'

'I see. Well I'd best be getting on with it,' He stood up and walked back towards the study, Gafton at his side. He tried not to notice the sad look in the President's eye. When they reached the door the pair turned and solemnly shook hands. 'I wish there was more I could do Myrddin. The Lord knows you've done more for the human race than anyone will ever know, but the Earth can't take another conflict.'

Myrddin held the President's hand in a vice-like grip and gave him a long, hard stare. 'Hey, Gafton,' he said with a impish grin, 'don't write our epitaphs before we're dead! We'll be back in time for the solstice.'

'I'm counting on it,' the President grinned back.

CHAPTER THREE

The tiny cubicle they called an interview room was beginning to make Hillmead claustrophobic. The grey metal walls and utilitarian desk which was bolted to the deck were austere even by the Navy's standards. The low gravity made him feel ill, and the questioning was getting him nowhere. Basically he was pissed off.

Lieutenant Shalock sat opposite a junior rating with a list of questions. Hillmead leant against a bulkhead and watched. The youth knew nothing, as did the other one hundred and thirty two officers, workers and troopers they'd interviewed in the past four days. This one was just the same as all the others. He entered the room looking as if he'd shit himself with fear, then after the first ten minutes, when he realised the line of questioning had nothing to do with him, fear turned to boredom. Just about everybody onboard this heap of metal had some misdemeanour they wanted to hide. Even in a closed military environment like the Dominator corruption was rife. Drugs, alcohol, leave passes, extra food rations, everything was up for sale. In fact Hillmead doubted that the Imperial Forces could operate without corruption; like everywhere else on Dyason it was a way of life.

Unfortunately, he wasn't here to investigate black-market activities and once it became clear that the interview was about something else, the subjects became bored and Hillmead got nothing, not even a whiff. The two known traitors died in the explosion and any evidence was destroyed in the fire and subsequent breach in the hull. It was entirely possible that there were only two conspirators onboard the Dominator in which case being here was a waste of time. In fact the sheer lack of residual evidence was suspicious itself. It was almost as if somebody had been here before him and made sure that there was nothing of worth for him to find out.

He opened the bulkhead door and left the interview to Shalock. He could feel the dirty look she was giving him without having to turn round. Still unused to the effects of low gravity, Hillmead stumbled off in search of some very black coffee. As usual the vending machine in the officers' quarters was playing up, but after giving the machine a serious kicking, he managed to get a cup of something that at least looked like coffee even if it didn't taste like it. He just got the scalding liquid to his lips when the ship's tannoy called, 'Colonel Hillmead to the communications deck. Colonel Hillmead to the communications deck.'

Damn it! Now what! He put the plastic cup on the obligatory steel table and went to the wall mounted intercom unit. 'Yeah, Hillmead here,' he snapped into the unit, purposely avoiding using his new rank. 'I'll be there in a minute.' Then he bounced into the corridor and headed for the communications deck, grabbing directions from a trooper as he went.

He had to admit it, the comm's deck was very impressive. Hillmead was used to cheap telephones that crackled and scratched, while police radios had to be kicked and thumped to make them work. Not so this place—it was full of equipment he could not even begin to understand. Rows of consoles flickered from the light of numerous display screens and the air was thick with the smell of electrical ozone. There was a continuous background sound of voices as the operators received and transmitted hundreds of communications.

A comms officer looked up from his console, noticed Hillmead and made his way over. 'Colonel, we have two audio-visual links for you. We have given priority to the link with Imperial Command. If you would step this way you can use this console to receive your message.'

Hillmead followed the comms officer to a console set aside from the rest. He could guess who the first link-up would be with, but who else wanted to talk to him? 'Who's the second link with?' he asked.

'Someone from your old police precinct in Caranak Colonel,' the officer replied with a shrug. Hillmead smiled to himself; he knew who that would be. He eased himself into the seat facing the communications monitor, the comms officer showed him how to operate the unit and quietly left. The screen came to life and the image of the Envoy Nimue appeared.

'Ah, Colonel Hillmead, at last,' the Envoy smiled at him and he shifted in his seat uncomfortably. There was something about the way Nimue looked at him that made him very uncomfortable. 'How is the investigation proceeding? Have you any leads as yet?'

Hillmead sighed inwardly before answering, 'No Envoy. As yet I have not found anything more than the original MDC investigation. We're interviewing everybody who was onboard at the time of the incident, but it is entirely possible that only the two traitors who died in the explosion were involved. Any other evidence was largely destroyed in the fire and ensuing hull breach. Lieutenant Shalock and I are continuing with the interviews and I am reviewing the files from the MDC investigation. However, I am *not* confident that there is anything else to be learnt aboard the Dominator.'

A frown appeared on the Envoy's face. 'I see. That's disappointing news. You don't believe that any other members of the crew, or construction workers were involved?'

'No, not if I'm honest,' he replied. 'Hurzon, the traitor who placed the charges, had a faultless record up to then. He was a hard-working, diligent technician whose references were excellent. I really need to trace his movements before he came onboard the Dominator if I am to find out what or who was behind his treason. The same can be said for the security office Goldmead. Both these people were to all intents and purposes model Imperial subjects up to the day of their treachery.'

'You wish to expand your inquiry Hillmead?' the Envoy asked.

'We'll have completed interviewing everybody who was onboard at the time of the event in another couple of days, except for one person—Security Leader Gulag. I need to know what it was about those two traitors that raised his suspicions.'

'Why don't you ask him yourself Colonel?' she replied. The camera viewpoint changed at the other end and the face of the clone appeared on the monitor. 'What can I do for you Hillmead?' Gulag asked his expression stony and unreadable.

The sight of the clone made him shudder. The meeting in the study when Gulag had plucked his thoughts out his head was still fresh in his mind. 'I wanted to ask you what it was about the two that aroused your suspicions,' he asked.

'They were blocking their thoughts,' the clone answered immediately.

'Sorry?'

'Most people on Dyason don't know how to block casual telepathic scanning. Why should they? Except for a few prisoners from Earth and myself there are no telepaths on Dyason,' Gulag explained. 'There are a few people who seem to have the natural ability to control the thoughts at the front of their mind—you happen to be one of those people—but the majority of the population just broadcast any old crap.'

'And this pair were attempting to control their thoughts?'

The clone nodded. 'The officer Goldmead, I'd been watching for a while and I was there when Hurzon came onboard. The almost contrived way in which they controlled their upper thoughts suggested some sort of training. I decided to put the two under close observation.'

'Obviously not close enough,' Hillmead said before he could stop himself.

Gulag smiled slightly. 'You are quite right Inspector, Colonel. I should have been more diligent.'

The camera moved once more and the Envoy reappeared on the monitor. 'I presume you want to pursue your inquiries into the traitor's past here in Caranak once you have finished onboard the Dominator,' she asked.

'That's right Envoy,' he confirmed. 'I think that will be our best line of inquiry.

'Fine,' she replied. 'When you return there will be a dossier awaiting you containing other recent events that may be connected. I look forward to seeing your report.'

The monitor went blank as the Envoy severed the connection. Hillmead tried not to let the Envoy and her clone get to him—and failed. Damn, but he really couldn't stand the bitch and her play thing. Sometimes he almost felt like supporting the traitors if they were intent on ridding Dyason of the likes of Nimue and Gulag. They represented everything that was rotten about the military government that ran Dyason. He sighed and hit the connection button for his second call. The weasel face of Pollowzki appeared on the screen grinning like a lunatic.

'Hi boss!' the police adjutant said merrily. 'Or should I say Colonel sir? Sorry to bother you sir! Nice uniform, better than the cheap crap us poor street fodder have to wear.'

Hillmead tried to keep a straight face but ended up grinning back at his old friend—it was good to see a familiar face and he knew he looked ridiculous in his Imperial costume.

'You're a nasty piece of slime Pollowzki,' he answered with a smile. 'What's the problem? Can't the Caranak police force manage without me for a few weeks? You've got to learn to stand on your feet some time you know!'

The adjutant held up a file to the camera lens. It was clearly labelled, 'Expenses'.

'Err... well, actually boss, we're all managing quite well without you. The arrest rate has shot up since you left—well, by a least two or three anyway. No the reason for calling such an important Imperial officer sir—of which I know you are one, sir—is to inquire about your expenses sir. The accounts department are throwing a fit over your incomplete expenses form.'

Hillmead kept smiling, but he sat up straighter in his chair. 'Expenses' was the code-word that Pollowzki and he had come up with, to let him know when Pollowzki had some information for him from his many 'sources'.

'Well I guess I did have to leave in a bit of a hurry, but you know how much I hate bureaucracy,' he said. 'I guess that if it's that important, you can send the file over to the spaceport and put it in the dispatch bag. There's a shuttle leaving later today, so I should get it by this evening. I'll check over the expenses in my quarters this evening and get the file back to you on the next return flight. Will that keep the tight-arsed accounts people happy?'

'I'm sure they'll be delighted to hear that boss. By the way how is your hush-hush mission getting along?'

Hillmead gave a very convincing sigh and said, 'To be honest Pollowzki it's going nowhere at the moment, but I'm still hoping to be back in the precinct before too long. Well I'd better get back to it. I'll make sure I look at the file this evening and get back to you if I have any problems.'

'Okay boss.'

The connection cut. Hillmead got up and left the comms desk, wondering what his long-time assistant and friend had discovered. When he got back to the interview room, Lieutenant Shalock was interviewing another member of the construction gang. After listening for five minutes Hillmead decided that the guy knew nothing. To relieve the boredom he stood and wondered idly what the young lieutenant was like without her uniform on. As if reading his thoughts, she turned and gave him a dirty look—ah well maybe not.

By the time ship's evening arrived both Hillmead and Shalock were tired and irritable. It had been another fruitless day of long dull interviews. They sat at a small table in the officer's mess sipping at fruit punch which was as colourful as the military grey bulkheads. Hillmead made a face, 'Eeargh...this stuff is disgusting. What kind of life is it when you can't have a decent bolt of blood poisoning alcohol after a hard day?'

'A healthy one,' Shalock replied primly. 'I'd hate to see the state of your liver. The Dominator like all Imperial Space Fleet vessels is a dry ship.'

Hillmead looked at the pretty young lady over the rim of his glass. 'Tell me Lieutenant,' he said, 'do you actually know how to have a good time? I mean underneath that starched, frosty exterior is there a fun-loving person? A person who likes to party occasionally? I mean, you're an attractive young lady—have you ever been flat on your back with your clothes off?'

A blush rose up her face and she looked away. 'As it happens, I have a boyfriend if you must know—Colonel. He's also an officer in the Imperial Military Detective Corp and we had many amusing times together at the academy.'

He looked at her again. The blush on her face made her look even more attractive—what a waste. 'Yeah, I bet you guys were a real barrel of laughs. Ha, bloody ha.'

She ignored his retort and stared into the distance ignoring both Hillmead and the other admiring junior officers sitting at other tables in the mess. A steward threaded his way over to their table.

'Colonel Hillmead?' the steward asked. Hillmead turned round to look at the small Dyason in his white serving uniform.

'Yeah, I guess that's me,' he answered without enthusiasm. 'What's the problem?'

The steward passed over a brown manila envelope. 'This just arrived for you sir.'

Hillmead looked blank for a moment then twigged, it was the 'expenses' file from Pollowzki. The shuttle from Caranak must have just arrived. He took the folder and dismissed the steward.

'What's that about?' Shalok asked curiously.

'Hmmm? Oh just my police expense sheet. I was pressed-ganged into the military so fast I didn't get a chance to complete all my paperwork,' he explained. 'Well, as you and I are getting on so famously I'm going to retire to my plush cabin and plough my way through this shit. If you get bored you know where I am.'

She gave him a cold smile and said, 'Don't wait up.' Hillmead shrugged and walked away.

In the privacy of his quarters he opened the folder. As to be expected it contained nothing but figures supposedly relating to his expense account. He sat down at the desk and got out another sheet of paper. Then, by using the code that he and Pollowzki had devised and memorised before he left on this assignment, he began to decypher the numbers. After two hours he had completely decoded the pages. He re-read the information in disbelief. Could it be true? If it were, then it shed a whole new light on the case, but the consequences! He soaked the decoded message in a solvent that slowly disintegrated the paper and threw the pulp in the waste chute. Then he threw himself on his bunk and switched the light off. Fear gripped his heart like a vice; everything was at risk!

EXCALIBUR 0900HOURS JUNE 23RD 2031

The intelligence officer leant back in his chair and crossed his arms. 'Well that's about it really. The *Observer* will be ready to leave in just over eighteen hours. The voyage back to Dyason takes twenty-three days at the light speeds the scout ship is capable of. Once in the Dyason home system you take up station employing full "stealth" capability. After that any further action is decided upon by the mission commander, which of course is you Group Captain.'

Paul Jenson sat on the other side of the conference table and looked over the briefing notes once more. 'Let's run through this just once more so there can be no mistake as to the purpose of this mission,' he said. 'The images brought back by the *Observer* a few days ago are of a new Dyason battle-cruiser that has light-speed capability. Or at least that's what you suspect it is.'

'That's right Group Commander,' the intelligence officer confirmed. 'We believe the design and configuration of this new vessel will give the Dyason an interstellar capability they have never had before.'

Jenson nodded. 'Okay I get all that, but what I can't quite get my head round is, just where the Dyason have got this technology from. We know now that in a lot of areas the Dyason are a lot less technologically advanced than we are. They only managed to reach our star system last time thanks to a convenient worm-hole, yet all of a sudden they're able to match our own technology. How is this possible?'

The intelligence officer looked down the table at Myrddin and said pointedly, 'I think the senator can explain that one.'

Myrddin looked at all the faces around the conference table and began, 'Well, I guess I probably can at that. If you cast your mind back to the final battle in the hangar here onboard the Excalibur, you'll remember that Moss here dispatched the little bastard Gulag.' Everyone glanced at Moss who sat stony faced in his WDF uniform next to Jennifer. It was hardly something that anyone of them would forget.

'At the time,' Myrddin continued, 'I made the mistake of thinking that when Gulag was frying on the hangar deck, Nimue's main concern was to save her bastard son. She leapt forwards and touched the burning remains of his body. I should have realised then the significance of this action.'

'What significance is that?' asked Captain Black.

'Gulag was an operant of extraordinary powers the same as Nimue. One of the talents the pair shared was the ability to absorb the contents of another person's mind just by touching that person,' Myrddin answered.

'So Nimue took the contents of Gulag's mind before fleeing herself?'

'That's right.'

'Okay, so let's presume that Nimue absorbed Gulag's mind before he became charcoal and she somehow managed to take the stolen Sukhoi back to Dyason,' Jenson interrupted. 'They're big presumptions, but we'll run along with them for the time being. That still doesn't explain how the Dyason got their hands on faster-than-light technology. Gulag was no technician and the Sukhoi certainly wasn't capable of more than orbital flight.'

'Luke Brabazon,' Moss said. Myrddin nodded.

'My brother?' Josh Brabazon said in surprise. 'What's this got to do with him?'

'Luke knew just about everything there was to know about the Excalibur,' Myrddin answered. 'The pair of you got her space-worthy again when she was sealed in the caverns. When Gulag killed Luke he raped his mind of everything he knew.'

'So when Nimue took the contents of Gulag's mind, she inherited all of Luke's knowledge?' asked Josh.

'That's about the size of it,' Myrddin confirmed.

'Which means that the Dyason possibly have access to some or all the technological information concerning Excalibur?'

'It's beginning to look that way.'

'Ah.'

'Exactly.'

A frown crossed Jenson's face. 'Why haven't we been told any of this before Myrddin?' he demanded.

'Well to be fair Paul, we had no real evidence until now that Nimue had returned to Dyason and had access to this knowledge. As far as I knew she was lost in the depths of space when the propellant in the Sukhoi expired. You were with us when we searched for her, but found nothing. It's only now with the construction of this new craft that the evidence is pointing towards her making it back there. How I don't know, but what we do need now are hard facts. If the Dyason are building a whole fleet of these ships, then we are in *deep* shit.'

'Hence the reason for this mission?'

'That's right.'

'Okay I understand why we need to go, and I understand that we can't risk taking the Excalibur,' said Jenson. 'But how do to you intend to get us down to the planet's surface undetected Myrddin? Once there how do you intend to make contact with any anti-imperial factions?'

Myrddin leant forward and placed his hands on the table. 'The *Observer* was designed to be capable of atmospheric flight. With her stealth capability we should be able to avoid detection although there is no guarantee of this. The plan is to land in one of the more desolate areas of the planet and rendezvous with the anti-government movement.'

'You're taking a big risk there Myrddin,' said Moss. 'If the Dyason are capable of building a light-speed battleship, then they are probably also capable of producing sensors that can detect a breach of their airspace, regardless of stealth.'

'I know son,' Myrddin replied looking at his descendent. 'That's one of the reasons why you and I are going on this mission. We'll have to divert any unwarranted attention.'

'If we do get onto the planet's surface in one piece, how do you intend to contact this underground movement?' Moss asked.

'They'll meet us there.'

'Eh? How will they know we're coming when we've made such an effort not to announce our arrival?' asked Jenson from the head of the table. 'There's something you're not telling us old man.'

Myrddin fidgeted and looked uncomfortable. Jenson saw this and demanded, 'Come on Myrddin we've all been through a lot in the past. This is not the time to hold back on us.'

He looked up at Jenson and said, 'I was going to tell you all just before departure. I didn't see any point in rocking the boat unnecessarily.'

'What do you mean?'

The old man got out of his chair and stepped towards the picture window which gave an incredible view of the Earth slowing rotating below them. After a pause he turned and looked at the others. 'After the occupation, the UN held several thousand Dyason in camps all over the planet. All the prisoners were interrogated in depth and after a period of time it became clear that not all of them were ardent supporters of the planet-wide totalitarian regime. Of course many of them would say that in an attempt to get more privileges, but the depth of feelings expressed appeared genuine in some cases.'

'This is what makes you think there is an underground movement on Dyason?' asked Jennifer.

'That and recent events,' the ancient answered. 'If such a group exists then we have to find it. That's why we are going to take a Dyason with us on this mission.'

'What?' exclaimed Jenson. 'You've got to be kidding Myrddin? I presume one of the POW's declared he was a member of the Dyason underground, so you're going to take him home? The bastard will make a run for it as soon as we get there!'

'No, I don't think so,' Myrddin replied. 'I've met the prisoner in question and I believe he is genuine.'

Jenson shook his head. 'Hell, this mission is beginning to sound more and more like a one-way ticket,' he said. 'What do you think kid?'

Moss though for a moment before answering. 'If Myrddin believes this guy will get us in touch with the Dyason underground movement, then that's good enough for me. Besides there really is no choice, we have to discover just what those bastards are up to.'

'I guess you're right,' Jenson replied. 'But I can't order anybody to go on this mission. It'll have to be volunteers only. So I'll give you the choice now— does anybody want to stay at home?'

He looked at the faces around the room one by one. Myrddin, Moss, Sandpiper, Brabazon, Jennifer and Black all remained quite. 'Well don't say I didn't warn you,' he said.

Sandpiper leaned back in his chair and put his flight boots on the highly polished conference table a wide grin on his face. 'Ah,' he sighed. 'It'll just be like old times!'

01.23 HOURS, BUSINESS QUARTER, CARANAK, DYASON

The smog was so thick, visibility was reduced to only a few metres. The wipers ineffectually scratched away at the windscreen wiping away the grimy moisture while the dull headlights simply reflected light from the droplets of water and pollution. Lieutenant Shalok shivered, despite the blast of warm air from the battered car heater.

'Where are we going Hillmead?' she asked miserably. 'This area of the city is virtually deserted except for a few roving gangs of Lobos. What the hell are we doing here?'

Hillmead leant forward over the steering wheel peering through the gloom, finding his way by memory more than sight. Huge derelict warehouses appeared from the muck then disappeared again. Once this was a prosperous business district with merchandise arriving from all over the planet to be redistributed to the citizens of Caranak. But that was back in the days before the great patriotic war when Dyason still had an economy to speak of. Now the whole area was slowly turning into dust and rubble, the only occupants being gangs of the sub-life, Lobos. Shalok was right, the place was a shit-hole, but it was also the perfect place for the kind of meeting you didn't want anybody else to know about.

'We've got to talk to somebody,' he answered.

'What here? Just what kind of person is it that you have to drive all the way out here to meet?' she replied pulling her overcoat tighter around her shoulders. Hillmead turned and looked at her, a small smile on his face.

'Tell me Lieutenant,' he said, 'just how many investigations have you been on?'

She shifted uncomfortably in the worn seat. 'Four,' she replied abruptly.

'Four?'

'Four simulated. At the academy.'

'Simulated? I see. Well, how many real ones — like this one?' he prompted dryly.

A blush rose up her cheeks. 'This is my first.'

'Well, I'll tell you what rookie,' he said with a deadpan voice. 'You stick to taking notes and wearing skirts —I'll make the decisions okay?'

Shalok turned in her seat and opened her mouth to respond. At that moment Hillmead swung the wheel and the battered vehicle descended down a ramp coming to a halt in an underground car park littered with the rusting hulks of other cars that never quite made it.

'Shut up,' he snapped. 'We're here. Put your environment mask on and follow me.'

He halted the car and cut the engine, then he flashed the lights four times. From the otherside of the derelict car park headlights from another vehicle flashed twice, then twice again in response. That was the signal. Hillmead opened the door and got out, motioning to Shalok to do the same. Despite the small breathing mask, the air was rank and very damp. He pulled his greatcoat tighter around him and walked in the direction of the other vehicle's lights. The eerie shadows cast by the headlights and the constant dripping of water made the place feel more like an ancient underground cavern than a disused car-park. Behind him he could hear the sound of Shalok's boots on the concrete, her breathing laboured, probably from fear. He could remember how shit scared he was on his first 'rendezvous'— just.

A figure materialised from the gloom and stepped towards him. They met in the pool of light between the two cars. Hillmead kept his hand on the hilt of his small automatic until he was sure of the person's identity.

'Hello boss. Lovely day ain't it?'

Hillmead smiled at his weasel-faced friend from the precinct. 'Hello Poll. Remind me never to go on a date with you. You seem to know all the best places,' he answered dryly.

'Don't worry boss, you're not my type.'

Shalok stepped forward and peered at the policeman. 'You?'

'Oh, hello gorgeous,' Pollowzki said with a lecherous grin. 'Nice get up—very practical. You'd never stand out in the crowd in that lot.'

'What the hell's going on here?' she asked ignoring his jibe at her fashionable street clothes.

'Poll here has some information vital to our investigation,' answered Hillmead.

'What can be so vital, that we have to play these silly cloak and dagger games?' she retorted sharply. 'What's wrong with the police station or our office at the MDC?'

Hillmead turned to the young lieutenant and snapped. 'For the god's sake shut up woman! Just for once keep your mouth closed and you might just learn something. What Pollowzki has for us is far too sensitive to be shouted all over Caranak. Do you think we enjoy meeting in shit-holes like this? Now, please, shutup.'

Shalok gave him a dirty look over the top of her breathing mask but said nothing. 'Thank you.' He turned back to Pollowzki and said, 'Okay Poll. I read the message you sent me on the Dominator, but I have to say I find it hard to believe. I know things are bad, but I never dreamed they were that bad. Do you have any proof to back your information?'

Pollowzki pulled an envelope out from under his coat and handed it to his former boss. 'It's all in here. The facts, the figures and the research. I don't think there can be any doubt about the conclusion. My contact says the information comes from the highest source.'

Hillmead broke the seal and opened the envelope. He looked at some of the contents but realised it would take a while to look through all the pages. 'Okay, great,' he said. 'How about a quick resume for now?'

'Well,' the policeman began, 'the bottom line is that the environment on this planet is completely fucked. The atmosphere has become poisoned to the point where it will soon be unable to sustain life. Food production has all but ceased and the seas no longer contain life.'

'How long have we got?'

'Ten years at the most. More likely five.'

'And then?'

'The planet becomes a lifeless desert.'

Shalok took in a sharp intake of breath. 'By the gods,' she breathed, 'this can't be true. I know things are bad in the cities, especially here in Caranak, but surely things are still okay in the countryside?'

Pollowzki shook his head sadly. 'If only it were a pack of lies gorgeous, but I'm afraid even an idiot can understand those figures,' he said nodding towards the envelope in Hillmead's hand. 'There is no countryside anymore, just desert. There are still a few small oases of life, up in the mountains for instance, but these are becoming few and far between. Even in these places the crops are diseased and the animals mutated. There's no doubt about it, in a few years' time the whole planet will become history.'

Hillmead shook his head. Even now he found it hard to believe. As Shalok said, they all knew things were bad, but not that bad. However, he would trust Pollowzki with his life and in fact had on more than one occasion. Once more he didn't know where he got his information from, but he had no doubt about its accuracy.

'Okay, let's take it as said that we're all going to die in a few years' time, what exactly has this got to do with our current investigation?' he asked, fairly sure he knew the answer already, but wanting to hear it from his former adjutant.

'The military have known that the environment is on a downward spiral for years,' Pollowzki explained parking his rear-end on the bonnet of his battered vehicle. 'The writing's been on the wall since the "great patriotic war". That's what was behind the invasion of planet Earth after the discovery of the "artefacts". With nowhere to expand to on our own planet and star system the re-occupation of Earth would enable the military to keep all their rank and privileges and have somewhere to go when things became intolerable here.'

'And once firmly entrenched on another planet, they could start the search for other planets that would support life,' Hillmead added. 'Imperial colonialism at its most ambitious.'

'You got it boss.'

'I can't believe any of this,' Shalok butted in, stamping her boot on the crumbling concrete floor. 'The Imperial forces are dedicated to protecting the life, family and moral values of every single Dyason citizen. The accusations you are making are treasonous, I mean they are simply not compatible with the beliefs and orders of the Imperial forces!'

Hillmead and Pollowzki looked at each other then at her. 'Oh please!' they said in unison. 'Save me the sermon.'

'Look gorgeous,' Pollowzki said almost gently. 'You're not in the academy now—this is the real world, and it ain't very pleasant. I admire your loyalty, I just wish it was aimed at something that deserved it.'

'But it's all madness,' she cried. 'If the planet is going to die, why aren't we doing something about it? Why aren't the scientists looking at ways to clean up the environment rather than spending all our resources on building ships like the Dominator?

'Hurrah!' Hillmead said lifting his head towards the heavens. 'At last she gets the point!'

'What point?'

'The reason behind this sham of an investigation!'

'What reason?'

'It's obvious isn't it?' Hillmead answered. 'One faction in the Imperial Forces believes in exactly what you suggested—that we should putting all our resources into finding a way to revitalise the biosphere. The other faction believes we should build a new fleet of battle-cruisers to retake and colonise the Earth. At the moment this faction has the upper hand, but with a few more explosions and assassinations the environment faction could gain the upper hand.'

'Your friends, the Envoy Nimue and her clone Gulag belong to the colonisation faction,' Pollowzki added. 'And the reason they've got the boss here on the case is because they don't know who among the military they can trust anymore. They're hoping that he will unearth the information they need to put an end to the environmentalists once and for all.'

Shalok's mind rapidly thought through what she was being told. Despite her dislike for the upstart police inspector and his scruffy side-kick, she had seen enough of him to know he was a shrewd investigator and played a straight hand. She didn't like it, but she couldn't dismiss his obscure theories out of hand.

'Okay,' she said. 'So where do you stand with all this. You've obviously thought about it—are you with the colonists or the environmentalists?'

Hillmead sat on the car bonnet next to his friend and crossed his arms. 'Well Lieutenant,' he answered, 'it's obvious that something has to be done or we're all going to die in our own shit. But as far as I'm concerned the jury is out on which faction has the answer. That's why these figures are so important—we have friends who can give us an independent opinion on whether the collapse of the biosphere is irreversible. If it is then the only answer is to move the population to another planet. As that place Earth is the only other planet we know of that can support life, then that's the place to go.'

'The humans aren't exactly going to invite us back with open arms though, are they?' Pollowzki added.

'No they're not,' Hillmead agreed. 'In which case brute force is the only answer. However, if the state of the environment is reversible—then we should be halting all military research and putting what resources we have left into making this damn place habitable.'

'So you're going on with the investigation?' she asked.

'Yes—for the moment at least. I don't like Nimue, that clone of hers or the military, but for the time being our aims are the same. I can't say any more than that.'

'So where are we going from here?'

'We?' Hillmead said raising an eyebrow. 'I would have thought you'd want to have nothing more to do with me. After all, it could have an adverse effect upon your career.'

Shalok crossed her arms and looked Hillmead in the face. 'You just said that for the time being at least the investigation goes on, so why would I want to quit? Besides, like you said, I might learn something. I…' she got no further. A sharp crack reverberated around the car park and the floor in front of her feet erupted in shards of concrete. 'Shit!'

The three of them leapt in different directions diving for cover, out of the light of the headlights. There were another five gunshots, one of the headlights on Pollowzki's vehicle disintegrated along with the windscreen. The other shots entered the radiator and bonnet sending a plume of steam towards the carpark roof.

'Shalok?' Hillmead called from behind the cover of a rusting hulk, automatic pistol in hand. 'Are you okay?'

'Yeah,' she shouted back from behind the hulk of a delivery van. Her own pistol was in her hand and she peered into the gloom trying to get a fix on the sniper. There were another two sharp reports and the other headlight disintegrated. The only light in the underground car park now came from the twin beams of Hillmead's vehicle.

'Poll?'

'Yes boss?'

'The bastard is somewhere to our one o'clock position. You head anti-clockwise, I'll go the other way. Let's see if we can flush this bastard out.'

'Will do.'

'Shalok, you stay put.'

'Piss-off Hillmead,' she replied testily. 'I did learn some things at the academy. If this guy has got a night-scope we're in deep shit.'

'If he has a night-scope he's a piss poor shot. Okay you cover my back. On the count of three. One...Two...Three!' Pollowzki ran right, Hillmead and Shalok ran left. Three more shots rang out kicking up the dirt behind them. Hillmead collapsed behind the remains of a luxury limousine, a dinosaur from a bygone era of plenty. Shalok fell in a heap beside him.

'Shit, Hillmead, you really know how to show a girl a good time.' she said breathing heavily. 'Never a dull moment.'

He put his hand on her arm and gripped it. 'Watch this,' he said bluntly. Across the car park a small light arced through the air and landed with a clatter on the concrete floor. A hail of bullets ripped the small lighter to pieces.

'Works every time.' he said with a smile. 'There. Just by that old truck. That's where the gunfire came from. This guy is an amateur—no night-scope and no silencer. Nice one Poll. Okay, follow me.'

He ran for the cover of a group of rusting hulks pushed up against the dripping concrete walls. Another couple of rounds were fired, but they went far off the mark. As Hillmead thought, the sniper didn't have a night-sight and had been aiming using the beams of the vehicle lights. Quietly he edged his way around the edge of the car park constantly keeping an eye on the spot where he saw the muzzle flash, gradually moving toward it. He couldn't hear anything except for the dripping water and the slight hiss of the shot-up radiator—which was good; at least Shalok knew how to move quietly. There was hope for her yet.

It took him several minutes to move from the cover of one derelict vehicle to another, several minutes in which his eyes slowly became accustomed to the gloom. Eventually he neared the spot he'd marked as being where the gunfire came from. Slowly he crept around the edge of a concrete support pillar until—there, in the gloom he could just make out the silhouette of a figure with a rifle still looking in the direction of the illuminated vehicles.

There was a clatter behind Hillmead and a barely whispered 'Shit!' The sniper whirled round and loosed off a volley in the direction of the noise.

Sparks flew off the body panels of an ancient saloon car. Hillmead stepped out from the cover of the pillar flicked on his small torch, illuminated the gunman and aimed his automatic. 'Police! Put down your weapon!' he shouted. Surprised, the sniper raised his arm to shield his eyes from the glare of the light, letting the muzzle of the rifle point toward the ground. 'I said, put down your weapon!' Hillmead called out again. Realising he was out-manoeuvred the gunman began to lower his weapon to the ground. There were two sharp cracks and the sniper was literally picked up off his feet and hurled against the side of a truck his chest blown wide open.

Hillmead ran over as the sniper's body slid onto the floor in a pool of crimson blood. He didn't even bother to check if the sniper was dead, it was a foregone conclusion. 'Bastard!' he shouted in frustration. Shalok appeared at his side breathing heavily, her gun still smoking slightly. In a blaze of anger he whirled round, gripped her by the throat and pushed her up against the side of the truck.

'You stupid bitch!' he shouted. 'We needed him alive! He was the best lead we've had!'

'He was going to shoot you!' she gurgled trying to prise his big hands off her throat.

'He was putting the sodding gun down!'

Another hand gripped Hillmead's arm and eased it down. 'Okay boss, calm down,' Pollowzki said evenly. 'It's too late now. There's no point in killing her as well. Come on—let go. That's it.'

The red faded from Hillmead's eyes and he released the pressure from Shalok's throat. She collapsed on the floor next to the corpse fighting to get her breath back. 'Don't you ever. 'Don't you ever...ever...get in the way of an investigation like that again.' he snarled. Shalok just sat on the ground massaging her throat.

'Heh boss, you'd better come and take a look at this,' Pollowzki said leaning over the body of the gunman. Hillmead tore his eyes away from Shalok and went to see what Pollowzki was looking at.

The gunman was wearing the tattered clothing of a Lobo, one of the underclass, with no environmental mask. However, Hillmead wasn't fooled by any of this. Underneath the dirty hair and grimy skin was a face devoid of the open sores and rashes that were a result of long-term exposure of unprotected skin to the atmosphere. The rifle despite being an ancient design dating back to the great patriotic war, was well oiled and obviously lovingly maintained.

Pollowzki opened his hand and showed Hillmead a set of dog tags. 'Our Lobo here boss, would appear to be a member of the Military Detective Corp. He followed one of us here, but if you ask me, he was just playing with us. That old sniper's rifle is a classic piece—there's no way he could have missed us from this range, despite the low light levels.'

Hillmead grunted in acknowledgement and peered at the name on the dog tags. Suddenly there came the sound of an awful wailing from behind them and the two men turned to find Shalok hugging her knees to her chest and bawling like a child.

'Shit. What's got to her?' asked Pollowzki. 'She looks like she's seen a ghost!'

Hillmead slipped the bloodied dog tags in his coat pocket. 'I think you'll find the lieutenant has just found out she shot her boyfriend,' he replied.

CHAPTER FOUR

0900 HOURS GMT. JUNE 25TH 2031

M oss sat in the helmsman's couch on the bridge of the *Observer*. The control system was a direct copy of that on the Excalibur which meant he could feel the ship as if it were an extension of his own limbs. The twin powerplants that held replicant singularity drives were a fraction of the size of those on the ancient alien ship, but they still throbbed with power undreamed of only a few short years ago.

'Excalibur control this is the *Observer*,' he called traffic control.

'Go ahead *Observer*,' came the reply.

'Permission to depart from docking bay three.'

'You are cleared to depart docking bay three *Observer*,' traffic control informed him. 'Steer delta nine, decimal four one seven and accelerate to light speed at your discretion.'

'Confirm heading delta nine, decimal four, one, seven,' Moss automatically responded.

'Good hunting *Observer*.'

'Thank you Excalibur.'

The locking bolts released and Moss gently eased the *Observer* away from the massive hull of the Excalibur. As they slipped along her underside Moss took one more look at the ancient vessel that had become his home then banked the *Observer* round until she was heading towards open space. Once in open space he gradually released more power from the singularities and felt the ship surge ahead accelerating faster and faster. The moon slipped beneath the hull and within seconds she was beyond the limits of the Earth's and moon's gravity and heading into the depths of space. He felt a familiar presence at the back of his mind.

'I'm still not very happy at the thought of you going without me,' the sentient computer of Excalibur said to him.

'We've been through all that,' Moss replied gently. *'It's important that you stay to protect the Earth. If anything should happen to us or our mission should fail, you will be the only thing that will keep the Dyason from retaking what they once had.'*

'I understand that, it's just that I don't like it.'

'Learning to accept responsibility is a part of growing up Excalibur,' Moss thought at the sentient computer that was the soul behind the ancient craft. *'Believe me—I should know!'*

'Indeed, you speak wisely,' Excalibur replied. *'You will shout if you need me?'*

'You can be sure of that old friend. In the meantime, be good and do as you are told.'

'I shall. Farewell.'

'Farewell,' thought Moss.

'Hyperspace entry point coming up in ten seconds,' said Jennifer from the *Observer's* navigator's position. 'Five, four, three, two, one...'

Moss extended his perception beyond the three dimensions of space and on into the fourth dimension—time. He perceived the route through the vast distances of space and time to a spot in the star system of the Dyason. He kept this point uppermost in his mind as if it were a point on a distant shore and set course accordingly. The stars bunched up before the *Observer* until they merged to form one huge solid wall of light. Moss felt their resistance against the hull of the ship, but ignored them and released the two singularities until the very substance of space was screaming through the engines at full power. He felt the solid wall of light begin to part as a needle slips through the toughest material. Then the ship slipped through the tear in space and slipped into hyperspace with barely a ripple.

11.00HOURS. JULY 16TH 2031

Jenson sat in the captain's chair on the small bridge of the *Observer*. For the umpteenth time he scanned his panel and checked that the others were all at their stations. He was particularly careful to check that the electronic countermeasures were fully operative. Without them, they risked appearing on the scopes of the Dyason as soon as they popped out of hyperspace. He'd been in charge of several surveillance missions in the past and always felt tense when they entered the Dyason home star system. He knew the others would be feeling the same.

They had used the three-week voyage through hyperspace to prepare as best they could for the mission ahead. Hard information about the new Dyason battle-cruiser was scarce, so it was hard to make detailed plans, therefore it would be necessary to improvise to a great extent—which was something Jenson was very unhappy about. He realised the importance of their mission, but was privately alarmed at the speed at which this operation had been put together. Having the Dyason, Tychivesk as part of the team didn't help matters either. Moss flatly refused to talk to the ex-Imperial officer and to be honest the Dyason hadn't been any great help so far. The Dyason Tychivesk didn't know anything about the new battle-cruiser; it's construction had begun some time after he became a prisoner of war and only time would tell if he really was a member of the Dyason 'Democratic Front'. If he were, then he would eventually be a great asset. If he was lying, well they were about to walk into a trap.

'All stealth systems fully operational,' Sandpiper said from his position at the weapons defence panel. 'All weapons on line.'

'Powerplants fully operational. There is a slight drop in the starboard status field surrounding the singularity, but it's well within limits,' Josh Brabazon said from the engineering panel.

'Acknowledged. Keep an eye on that Josh. Helm are you ready to leave hyperspace?'

'Helm is ready to leave hyperspace,' Moss answered from his couch where he was strapped up to the ship's inter-active flying controls. Jenson took a deep breath; they were as ready as they ever would be. 'Okay people let's do it. Nav, re-entry into normal space at your discretion.'

'Roger skipper,' Jennifer acknowledged from the navigators console. 'Leaving hyperspace in thirty seconds…ten…five…four…three…two…one…now.'

Through the bridge viewers Jenson saw the stars that had been streaking past the ship like meteors bunch up once more to briefly form a solid wall of light, then dissipate. There was no sensation of movement onboard the ship, the only notable difference was the return of stars as pinpoints of light rather than streaks of flame.

'Any sign of other ships?' he asked Sandpiper.

'Negative skipper. The scopes are clear at present and there appears to be no unusual telecommunications. I think we made a clean re-entry,' Sandpiper replied.

'Good. Tychivesk, I intend to make for the edge of the dark side of the second moon Alphebus. We should be near enough to observe any orbital activity there, without being at risk from casual detection. Good enough?'

Tychivesk turned from his position at the surveillance console and answered, 'That will be fine Group Captain.'

'Okay. Helm take us into orbit around Alphebus.'

'Roger skipper,' Moss answered and once more feeling the engines and thrusters of the *Observer* as if they were parts of his own body, he banked and rolled the ship until it was heading towards the smaller of Dyason's twin moons.

Jenson got up from his seat and walked over to the surveillance console where Myrrdin and Tychivesk were seated. The Dyason had the flaming red hair and almost oriental facial features that were the norm for his race. About thirty years old, Tychivesk still treated the others onboard the *Observer* with the rigid formality of an Imperial officer, despite the years he had spent in captivity.

'Let's go over this once more,' Jenson said to the two of them leaning on the edge of the console. 'We'll observe the planet for one full revolution, which will bring the Dominator into view and enable us to look for signs of increased military activity. Okay so far?'

'That would be sensible Paul,' confirmed Myrddin.

'Then you want us to send a pulse microwave burst to the specific co-ordinates you have given us?' he asked of the Dyason.

'That is correct Group Captain. The co-ordinates are for a remote communications centre in the southern desert regions. It was built during the great patriotic war as a listening post. It was manned and updated by sympathisers to the cause, just before the fleet left for Earth.'

Jenson shifted uneasily. 'This is the part of the plan that worries me,' he said. 'You've been gone nearly five years now Tychivesk. A lot could have changed since then. How can you be sure that the post is still manned? Your group of "sympathisers" could have been compromised and executed ages ago and you'd never know it. How do we know that the militarists haven't taken over this communications post and are just sitting there waiting for us to send our greetings?'

Tychivesk looked at Jenson and gave a small shrug. 'I'm sorry Group Captain, but I do not have an answer to that question. The latest information that I have came from a member of our faction that was posted to Earth just before the capitulation. At that time the "sympathisers" were growing rapidly in strength and numbers. There *is* a risk that our codes or the listening post have been compromised, but I would not be giving you the co-ordinates if I did not truly believe that this is *not* the case. I have every faith in my compatriots.'

Jenson scratched his head. 'Well that's all well and good Tychivesk, but perhaps what you don't realise is that our stealth capability works only when we are in "passive" mode. As soon as we transmit anything, we can be detected. Now a microwave beam is very narrow, so if your guys are at those co-ordinates, then the chances of being detected aren't too high. However, if they have been compromised, then we'll be advertising our presence to the whole Dyason space fleet! Are you sure that there is no other way of contacting your people?'

'Paul,' Myrddin spoke up, 'time is not on our side. Their new battle-cruiser is nearly complete and packs sufficient fire-power to easily take on the Excalibur. It could be ready for travel through hyperspace any day now. The militarists could launch another invasion against Earth at any time. We must find out what exactly is going on down there as soon as possible. I agree that transmitting anything is a great risk, but in this case it's a risk that we will just have to take.'

Jenson held up his hands in surrender. 'Okay Senator. We'll do it your way. I just wanted to be sure we had no other options before we committed ourselves.'

'Your caution is understandable and very wise under the circumstances Group Captain.' complimented Tychivesk.

'Thanks,' he replied dryly. He stood up and returned to the captain's chair. 'Okay helm, park us in a position around Alphebus where we can observe the planet for two revolutions. Sandpiper.'

'Yes skipper?'

'Prepare a microwave pulse signal and aim the dish at the co-ordinates.'

'Will do, boss.'

'Okay people, let's keep our eyes and ears open. There are a lot of hostile natives out there.'

Moss brought the *Observer* into position close to the moon of Alphebus. He programmed the ship's computer to hold their position in relation to the planet Dyason itself, rather than orbit around the moon. This kept the surveillance ship stationary while Dyason rotated through its normal thirtyone hour cycle. Jenson ordered the sensors to begin recording anything they could find, including radio and television emissions, infra-red signatures and atmospheric content. As soon as the data started to come in they began to analyse it. The orbit of the battle-cruiser Dominator was such that it circled around the planet every six and a half hours, giving them four opportunities to observe the huge vessel closely.

They took it in turns to monitor the sensors and computer readings, grabbing food and a few hours' sleep where they could. Josh Brabazon untiringly examined the digitally enhanced images of the battle-cruiser occasionally giving out a low whistle of appreciation that did nothing for Jenson's nerves. Eventually as the long hours of observation came to an end, Jenson decided he couldn't take the suspense anymore. 'Josh if you whistle once more, I'm going to throttle you! You've had plenty of time now to examine that piece of junk, do you mind sharing your findings with the rest of us?'

Josh Brabazon looked up from his computer console sheepishly, aware for the first time that everyone was waiting for him. The others had finished their observations hours ago. 'Hmm? Oh sorry skipper, I didn't realise you were all waiting on me. I'm just about done,' he replied.

'Okay then, lets compare notes. Josh you go first— tell us what you make of their new toy.'

'Well,' Josh began tapping orders to the ship's computer to project a three-dimensional image of the Dominator over the small conference table set to one side of the bridge. 'I have to hand it to these guys, it's quite a piece of machinery they've got there. Somewhat crude compared to Excalibur, but effective none-the-less.'

'As time is short, I think it would be best if we left the indepth analysis until another time,' said Myrrdin gently. 'Just give us the general picture for now Josh.'

Josh looking a little crest-fallen said, 'Er...yeah, okay. Well basically from what I can make out from only a preliminary external examination, I'd say you are definitely looking at a heavily armed battle-cruiser capable of faster-than-light speeds.'

'That's pretty well the conclusion we'd all come to, but what is it that brings you to that conclusion, Josh?' Moss asked leaning back in his chair and examining the holographic image closely.

'The shape for a start. It's a classic tear-drop design. You see, when a craft nears the speed of light, pressure builds up in the same way as an aircraft approaching the speed of sound. This pressure build-up causes shock-waves that cascade along the length of the hull and can cause the vessel to break up and disintegrate. These shock waves can be so intense they cause a failure in the hull and subsequent break-up of the vessel. BOOM!

'The way to avoid this is to streamline the hull. These guys are using a tear-drop shape. The needle nose pierces the light barrier and gradually slips the rest of the ship through with the minimum of resistance. It's basically another type of streamlining much the same as the *Observer* and Excalibur.'

Jennifer pointed to the short stub wings sitting at the rear of the hull. 'What are these things for?'

'Ah, they'll be for the engine intakes,' Brabazon replied. 'You see those large nacelles on the end of the stub wings? They do the same job as the belly scoop on Excalibur. They suck all those loose atoms and gases that float through space, accelerate them past the singularities and eject them out the rear, therefore providing thrust.'

'So in your opinion this ship will be capable of making the trip to Earth?' Myrrdin asked, a frown on his forehead.

'Without getting inside there's no way of knowing what state their powerplants are in, but certainly if they've got that end sorted out, there's no reason why this ugly brute can't travel to any point in the Galaxy and back.'

'That's what I feared,' Myrrdin said tapping thoughtfully on the table. 'What about her armament?'

'Once again, I can't be sure without getting onboard, but by the look of the numerous gun blisters adorning her hull I'd say she's armed to the teeth with everything from lasers to missile batteries.'

'Sufficient to take on the Excalibur.'

'More than sufficient. In fact I would say that the Excalibur is probably out-gunned.'

'Hmm...not good. Not good at all,' said Sandpiper. 'If Josh's observations are correct we're in deep trouble. If they build more of these babies, we won't stand a chance. Somehow we're going to have to get onboard and find out for sure what her capabilities are.'

'Well that pretty well covers the Dominator. We know what we've got to do there—get more intelligence and disable or destroy the beast if possible,' Jenson said decisively. 'What about the rest of the planet? What's the state of the Dyason atmosphere Jennifer?'

Jennifer instructed the computer to project an image of planet Dyason with a spectral analysis of the atmosphere next to it. 'It's not looking good. There's no sign of a reduction in the amount of industrial pollutants and toxins being poured into the oceans and atmosphere. If anything there's an increase in the level of pollutant discharge rather than a decrease. This would seem to indicate an increase in heavy production.'

'You mean to tell me that even though the whole ecology of the planet is taking a nose-dive the Dyason are doing nothing about it? They're actually speeding up their deaths by discharging even more shit into the environment? It's hard to believe,' exclaimed Sandpiper.

Tychivesk looked at the figures and charts displayed and shook his head sadly. 'As one born and raised there, even I find this difficult to understand. Now my friends you can understand why there is dissent among my people. Ah...how could they be so stupid?'

'Tychivesk, could the increase in output be a sign that the militarists are exhausting the planet's resources on building another invasion fleet?' Myrrdin asked.

'Possibly,' the Dyason shrugged dejectedly. 'Without being there it's hard to say.'

'Bearing in mind that it's a controlled economy, it's equally possible that the government has ordered an increase in the production of consumer goods to keep the good citizens' minds off the fact that they can't breathe the air anymore,' Moss suggested.

'I wouldn't be surprised,' agreed Sandpiper. 'Can you imagine the uproar if everybody realised just how bad things actually are? The planet would become ungovernable.'

'I would say that's exactly what the Emperor and his cronies are worried about. I would imagine that their biggest fear would be to lose control of the population before they have time to complete the new fleet and sail away, leaving a dead world behind them,' added Myrrdin.

Jenson switched the holographic projector off and stood up. 'Well people that decides it. We have to try and make contact with Tychivesk's people and at best, help in their attempt to overthrow the militarists. At worst, we need to gather enough intelligence together to give ourselves a fighting chance of beating off a new invasion force.'

Tychivesk looked at Jenson, a determined glint in his eye. 'Group Captain, if my people stop the Imperial Navy from building a fleet of these new starships can you stop my planet from dying?'

Jenson returned the Dyason's stare and said sincerely, 'I can't guarantee that Tychivesk. We don't know just how bad the damage is. But God knows we'll try, that's one thing I can guarantee. I can tell you this though, if they succeed in launching a new fleet, the only people to benefit will be the Emperor and his henchmen. The rest of the population, your family and friends, everyone, is going to die a slow and painful death.'

Tychivesk sat and said nothing for a moment, his eyes focused on some point beyond the hull of the *Observer*. Eventually he turned and addressed everyone on the table his face angry and determined. 'You're right. There's no other option, I shall give you the codes with which to contact my people. The time has come to make the Emperor pay for the horrors he has brought upon my world.'

CHAPTER FIVE

IMPERIAL AIR STATION GACCIO

The transport aircraft touched down with a screech of protesting rubber and taxied towards a group of buildings at the far side of the airfield. It came to a halt near a large hangar and the massive six-blade propellers on the four huge turboprop engines gradually came to a standstill. A small door opened near the front of the massive desert camouflaged fuselage and two people climbed down the crew ladder. A moment later their baggage was passed down to them and they stood wearily under the shadow of the huge wing.

The heat was intense, it shimmered in waves across the concrete apron and sweat dripped off Hillmead's face. The contrast between the cool air-conditioned interior of the transport and the blistering desert air was indescribable. He pulled a handkerchief out of the pocket of his tropical uniform and wiped his face, peering up at the dirty blue-green sky. He wasn't sure which was worse, constantly having to wear environment masks in the traffic polluted cities, or not having to wear a mask but risk being sunburnt to death in the outland regions. As he travelled around the planet it became more and more obvious that the environment was in terminal decline.

'What a dump!' Shalok commented dryly, wiping the sweat dripping from her forehead. 'I can't believe they've got a security problem here. You'd have to be completely insane to want to spend any time out in the open here. Who the hell would come to this place?'

'That's what we're here to find out,' Hillmead replied. 'Here comes our transport.'

Through the shimmering haze a crew transporter appeared and came to a halt beside them. The driver wound down the window and shouted, 'Colonel Hillmead? Lieutentant Shalok?'

'Yeah, that's us.'

'The base commander sends his compliments. If you'd like to climb aboard I'll take you to his office.'

Hillmead and Shalok opened the rear doors threw their kit inside and climbed onboard. Thankfully they collapsed onto the bench attached to the side of the vehicle. At least the air conditioning was partially working and the interior was a few degrees cooler. Shalok leaned forward towards the conscript driver. 'Is it always so bloody hot here?'

The driver glanced over his shoulder and gave her a big grin. Hillmead couldn't help thinking just how young he looked. He was no more that seventeen maybe eighteen years old, with a spotty pock-marked face and downy cheeks. 'Sure is Lieutenant,' the driver replied. 'Every day of the week, every month of the year, it's hotter than between a whore's legs—begging your pardon Lieutenant.'

'This must rate as the posting from hell,' Shalok said ignoring the youth's language.

'It is if you're stuck outside on patrol or guard duty. Then you just sweat like a smelly pig. But the barracks and hangars ain't too bad. They've at least got working air conditioning and the CO, he makes sure there's always plenty of entertainment from the cities laid on—if you get my drift.'

'Has it always been like this here?' Hillmead asked.

'I've only been stationed here a few months sir. But some of the old sweats reckon that the whole area around here used to be farm land with fields and crops and trees and all sorts. Then over a period of time it became a desert. You can still find the remains of old buildings and dry riverbeds.'

'When did all this happen trooper?' Shalok interrupted.

'I don't rightly know Lieutenant. Four maybe five years ago—you'd have to talk to the old sweats. One thing I do know.'

'What's that?'

'It's getting hotter every day. Ask the met officer.'

Shalok and Hillmead exchanged knowing looks as the driver pulled up outside some two-storey buildings made of some local heavy stone blocks and painted white to reflect the sun.

'Well here we are. It ain't Caranak but it is home. Welcome to Imperial air station Gaccio.'

Shalok and Hillmead picked up their bags, climbed out of the transport and entered the offices. The driver bade them farewell and drove off again. The interior was cool and dark in contrast to the blazing heat and sunshine outside. The tiled floors and white-washed stone walls were very different from the declining, acid eaten, ornate decor of so many buildings in Caranak. A junior officer stood up from a large metal desk and made his way across the floor to greet them.

'Colonel Hillmead, Lieutenant Shalok, welcome to air station Gaccio. Group Leader Baccia apologises for not meeting you personally. Unfortunately something has arisen that needs his urgent attention. He will be with you as soon as he possibly can. In the meantime can I show you to your quarters? I'm sure that you would both like to freshen up after your long journey.'

Hillmead ignored the flight Lieutentant, dropped his bags on the tile floor, lit a weed and looked around at the pictures on the reception wall with curiosity. Shalok gave him one of her best dirty looks.

'You'll have to excuse the Colonel,' she said. 'He's very tired. We would both be very grateful if you could show us where we might get a show...' Her sentence was cutoff by the wailing of a siren. Hillmead dashed outside to see what was going on, closely followed by Shalok and the flight Lieutenant.

What was only a moment ago, an apparently deserted air base, was suddenly a hive of activity. Vehicles raced across the apron and troopers ran to their posts. At the far end of the airfield Hillmead watched as the blast doors to rapid reaction aircraft shelters slid open and through the heat haze emerged menacing all-black machines.

'What's going on?' he asked the junior officer.

'It's just an exercise Colonel. Please come inside out of the heat.'

Hillmead ignored him and continued to watch as the evil-looking aircraft moved onto the main runway. He counted five of them, all of a strange design he'd never seen before. The heavily glazed cockpits blended into a contoured fuselage and small stub wings—canards if he remembered the term correctly. The intakes were huge and hung below the body like massive scoops. The twin fins were cantered outwards and stood as tall as a two-storey building. There was no doubt about it, these beasts were a new type and by the looks of them they were big vicious bastards.

'These beasts are destined to be part of the new invasion fleet?' he shouted at the flight Lieutenant above the noise of the sirens and roaring engines.

'I don't know anything about that Colonel. Please sir, I must insist that you step inside.'

'What's the matter? Scared I'll see something I shouldn't?'

Shalok stood next to him peering at the machines as they lined up on the runway. 'I've never seen anything like them before. Could they be connected to the new prototype that crashed?' she hollered into his ear.

Hillmead's reply was drowned out as the five aircraft opened their engines and piled on the thrust. Within seconds they were roaring down the runway, clawing the air. Just as it looked as if they would hit the end of the runway before they saw light under their wheels, the needle noses pointed towards the sky and the formation took off. The bizarre machines accelerated with incredible speed climbing vertically into the dirty blue atmosphere. Hillmead and Shalok stood rooted to the spot watching them disappear into the haze as a double sonic boom reverberated across the desert. Eventually, Hillmead turned to Shalok and said, 'In answer to your question, I think the answer is almost definitely yes.'

'The Air Commander will see you now,' said the thin junior officer,' his tone quieter now that peace had descended upon the airfield once more.

'Yeah,' said Hillmead sarcastically, 'I bet he will. Come on let's find out just what's going on here.' Then he turned and marched back into the building.

'Microwave pulse sent. I'm scanning all frequencies for a reply,' Jennifer stated from her position at the navigation and communications console. 'No reply at present.'

'Give them time. They're probably running around wondering who the hell's calling,' said Mryriddin feigning nonchalance.

'The question is who are *they*? The rebels or Imperial forces? It's going to ruin our day if we're busy sending greetings to the wrong bunch,' said Hanson.

Jenson leaned forward in his captain's chair and spoke quietly to Moss. 'What do you reckon kid? Do you feel any unusual activity?'

Moss sitting in the helmsman's couch shook his head. 'Sorry skipper. I'm not feeling a thing. It's all quiet out there at the moment.'

'Hmm...Okay, just be ready to move us away from here and make the dash back into hyperspace if neccessary.'

'Will do boss.'

Jennifer sat up straight in her chair, her hand to the remote amplifier in her ear. 'That's it...' she whispered quietly to herself, then with more assurance, 'that's it! That's the recognition reply code!'

Tychivesk leapt up and dashed over to Jennifer. He leant over her shoulder and scanned the digital read-out. 'Yes!' he said with evident relief. 'I knew they'd still be scanning the frequency!'

'Are you sure that's the correct code?' Jenson asked cautiously.

'Yes, yes! Only a select few among the underground movement know that code! It's as I have said—the movement is going from strength to strength. I am sure of it!'

'Okay, let's not get too excited Tychivesk. Jennifer?'

'Yes skipper?'

'Pulse the prepared message down to them. Moss, move us closer to the planet, but keep scanning for any sign of hostiles. If you sense anything, anything at all, then get us out of here.' Jenson sat upright in his chair and scanned the bridge. 'Everyone keep on their toes. There's still no guarantee that we're not walking straight into a trap.'

Moss moved the *Observer* away from her holding position in the shadow of the moon and eased the ship towards the planet. He scanned ahead of them with his mind and the ship's probes but found nothing accept for the usual low-orbital traffic to and from the space stations. It would seem that Tychivesk was correct in his belief in the underground movement.

'Im receiving a narrow beam message now.' said Jennifer. 'I'll get the computer to decode it and project it on the main monitor.

Sandpiper looked up at the row of displayed figures on the monitor. 'Co-ordinates. I presume that's the position we're supposed to head for. Where exactly on Dyason is it?'

Jennifer tapped the numbers into the nav console and a three-dimensional projection of the planet was displayed on the monitor. A red marker pulsed on a land mass in the southern hemisphere of the planet.

'That's the wastelands near to the ground station,' said Tychivesk examining the projection. 'Most of that area was devastated and abandoned during the war. Much of it is supposedly uninhabitable, which is why the underground have made the land their own.'

'What about Imperial forces?' asked Jenson. 'Are there any military bases nearby?'

'The nearest is about 900 klicks to the north on the edge of the desert.' replied Jennifer. 'If what

Tychivesk says is correct then we should be able to land without being detected.'

'What's actually at those co-ordinates Tychivesk?' Sandpiper asked.

'There's an old airbase there that was abandoned when the area became too radioactive. The buildings are all derelict now, but the runway is largely intact. We can put down there,' came the reply.

'What about the radiation? We're protected here inside the *Observer*, but what happens once we get out?' asked Jennifer.

'The radiation is gradually decaying though still toxic if you're exposed to it for too long,' replied Tychivesk. 'The atmosphere is unbreathable anyway, so as long as we wear the lightweight environment suits, we'll be okay.'

'Great. Sounds just like the location for a holiday.' said Sandpiper drily. 'We get to go to all the glamorous places.'

'Well I guess we haven't really got any choice but to get down there and find out what's going on. Moss, head for those co-ordinates carefully! Keep us at full stealth and be prepared to make a run for it if it looks like something is wrong.'

Moss eased the *Observer* towards the planet surface. The landing site was on the daylight side of the planet which was undesirable, but by entering the atmosphere on the darkside he could set a trajectory that would minimise the amount of time they would spend in daylight. Although they were effectively invisible to electronic surveillance, they could still be seen by the naked eye and the *Observer* wasn't the smallest of vessels. Hopefully anybody who did see them pass over the wastelands would think they were some sort of new Imperial Navy ship.

'I've got to make a trajectory from the night side of Dyason which will take us uncomfortably close to that orbital construction site, but I'm not reading any signs of unusual activity. I don't think any body's looking our way.' Moss announced.

'Do what you have to Moss,' Jenson acknowledged. 'Josh, this will be your chance to get a closer look at the *Dominator* as we pass it. Make as many readings as possible, but make sure you only use the passive scanners. We don't want to announce our presence.'

'Will do skipper,' the young scientist answered, setting about his task with relish.

As the first wisps of atmosphere passed over the ship's stub wings, Moss engaged the aerodynamic field and cut the artificial gravity. Like the Excalibur, the *Observer* was designed as an interstellar craft not an aircraft. She had slightly better flight characteristics than a brick, but not much. However, by engaging the 'aerodynamic field' the flight envelope became more akin to a large airliner. Developed aeons ago by the race that built the Excalibur, the aerodynamic field created a low power force field which smoothed the airflow over the fuselage and stub wings creating lift. It made the *Observer* equally at home in the atmosphere or in space.

Gradually Moss eased them down through the atmosphere. Initially he used the power from the singularities to counter the planet's gravity. The last thing they wanted to do was to enter the atmosphere on a free-fall trajectory like some ancient space capsule. The heat and flames caused by such a traditional re-entry could be seen across half the planet. As the atmosphere thickened he could feel the aerodynamic field creating lift, and he gradually reduced the vertical component of the thrust until the *Observer* was flying like a normal aircraft. He decelerated until they were cruising at 1500 kilometres per hour.

'I'm taking samples of this atmosphere,' said Jennifer from her work station, 'and it's an environmentalist's nightmare.'

'What's it consist of?' asked Myrddin.

'Well it's basically the same as the atmosphere on Earth, which is what we already knew. But I'm reading extremely high levels of background radiation, plus an almost lethal cocktail of industrial pollutants. Oxygen levels are way down on what you would expect. Carbon dioxide levels are extremely high. It's a mess. No wonder the planet is on the verge of dying.'

'The radiation you are reading is from the 'great patriotic war', when atomic weapons were used almost indiscriminately,' said Tychivesk examining the read-outs on his monitor. 'But there is a huge increase in pollutants and carbon dioxide since I left for Earth. Industrial output must have been increased ten-fold, but why?'

'We'll find out soon enough,' said Moss. 'We're going to see the sun rise in ten minutes and the landing site will come up in eighteen minutes.'

'There doesn't seem to be much sign of life down there,' commented Sandpiper, looking out of the windows at the oceans and land masses of Dyason passing beneath them. 'If this were Earth, there would be pinpricks of light from towns and cities everywhere. There's nothing but a black void down there. Not even the light of a ship crossing the ocean.'

'The great patriotic war was basically total war between the empires of the northern hemisphere and the southern states. The north only won by nuking the southern hemisphere into obliteration leaving most of the land lifeless,' said Tychivesk.

'And then the northern empires set about destroying each other?' asked Myrddin.

'That's right. It was a period of madness not unlike the two world wars on Earth. Only the formation of the one empire under the one "Imperial Dynasty" stopped the fighting.'

'When did all this happen?'

'It all started just over a hundred Dyason years ago, about the time of your own world wars.'

'Attempted mutual annihilation seems to be something all civilisations go through at some stage in their development. It's almost like the "'rutting" phase adolescents go through. It's simply that the people of Dyason got a little carried away,' said Myrddin philosophically. 'Earth could just have easily turned out the same way.'

'At least commonsense prevailed eventually on Earth. That's something the people of Dyason seem incapable of, even now,' replied Tychivesk sadly.

As the *Observer* sped through the skies above Dyason the sun rose above the horizon and daylight flooded the bridge through the large windows. The sun's rays were diffused and discoloured by the pollution in the atmosphere. It was a beautiful and dangerous sight.

'Okay folks, we're visible with the naked eye now. That makes us very vulnerable until we land so everyone pay attention to their scanners. If we get interrogated by their radar or another aircraft gets closer than 300 kilometres, I want to know about it. Okay?' asked Jenson. The others gave their acknowledgement. 'How's it looking Moss?'

More than any of them Moss was aware of what was going on around them. Through the interactive flight controls he could feel the rush of air across the aero-field, he could feel the lift and thrust of the powerplants and information from the *Observers* numerous passive sensors were fed directly into his neuro system. 'I'm decelerating to below local mach one. We don't want to leave a supersonic footprint right across the continent. There's a fair amount of activity at the edge of the wastelands to the north, but I think that's just normal aircraft movements. There's nothing heading our way,' he said aloud.

'The cameras are picking up the landing site now,' said Sandpiper. 'I'll display it on the monitor. As you can see it looks deserted. There's no sign of any life and the infra-red scan is also blank. If there's anybody home, they're doing a very good job of concealing the fact. At least there aren't hordes of Imperial troops down there with a welcoming co...' Suddenly the ship lurched to one side, unfamiliar g-forces pushing them into their couches. 'What the hell...?'

Moss called out in pain as his neuro-system was nearly overloaded. Desperately he hauled the Observer in a tight bank and tried to pile on the power. 'We're under attack!' he cried out through gritted teeth. 'There's three interceptors of some sort on our tail.' As he said this a menacing black shape passed directly across their bow, clearly visible through the bridge windows.

'Evasive action! Get a lock on them and ready missile battery,' Jenson ordered. 'Moss get us out of here!'

'I can't skipper,' he replied his teeth still gritted. 'We took a hit in the intake on the first pass. I've only got thirty percent power. We haven't got the thrust to get us back into orbit.'

'Shit! Where the *hell* did they come from?' Jenson demanded.

'They're not reading on any of our scanners, active or passive. They must be using some advanced type of stealth to slip up on us without warning. Here they come again!' Sandpiper called out. 'The computerised gunsight isn't able to get a lock-on. I'm putting the laser turrets on manual.'

Moss hurled the *Observer* into another gut-wrenching turn, but they were no match for the far more manoeuvrable fighters. The three black machines formed a 'Vic three' and closed in on their prey. Moss thought back to his combat training in the Flyship and an idea came to mind. He levelled the stub wings and paused as the fighters wheeled in for another pass. He waited until he judged the pilots figured they had a certain kill, then hauled the nose up to the vertical and pulled back the power. It was as if the *Observer* had hit a brick wall, she decelerated rapidly, then fell away towards the ground. The three fighters overshot their target, only one managing to get off a glancing shot a them. Sandpiper opened fire with the laser gun turrets situated fore and aft and smiled grimly when he saw the last fighter take hits along its port wing. By the time Moss had got them back to level flight they'd lost several thousand metres in altitude and the fighters were regrouping, one of them trailing a thin plume of smoke.

'Those are beam weapons they're using against us, not missiles or gunfire. I can't get a lock on them to fire our own missiles. They're blanking out our weapons system somehow. The only option is to aim manually, but those mothers are really moving. I've winged one of them but it's hard to pin them down,' said Sandpiper urgently.

'I can only pull that manoeuvre off once more,' cried Moss. 'If I try it after that we'll be on the deck. Power is down to twenty-five percent. They hit something vital.'

'We're losing coolant. The powerplants are beginning to overheat. The singularities will go to automatic shutdown in eight minutes and forty-two seconds,' called out Brabazon.

'Just what the *fuck* have your dropped us into Tychivesk?' Sandpiper snarled.

'This has *nothing* to do with me!' the Dyason exclaimed.

'This isn't the time for recriminations!' Jenson shouted. 'Moss! Can you evade them once more?'

'I think so...yes I can, but there won't be enough height left for any more evasive action after that. I'll have to put her down somewhere.'

'Can we make it to that landing site?'

'Only if I fly in a straight line. As the power drops the aerodynamic field weakens. She's beginning to handle like a sinking whale.'

Jenson leapt out the commander's chair and headed for the deck transporter. 'Go for it! Do the best you can and make for the landing site. Han!'

'Yes boss!' Sandpiper got up and followed Jenson.

'You're with me. Jennifer, prepare the Snub fighter for launch. We'll give these bastards a taste of their own medicine and give you the chance to land before the power fails completely.'

'Jenson!'

'Yes Myrddin?'

'They're playing with us!' the ancient said from the spare crew position. 'If they really wanted to destroy us, they could have done it on the first pass and we'd never have known what hit us!'

'I know, Myrddin. But regardless of that we still need to hold them off long enough to try and get to

Tychivesk's mates, if they really exist. I don't know what their game is but we'll make them wish they hadn't started toying with us.' With that Jenson and Sandpiper entered the transporter and headed for the small launch bay.

'They're launching missiles at us! Salvo of four atolls incoming!' Jennifer called out urgently.

Tychivesk hauled himself into Sandpiper's vacated work station and took control of the weapons system. Watching the gunsights on the monitor, he took hold of the small joystick and turned the aft turret towards the incoming missiles. Manually he locked onto each incoming atoll and fired a short burst. The multiple lasers turned three of the four missiles into vapour, but the fourth continued unscathed. Swearing loudly Tychivesk reset the turret and tried to lock onto the last remaining missile. He took a deep breath and manually fired the lasers once more. The atoll followed the others into oblivion.

'Good shooting!' said Jennifer. 'Snub One, are you ready for launch?'

'*Observer*, this is Snub One. We're all strapped in and fired up,' came the reply.

'Launching in five, four, three, two one...launch!' Doors along the underside of the Observer swung open revealing a small docking bay inside. Shackles opened and the released two-seat Snub fighter fell away. Much smaller than the standard Flyship, the Snub fighter was designed as a short-range, hard punching defence craft. The engines were hydrogen-oxygen hybrids which gave the craft the ability to fly in the atmosphere, or in space. Armament consisted of four of the latest kestrel missiles and 1000 rounds in the chain-gun. Traditional, but effective. Jenson sat in the pilot's seat in the front, while Sandpiper handled the weapons systems from the rear. Rapidly they peeled away from the Observer and headed for the Dyason interceptors.

'I've got visual contact, but my scopes are completely clear. These guys' must be taking a leaf out of our own book. There's no radar returns, no infra-red signature, nothing,' said Sandpiper.

'From nowhere, the Dyason seem to have caught up with our technology. It's a worrying trend. They must have a source of new technology somewhere,' mused Jenson.

'One of the fighters has broken off and is heading straight for us. The remaining two are engaging the Observer,' Sandpiper called out. 'I still can't get a lock, there's nothing for the missiles to track.'

'What about visual tracking?' asked Jenson. Can't you re-configure the warheads to use the opticals?'

Sandpiper quickly thought that over. 'No, the opticals are set for infra-red and these babies don't register, but we could use the laser designator. If you can keep the bastards in view while the kestrels are running, I can lock on with our laser designator and get the missile to follow the beam.'

'Do it Han! You just leave the flying to me!' Jenson replied as he flung the Snub fighter into a vertical rolling turn, narrowly missing a spread of laser fire. The Dyason interceptor shot past pulling hard to turn back toward the Snub fighter. Jenson pulled through the vertical and as he hung inverted in his straps he saw the other two interceptors closing in on the *Observer*. *'Moss break, break! You've got two hostiles closing fast on your six o'clock position!'* he called in his mind, knowing that Moss would be attuned to his thoughts.

'I see them, thanks Paul.' The *Observer* rolled hard left and the nose shot up as Moss repeated his evasive action. As one of the interceptors shot past the nose, the fore laser turret opened up and racked the Dyason craft from nose to tail. The interceptor already hit on the first pass began to trail very thick smoke. It rapidly lost momentum and span towards the ground. There was no sign of a chute. *'That was our last evasive manoeuvre boss. We've all but lost the aerodynamic field. I don't know what's keeping us up anymore!'* Moss thought painfully at Jenson.

'Okay kid. Stick with it and concentrate on getting that thing on the ground. We'll keep the other two bastards busy.'

As the third Dyason interceptor climbed towards the Snub fighter Jenson performed a half roll and half loop which brought them directly behind the Dyason interceptor which immediately began to jink desperately. *'They may be fast, but they ain't manoeuvrable.'* Jenson said to Sandpiper. *'Can you get a lock with the laser designator?'*

'I'm doing it now boss. Just keep us behind his tail,' replied Sandpiper concentrating on keeping the laser designator square on the Dyason interceptor. *'That's it, just a bit longer...just a bit longer...kestrel gone!'*

The missile sped towards the still wildly jinking Dyason, the flame and smoke from its solid fuel propellant reflecting the sun's rays with a deadly beauty. Jenson followed the interceptor's every move allowing Sandpiper to keep the laser designator locked firmly as the missile flew along the beam. Eight seconds later the kestrel exploded taking the black interceptor with it. The resulting fire ball consumed everything. If the Dyason had an ejector seat, he didn't get the chance to use it.

'Bingo! Good shooting skipper! That sure evens the odds a...*Oh shit!*' Laser light danced across the starboard wing scorching the resin finish and blowing access panels off. 'We forgot the third bastard!'

Warning lights lit up across Jenson's instrument panel. 'We've got an internal electrical fire Han. See what you can do!' Then he pulled the Snub fighter into a large barrel roll, pulling back the power and dropping the air-brakes. The rapid deceleration forced them against their straps, but the surprised third Dyason interceptor shot past. Jenson pulled in the brakes and shot after the black machine.

'I've pulled the bung on the extinguishers, but the weapons system is completely ballsed up. You'll have to make do with the cannon boss!'

'Well I guess we've got to give this guy a fair chance,' Jenson answered. 'At least the others have got the opportunity to get down safely. Here goes.'

The Snub fighter closed in on the bigger Dyason machine and Jenson peppered it with gunfire, then in a surprise manoeuvre the interceptor pulled the nose up, sat on its tail and decelerated rapidly. It was a classic 'cobra' manoeuvre. 'Holy shit! How the hell'd he do that?' Sandpiper exclaimed. 'Those babies must have some sort of vectored main thrust to achieve that!'

Jenson grunted and pulled the Snub fighter away and into a dive, keeping his airspeed as the Dyason interceptor sat almost motionless on its tail supported by the thrust of its engines alone. Jenson realised he'd lost the advantage once more. The Dyason pilot knew his machine well, perhaps too well—it was going to be a tough fight.

'He's coming down after us skipper!' Sandpiper called urgently. 'He's got a lock on us. Two missiles incoming! Break on my call...Break... *Now!*'

As the desert floor loomed dangerously close Jenson hauled back on the stick and the Snub fighter reared up like a startled animal, the g-forces pushing the pair deep down into their seats. The two missiles unable to follow the tight turn sped on and impacted on the desert floor below. Now the Dyason interceptor and the Snub fighter were coming at each other head to head. The Dyason was coming almost straight down and the Snub fighter was heading almost vertically up. Jenson saw his chance, if the Dyason pilot were concentrating on them as hard as they were on him, then they might just pull it off.

Jenson opened fire with his chain guns at the same moment the Dyason fired his lasers. He put the Snub fighter into a vertical roll, creating the smallest possible target for the Dyason who was still screaming down to meet them. It almost worked, but not quite. Jenson felt the impact of the laser fire somewhere back in the main fuselage. He ignored it and kept his finger on the trigger as the Dyason sped past them, his cockpit almost brushing their's. A thick plume of smoke began to pour out of the end of the interceptor as it headed towards the desert floor. Banking and looking back down below Jenson saw the Dyason desperately try to pull the nose of his damaged machine up. Too late, the Dyason realised he'd been conned and just as the machine began to reach the horizontal it ploughed into a tall rock face. The interceptor was obliterated.

'Sucker!' Jenson muttered.

The Snub fighter suddenly became very quiet— the engine died and the instrument panels lit up like a Christmas tree. 'Oh shit!' said Sandpiper. 'That's it, she's given up the ghost!'

'We took more hits in the engine. We were lucky the propellant didn't ignite...*Oh double shit!* We've got a fire in the electrics next to the main tank. We'll go up any second!'

Jenson didn't wait to be told. He pulled hard on the emergency handle on the left side of the cockpit. Someone came down, grabbed them by the shoulders and hauled them up. The cockpit, which also served as an escape capsule, was catapulted away from the rest of the Snub fighter which disintegrated into a fire-ball seconds after they punched out.

The parachute opened and the capsule slowly floated toward the inhospitable desert floor. 'Well it looks like you're about to get a long holiday in a hot, sunny climate Han,' said Jenson dryly.

'Great. You take me to all the best places,' came the equally dry reply.

'What makes you think this mission is going arse over tit?'

'Oh nothing. Nothing at all.'

CHAPTER SIX

Moss was in agony. The crippled *Observer* was almost impossible to fly. The last pass by the interceptors had caused even more damage and the aerodynamic field had all but collapsed. The interactive flight system sent pain shooting through his nervous system as if it were him rather than the ship that was damaged. He had to put them down and fast. Although Jenson and Han Sandpiper had drawn off the remaining interceptor, there was no chance of them staying in the air. As it was they were barely skimming over the surface of the desert.

'Power is down to fifteen percent and falling,' Jennifer called out, the concern in her voice audible. 'Moss you're going to have to put us down *now*. We're going to lose power completely any minute and then we'll simply fall out the sky.'

'I know,' Moss replied, his voice reflecting the pain he felt. 'How far is it to that old airfield Tychivesk?'

'It's about another 150 klicks Moss but…well…' the Dyason shrugged his shoulders apologetically. 'I don't know why were attacked. I can't be sure that the touch-down point, the airfield, hasn't been compromised. We could be walking into a trap.'

'Bloody hell Tychivesk,' Josh Brabazon exclaimed, 'surely you should know. You knew this would happen all along!'

'No! I swear this is not my doing!' the Dyason shouted back.

'Quiet both of you!' Myrddin demanded banging his fist on the console. 'Moss, Tychivesk is right we can't risk landing at the airfield. We don't what we'd be flying into. I suggest you put us down where you can.'

To Moss it was rather academic; he knew they couldn't stay in the air long enough to make it to the strip. They were going down *now*. They had less than a minute before the singularities went into automatic shutdown and they lost what remaining power they had. Frantically he looked around for somewhere to put down. Unfortunately this area of the desert was full of ravines and rocky outcrops, there didn't appear to be a flat area anywhere. Then they flew over what looked like a dried-out lake bed, surrounded by cliffs on all sides. That was it, that was where he would put them down. It was the only flat space in the whole area and the surrounding cliffs would give them some protection from searching Dyason patrols.

'Okay we're going in!' he announced. 'Strap yourselves in, this is going to be rough.'

As the others tightened their straps Moss banked the *Observer* round and back towards the lake-bed. It was like trying to fly through treacle with a lead brick. He was soaked in sweat and the effort was beginning to make him feel dizzy. He desperately fought off the urge to black-out. The pain of keeping the crippled ship flying was indescribable.

They sank towards the lake bed at an alarming rate. Moss lowered the landing gear and waited until the last possible moment before cutting the aerodynamic field. Then he poured all the remaining power into the landing thrusters and the *Observer* sank onto the lake bed with a sickening crunch. He didn't have to cut the engines, the singularities went into automatic shutdown and the bridge was plunged into darkness. They were down. The pain finally overwhelmed Moss and he gratefully let himself sink into unconsciousness.

It was unlucky, very unlucky. The escape capsule had floated onto the ground without any problems, it was just unfortunate that it had landed on top of a huge granite stack several hundred metres above the desert floor. The top of the stack was flat, indicating that this had originally been the level of the ground and aeons of erosion had taken away the rest of the desert. The walls of the stack were sheer, with very little in the way of foot and hand holds. Jenson and Sandpiper had looked all the way round the stack and were yet to come up with a sensible way of getting down without killing themselves. The sun was now high in the sky and the heat unbearable.

Jenson collapsed in a pile next to Sandpiper under the shade of the capsule, lifted up his environment mask and drank some of the water from their emergency kit. 'It's useless I can't find a way down,' he said.

'I hate to say it skipper, but I really think we're stuck here until at least nightfall. Once it gets cooler we can attempt to climb down. If we try it in this heat we'll just kill ourselves. Besides these emergency environment suits won't cope with the extra workload of physical exercise, we'll end up choking ourselves.'

'Oh shit! This is really turning into a farce!' Jenson replied expressively banging his fist against the side of the capsule. 'The others are stranded on a lake-bed and we're stranded on a bloody great rock. How did we get ourselves into this situation?'

'The usual way I should think,' Sandpiper answered deadpan. He cocked his head and listened, then stood up shaded his eyes with his hand and looked towards the horizon.

'What is it Han?' Jenson asked.

'There on the horizon,' he replied pointing at two small dots that were rapidly getting bigger. 'Look's like the welcoming committee. Two choppers by the sound of it. I presume they're Imperial forces come looking for their lost toys. They're heading straight towards us. Do you think we should find what cover we can and go out in a blaze of glory?'

Jenson stood up next to his friend and sighed deeply. 'I don't think that's the answer old friend. There's nowhere to hide and nowhere to run. Besides we've only got a couple of small automatics, which will be useless against a gunship. I think we'll have to go quietly. Our chance will come later, I'm sure of it.'

The pair stood there glumly awaiting the arrival of the helicopters. As they approached Jenson saw that one was a large troop carrier with big intermeshing twin rotors and the other was a bulbous gunship bristling with armament and looking for all the world like a pregnant fly. The gunship hovered in front of the stack, its weapons trained on Jenson and Sandpiper. The troop carrier circled around the stack checking the site over and then it hovered, blasting the pair with rotor-wash. A loud hailer screamed at them in Dyason.

'I think they want to surrender to us,' said Sandpiper with a quizzical expression on his face.

'Pillock. Your Dyason is lousy,' replied Jenson with a grim smile. 'They want *us* to surrender to *them*.'

'That must be it then.'

'Come on mate I know it hurts but we'd better put our hands up. If they'd wanted to kill us straight away they would have done it by now.' Jenson raised his hands over his head and Sandpiper followed.

The troop carrier landed on top of the stack next to the escape capsule and a squad of Dyason troopers in desert fatigues leapt out, weapons at the ready. They beckoned the pair forward and then shackled their hands behind them. Roughly Jenson and Sandpiper were bundled into the helicopter and shackled once more to a bench attached to the fuselage side. The troop squad piled back onboard, the rotors spooled up once more and the helicopter lifted off the top of the stack heading north out of the wasteland. Jenson tried to remember the last time he'd felt quite so depressed and failed miserably.

Hillmead sat with Shalock on the balcony to their adjoining rooms in the officers' mess apparently watching the sun go down. Hillmead paid little attention to his drink, his eyes were fixed firmly on the southern horizon. Shalock, showered and dressed in a fresh uniform, was content to enjoy the cooler early evening air.

Hillmead picked up the binoculars sitting in his lap and peered over the runway and hangars to a speck on the horizon. He peered through the lenses and grunted with satisfaction. 'Here they come.' He passed the binoculars to Shalock who also peered through the lenses.

'So you reckon there's something going on that they're not telling us about?' she asked putting the binoculars down and picking up her drink.

Hillmead scratched at his stubble. Unlike Shalock he'd not had a shower yet and he was beginning to feel grubby. However, he was convinced they'd walked into a situation the base commander and his officers wished to keep hidden from them. 'Well let's go through it,' he answered. 'Three interceptors of a secret design scramble and head south at full throttle. Several hours elapse during which time we have a chat with Group Leader Baccia who obviously has things on his mind and can't wait to get rid of us. The interceptors fail to return and two helicopters including a gunship head into the wasteland. Nobody is available to talk to us for the rest of the day and now the helicopters are returning just before it gets dark. You bet I think there's something up!'

'But what has it got to do with our investigation? Do you think there's been another case of sabotage?'

'Just sit quietly and watch Shalock,' Hillmead answered impatiently. 'If my suspicions are correct we'll find out as soon as those whirly-birds land. In the meantime why don't you just enjoy my company.'

Shalock tossed her hair and crossed her legs. 'If only I could inspector...if only I could.' Then she turned and smiled at him sweetly. Hillmead raised one eyebrow quizzically then turned back to watch the helicopters land on the apron close to their quarters. A squad of security troopers waited beside the troop chopper as the doors swung open and the squad inside climbed out pushing two shackled men in front of them. Hillmead watched intently through the binoculars as the security squad took the men roughly by the arm and frog marched them away. They both wore some sort of environment suit indicating they'd been in the irradiated wastelands. Their face masks had been removed and in the dying light Hillmead could just make out that one of them was tall with dark hair, while the other was shorter, stockier with skin like leather and sandy, fair hair.

'Just as I thought,' he said triumphantly. 'Humans!'

'What?' exclaimed Shalock grabbing the binoculars for herself and taking a look just before the prisoners were ushered into the back of a truck. 'How do you know they're human?' she asked.

'When have you ever seen features like those on a Dyason before?' Hillmead retorted.

'They could be mutants. They did come from the wasteland after all.'

'Nah...I've met humans brought back from Earth before and I can tell you that their facial features are very easy to recognise. *They* are human.' He leapt out of his chair and headed for the door.

'Where are you going?' Shalock asked also rising from her chair.

'Well if I am going to have to wear this stupid uniform and be a Colonel in the MDC I might as well make the most of it. I'm going to pull rank and interview those prisoners. Are you coming?'

Shalock looked at him with surprise, then smiled. 'Let's go.'

They could hear the sickening thuds of batons against flesh from the courtyard outside the guard's block. Hillmead frowned, it was just as well they were intervening, those thugs would beat the humans to death before a proper interrogation could begin. He barged his way into the front office and made for the cells at the back without pausing. The clerk at the front hastily pulled his feet off the desk and leapt up. 'Heh! What the frig do you think you're doing?' he yelled after Hillmead's disappearing back.

Shalock following close behind pulled out her identification along with her small automatic and levelled both at the clerk. 'Military Detective Corp,' she snapped. 'We have reason to believe you are holding two prisoners that come under our jurisdiction...close your mouth and sit down boy. You're out of your league here.'

The young conscript took one look at the expression on Shalok's face, glanced at the identity pass and automatic and collapsed back into his seat, a confused expression on his spotty face.

Hillmead followed the sickening sound of physical abuse to an interrogation room at the end of a long corridor. He reached for the door handle but stopped when Shalok grabbed his arm. 'Wait!' she whispered. 'These thugs aren't very bright, they have a tendency to shoot first and ask questions later. You'd better have your automatic ready.'

Hillmead looked at her and smiled. 'I already have,' he said.

'Where?' Shalok asked.

'Look down,' he replied. Shalok looked down and was surprised to see the muzzle of Hillmead's automatic pointed at her stomach, the rest of the gun hidden in the folds of his jacket. 'Ready?' he asked. Shalok nodded. 'Okay lets do it.' and together they piled through the door.

Inside the scene was just as Hillmead expected it. The taller dark-haired human was hanging by his wrists from a meat hook embedded in the ceiling. He was stripped to the waist and his back was covered in angry red marks caused by the cat-o-nine tails carried by the guard standing behind him. The human's face was beaten but defiant. The prisoner's had obviously already been softened up on the flight back to the air base. He held his head up and peered through the one good eye at Hillmead and Shalok. The other eye was swollen closed. Hillmead instantly realised that he recognised the human's face from somewhere—where exactly he couldn't be sure at the moment, but the face was definitely familiar. The other human was bound to a chair and by the look of his face he'd already received the same treatment. There were three guards, two of them troopers, the third a junior officer pretending to go through the motions of an interrogation. All three of them stood and stared at Hillmead and Shalok.

'Good evening gentlemen,' Hillmead began in a casual tone, his automatic still hidden in the folds of his uniform jacket. 'Would you be so good as to inform me what is going on here?'

The lieutenant looked Hillmead up and down, his face contorted in a sneer. '*We* are interrogating these mutants from the wasteland ...*Colonel, sir.* It is a standard procedure. The station commander will be here shortly to complete the interrogation...*sir.*' The lieutenant managed to make the 'sir' sound as if it were a terminal disease.

Hillmead looked at the young officer coolly and said, 'I see, well I think I might just complete the interrogation myself...if you don't mind.'

'I'm sorry *sir*, but I'm afraid I can't let you do that. This has nothing to do with you,' the officer snarled.

'Oh but I think it has lieutenant,' Hillmead replied his tone like ice. He pulled out his identity card and flashed it at the officer. 'I think these men have information vital to my investigation and I'm afraid that as a senior officer in the Military Detective Corp. I must insist that you hand the prisoners over to me and my assistant.'

'You're nothing but a gutter cop and you know it. Go fuc...' The lieutenant got no further. He collapsed on the floor hugging his right leg screaming loudly. His blood mingled with the other dried out blood that stained the floor and walls. Hillmead raised his still smoking automatic and trained it on the other two guards. Shalok did the same. 'Would either of you *arseholes* like to question my authority?' The pair took one look at their officer writhing in pain on the floor and dumbly shook their heads.

'I'm so glad you see it my way.' Hillmead pointed to the overweight guard standing with the cat-o-nine tails. 'You, cut the prisoner down. You,' he pointed to the other one, 'fetch some medics, there are three men that need attention here. Well, don't just stand there, move it!' The now frightened sadists leapt to comply. The tall human gave him a grin contorted by his injuries. Hillmead looked away to hide the smile on his own face—he'd just remembered who the human was.

One hour later and Hillmead had the situation under control. The two humans were being looked at by medics and were now placed in the more comfortable cells. Happily their injuries looked worse than they actually were. The thugs hadn't had the chance to really go to town on them and the medics reckoned they should be back to full health in a few days. Certainly he could start interrogating them first thing in the morning. The lieutenant was a different matter. Hillmead had shot him in the thigh and he would be laid up for several months. For some reason though he didn't feel any remorse. Group Leader Baccia had put in an appearance shortly after and seeing that he'd let the situation get out of hand, decided not to rescind Hillmead's orders. Now they sat in the station commander's office sipping rare Alderean brandy.

'What happened back there was very unfortunate Colonel. However, as you may have gathered we lost three aircraft in the desert today, and those men seem to be the ones responsible. The mutant scum that occupy the wastelands become more audacious with each passing day. We've lost many good men in the past to those freaks. You can't blame those conscripts for wanting to giving them a taste of their own medicine,' Baccia said standing at the open window breathing in the desert night air.

Hillmead said nothing, he just stared thoughtfully into the bottom of his glass. 'It was indeed unfortunate Group Leader,' said Shalok filling in for him, knowing he was in an awkward mood. 'I'm sure I speak for both the Colonel and myself when I say how much we regret having to intervene in such a manner. However, you must understand we could not risk their over-exuberance killing the prisoners.'

'Indeed,' Baccia mumbled into his drink.

Hillmead put his drink down abruptly and got up to leave. 'We'll I guess I'd better get an early night Group Leader, because in the morning I intend to find out what a pair of humans from Earth were doing in the wastelands. Where the wreckage of their vessel is and what exactly it is you're so desperate to hide. Good night.'

Baccia didn't answer, he simply stood there watching as Hillmead turned to leave, a dangerous look in his eyes. 'I think you had better get up *very* early Colonel.' the station commander said to his back, 'because first thing tomorrow morning we are having a surprise inspection from the Envoy Nimue and a certain Group Leader Gulag.'

Hillmead span around his face contorted with anger. He gave Shalok a meaningful stare. 'Nothing to do with me, I swear!' she replied to his accusing stare. 'I haven't been in touch with them for days.'

'That's right Colonel,' the station commander went on. 'We will *all* have to be on our *very* best behaviour tomorrow. It wouldn't do to upset the Envoy now, would it?'

Hillmead didn't bother to reply, he simply turned and slammed the door as he left.

'Another drink Lieutenant?' Baccia asked.

CHAPTER SEVEN

Between the peaks of distant mountains rose twin moons, climbing into a darkening sky. From horizon to horizon the snow of white-capped mountains reflected the glow of a huge red sun that set the world afire. Mist filled the valleys below and except for the gentle sound of the thin air whistling through the rocks, the world was beautiful and silent.

In the distance Moss saw a figure climbing up a gully towards him. Although it was hard to make out any details the figure seemed somehow familiar. Moss sat down on a rock and decided to wait for the climber to reach him. He felt perfectly at ease, almost serene. Despite the sinking sun and freezing air, he didn't feel the cold even though he was wearing nothing more than a thin flying suit. This place was obviously a world between worlds.

Eventually, the climber reached the flattened mountain top on which Moss sat. Dressed in lightweight climbing gear, complete with ropes and pitons, the stranger strode over to where Moss sat, dropped his rucksack to the ground and sat on a rock opposite with a contented sigh. 'It's another beautiful evening,' the stranger said.

Moss looked the climber over. He was somewhere in his mid-thirties of average height, lean and muscular. His mass of dark hair was shoulder length and framed an angular, handsome face. Of course Moss immediately knew who this person was.

'It certainly is a beautiful evening,' he replied. 'Where are we Arthur?'

'We're on my world son,' Arthur replied.

'Where exactly is that?'

'Somewhere between one dimension and the next.'

'Thanks, that's really precise,' Moss said sarcastically.

Arthur looked his descendent in the eye and smiled gently. 'I'm sorry Moss but time is short and there really isn't room for a lengthy explanation into the why's and where fore's of this place. Just accept that you're here and I'm here so that we can have a little chat.'

'Okay, I can accept that this is another of those weird dreams I have every now and then.' Moss shrugged. 'So what do you want to talk about?'

Arthur stood up, walked to the edge of the mountain top and looked out over the incredible landscape. The sun still hung as a huge orange ball on the edge of the horizon. Moss realised that it hadn't moved in all the time he'd been there. He got up and stood beside the image of his ancestor.

'Moss, events in your universe are rapidly heading towards a climax,' Arthur began turning to look at Moss.

'What, again?' he replied in surprise. 'I thought we'd been through all that last time. You know, with Gulag and I onboard the Excalibur. How many climaxes can you have?'

Arthur sighed, reached out and placed his hand on Moss's shoulder. 'I'm sorry son, that was only the beginning. The start of a whole series of events. The ball has really only just come into play.'

Moss turned and looked out over the landscape once more. 'You know, I'd really hoped I'd never have to use my *talents* in such a manner again. I don't enjoy being a *freak*.'

'You're no freak Moss,' Arthur said kindly. 'I realise how difficult all this is for you son, but I'm afraid like me, you really have no choice in the matter. Events are moving far beyond your or my scope of influence.'

'Why me?' Moss asked. 'What's so special about me that I have to become a pawn in some cosmic game? Surely there are other, stronger people more suited to these games than me—like you for instance.'

Arthur sat down on a large flat boulder and leant back on his hands looking up at Moss. 'I used to say the very same thing to Myrddin myself. I never got a decent answer either.' he answered with a chuckle. 'My time has passed Moss, the game I was a part of has finished. The present belongs to you.'

Moss sat down also. 'Is that what you wanted to tell me?' he asked.

'That was part of the message, yes. But what I really have to tell you is that things are not as they seem. There is a third party involved.' Arthur answered.

Moss looked at his ancestor and raised his eyebrows. 'Is that it? Come on—you'll have to be a little less cryptic than that. I never was any good at puzzles.'

'All I'm allowed to tell you is that there is a third party behind current events. I can also tell you that what everyone is after is something called 'Point Zero'.' Arthur added.

'Point Zero? What the hell is Point Zero?' Moss exclaimed.

Arthur didn't reply. Instead he stood up walked over to his rucksack and picked it up.

'Arthur! What the hell is Point Zero?' Moss shouted at his retreating back. 'Come-on don't leave me guessing.'

'Ask Josh Brabazon…he'll know. Just remember this, whoever gets Point Zero, goes on to the next player level. If you don't pass this stage, you'll be deleted…I've got to go…good luck…' Arthur disappeared over the edge of the mountain-top and the sun finally sank behind the mountain range. The white topped peaks faded from view and darkness descended.

Every bone in his body ached. He felt as if he'd been beaten with a very big stick and left for dead. He opened his eyes and groaned.

'Easy Moss, take it easy.' His focus swam in and out then finally focused on the anxious face of

Jennifer. She was wiping his forehead with a damp piece of cloth. Painfully, he raised his head and with her help managed to sit up. He looked around. He was lying on a cot in what would appear to be some sort of room carved out of rock. Small, heavily glazed windows looked out on the desert as the sun lay low on the horizon. Wherever they were was obviously built into a cliff face. He groaned again and lifted a hand to his head. 'Where are we?' he asked.

'It's okay we're safe. We were found by a patrol from Tychivesk's Democratic Front,' she told him. 'Your neural network was overloaded by the collapse of the *Observer's* aerodynamic field—you passed out. I was worried you'd gone into a coma.'

'Coma? God! How long have I been out for Jennifer?' Moss asked in alarm.

'Only a few hours Moss. Don't worry, for some reason your mind closed down completely for a while then switched back on only a few minutes ago. It's as if you've been off travelling somewhere but left your body behind.' Jennifer informed him, her mind gently probing his, scanning his mind for damage.

A curtain covering the doorway was pulled open and Myrddin stepped through. 'How's the patient?' he asked.

'He came around a few minutes ago,' said Jennifer.

'I know. I felt his mind return home. How're feeling kid?'

'Like shit,' Moss answered. 'It feels like I've had the crap beaten out of me, but I haven't got the scars to show for it.'

'Your nervous system's taken a pounding, but I don't think there's been any long-term damage,' Myrddin informed him.

'What happened to the *Observer*?' Moss asked swinging his legs onto the floor and rising to his feet carefully. He felt Myrddin was right, he ached everywhere, but it didn't feel as if anything important was damaged.

Myrddin walked over, sat down on the edge of a cot opposite and looked him over. 'I'm afraid the *Observer* is grounded permanently Moss. Those interceptors breached the hull in a couple of places and the status field collapsed moments after you put her down. The artificial singularities went into safe dissolve. She's not going anywhere.'

'What about Sandpiper and the boss?'

'They're being held at an Imperial airbase on the edge of the desert. I've managed to locate their position, but neither Paul nor Han are very good telepaths and without any amplification equipment I couldn't get through to them,' he answered shaking his head.

'God, this operation really has gone arse over tit,' Moss said with feeling, rubbing his forehead in agitation and proving to himself that he could still co-ordinate his battered limbs. 'We're going to have to go and get them out. We can't leave them in the hands of Imperial thugs. They'll happily tear them apart, especially if they find out their real identity.'

'I know Moss. We're working on a plan of action now. Do you feel strong enough to join us?' Myrddin asked.

'Yeah—I guess.' Wearily he made his way to the door, his arm around Jennifer's shoulder. 'You know I had this really *weird* dream. I'll have to talk to you about it later.'

Myrddin raised an eyebrow and followed the couple into the stone corridor. The corridor had been carved out of the rock by some sort of tunnelling machine by the looks of the marks on the walls. It reminded Moss of the hideaway on Earth, during the darkest days of the resistance, except that the base then was in the depths of the Arctic, while this place was in the desert.

They followed the line of low-wattage light bulbs until they came to a door set into the rock like an entrance to an underground vault. An armed guard stood at each side of the door. They were both dressed in desert fatigues, not dissimilar to those worn by the WDF on Earth, and they carried lightweight automatic rifles. However, the similarity ended there. Both their faces were swollen with open sores that distorted their features. Moss noticed that the fingers of the guard on the left were webbed, whilst the guard on the right had no nose at all, just two small orifices. These poor wretches were obviously mutants, their bodies deformed by the radiation and pollution of the wastelands outside the sealed confines of their base.

They stepped aside and the huge steel blast doors hissed open. The three of them stepped through into a cavern thrumming with activity. Crates of equipment were being off-loaded from balloon-tyred vehicles on one section of the floor, whilst some sort of desert buggies were being armed and serviced in another area. A familiar face was organising the unpacking of crated equipment. Josh Brabazon saw Moss on the gantry, stopped what he was doing and joined them.

'Good to see you up and about Moss,' he said with evident relief. 'I was really worried that your brains had been frazzled when the interactive flight system overloaded. That's something we're going to have to rectify when we get home—whenever that is.'

Moss looked around the cavern once more. 'What's going on here Josh? Those are equipment pallets from the *Observer* down there, aren't they?'

'Yeah, I'm afraid so Moss,' he answered, wiping his hands on the back of his flight suit. 'After you got us down on the ground, Tychivesk's mates turned up. Jennifer and Myrddin got you back here first, whilst I stayed with a couple of the mutants and checked out the damage on the *Observer*.'

'And?'

'Well, she ain't going anywhere in a hurry,' Josh said shaking his head sadly. 'The hull has been breached in several places, but the main problem is that the status field collapsed completely, causing the fail-safes to cut in. The artificial singularities have been neutralised and there's no way of bringing them back.'

'So I heard,' replied Moss. 'You're bringing all the equipment to this place—wherever it is.'

'That's right. The Imperial forces have overflown the crash site twice already. Tychivesk's mates had some huge camouflage netting with them, which we managed to haul over the Observer, but it's only a matter of time before they find her. So we've been stripping her of anything useful.'

'How much more have you got to do Josh?' asked Jennifer.

'That was the last load.'

'Did you set the demolition charges?' Myrddin inquired.

'Yeah. All that will be left now is a smouldering heap of metal, kevlar and carbon fibre. We're going to have to look for another way home.'

'Great, this mission just gets better and better,' said Moss bitterly. 'Come on, let's go and meet our hosts. It looks like we're going to need their assistance, rather than us giving them our assistance.'

The gantry lead to a series of communication and briefing rooms. There they found Tychivesk deep in conversation with a woman of Amazonian proportions. She stood head and shoulders above Tychivesk and filled her desert fatigues with a lean, well-muscled figure. Her bald head was tattooed with the image of some sort of serpent and as she turned to look at him, Moss saw that her eyes were completely black, devoid of any white at all.

'Ah, I see you have recovered my friend Moss. For a while we were worried. I am afraid that our medical facilities here are very basic,' the Amazonian woman said in Dyason.

'Moss I would like you to meet Colmarrie, head of the southern chapter of the Democratic Front,' said Tychivesk stepping forward and taking Moss by the arm.

Moss shrugged him off and offered the woman his hand. She grasped it in a grip that made him cringe. 'Your reputation precedes you. I am honoured to meet such a noble person.'

'Likewise I'm sure,' Moss replied in Dyason, a quizzical expression on his face. 'Thank you for rescuing us from the desert. We would all be in Imperial hands if it weren't for you and your people.'

Colmarrie offered Moss a chair at the briefing table, which he happily accepted as he still felt drained. 'I only wish we could have done more friend Moss. We are all fighting on the same side and the destruction of your vessel is a great loss to the cause,' she said.

The others filled the spare seats around the table and Myrddin asked, 'Colmarrie, do you think you could briefly fill Moss in on what you have already told us. I'm sure he is anxious to know where we are and what your organisation is about.'

'Surely Myrddin.' The mutant leader fetched a large globe from the side of the room and placed it in the centre of the table. She spun the planet around, then slammed her finger on the southern part of a large continent. 'This base is here, in the wastelands of Ecosia in a land once known as Sarangetta. This whole area was once fertile, with beautiful, cultured cities and an intelligent, peaceful population, but that was before the Imperial wars.'

'This is a nuclear wasteland?' asked Moss.

'Yes. Ecosia sided with the allies against Imperial domination and lost. This was their reward.'

'How much of this land is uninhabitable?'

'Several thousand square klicks. Basically from the coast up to the fifty-third parallel,' Colmarrie replied, tracing a finger over a huge tract of the southern continent. The Emperor ordered that the area be sealed so that none of the surviving Ecosians could leave the wastelands. They set up bases around the perimeter and forced the surviving population to remain in the radioactive ruins of the cities.'

'God, that's awful,' exclaimed Jennifer. 'It's amazing that any of you survived at all.'

'The early years were the worst,' continued Colmarrie. 'It all happened before I was born, but the account of that time is engraved on our hearts. Millions died from radiation sickness, disease and starvation until only a handful remained. Some managed to break the Imperial blockade and flee, but only a very few.'

'Blockades seem to be an Imperial speciality,' said Moss. 'London, my home city on Earth suffered the same treatment during the Dyason occupation.'

'I am aware of the events that took place on your world friend Moss, and you have my sympathies. It is another example of the cruelty our peoples have suffered under the Empire. It is another reason why our cause is the same.'

'Did the people from your country who survived the holocaust go on to form the Democratic Front?

Were the remains of Ecosia the birthplace of the anti-Imperial movement?' asked Josh Brabazon.

'The actions the Empire took against Ecosia and numerous other once independent states caused resentment and sympathy amongst people all over the planet. However, for many years there was no organised resistance against the Empire. The Imperial grip on the planet was absolute. Any country that so much as demonstrated against the Emperor was crushed ruthlessly. Here in Ecosia the few survivors of the radiation sickness set about organising themselves. Bases such as this were built into the sides of mountains and ravines throughout the wastelands. Sealed, with filtered air and water, they became sanctuaries from the radiation outside.'

'By then, the radiation must have filtered into the local food chain and entered your bodies regardless of any sanctuaries,' Jennifer thought aloud.

'Unfortunately, you are correct sister,' Colmarrie continued. 'By the time we had moved our people into these shelters the damage had already been done. As you can see we are a population of mutants.'

'That's a terrible story Colmarrie. Nobody should have to suffer as you and your people have,' Moss said.

'What is done is done friend Moss. We cannot change the past, but we can change the future. I am very proud of what the survivors of Ecosia have achieved. Our hydroponic labs and underground farms supply us with radiation-free food. The irony now is that as the rest of the Empire chokes on its own filth, these sanctuaries are the only places on the planet where you can eat food that won't eventually kill you. Our medics are researching ways to control the mutations in our population. Indeed not all the mutations have been unbeneficial.'

'Really?' Myrddin asked, pulling at his beard thoughtfully. 'What sort of mutations have proved beneficial?

'Well, all mutants have an in-built resistance to the radiation that remains in the wastelands. Whereas you need to wear environment suits and masks when outside, we do not,' Colmarrie answered 'As for the other benefits, these will become apparent in time.'

Moss opened his mouth to speak. He was curious to know more about these mutant 'benefits' but he caught Myrddin's eye, who gently shook his head. Maybe later. Instead he asked, ' So how did the Democratic Front evolve?'

'For decades there have been many factions against the Empire, but they have always remained disorganised and fractional,' informed Tychivesk getting up from his chair and striding around the room in an almost agitated manner. 'In the past it was always easy for the Empire to crush any resistance. However, this all changed with the discovery of the worm-hole that led to Earth. There was disquiet amongst the Imperial forces that an expeditionary force to your planet would seriously drain resources here on Dyason and give the anti-Imperial forces a chance to organise themselves—which is exactly what happened. The drain on manpower and resources was incredible. Our planet's mineral resources were almost depleted by years of war and military expansion, the construction of a space fleet was the last straw that broke the camel's back, to use one of your own phrases.'

'Hold on Tychivesk,' interrupted Josh Brabazon. 'You guys shipped thousands of tons of goods and materials back from Earth to here. Surely this compensated in some part for Dyason's depleted resources?'

'You're right Josh, we did import large quantities of materials from Earth,' answered the ex-Imperial officer, pausing in his agitated pacing, 'but this was a mere drop in the ocean compared to what had been exhausted in the years leading up to the 'great patriotic war' and after. Anyway, by the time of the invasion, not only was Dyason's entire populace under an oppressive regime, starved of any sort of consumer goods, the ecology was also in terminal decline. Storm, drought and famine were added to the general population's list of problems.'

'The defeat of the Imperial Navy by you and your rebels directly led to the formation of the Democratic Front, added Colmarrie.

'You finally found yourselves a leader to unify the different factions?' asked Moss carefully trying to keep track of the story despite a woollen head.

Tychivesk pointed at him and snapped, 'That's right Moss. We *finally* got ourselves a leader worthy of the cause and one day our leader and your people will join together to create a *new* Empire. A just and caring Empire that will unite *both* our worlds.'

A somewhat embarrassed silence descended on the briefing room after Tychivesk's surprising outburst. Moss saw Colmarrie lean back in her chair and examine the ex-officer with a calculating look.

'There's something going on here,' Moss thought at Jennifer and Myrddin.

'Tychivesk's hiding something from us, but I don't know what it is,' replied Jennifer.

'Whatever it is, he's got it hidden in the very depths of his mind,' added Myrddin. 'There's no way I can access what he's hiding from us without him knowing.'

'I'm so glad you realise there is more to this Dyason officer than meets the eye,' Exclaimed a new mind.

Moss turned and looked at Colmarrie in surprise. She met and held his eye, a small smile curling her mouth.

'One of the beneficial mutations, my friend.'

Jennifer, Myrddin and Moss exchanged looks, then Myrddin said aloud in a careful, measured tone. 'I think this would be a good time to talk about how we are going to rescue our friends Colmarrie. If I may be so bold, I have a plan.'

CHAPTER EIGHT

The swelling on the human's face had eased a little and Hillmead could observe the man's features better, now that the blood had been washed away. He sat handcuffed in a chair in the centre of the room facing the desk Hillmead casually leant against. Through his one unswollen eye the human scanned everyone and everything in the room, from the early morning sunlight pouring through the barred cell window, to the armed guards at the door. Hillmead realised he was in the company of a dangerous professional.

'Good morning Squadron Leader Jenson,' Hillmead began in faltering English. 'How are you feeling today?'

The human remained silent staring up at the cell window. 'There is no purpose to your silence,' Hillmead struggled with the alien language. 'We have a complete dossier on your activities Squadron Leader.'

The human turned his head and looked at Hillmead with his one good eye but said nothing.

'You realise that if these Imperial conscripts continue to believe you are one of the wasteland mutants, they will kill you and your friend. I cannot protect you forever. Now perhaps you would like to tell me why you are here on Dyason.'

The human looked at him thoughtfully then shrugged his shoulders. 'The name is Paul Jenson and I'm a Group Captain not a Squadron Leader. Someone promoted me.' Jenson said in almost faultless Dyason.

It was Hillmead's turn to be surprised. 'You speak Dyason? I'm impressed.'

'Yeah, I made it a point to know how to tell you shits to shove it up your arse when we kicked you off the Earth.'

'And you have been promoted to Group Captain? Well, you've obviously become an important person Paul,' Hillmead continued, 'which brings me back to my original question: what are you doing here on Dyason?'

'Piss off mate!' Jenson grinned at him. 'That's as much as you'll get out of me!'

One of the guards stepped forward and raised his rifle butt. Hillmead raised his hand and ordered 'Stop! There's no need for that! We're not *all* uncivilised scum!' The conscript looked at him strangely, shrugged then returned to his post. There was a knock at the door and a junior officer stepped into the cell and gave Hillmead a note. He read through the message then handed it back to the messenger. 'Make sure that Lieutenant Shalok gets to see this. She's in the next cell interviewing the other prisoner.' The messenger nodded then left.

Hillmead clasped his hands together on the table-top, leant forward and said, 'A search team has found the wreckage of your fighter craft and your interstellar vessel, the *Observer.*' He paused and looked Jenson straight in the eye before continuing, 'Unfortunately there is very little left of the ship except scrap metal, poly composite and the flight recorder. They found the bodies of the crew still inside the wreckage.'

Hillmead watched Jenson closely, looking for signs of stress and was deeply satisfied when he saw the muscles in his neck tighten and the veins throb. 'So you see, you and Han Sandpiper are the only survivors of your mission. We can easily gather the details on your flight from your vessel's computer, but it would save time and effort if you were to tell me now. So, once again Group Captain Jenson, what was the purpose of your mission?'

Jenson sat up straight in his chair and spat at Hillmead venomously, 'You're lying shitbag! Go fuck yourself!'

Hillmead smiled to himself. Despite Jenson's show of bravado he knew he'd managed to crack the man's armour. The seed of doubt had been sown. All that remained was to widen the gap.

There was a loud 'crump' and the cell was suddenly filled with smoke, dust and the smell of cordite. A series of further explosions shook the concrete walls threatening to bring the whole place down in a pile of rubble. By the gods that was an explosion from outside! Just what the frig was going on? Jenson had instinctively thrown himself on the floor and the two guards were looking around in confusion. Hillmead leapt out of his chair and ran for the door. 'You two watch *him*. Don't let him out of your sight. I'll be back as soon as I find out what the hell's going on!'

He rushed into the corridor and out into the main foyer. Shalok was already there, her small automatic in her palm. 'Shit Shalok! What's going on?' he hollered at her. She waved him to the ground and he hit the deck just as a hail of automatic fire wove a pattern on the wall behind him. He pulled his own automatic and crawling on his hands and knees he made his way to where Shalok was taking cover behind a concrete pillar.

'Over there!' she pointed to a number of strange looking vehicles screaming across the airfield, their large balloon tyres kicking up plumes of dust. As he watched one of the buggies fired a missile and a hypersonic transport taxying towards a hangar erupted in a huge fire-ball that shook the ground. Other buggies swept past workshops and quarters raking the area with cannon fire. The scene was chaotic, surprise total.

'By the gods! Who the hell are they?' he shouted into Shalok's ear.

'Mutants,' she shouted back. 'They must have driven out of the wastelands during the night.' A buggy swept past them, its chain-gun rattling. Shalok ineffectually opened fire with her automatic.

'Mutants? Mutants have never led a direct assault on this place before. That's why there's no real perimeter defence,' Hillmead yelled over the sound of further explosions. 'So why are they attacking now?' Realisation hit him like a smack in the face. 'The humans!'

Hillmead and Shalok stared open mouthed at each other. 'The rest of the crew must have been picked up by the mutants and then persuaded them to make a rescue attempt,' she said.

'That's exactly what's happening! Come on move it! We've got to get them away from here before those mutants get their hands on them!' he shouted, grabbing her hand and literally hauling her towards the interrogation cells. He stormed down the corridor, threw open the door to Jenson's cell and stepped through, closely followed by Shalok. The door slammed shut behind them. Hillmead came to an abrupt halt and slowly looked around the cell. He saw the gagged and bound guards, he saw the group of armed humans and one mutant and he saw Jenson and Sandpiper standing before them automatics raised. They were obviously too late.

'Looks like my friends have returned from the grave Colonel,' Jenson said aiming his stolen weapon at Hillmead's head.

'Leave them to me,' the mutant muttered dangerously, 'I will happily dispatch these scum. They have tortured and butchered many of my people.'

Hillmead took a step back as the giant mutant woman stepped towards him holding a large double-edged blade in her hand. Jenson stepped forward and placed a restraining hand on her arm. 'Wait,' he said. 'These two aren't the same as the others. They stopped Han and me from being beaten to death last night. We owe them a little bit of mercy.'

Hillmead could see the disappointment in the mutant's face as she reluctantly lowered her blade. 'If you say so, friend Jenson. Are you sure I cannot cut them just a little bit?' she asked hopefully.

Jenson grinned. 'Not even a little bit friend Colmarrie. There's something different about these two. I think they know a lot about what's going on. Besides, they'll make good hostages.'

Colmarrie frowned then smiled. 'That is so, very wise. I understand why you are regarded as a great leader.'

Another of the humans handcuffed Shalok and Hillmead together. As he did this Hillmead took the opportunity to look at the younger man's face more closely and with a shock realised that once more the face matched the description as did that of the older human standing in the corner. He recognised all of them except for the giant mutant woman— incredible! Those responsible for the collapse of the Dyason occupation forces on Earth were all here in this one room together! What by all the gods were they doing here? Shalok gasped behind him; she too recognised the humans. He elbowed her in the stomach in an attempt to get her to shut up.

'Time to make moves Paul,' the old man said in English. 'Are you up to this?'

'Yeah, I'm fine. A bit battered and bruised but nothing broken,' Jenson replied.

'There are two buggies waiting for us out the back. Jennifer, Tychivesk and Josh are with the assault team outside,' the old man said. 'So let's go people!'

Hillmead and Shalok were bundled out of the cell and down the corridor. Colmarrie gave the two guards a swift kick each for good measure then locked them in the cell. They'd got halfway down the corridor when Jenson turned and said, 'Wait, we nearly forgot somebody.'

Moss stopped and asked, 'Who've we left behind boss? There was only you and Han, wasn't there?'

'Just wait here a minute. Colmarrie can you give me a hand?' The mutant woman nodded and followed Jenson to another cell door. Using the keys taken from the guards they opened the door and went in. A few moments later they re-emerged half carrying, half dragging the body of a mutant girl between them. Myrddin stepped forward and lifted the girl's face. 'She's been badly beaten and half-starved. She needs medical attention. Who is she?'

'I don't know,' answered Jenson. 'I heard her moans during the night. God only knows how long she's been stuck in this hell-hole.'

'Her name is Neehmad, ' Colmarrie said. 'She's a member of my unit. She went missing whilst on patrol four months ago. We thought she'd been killed.'

'Well let's not stand around. I for one don't want to be locked up again,' Sandpiper said with feeling. Nodding in agreement Jenson and Colmarrie set off once more, supporting the girl between them.

At the back of the building was a small access door which was wedged open. Hillmead and Shalok were herded through the door and out into the blistering morning heat. In a rear courtyard sat two of the strange desert buggies looking like alien machines next to the standard Imperial trucks and vehicles also parked there. Close up the buggies looked even more lethal. They seemed to consist of a basic stripped-down chassis onto which had been added all sorts of nastiness. A huge engine at the front led to an open driver's cockpit. Behind the driver's position was a gunner's position, with a chain-gun mounted on a flexible mount. At the rear of the vehicle were a few jump seats plus spare cans of fuel and water. Simple, but effective.

'Okay folks let's climb aboard,' Moss called out. Mutant drivers sat in the cockpits of the buggies, their faces completely covered by face masks and goggles. They waved their arms encouraging the group to climb aboard as quickly as possible. Hillmead and Shalok were unceremoniously dumped into the back of one of the buggies followed by Sandpiper and Moss, who kept their weapons loosely at the ready. Hillmead saw the giant woman Colmarrie try to lift the girl Neehmad aboard the other buggy, but she started to struggle looking around the compound with wild eyes. Colmarrie tried to calm the girl, but she wasn't helped by the agitated driver who started to gesticulate, waving his arms everywhere. Suddenly the girl kicked Jenson smartly in the balls making him double up in agony. Colmarrie let her go in surprise and she bolted for the door, heading back towards the prison cells.

Jenson painfully got up off the ground, holding his wounded testicles in one hand, 'What the hell is wrong with her...' his voiced trailed off when he saw the buggy's chain-gun pointing directly at Colmarrie and himself. Hillmead was as surprised as the group of humans, especially when the driver of his buggy turned his chain-gun on the rest of them. Colmarrie snarled and cursed but stopped short of attempting to reach for her own weapon. There was a clatter from the direction of the other vehicles in the compound and Hillmead turned just in time to see a whole platoon of Imperial troopers move out from their hiding places.

'Oh shit, not again!' Sandpiper said expressively. 'This is getting to be a *real* bad habit!' Reluctantly the group lay down their weapons and put up their hands.

Any sense of relief Hillmead may have felt at being apparently rescued was dashed when a tall, darkly beautiful woman and a chisel-faced Imperial officer stepped forward and faced the group.

'Gulag!' Moss hissed in disbelief.

Jennifer gripped the handles of the chain-gun and loosed off another burst at a group of Imperial troopers dug in behind a blast-pen. The surprise of the initial attack had gone and the airfield's resident defence regiment was finally putting up an organised resistance.

The buggy driver kept his foot hard on the accelerator and constantly swerved in an attempt to throw off the Imperial troops' aim. Unfortunately, Jennifer found her own aim being thrown off more than those of the defence regiment. She'd tried to get the driver to co-ordinate his driving with her firing, but this was a concept the Dyason mutant couldn't grasp. Aggressive enthusiasm was no substitute for discipline and training and Jennifer knew it was only a matter of minutes before the mutants would have to withdraw before their losses became too high.

'Avenger three, this is Avenger one—Jennifer we're beginning to take heavy casualties here,' called Tychivesk over the radio. 'We must start a withdrawal. These people can't take much more of a pounding! Is there any sign of the others? Over.'

Jennifer cursed, stopped firing and called into the mike, 'Negative, Avenger one. We're in position opposite the detention centre, but there's no sign of activity.'

'Avenger three, something must have gone wrong. They should be out of there by now. I'm going to order a withdrawal. We must cut our losses.'

Jennifer was crestfallen. 'Negative Avenger one. Hold your position. I'll try to contact the group and assess the situation.'

Whilst the driver continued to scream around the airfield in an almost random manner, Jennifer called out in her mind, *'Moss, what's going on? Where are you? The mutants are threatening to withdraw. We're running out of time what's happening? Moss?'*

The answer she got was not the one she was expecting. Instead of the familiar presence of her man she felt a cold, soulless mind enter her own. Immediately she clamped down her mental barriers as a greeting entered her thoughts. *'Ah Jennifer, I'm afraid your friends are a little, shall we say, tied up, at the moment. '* Jennifer immediately recognised the sick mind and let out an involuntary scream, 'Gulag!'

A lone figure ran out of the front of the detention cell, automatic fire kicking up the ground around the person's feet. Praying it was Moss, Jennifer kicked the driver in the shoulder and pointed to the running figure. The driver nodded in understanding and screamed off in that direction whilst Jennifer lay down a covering fire with the chain-gun. As they got nearer the return fire from the Imperial troopers became more accurate with shells ricocheting off the buggy's armour plating. Her heart sank as she realised the figure was not Moss but a mutant, but she kept laying down a covering fire regardless. Skilfully the buggy driver intercepted the running figure and went into a skidding turn that stopped just in front of the escapee. Jennifer leant over and literally hauled the skinny body of a mutant girl into the back of the buggy, then screamed. 'Go! Go! Let's go!'

The driver didn't need to be told twice, he put his foot down again and sped off toward the airfield perimeter.

'Jennifer, this is Tychivesk. We're withdrawing! I repeat we are withdrawing! We've come up against heavy armour! We must withdraw!' the Dyason officer called over the radio.

Desperately Jennifer screamed into the mike, 'Tychivesk you complete shit! They're not out yet. Hold your position—something has gone wrong. I repeat—hold your position—please...!' She got no further, her shoulder turned to fire and she just glimpsed blood starting to pump out of a deep wound before she blacked out completely.

CHAPER NINE

The heavy steel cell door swung open and two troopers stepped inside pointing their short-barrelled automatics at Moss. He casually opened one eye and looked them over. These were no conscripts, they carried their weapons in a confident professional manner and their uniform insignia identified them as belonging to the elite Imperial Guard.

'The Group Leader wants to talk to you,' one of them snapped at him. 'Now!'

Moss got up off the bunk and stepped out into the corridor. For a moment he considered taking the pair of guards on, but he decided against it. There was something strange going on here and the man with the answers was the clone Gulag. The strange dream he'd had on that fateful first day was still fresh in his mind and he was a firm believer in following his dreams.

After the trap was sprung on them back on Dyason they were all thrown into the back of an orbital shuttle that had already been flight prepared before the mutant attack had even begun, which was just a little bit suspicious. They'd been brought here to the nearly complete Dominator and then put into separate cells, but not before Colmarrie had given Moss some background information on the cloned version of Gulag.

He followed the Imperial Guards down the steel-plated corridors of the Dominator for over ten minutes before they finally arrived at a section of the ship closed off from the rest. He was carefully searched and electronically scanned in some sort of reception area before being ushered through another set of blast doors and into another suite of rooms. Moss noticed that these rooms were completely different from the rest of the ship. They were carpeted for a start and the fixtures and fittings would be more at home in a luxury cruise liner than a naval battleship. He was led into a lounge area, fitted with big leather sofas and soft, diffused lighting in contrast to the harsh fluorescent strips fitted in the rest of the Dominator.

Moss was led to a leather couch and his shackles were removed. The guards then turned and left. He sat quietly for a couple of minutes waiting for something to happen and when it didn't he got up and started to look around. His attention was grabbed by a series of bookshelves filled with beautifully bound books. He wandered over and casually took down a volume, it was a copy of Shakespeare's *Merchant of Venice*. Surprised, Moss took down another volume. This time the book was a volume of Dyason poetry which Moss attempted and failed to translate properly. He regretted not spending more time at the learning terminals onboard Excalibur. There was one book open on a small study desk which Moss picked up. The gold-leaf title on the leather-bound cover was, 'Point Zero—experiments in power from water'. His heart beat a little faster, the words of Arthur in his dream came back to him: 'Everybody is after something called Point Zero,' and here it was in front of him in black and white. Moss sat down at the desk and started to read the book.

He lost track of the time, he guessed he'd been reading solidly for at least two or three hours when he finally became aware of another presence in the room. Gulag sat on a couch not far from him, sipping from a cognac glass. The Dyason got up and poured another tumbler full of a light red liquor and brought it over to where he sat. Moss took the glass and had a sip, it was good.

'Interesting reading don't you think?' Gulag said.

'Very,' Moss replied. 'I take it you left it out for me to read? That's why your goons brought me here.'

'That's right. I thought it was time that you and I had a little chat and I wanted you to know about Point Zero before we spoke.'

Moss gave the cloned Gulag an appraisive look. This was a different animal to the Gulag he had met on Earth. This guy was colder, more calculating, but apparently not a psychopath like his predecessor.

'You're not the Gulag I knew,' he said simply.

Gulag shrugged, pulled up a chair and sat down opposite him. 'I may be a clone, I may have had all the original's memories downloaded into my own mind, but it is my *own* mind, not his. My feelings, thoughts and actions are independent of his. Besides, he was a complete *arse hole*.'

Moss smiled at that last comment. 'On that we can safely agree,' he said. 'So tell me, how did your existence come about? I thought I'd fairly well incinerated your predecessor.'

Gulag took a sip from his tumbler, looked towards the ceiling for a moment, then answered. 'Nimue created my predecessor from a witch's brew of genetic experiments then had herself impregnated with an egg fertilised with her created DNA. The result was the original Gulag, complete with all his neuroses and mental instability. When you incinerated him Nimue took his memories from him in the moments before his death and stored them in the back of her own mind. When I was born and created in the genetics lab, those memories were downloaded into my own mind as part of my accelerated growth. A lifetime of experience gained in a few short minutes. It's just a shame they are the experiences of a psychopath.'

'So Nimue decided to skip all the pain and effort of child-birth and waiting for a normal child to grow up?' Moss probed. 'I'm surprised those mad scientists of hers managed to achieve accelerated growth. It's been tried several times on Earth, but without success.'

'Dyason scientists aren't held back by the same ethical and moral considerations that your scientists are. There were plenty of monstrous failures before they got the process right and created me.'

Moss put his glass down and looked at the clone carefully, at the same time he probed Gulag's mind and found firm barriers. He saw no immediate hostile threat, but at the same time the clone wasn't about to let him know any more than he wanted him to. Moss decided the direct approach was called for.

'Why are you telling me all this?' he asked. 'What is it you're after exactly?'

Gulag ignored the question and asked one of his own. 'What do you make of the book Moss?' he asked.

'Point Zero...? It's interesting,' he replied guardedly. 'Once again I've heard of experiments into turning water into a viable power source on Earth, but nothing concrete was achieved before your thugs invaded. Towards the end of the twentieth century a few half-baked inventors came up with machines that could supposedly split water into its main elements of hydrogen and oxygen. They reckoned they got more power out of them than they put in. Their experiments were hard to repeat, so nothing was proved.'

Gulag got up, walked over to the desk and thumbed through the still open volume. 'Scientists had a little more success with their experiments on Dyason. It was proved that if you passed a certain frequency through water, some sort of reaction caused it to split into its main elements. However, for some reason the experiments never worked on a large scale.'

'So why all the interest in some part-successful experiments? What has any of this to do with me?' Moss asked him, keeping his face poker straight.

Gulag turned to look at him. 'Do you have any idea as to the effects such an invention would have on both our worlds? We're talking limitless power—clean, pollutant-free power. You know the ecological state this planet is in; it's a disaster, but if we were able to replace all our fossil fuels with powerplants based on water we could turn the environment around, repair the damage that has been done.'

Moss stared at Gulag shrewdly, he wasn't taken in by the clone's act. Despite what he'd been told, he couldn't quite believe that this new Gulag was an environmentalist. There had to be more to it than that. *'Point Zero'*, a reaction that turned water into hydrogen and oxygen, possibly the ultimate power source. Clean, renewable and available in just about every corner of the universe...of course! That was it!

'You know Gulag,' Moss began, keeping his face expressionless, 'it seems to me that whenever a new power source is discovered, there's always two ways in which it can be used. Usually, this means it can be used to provide the power that drives civilisations, or it can be corrupted and used as a weapon to destroy these same civilisations. Would I be right in thinking that *Point Zero* relates not just to creating energy? I mean, what would happen if you started your chain reaction in an ocean? That ocean is split into pure oxygen and pure hydrogen, you light a match and hey presto! The seas are ablaze!

'Just *imagine,* you could set whole worlds on fire and when the chain reaction finally die expires what's left? The hydrogen and oxygen become water again. Admittedly the seas and continents will probably have changed around a bit and everybody and everything will be dead, but so what? Given your techniques for cloning, you could repopulate the planet with perfect specimens of plants, animals and people. You could create a world of your own design, not in a matter of years, but in a matter of weeks! *You* would become a God!'

Gulag said nothing, which was a good enough admission for Moss. 'You're right, you are different from your predecessor. He was a sick psychopath whilst you're a megalomaniac.'

Gulag turned to look at him, his face remaining expressionless. 'I refuse to be baited Moss. You know as well as I do that the two of us are very evenly matched; our minds and talents are equally potent. There is no need, no point, in us being enemies; it serves no purpose. The universe is big enough for the two of us. The acquisition of Point Zero would enable both of us to solve our worlds' problems, *that* is something you cannot deny.'

'If you're so keen for us to become allies why have you built this battle-cruiser? Why are you in the throes of creating another invasion fleet?' Moss retorted.

'I needed something to bring you here,' Gulag answered simply. He sat down on the couch next to Moss and looked him in the eye. 'Look, you have something I need and I have something you need.'

'I'm listening.'

'When Excalibur was first discovered Luke and Josh Brabazon spent some time examining the huge onboard data library. One of the things they discovered was a reference to Point Zero. Luke Brabazon started examining the files and discovered that there is a formula, a method for turning water into fuel on a huge scale. However, only half that formula was onboard Excalibur's computer.'

'That's not possible,' interrupted Moss. 'Excalibur's data-banks have been minutely examined since then and so far as I'm aware, no reference to Point Zero was ever found.'

'That's because Luke Brabazon put a lock on the file and changed its name to prevent access by anyone other than himself. Realising the importance of what he'd found it was his intention to go back and examine the files later.'

'How do you know all this?'

'When my predecessor in his madness killed Luke Brabazon, he raped his mind of everything he knew,' Gulag answered.

'And of course you acquired this knowledge when you inherited the original Gulag's memories,' Moss finished. 'But I still don't get what you're after from me.'

'Luke Brabazon managed to hide the formula from my predecessor's probing, so the information is locked somewhere in the data-banks. You know Excalibur. You can get the computer to open up that file.'

'What good will that do. It would still only give us half the formula. What about the rest?' Moss queried.

'You give me the information that's locked on Excalibur and I'll show you where the rest of the formula is,' replied Gulag.

'Where is it?'

Gulag smiled and held up his tumbler. 'Now that would be telling my friend, but rest assured I *do* know where the rest of the formula is hidden.'

'How do I know that you're telling the truth?'

Moss felt Gulag's mental barriers drop, just a fraction, just enough for Moss to get a brief glance...he was telling the truth. Gulag put his drink down and got up to leave. 'Just remember this Moss. There are powers and minds behind everything that is happening to our two worlds. At the moment we're powerless pawns in a cosmic game. Point Zero will even the score. High stakes are being played for a big prize. Think about it!' Then he left, leaving Moss looking thoughtfully into the bottom of his glass.

'Your dossier makes interesting reading Myrddin,' Shalok said.

Myrddin leant back in his chair and stretched expansively before fixing his eye on the young Dyason woman. 'You know, as much as I hate to admit it,' he said with a sly grin, 'for an Imperial lackey, you're a damned fine attractive woman. How about visiting my cell tonight?'

The solitary guard standing in front of the door to the interview room tried hard to suppress a smirk. Despite herself, Shalok found a flush rising up her neck. There was something about the way this old human looked at her that she found disturbing, or should that be exciting? 'Don't change the subject Myrddin,' she snapped, trying to regain control of the interview. 'What exactly was the purpose to your group's mission here to Dyason? What do you know of the Democratic Front?'

Myrddin kept his eyes glued on Shalok's face. 'That's boring. You know the answer to that question already. Why don't you ask Gulag or Nimue? They appear to be behind everything that's going on here. Let's talk about something far more interesting. What's going on between you and that policeman Hillmead? He's got the hots for you, you know. Personally, I think you would make a great couple...'

Shalok slammed her folder down on the metal table as her face broke into a huge red flush. 'We are not here to discuss *my* private life human!' she shouted. '*You* are the prisoner here. *You* are the enemy of the state, not me! You would be wise to remember that!'

'Oh so you do fancy him!' Myrddin laughed.

Shalok rose out of her chair and raised her arm to strike Myrddin across the face. As her hand descended the old man grabbed her wrist with surprising strength. She screamed at the guard to intervene but the trooper remained at the door unmoving. She felt a force enter her mind and command, '*Sit down you foolish girl!*' Shalok collapsed back in her seat her face a picture of surprise. She turned and looked at the guard, he remained at the doorway unmoving.

'What have you done to him?' she demanded.

The jovial Myrddin had been replaced by a man with a deadly earnest face. 'I've done nothing to him,' he replied. 'The trooper simply believes everything is as it should be. He is simply seeing what he wants to see, rather than what is actually happening. Time is short, I don't know how long we can talk like this before Gulag intervenes.'

'I thought that the stories about ESP and telepathy were nothing but legends,' she blurted.

'Well you were wrong, they're for real. Now listen carefully and answer me through your mind.... Where is the Envoy Nimue?'

Without even thinking about it Shalok replied in her mind, *'She's back in Caranak.'*

'That's good. What about Gulag?'

'He's here onboard the Dominator.'

'That's not so good. Now I need you to check out something here on the Dominator, something I have a suspicion of.'

'Why should I help you? This is ridiculous!'

'The reason is that you want to know who was behind sending your boyfriend to try and kill you-that's why.'

Shalok took in a sharp intake of breath. 'How do you know about that?' she asked aloud.

'Because it dominates your waking thoughts. You want to know who set your boyfriend up? You want to know whether it's true that the Empire is killing your planet? I can help you find the answers. That's why you must do what I ask. You and Hillmead aren't like the others. You have open minds—use them! I'll give you a glimpse of what I know and what we're looking for...'

For a brief moment Shalok could see the human's thoughts displayed before her like an open book. Information swept past her eyes as if she were looking at a holo-screen. She gasped, the enormity of it all was almost too much to comprehend. By the gods, what he was proposing was incredible! Could it all be true? Could she have been *so* wrong? Questions poured into her mind at the same speed as the information. She felt a hand on her shoulder, turned and saw the guard looking at her with a strange look on his face.

'Is everything all right Lieutenant? You look a little faint,' he asked.

Shalok brushed the trooper's hand away and blurted, 'Yes, yes...I'm fine. Thank you.' The trooper looked at her, shrugged then moved back to his position by the door. She turned to look at Myrddin. He was slouched in his chair once more, arms crossed about his chest, a grin on his face.

Hurriedly, Shalok picked up her papers and the video tape of the interview. 'I'll talk to you later,' she said pointedly, then fled the room.

CHAPTER TEN

SOUTHERN WASTELANDS

'Well, you'll live,' said Josh Brabazon, placing the last dressing on Jennifer's shoulder wound. 'You're lucky, the bullet simply grazed you. If the bullet had entered a few centimetres lower down we wouldn't be having this conversation. Honestly Jennifer, that was a bloody stupid thing to do, dashing off like that. You could have been killed!'

Jennifer pulled her flight suit over her shoulder and zipped it back up. 'It's funny,' she replied. 'I don't feel lucky. We've still lost the others.'

'Moss will be okay. He can look after himself, remember who he is.'

'So how come I can't touch his mind. Can you?'

Josh didn't answer. 'That's what I thought,' Jennifer said.

There was a cough at the entrance and Tychivesk pulled the curtain aside. Jennifer looked up and snarled. 'I'm not talking to you, you bastard!'

'Please, Jennifer. It's not my fault, we stayed as long as we could. We were up against heavy armour that appeared from nowhere. We could do no more. Nobody is more sorry about what happened to the others than me...'

'Yeah right,' she said sarcastically.

'Jennifer,' Josh intervened, 'be reasonable. I was there, what happened to the others wasn't

Tychivesk's fault. The mutants were taking heavy casualties. You can't blame them for cutting their losses, it was the only sensible thing to do.'

Jennifer ignored them both and stared moodily out the window at the star-lit desert.

'Look, I need you to meet somebody,' Tychivesk continued. 'The girl mutant you rescued, Neehmad, has something important to tell us. I think you should hear what she has to say.'

Jennifer continued to ignore the ex-Imperial officer. Tychivesk sighed and said, 'If you change your mind, we'll be in the briefing room.' Then he turned and left.

'I'll go,' said Josh. Jennifer got up off the cot and made her way to the doorway. 'No Josh, we'll both go, but I still don't trust the little bastard.'

'Really? You surprise me,' Josh replied deadpan, following Jennifer into the corridor.

When they got to the briefing room, the mutant girl Neehmad was sitting next to an artist making sketches with a pen and paper. The girl looked up at Jennifer and despite her injuries smiled warmly.

'Hi Neehmad,' Jennifer said gently in Dyason. 'How are you feeling?'

'I'm okay,' the mutant replied shyly. 'I wish to thank you and your friends for rescuing me. I'm sorry that they were captured.'

Jennifer took her hand and squeezed it. 'It was the least we could do. Think nothing of it. You're not responsible for their capture.' She glanced down at the pictures being drawn by the artist and picked one up. It was a rough sketch of some sort of craft she'd never seen before. 'What are these Neehmad?' she asked.

'I saw them out in the wastelands. I was watching them when I was hit on the head and captured,' the mutant replied.

'Inside the wastelands?' Josh asked. 'I thought there were no Imperial bases inside the wasteland boundary?'

'There weren't until a few months ago,' the officer debriefing Neehmad answered. 'Imperial forces have set up some sort of secret weapons establishment some 200 klicks north-west of here. We've been keeping an eye on the place since it was built. They've been testing some sort of new aircraft there.'

'Are these sketches the aircraft you saw?' Jennifer asked. Neehmad nodded. 'What do you think Josh?'

Josh picked a couple of the sketches up off the table and looked at them appraisingly. He stared hard at them, turning the sketches around and looking at them from different angles.

'Well?' Jennifer demanded impatiently after a while.

'It certainly isn't good news I'm afraid,' he finally replied. 'These stub wings are useless in terms of generating lift,' he continued, pointing to a couple of the sketches, 'and this large set of intakes looks very familiar.'

Jennifer peered at one of the drawings herself. 'They look like variations on a theme. A little like our own *Observer*. Could they be some sort of scout-craft with hyperspace capability?'

'That's exactly what they look like to me,' Josh agreed shaking his head. 'Neehmad, can you talk us through exactly what happened when you saw these craft?'

The mutant girl went on to explain how she saw several prototype vessels of different design during her period of observation. She told them that all of them made terrible whining noises and eventually blew up, except for the very last machine she saw before her capture. That machine managed to get off the ground but apparently blew up in the upper atmosphere, although there was no explosion, just an incredible flash of light.

'So what do you make of that Josh?' Tychivesk asked, rubbing his hands in an agitated manner.

'Well it sounds like they're trying to perfect the kind of drive we used in the *Observer* and have installed in our Flyships. The spooling-up sound is the status field applying a distortion to the singularities. It sounds like they're having a problem harmonising the field to the singularities' resonance.'

'Obviously,' said Jennifer. 'What about the one that got off the ground though?'

'They must have managed to get the harmonisation right, or at least for a while. The field must have gone out of synch a few minutes after launch and oops! The prototype is no more. The flash without the bang would suggest that the singularities blinked into another dimension leaving nothing but wreckage in this dimension.'

'Sounds painful, but do you think they could be on the verge of getting their sums right? If they are, these machines could form part of a new invasion fleet,' Jennifer asked worriedly.

'I'd say the Imperial Navy are only a few weeks, maybe a month away from getting their calculations right, if they've got any more prototypes to play with. When we built the *Observer* we had to spend months working through computer simulations before we could safely carry out any trial flights, even with the help of Excalibur. If you're not worried about killing a few test pilots along the way, the whole process could be speeded up enormously.'

'Which would appear to be what the Imperial forces are trying to do,' agreed Tychivesk.

Jennifer tapped thoughtfully on the stone table-top for a few minutes before asking Josh, 'Would you be able to harmonise the status field in one of the prototypes?'

'It would depend a lot upon the quality of the control equipment they've installed,' Josh answered. 'In theory yes, but I'd hate to have to rely on equipment from down-town Dyason—no disrespect,' he added nodding at Tychivesk. 'Why? What have you got in mind?'

'We're stranded here on Dyason right?' she said decisively.

'Ye...s,' he answered slowly.

'And you reckon the others have been taken to the Dominator?' she asked of Tychivesk.

'Yes. That's what our intelligence reports,' he acknowledged.

'So we need to find a way to get off the planet, rescue the others and get back to Earth with the information that the Imperial forces are trying to build another invasion force. Right so far?'

'I really don't think I'm going to like this!' Josh said worriedly.

'You're not really suggesting we try to steal a prototype ship are you?' Tychivesk asked unconsciously rubbing his hands again.

'That's exactly what I'm suggesting we do,' Jennifer snapped back. 'Now hear me out.'

Shalok slipped from shadow to shadow using the poor lighting in the servicing conduit to her advantage. It was the middle of ship's night and a rest period for those work gangs still fitting out the interior of the Dominator, consequently there was only a skeleton crew manning the engineering section which gave her the chance to check something out.

Her meeting with the human Myrddin had affected her more than she was willing to admit. The manner in which he appeared to read her thoughts was alarming, it was as if she stood naked before him. He was correct about her desire to find out the truth behind her fiance's attack in the underground car park. As much as she hated to admit it he was also correct about her growing feelings for the uncouth, uneducated gutter cop Hillmead. It was ludicrous, she knew, but she had to find out if the other thing he said was true, if only to satisfy her own mind that it was all nothing but a series of coincidences.

Crawling on her hands and knees she moved down the servicing conduit until she came to a hatchway marked with a number that matched the one on her hastily drawn map. The service conduit exited into the main propulsion hall where the artificial singularities were maintained in status by a series of powerful electro-magnetic fields. Using the special tool from the pocket of her flight suit, she quickly undid the six release bolts and opened the hatch carefully. The propulsion hall was gigantic, the size of an aircraft hangar. All around the edge of the hall were control panels and monitors. However, the centre of the hall was dominated by two huge generators that pulsed and glowed with an eerie blue light. These generators took up nearly all of the hall space and reached up for tens of metres. The latest in Imperial technology blended strangely with more traditional materials and despite being controlled by futuristic computers, the generators were still a mass of hissing, venting pipes and wires. It was as if they were a pair of living, breathing monsters.

From her position she could just make out a pair of technicians sitting at some control desks on the other side of the generators. Other than that, the hall appeared to be deserted. Quickly she climbed out of the servicing conduit and padded across the hall to the two main field generators. Keeping the mass of pipes and cables between her and the two technicians she started to look for the status field focus points that the human Myrddin told her should be at the epicentre of each generator.

The human had told her that if the Dominator was all but complete, as had been stated by Imperial Command, then the singularities should be up and running. These singularities would be at the focus point of the status fields, a fact she had confirmed in a casual conversation with one of the engineers the previous day. Carefully, she walked all the way around the port field generator, eventually finding the control panel she was looking for. She began tapping at the keys but it took her a few minutes to figure out how to use the complicated monitoring systems before she could get the results she was looking for. When the monitor finally displayed the information she was looking for her heart began to pound furiously, as if it were attempting to escape the confines of her chest. Could the old man be right after all?

It wasn't enough, she needed more proof, and there was only one way to get it. Quietly she wormed her way through the mass of pipes and cables then climbed over the safety rail to step into what should have been the pulsating heart of the status field. She should have immediately been turned into her base elements, but nothing happened. She stood there for several seconds, not daring to move or breathe, but still nothing happened. 'Oh my God!' she mouthed to herself. The human Myrddin *was* right! So how much more of what he said was truth?

'Oi! By the gods, what do you think you're doing?' One of the two technicians shouted at her from the other side of the hall. 'Get out of there. You'll be fried alive!' The two technicians grabbed at their gun holsters, pulled out small automatics and ran toward her.

The movement snapped Shalok out of her thoughts and her training took over. Nimbly she leapt out of the status chamber and ran for the still open hatch to the service conduit.

'Stop! Stop, or I fire!' the technician shouted at her retreating back.

Shalok wasn't about to get shot at, what she now knew was of vital importance to every living Dyason and she was determined that everyone would know. She rolled onto the floor and pulled out her small automatic in one movement. The technician aimed his pistol at her, but she loosed off a round before he could fire. The weapon flew out of the technicians hand and he fell to the floor screaming in pain. Shalok took aim again and loosed a round at the second technician. The second technician collapsed silently onto the deck floor. Not waiting to see if she were still being pursued, she dived for the conduit and began to crawl along as fast as she could, ignoring the knocks and cuts her knees and shoulders were suffering in the cluttered conduit.

The sirens began to wail just as she dropped back into a main corridor, outside the engineering section. The whole of the Dominator reverberated to the sound of the alarm and Shalok knew she had very little time left. As quickly as she could, she strode along the corridor ignoring other crew that ran past her to get to their emergency stations. With any luck, they would all think this was just another emergency drill, at least for a little while.

She finally got to the officer's deck and made her way to Hillmead's tiny cabin. Without bothering to knock, she barged in, slamming the door behind her. The lights came on and Hillmead sat upright in bed, pulling his pistol from under his pillow and levelling the tiny automatic at her head. 'Just what the frig is going on Lieutenant?' he demanded.

'I think we have a problem,' she panted. 'The shit is about to *really* hit the fan!'

Moss lay on the bunk in his cell, hands behind his head, staring up at the ceiling. *'So there you have it, this is all about Point Zero,'* he said in his mind. *'Gulag and Nimue have some half-baked plan to colonise planets that have large reserves of water, either at their polar caps, or in oceans. Turning water into fuel will give them an almost limitless power source.'*

'Of course, they could simply return to Earth, set off a chain reaction in the oceans and inherit the world once the reaction has cleansed the world of life,' added Myrddin from his own cell.

'That's right,' agreed Moss. 'What's really frightening is the concept of them repopulating the planet with cloned people, animals and vegetation of their own making. It's almost too incredible to believe. You realise of course, that although we can *keep Gulag out of this conversation, he'll at least know that we're talking to each other.'*

'He'll be counting on us talking together son.'

'So how are we going to play this?'

'What were your impressions of this new cloned Gulag, Moss?'

'Well, he's a very different animal from his predecessor. This guy is cold, clinically cold and his thinking reflects this. He's very calculating but I don't think he's a psychopath like his earlier incarnation. I can't be sure, but I got the impression that he thinks independently from Nimue. He may be a creation of her making, but he's got plans of his own and I'm not sure what they are.'

'It may be that his relationship with Nimue is a weakness we can work on,' Myrddin added thoughtfully. *'Hang on Moss...I've got visitors. I'll get back to you in a moment.'*

Hillmead and Shalok stormed into Myrddin's tiny cell. Hillmead pulled out his pistol and fired two rounds into the lens of the ceiling mounted surveillance camera, then he reached behind the back of the small metal-framed bunk and pulled out a small device. This he crushed beneath his feet.

'I thought about doing that myself,' Myrddin said flippantly, 'but decided it wasn't worth the effort. To what do I owe the pleasure this evening?'

Hillmead whirled on Myrddin and faced him angrily, 'What the frig is going on you old git?' he demanded.

Myrddin shrugged expansively and said, 'You tell me. I'm the prisoner here.'

Hillmead's face flushed bright red with anger and he leapt towards Myrddin, hands reaching for the human's throat. Almost contemptuously Myrddin gave a flick of his wrist and Hillmead found himself thrown against the far wall of the cell. The ex-police inspector slid to the floor with a groan.

'Now, now... be nice,' Myrddin chided gently.

Shalok looked at the immobilised Hillmead, then at the white-haired human in amazement. For a few seconds her mouth opened and closed wordlessly, then overcoming her momentary handicap she blurted, 'I went to the propulsion hall as you suggested!'

'And?'

'There's nothing there... *nothing* but bits of wire and pipes that do nothing. There *are* no status fields, there *are* no artificial singularities,' she answered frantically.

'It's just as I thought,' Myrddin said thoughtfully, shaking his head. Hillmead groaned so Myrddin got up off his bunk, stepped over to the semi-conscious policeman and with surprising strength hauled him to his feet. 'Did anybody see you go in there?' he asked Shalok.

'I was spotted by two technicians. There was a fire-fight and I shot them both. I'm not sure if they're dead or not,' she answered in a panicky voice. 'What do we do now?'

'Oh dear, that is unfortunate. I guess that explains the alarms.'

Hillmead shook his head and mumbled, 'What's going on?'

'I'm afraid your assistant has stumbled across a rather big Imperial secret,' Myrddin answered, letting go of Hillmead and heading for the door.

'What secret?' Hillmead asked as he became more aware of his surroundings once more.

'We've all been had Inspector-Colonel. You...me...all of us!'

'What do you mean, *had*?' Shalok demanded.

'I mean that the Dominator is one big hoax. She's nothing more than a huge motionless space station—a space station that is incapable of going *anywhere*!'

'What?' Hillmead blurted in surprise.

'My friend,' Myrddin said, facing the still swaying Dyason policeman, 'we've all been led to believe that this contraption is the prototype battle-cruiser of a fleet that will conquer the universe. Now it turns out that this is all nothing but an elaborate hoax. Of course, the real question is why?'

'Oh shit. That's what I thought,' Shalok said in a voice that was now *very* panicky. 'We're in *deep* trouble now Hillmead! What are we going to do?'

'Well I know what I'm going to do,' Myrddin interrupted.

'What?'

'I'm going to break jail and get the hell out of here.' After another quick gesture of his hand and a frown on his forehead the cell door sprang open. 'And I highly recommend that you both do the same if you want to live to see another sunrise.'

Myrddin stepped into the corridor and beckoned the two Dyason to follow him. 'Come along children. There's no time to lose. I guess you're both going to have to get used to the idea of playing for another team.'

Shalok stood rooted to the spot, her mouth opening and closing like a fish. This was a nightmare! All of a sudden she was an outcast; she'd shot two technicians, discovered possibly the Empire's biggest secret and a prisoner officially under her charge was walking out of the cell on his own accord! She pulled out her small automatic and pointed it uncertainly at the human.

'Wait... you can't, I mean...well, this is wrong,' she blurted, sounding confused and unconvinced, even to her own ears.

Hillmead, finally grasping the situation put his hand on Shalok's arm and slowly lowered it. 'He's right Shalok,' he said. 'There's no way Nimue and Gulag are going to let you, or me live now that we know their biggest secret. If the Dominator is nothing but one big hoax, then many of our other suspicions are probably true as well. It's time to leave the sinking ship.'

For a moment she remained rooted to the spot, her uncertainty obvious, then there was a distant shout and the sound of boots on metal decking. 'They're on their way young lady. Time's short, but I think you would be wise to listen to your friend's advice,' said Myrddin.

'Come on Shalok, let's go,' Hillmead urged.

Hesitantly she took a step forward towards the corridor, then another and another, knowing that her ambitions, hopes and dreams had finally been dashed forever.

Myrddin extended his consciousness and said, *'Moss we're on our way—it's time for a jailbreak.'*

Jennifer lay on top of the sand dune next to the mutant girl. She wore her lightweight environment suit and peered through the night-glasses at the group of concrete buildings laid out before her. The area appeared deserted but she could see track marks in the sand and other signs of recent activity. Neehmad pointed out the concrete apron where she had watched the attempted launch of the prototype space vehicles. Jennifer could see that although the remains of the disintegrated prototypes had been removed for examination, there were still clear signs of recent blast damage. She passed the night-scope to Josh Brabazon who examined the test site carefully.

'What do you think Josh?' she whispered after a couple of minutes.

'Well there's clearly been a lot of activity here, although it looks pretty quiet at the moment. There's no runway, so these prototype craft of Neehmad's must have vertical take-off capability. The fused concrete and sand around the launch apron would indicate intense heat and pressure,' he whispered back.

'Evidence to support Neehmad's story?'

'Well it's looking good so far, but I'll need to see more than fused sand and concrete.'

'There are no sentries and no other visible signs of security. I suggest we take a closer look at those concrete domes, they may have been the hangars where they kept the prototypes. The place looks abandoned to me,' Tychivesk suggested.

Jennifer thought it over for a moment. Somehow this seemed too easy. She'd been expecting perimeter fences and heavily armed security patrols, but there was none of that. The fact that this site was deep in the heart of radio-active wastelands may have something to do with it. Alternatively, it was possible that the site had been abandoned after the destruction of the prototype Neehmad watched, but the single road leading to the site showed signs of much more recent activity. However, she certainly wouldn't find out any more if they stayed where they were. She had to find a way to rescue Moss and the others, and get them all home. The answer didn't lie on top of the sand-dune.

'Okay, let's get down there and take a look, but be careful. We can't be sure that this place is deserted,' she finally agreed.

Neehmad led a squad of mutant fighters down the back of the sand dune then carefully edged towards the concrete domes. Jennifer, Josh and Tychivesk followed, cradling their own MG303 automatics, the mutants carrying arms fashioned in their own underground factories. After twenty minutes of carefully sweeping the launch site they arrived back at their start point.

'Nothing, nothing at all,' declared Tychivesk, lifting the face-plate of his environment suit and sipping from his water bottle. 'The place has obviously been abandoned. We're wasting our time here. Let's go before it starts to get light.'

'I've got to admit Jennifer, there's not a lot here to look at,' Josh agreed wearily . 'Whatever toys they had here, they've moved. Maybe they were spooked when they found Neehmad spying on them.'

Jennifer sat down on a nearby boulder and drank from her own water bottle. There was something not quite right here. It was as if...well, as if the place had a somehow familiar feel to it...

'Josh,' she asked. 'Does this place remind you of anywhere?'

He looked at her quizzically, 'How do you mean?'

She shrugged expansively, 'I don't know. I've just got a strange feeling about this place—it's almost as if it were familiar, yet I know we've never been here before.'

Tychivesk walked over, sat on the boulder next to her and put his arm around her shoulder. 'Jennifer, you're just worried about Moss and the others, that's all. You're tired and disappointed that there's nothing here. Let's go back and think this through again.'

Jennifer elbowed Tychivesk hard in the stomach and stood up. 'Piss-off Tychivesk,' she said as he fell backwards off the boulder. 'You give me the creeps.'

She wandered towards the first of the concrete domes embedded in the desert and examined the huge steel doors that must have been at least fifty metres wide and thirty metres high. The answer was in there somewhere, she knew it. Her eyes followed the line of the doors and came to rest on a much smaller entrance set in the left hangar door itself, which she'd never noticed before. She walked over and took a closer look.

This entrance was just big enough for one person to step through and was obviously there to allow access to the interior of the dome without the need to open the main doors. The entrance had a pull-down lever handle which she tugged at but to no effect. There was some sort of electronic combination lock next to the door labelled in Dyason letters. Jennifer punched in a few numbers experimentally, but nothing happened. Josh got up and came over to look.

'It's a six number, multi-combination, double-reverse sequence code. No wonder there's no security round here. You'll never crack that combination, not even with a computer the size of Excalibur,' he declared.

The mutant girl Neehmad took one look at the electronic lock and promptly fired half an ammo-clip from her automatic into it. The lock disappeared in a shower of sparks and the door sprung open.

'Imperial locks—pah! Only good for keeping out dumb animals!' she stated with a warped grin.

Jennifer pulled out the night-scope and peered into the dome. 'What do you see?' Josh asked.

'Not a lot,' she replied. She put the night-scope back in it's pouch and pulled out a torch and clipped it onto a holder above the barrel of her MG303. 'Well don't just stand there Josh. Are you coming with me or what?'

Josh sighed, pulled out his own torch and followed Jennifer into the dome. Inside it looked much like any other hangar, the concrete floor was stained by oil and hydraulics, work gantries stood at the edges and tools sat on neatly labelled trolleys. Neehmad's squad quickly searched the area, including offices and storerooms at the back of the dome. When they declared the site clear Jennifer switched on the hangar lights.

Jennifer could now see that the dome was quite large, not big enough to house a craft like their own *Observer*, but big enough to contain several B11 bombers. Her attention was drawn to the centre of the dome where the concrete floor gave way to an area of heavy steel plates.

'An elevator,' Josh stated. She gave him a quizzical look. 'That's what it looks like to me,' he continued. 'You can see a slight gap all around the edge of the plates. It's a huge elevator of the type you get on those old aircraft carriers—God only knows where it goes though.'

'Could there be some sort of underground hangar, maintenance or storage area?'

'Possibly. This whole site consists of only three domes without any out-buildings. If the other domes are like this one, it would make sense if all the equipment were stored underground. It would also make sense if the personnel quarters were down there as well, they'd then have protection from the reasonably high levels of radiation on the surface.'

'You mean that there could be shit-loads of Imperial troopers sitting under our feet?' Tychivesk asked in alarm. 'Don't you think we're getting in a little over our heads here?'

'Stop being such a snivelling coward Tychivesk,' Jennifer said with disdain. 'I hardly think they'd leave this place unguarded if the site hadn't been deserted. Do you?'

'Then how come the powers still on?' he retorted.

Jennifer chose to ignore him and continued to look for the panel that controlled the elevator. One of the mutant squad called out and beckoned them over to a door at the very back of the dome. When they got there the mutant excitedly held the door open and pointed to a spiral staircase that descended below ground level. 'That must be the emergency exit for the rooms underground,' said Neehmad.

'I think you're right,' agreed Jennifer, 'how long have we got until daylight Neehmad?'

'About two hours, friend Jennifer.'

'Good, then we've got time to take a look and still get away before daybreak. Any objections?'

Tychivesk looked at her sullenly but said nothing. 'Let's do it then.'

Neehmad ordered two of her squad to guard the entrance to the stairs and the remainder started down the stairwell, weapons cradled at the ready. They moved steadily down the stairwell as quickly and as quietly as possible although their boots did make a very unnerving clatter on the steel steps. They'd descended maybe fifty metres when they reached the first sub-level. Neehmad insisted on going through the fire-door first, followed by the remainder of her squad. Once more they performed a sweep of the rooms beyond before coming back to report.

'There is nothing on this level except for offices. No signs of current occupation,' she reported.

'What about papers, files, anything that might suggest what this place is all about?' Josh asked her.

'We saw nothing.'

'Okay let's press on down to the next level,' said Jennifer. 'We can have another look at this area if we don't find anything else of interest. I don't know about you guys, but I'm sure I can hear a humming, like heavy machinery.'

'Now you mention it, I can hear it too,' Tychivesk confirmed. 'It does sound like it's coming from below. Let's be careful people.'

Once more the squad descended the stairs to the next sub-level. The humming was by now much louder. Again, Neehmad and her mutants went through the fire-door first. A few minutes later one of the squad returned on his own.

'The noise gets louder in here,' the mutant told Jennifer. 'This level contains workshops and store-rooms, but there's no sign of Imperial scum. Neehmad wants you to come. There is something she thinks you should see.'

Jennifer nodded and followed the mutant fighter into the second sub-level. The corridor was reasonably well lit with fluorescent tubes hung from a ceiling swamped by power cables and pipes. Store-rooms and workshops led off the main corridor, each one carefully numbered and labelled in Dyason.

The humming noise was certainly more intense here and appeared to be emanating from somewhere up ahead. Neehmad was standing waiting, next to a set of large blast doors.

'Jennifer,' the mutant began, 'I think the source of the sound comes from beyond these doors.'

Jennifer put her ear to one of the large blast doors, the sound of heavy machinery made it vibrate gently. Neehmad was right.

'Can we get these doors open?' she asked.

Josh looked at the small panel set in the wall beside the doors. 'They're closed, but not locked,' he announced. 'I think it's this button here, I'm not sure, but here goes.'

Servos kicked in and the blast doors silently slid open. Neehmad drew in a short intake of breath, for there in front of them sitting in some sort of hangar was one of the prototypes she had described. 'There,' she whispered excitedly. 'There, you see... I told you they were here. That is one of the machines I saw them try to fly up there on the desert.'

'Wow!' Josh Brabazon uttered appreciatively.

The craft was about the size of a commercial airliner. A heavily glazed needle nose led into a wedge-shaped body that sprouted contoured, swept-back wings. Huge intakes sat above the wing, just below two large fins that were cranked out at opposing angles. Painted an all-over black, it was big and ugly.

Neehmad's squad quickly dispersed around the bay, once more looking for signs of Imperial troops. When they discovered nothing Josh ventured toward the Dyason craft and began to examine it in detail.

Jennifer walked around the perimeter of the bay looking at the machine from all angles. 'Well, what do you think Josh?' she called out to the wiry scientist who was busy peering in through the glazed nose.

'Well it certainly fits the description Neehmad gave us of the prototype that actually managed to get off the ground,' he called back. 'The question is, what's it doing here?'

'What do you mean?' Tychivesk asked from a gallery he'd discovered that over looked the machine. 'Why shouldn't it be here?'

'I would have thought it was obvious,' Jennifer answered. 'This place is deserted, no troops, no security, nothing...but, the power's still on and someone's left all the toy's out. In short, the lights are on, but nobody's home.'

'I guess I hadn't thought of it like that.'

'Yeah right...I can still hear that humming, is it any louder up there?'

Tychivesk cocked his head to listen more carefully, 'Yeah, maybe.'

Jennifer climbed up onto the gantry that surrounded the prototype. The Dyason machine was even more impressive from up there and despite her hate for the Imperial regime she had to admit to herself that it looked a very efficient, lethal space-fighter. If the Dyason ever managed to produce it in numbers, Earth would once more be at great risk. The idea of a fleet of battle-cruisers like the Dominator and several squadrons of these space-fighters didn't bear thinking about.

There was something bothering her. The constant background humming—It was a familiar sound, if only she could put her finger on it...

'Josh!' she called down to the scientist. Brabazon ignored her and continued to examine the control thrusters on the tip of the port wing. 'Josh get up here!'

'Jennifer I'm busy,' he yelled back. 'Can't it wait?'

'No, I think this is important. Get your skinny arse up here!'

Reluctantly, Josh pulled himself away from the prototype and joined Tychivesk and Jennifer on the gantry.

'Despite some external differences, this prototype is generally the same design as the larger space fighters on the drawing boards at home. The Imperial Navy has basically got its sums right, they just need to fine tune the.....'

'Josh!'

'...status field a bit. Then...'

'Josh!'

'What?'

'The noise, I think I know where I've heard it before,' Jennifer said, finally getting his attention.

'Where?' he asked.

'It's the same sound that reverberated through the caverns beneath Stonehenge when Excalibur first came to life,' she answered.

Josh raised an eyebrow, 'You're imagining it Jennifer.'

'Listen carefully.'

Josh tuned his ear to listen to the constant background humming more carefully, after a minute he said, 'Possibly...I admit it does seem familiar.'

'The sound is coming from the direction of that passageway at the end of the gantry. Let's go take a look,' Tychivesk added, striding off in the direction he indicated.

'Hang on a minute Tychivesk, wait for Neehmad's fighters, let them take the lead. There's no point in taking any unnecessary risks,' Jennifer called after the ex-Dyason officer, but he ignored her and carried on. 'Tychivesk...wait! Ah, shit!'

Reluctantly Jennifer headed after him, her MG303 at the ready. Josh Brabazon called Neehmad to catch up with them, then followed her. The gantry led to another blast door which was open, and a passageway beyond. Tychivesk had already disappeared around a corner by the time Jennifer, Josh and Neehmad had stepped through the second set of blast doors.

'Shit, where's that arse-hole gone?' Jennifer swore. There was the whirl of servos and she turned around just in time to see the blast doors close behind them, leaving Neehmad's mutant squad still in the underground hangar.

Josh leapt for the control panel and punched the buttons to no effect. 'Oh bloody wonderful!' he swore.

'Leave it,' Jennifer said, 'we're nearly on top of that sound now. I've got a bad feeling about this, but let's push on.'

The three of them carried on down the passageway in the footsteps of Tychivesk. They rounded a corner and found the Dyason. He stood on a viewing gallery looking out over a huge cavern. Jennifer, Neehmad and Josh Brabazon joined him and followed his gaze.

'Oh my God! I don't believe it!' Jennifer whispered. 'It can't be true. This can *not* be happening.'

'Oh but it is Jennifer,' Tychivesk answered in a awed voice, his eyes glazed over. 'Oh but it *is* my dear.'

The Dyason, mutant and two humans stood on the gallery and looked out over the huge cavern at an exact replica of Excalibur.

CHAPTER ELEVEN

Myrddin ran along the steel plating hitting the door release panels to the cells as he went. Jenson, Sandpiper, Moss and the mutant Colmarrie emerged from their cells all looking confused except for Moss who immediately went to the blast doors at the end corridor.

'What's going on Myrddin?' Jenson demanded.

'There's no time for explanations Paul,' Myrddin answered. 'We've got to get off this thing and back to the planet surface.'

'What do *they* want?' Sandpiper asked, gesturing toward Hillmead and Shalok.

'They're with us.'

'Why?'

'Han,' Myrddin snapped, his face going red. 'This is neither the time, nor the place. Now are we all going to stand here and get shot, or shall we get the hell out of here?'

'Quick, everyone out of sight!' Moss called urgently from the blast doors. 'There's a squad of troopers on their way.'

Hillmead and Shalok pounded up to the blast doors. 'Hide, we'll deal with this,' Hillmead demanded pulling out his automatic. Moss gave him an appraisive look before nodding.

'All yours,' he agreed.

They all slipped back into the cells as the blast doors opened and a squad of troopers marched through. Hillmead gestured with his gun toward the nearest open cell door and yelled, 'One of them attacked us. Quick in there!'

Shalok staggered and held a hand to her temple for good effect. The squad leader caught her by the arm as the remainder of the squad ran into the cell, closely followed by Hillmead. 'Are you all right Lieutenant?' the squad leader enquired.

'I'm fine thank you, but you'll be dead in a second if you don't do what I tell you,' she hissed, shoving the muzzle of her gun into the trooper's gut. 'Drop your weapon!'

The squad leader open and closed his mouth wordlessly a few times, then dropped his weapon onto the deck. Colmarrie leapt out of her cell, picked up the weapon and disappeared after Hillmead. Less than thirty seconds later she reappeared carrying all the weapons of the other Imperial troopers. Hillmead followed her out and sealed the cell door. 'Let's go!' he called to the others.

'Where to exactly?' Jenson demanded picking up an automatic rifle.

'You can fly a ship?' Hillmead asked.

'Yeah, I guess. Although I've never flown a Dyason machine before.'

'Well you'll have to make it up as you go along,' Hillmead told him. 'There's a shuttle docked at bay four now, it's fuelled and ready to go. If we can get there, we might stand a chance.'

'How do we get there?' Moss asked.

'I saw a service conduit marked on the plans that leads from level three, which is the level above us, to docking bay four. It should just be big enough for us to squeeze through,' Shalok answered almost reluctantly. She was still having problems accepting the situation had gone so badly against her.

'What even me?' the giant mutant leader asked. Shalok nodded.

'Let's get on with it then people,' Myrddin ordered decisively. 'We'll follow you Lieutenant.'

'Wait! I've got a better idea,' Jenson snapped.

'What's that?' Moss asked.

'Follow me kid and you'll find out. Colmarrie, can you give us a hand?'

'Of course friend Jenson,' the giantess agreed, following Jenson and Moss to the cell where the troopers were being held. The three of them disappeared inside, there were a couple of sickening thuds and a suppressed scream, then they reappeared, Jenson and Moss wearing Imperial uniforms.

'We'll get further if it looks like we're taking prisoners for interrogation,' Jenson stated, tightening up the heavy leather belt on the Imperial grey flight uniform. Moss clamped a pair of handcuffs on Colmarrie, leaving them unlocked. He winked at her and she grinned in return. Moss got the impression that the giantess hadn't had so much fun in a very long time; crushing Imperial heads was her favourite occupation. Cuffs were also placed loosely on Myrddin and Sandpiper then the unlikely troop headed out of the brig and down the corridor.

They hadn't gone far before they reached the first obstacle, the brig officer. He sat behind a large grey metal desk that was bolted to the steel floor. He sat reading a report from a computer monitor, but looked up in surprise when he saw the group approach from the direction of the cells.

'What's going on Colonel?' the officer asked. 'I sent a squad down to the cells a few minutes ago to check on the prisoners. There's been an intruder and gunfire in the engineering section. The ship is on alert level Alpha I'm afraid you can't take these prisoners for interrogation now. You must return them to their cells. Who are those troopers with you? I don't recog....' The officer's voice died with a gurgle when Colmarrie leapt forward and slashed his throat with a stolen combat knife.

'What the flying-frig did you do that for you stupid bitch?' Shalok screamed in horror. The nightmare was getting worse every minute. 'You can't go around butchering everyone!'

Colmarrie look at the lieutenant in confusion. 'Why not?' she asked. 'Besides he was talking too much.'

'Mutant, I'm going to have to explain to you that not everyone in the Empire is personally responsible for your people's predicament,' Hillmead said with a sigh. 'Shalok and I are in enough shit as it is without you murdering every member of the crew. Please try and show some restraint!'

Colmarrie turned and looked at Moss, 'I don't understand, are these people on our side or not? If they are, then why must I not butcher everyone?'

'That's a tough one Colmarrie. Yes, these people are on our side, but you'll have to trust me when I say that you've got to show a little bit of restraint. I promise I'll explain everything to you later.'

Colmarrie looked at him very seriously and said, 'That would be appreciated friend Moss. I will do as you say, but I must admit it does detract from the pleasure of the kill.'

'Yeah, I realise that Colmarrie and I sympathise with your predicament, I really do.'

They sealed the blast doors of the brig behind them and set off towards the nearest elevator. The sirens had stopped their wail, but green flashing lights still announced the alert status and gave everyone a strange hue. Squads of troopers pounded past them, their movements taking on a strange almost dance-like form in the low gravity. Happily, no one paid them any attention and they reached the elevator without further incident.

'Where to now Lieutenant?' Myrddin asked once they were all inside.

'Up to the next level, then along to workshop 37. There's an entrance to the service conduit from there,' she replied.

'How long will it take to navigate along the conduit?'

'I'm not sure. The docking bay is quite a distance, but if we're quick maybe ten, fifteen minutes.'

'Good. At the moment the confusion is to our advantage, but that won't last forever. Once they realise you were the intruder, they'll inevitably shift their attention to the brig and find that we're gone as well. Time is of the essence.'

The elevator stopped and they stepped out onto level three. This level was a light engineering area with a series of workshops and was now largely deserted as everyone had fled for their alert stations. They made rapid progress and quickly found workshop 37. Hillmead had just hit the entrance code when a shout went up from further up the corridor.

'There she is! This way!'

A squad of troopers appeared their automatics at the ready. 'You lot freeze! Lieutenant Shalok you are under arrest. Do *not* move!'

Jenson and Moss didn't wait to be shot at, they fell to the floor and opened fire, their rounds ricocheting off the steel plates. A couple of the squad immediately collapsed whilst the others fell back in surprise.

'Come on Hillmead, get that bloody door open,' Jenson yelled. 'They'll be back any minute with their friends in tow!'

The doors opened and they piled into the workshop. Moss closed the doors and fired a couple of rounds into the mechanism. 'That should hold them for a little while, where's this service conduit.'

'They wanted me!' Shalok cried in anguish. 'They know!'

'Of course they bloody know Shalok! What did you expect?' Hillmead shouted at her, grabbing her by the shoulders and shaking her. 'We're now on the wrong side of the fence, you've got to accept that! At least for the time being. Now where's that bloody service conduit.'

Shalok seemed to pull herself together and made her way to the rear of the workshop which was filled with various machine tools. She pointed to a hatchway cut into the plates above them.

Moss and Jenson pulled an ali-case under the hatch and climbed up onto it. Together they released the hatch and with a hand from Moss, Jenson easily hauled himself up in the reduced gravity. He took a quick look around, then gave the others the thumbs-up.

'It's clear. Let's go folks. We wouldn't want to miss the flight.'

The service corridor was just big enough for them to run along if they kept doubled over. Moss and Jenson took the lead with Shalok shouting directions from behind them. Colmarrie and Sandpiper took up the rear with the Amazonian woman cursing as her head kept hitting pipes and conduits the others managed to avoid. After about ten minutes of following the conduit through numerous bends and junctions, Jenson raised his hand and brought them to a halt.

'What's the problem?' Moss asked.

'Listen.'

Moss complied and after a moment whispered, 'There's someone else in the conduit. They've twigged that we're in here.'

Jenson nodded, 'It sounds like they're getting closer as well. This is bad news Moss. We're very vulnerable in here.'

Moss looked around, Jenson was right. There simply wasn't room for a fire-fight in here, they had to come up with another solution. He saw another intersecting junction ahead of them and an idea came to him.

'I've got an idea boss,' he said. 'I'll need everyone to keep perfectly still whilst I attempt some subterfuge. That means you Colmarrie; try and control your blood-letting instinct for the moment.'

'You can be most hurtful at times friend Moss,' came the quiet thought in his mind. *'I look forward to seeing a master at work.'*

'Then watch.'

The troopers came towards them from the opposite direction, swearing and cursing as the combat kit kept catching on the numerous sharp corners apparently designed to cut and bruise limbs.

'Frig me, what a job!' one of the Imperial troops cursed. 'Who said it was a hero's life in the Imperial Navy?'

'Shut your ugly face Grodisky,' the squad leader snapped, 'you're constantly complaining. Just concentrate on the job at hand will you?'

The troops came to the junction and halted. 'Now which way?' one of them asked.

'Straight ahead according to this map. They entered through a workshop that's down that way somewhere,' came the reply.

There was a sound like a shout from the direction of another tunnel. 'Did you hear that?' the squad leader asked. 'The bitch and her friends must have pegged it that way! Come on lads, there's extra rations for everyone if we get our hands on the slag, dead or alive!'

The troops turned and headed off up the other tunnel as fast as they could. Once they had disappeared out of sight, Moss let go of the illusion in his mind. *'That was well done son,'* Myrddin thought to him. *'Practice makes perfect,'* he replied.

Hillmead reached for Shalok's hand and squeezed it hard. Her face was deathly white—she'd heard what the troops had said. 'Hang on in there kid,' he whispered almost gently. 'This isn't the time to give up on me.'

She swallowed, nodded at him and together they moved on. A few minutes later they reached a ladder and hatch that Shalok believed exited into the main docking bay. Jenson descended and very cautiously eased open the hatch just enough for him to see out. He sat there quietly for a minute observing the scene beyond, before rejoining the others.

'Well?' Myrddin asked.

'The shuttle is still docked and the port is open. The area looks fairly deserted though,' Jenson answered.

'Doesn't that seem a bit odd boss?' Sandpiper queried. 'I mean, you would think they would expect us to try and get off this heap and stealing a shuttle is the obvious answer.'

'Maybe they're only looking for Shalok and know she can't pilot a ship,' Hillmead suggested.

'I agree it does seem a bit suspicious, but we're committed now. We'll continue the charade of escorting prisoners and if anyone asks we've been ordered to get them to the planet's surface,' Jenson said decisively.

Jenson climbed down the ladder once more and after checking the coast was clear, he beckoned down the others. They all squeezed through the hatch and into the docking bay. The bay consisted of two sets of heavy blast doors which also acted as air locks, and a small control room. The shuttle itself was clamped to the outer hull connected by a short retractable gangway. Moss and Jenson entered the control room where they found the docking bay officer and three technicians. The officer looked up from his control panel and gave them a suspicious glare.

'What are you troopers doing here?' he demanded.

'We have orders to escort these prisoners to the planet surface sir!' Jenson snapped gesturing to the others in the bay who were shackled once more.

'I've heard nothing about this,' the officer replied waving his hand dismissively. 'There's an alert on. No craft are to leave until the all-clear is given. You'll have to wait.'

'Sir!' Jenson persisted. 'We have special orders. These prisoners are required at Caranak at the earliest opportunity, by order of the Envoy Nimue, herself, sir!'

The officer glared suspiciously at Jenson once more. 'Where are your orders then trooper?'

Moss decided that the Imperial officer needed some gentle persuasion. He concentrated his mind and gently probed the Dyason's thoughts. Moss planted a seed in the officer's mind who looked blank for a moment then turned to the three technicians saying, 'We don't need to see any written orders. Their mission obviously has the highest priority. Open the air locks.'

'But sir!' one of the technicians exclaimed in surprise. 'This is strictly against procedure!'

A flush rose up the neck of the docking officer and he yelled, 'Do you wish to explain yourself to the Envoy Nimue, you snivelling piece of slime?'

The technician shrugged and shook his head. 'I thought not. Now do as I order and open the air locks!'

Jenson looked at Moss and raised an eyebrow. 'Thank you sir!' he said to the officer who was looking slightly confused. They fled the control room and gesturing to the others moved through the air locks as fast they could without appearing to run. Once inside the shuttle Sandpiper immediately set about strapping the others into the acceleration couches whilst Moss and Jenson made their way to the cockpit. The shuttle pilot and co-pilot were already strapped into their seats going through their pre-flight checks. The pilot looked up in surprise when they entered the cockpit. 'Who the bloody hell are you?' he demanded.

'We have orders to deliver prisoners to Caranak,' Jenson answered sticking to their cover story.

'Caranak?' the pilot uttered in surprise. 'We've got no flight-plan for Caranak. This shuttle is going to Laques in the south, not Caranak.'

Moss saw the co-pilot reach down for his holstered automatic. Not giving the co-pilot the opportunity to complicate matters Moss clubbed the Dyason over the head who then slumped forward unconscious. Jenson shoved the muzzle of his rifle in the face of the pilot, who undid his straps, raised his hands and quietly got out of his seat. A few minutes later Moss was sitting in the pilot's seat and Jenson sat in the co-pilot's seat. 'What do you reckon kid? Do you think you can fly this contraption.'

Moss scanned the instrument panel and took hold of the controls. 'I hope so, after all I just stole the instruction book from that pilot's mind. He's feeling a bit woozy now.'

'Good lad!'

Jenson opened a comm's channel to the docking bay control room. 'Control, this is the shuttle Opris requesting permission to depart.'

'Shuttle Opris, request denied. Return your passengers to the concourse. 'I repeat, request denied!'

'That doesn't sound good,' Moss commented. 'That wasn't the voice of the control officer. He must have been out-voted by the technicians.'

'What's going on?' asked Sandpiper from the cockpit doorway. 'They've re-opened the air locks and there's a nasty looking bunch of troopers heading this way!'

'Is the shuttle's hatch closed and sealed?' Jenson demanded.

'Yep, and everyone's strapped in, including a rather pissed-off pilot and co-pilot.'

'Good. Moss, can we unclamp from the docking bay from here?' Jenson asked urgently.

'Yes we can, there's an emergency override switch which blows the docking bolts and blasts us away from the hull. Initiating...now!'

The shuttle was blasted away from the docking port and Moss just caught a glimpse of bodies being sucked into space as the troopers in the air lock suddenly found themselves in a vacuum. The massive hull of the Imperial battle-cruiser swept past the cockpit as Moss ignited the main engines, rolled and peeled away towards the planet surface.

'Shuttle Opris, halt and return to the ship, or you will be fired upon!' came the call over the radio. Sandpiper and Jenson exchanged alarmed looks. 'They're joking,' said Sandpiper. 'Their armament isn't up and running yet.'

The shuttle was rocked by an explosion nearby. 'Apparently not!' Jenson replied. Another blast rocked them, then another and another, but although the craft was badly shaken, it carried on plunging toward the atmosphere.

'Either they're bad shots or the weapons system has got a few bugs in it,' said Moss as he continued to take evasive action. 'We should have been turned into shrapnel by now.'

The Opris was hit by another explosion and the lights momentarily went out. 'Are you sure about that?' asked Sandpiper, sounding very unconvinced.

'We'll be entering the atmosphere any second now. They'll be unable to fire on us then. Their missiles will break up,' said Jenson and sure enough as the nose of the shuttle began to glow from the first wisps of Dyason's atmosphere, the explosions trailed off. They all began to sigh with relief. The situation was finally under control.

Sandpiper looked thoughtful for a moment, then said, 'That was too easy. They let us get away.'

'I know,' replied Moss a serious frown on his forehead. 'The question is why?'

'The answer lies with those two, Hillmead and Shalok, if you ask me,' Sandpiper speculated.

'You might be right there...' Moss's voice trailed off as a scream of anguish filled his head. '*Moss! Help! I need you! It's here!*'

He checked the angle of descent and banked the Opris to a new course. Jennifer was in trouble and he *had* to reach her!

Gulag stood at the observation port watching the shuttle craft speed away from the battle-cruiser. He quietly admired Moss's piloting skills; he deftly handled the Opris, guiding the ship towards the planet's surface and taking evasive action at the same time. Not that they were ever at any great risk. Gulag had made sure of that.

The last of the missile salvo exploded harmlessly in the shuttle craft's wake and the Oris slipped into the upper atmosphere of Dyason. *They're on their way*, he expanded his thought.

'The girl, she discovered the secret?' The message entered his mind.

'Yes, it all went as planned and others have discovered the cavern as expected.'

'Excellent my son! Excellent! it merely remains for Myrddin to make his way to me for the plan to be complete.' Nimue's thought positively purred across the ether.

'You think he'll do that?' Gulag asked.

'Fate decrees it my son. The time for our final battle draws close.'

'Yeah, right,' he thought to himself.

'You will take command of the situation at the cavern?' Nimue asked.

'My ship's ready waiting for me now,' he replied. *'I'll be there in a couple of hours. You will keep me informed of the situation in Caranak?'*

'Of course son. Matters are coming to a climax, the end of the game is in sight. Until later.'

'Until later Envoy.'

As the initial shock wore off a realisation came to Josh Brabazon. He tore his eyes away from the huge vessel and looked at Tychivesk. 'You knew!' he said pointing an accusing finger at the Dyason. 'You knew it was here all the time! Trying to dissuade us from entering these caverns was nothing but a charade. It was your plan to get us here all along.'

Tychivesk returned Josh Brabazon's stare and levelled his MG303 on the scientist. 'How astute of you Brabazon,' he replied. 'I realised from early on that your natural prejudice against me would cause the two of you to do the opposite from what I suggested. Which is exactly what happened.'

Neehmad, who had been as stunned as the rest of them by the sight of the ancient interstellar vessel, reacted to Tychivesk's hostile moves by raising her home-made rifle. She wasn't quite fast enough; Tychivesk shifted his aim and loosed off a short burst. Neehmad let out a short cry and fell to the balcony floor blood pouring from several horrendous wounds.

Jennifer felt as if she were moving through a bad dream, time seemed to slow down and events appeared to happen in some sort of slow motion over which she had no control. The sight of the ship had shocked her to the core, but the shooting of Neehmad broke the spell. She dropped beside Neehmad and felt for her pulse already knowing that the brave mutant girl was already dead. She whirled on Tychivesk. 'You bastard!' she screamed. 'I should have killed you when I had the chance! You've been working for the Empire all along, haven't you! You deceived us all!'

Tychivesk took a step back to make sure he was able to cover them both. 'I've deceived nobody, Jennifer,' he answered with a smug smile. 'I told you that I'm working for the democracy front, and so I am. I'm no Imperialist, in fact this whole operation is an anti-Imperialist activity.'

'What?' Josh Brabazon exclaimed. 'This has nothing to do with the Empire? So why have you just killed that poor wretch?'

'I regret killing the mutant, I really am working on her side, but for security reasons I cannot allow just anyone to know about this site,' Tychivesk replied unconvincingly. 'If it helps, this is the first time I've seen this incredible place. I received my orders to bring you here, soon after we arrived at the mutants' hideout. The rest of the explanations can wait until later, now please, place your weapons on the floor—slowly.'

'Piss off Tychivesk, I'm not doing anything you say,' Brabazon stated.

There was a clatter from behind them and Jennifer turned to see a squad of Dyason in uniforms she had never seen before. Each one of them carried an assault rifle and with a sinking heart she let them disarm her.

'I think you will co-operate Brabazon,' Tychivesk said with a sick smile. 'After all, Jennifer is a very attractive young lady and there are a lot of males around here who haven't seen female flesh in a *very* long time.'

'You're a sick bastard!'

'Quite possibly my friend. Now, shall we take a closer look at this wonderful machine?'

The troops placed shackles around their wrists and led them away. Jennifer opened her mind and called out to her man with all her strength. The cosmic game in which they were all players had taken a frightening direction. Like flotsam in a raging river, Jennifer felt for the first time in her life that she had no control over her destiny, and it scared her.

As the atmosphere became more dense, the shuttle behaved more like a normal aircraft and Moss was able to control the descent. Using the information obtained from the mind of the Dyason pilot he laid in a course for the wastelands in the southern hemisphere.

Myrddin unstrapped himself from his acceleration couch and made his way to the cockpit. 'Where are you planning on landing son?' he asked.

Moss didn't reply, he kept his eyes firmly fixed on the instruments and the horizon outside the cockpit. However, Myrddin could see that the tendons on his neck were as taught as guitar strings and he held the control stick so hard the knuckles on his hand were white.

'Moss there's no point in hurtling down there in a futile rescue bid that is doomed to failure,' Myrddin said as kindly as he could. 'We've only just got ourselves out of a tight spot. We're in no position to help Jennifer at the moment, that time will come later.'

Jenson turned in his seat and exchanged looks with Sandpiper, who raised an eyebrow and shrugged his shoulders. 'Would one of you two mind telling me what the hell is going on,' Jenson demanded.

'There's been a bit of a drama,' Myrddin answered carefully.

'What another one? What's going on Moss?'

Anger still filled his heart, they were being manipulated and he didn't like it. Ever since they'd arrived in the system, they'd been on the run, constantly one step behind events. Somebody was yanking their strings and now Jennifer was in real danger, this was becoming personal. Moss remained tense and angry ignoring the others.

'You know Jennifer is in no real danger—at least for the time being, don't you?' Myrddin said to him. 'They need Josh's help in getting the ship operational and Jennifer will be the lever they'll use to get his co-operation. Come-on Moss, this isn't the time to fly off the handle. Save your anger for those that deserve it.'

Moss took a deep breath and forced himself to relax. In his heart he knew Myrddin was right and he owed it to his friends to let them know what was going on. They weren't responsible for what was happening to them all. He forced himself to relax his grip on the controls. 'As we started re-entry I had a mental call from Jennifer,' he said finally.

'What did she say?' asked Sandpiper.

'Basically, Josh, Tychivesk and Jennifer took some of Colmarrie's mutant fighters and went to check out reports about a secret Imperial launch site,' he replied.

'That was foolish, they should have stayed at the mutants' base,' Jenson stated with a frown. 'What did they find?'

'They were hoping to find a ship they could use to rescue *us*, but they found more than they bargained for. It turns out that Tychivesk knew about the site all along and led them there. He's working for somebody but it ain't us,' answered Moss.

'Shit! I knew we couldn't trust that creep!' exclaimed Sandpiper. 'There was always something weird about the guy.'

'Go on Moss tell them the rest,' Myrddin encouraged.

Moss kicked on the auto-pilot and turned in his seat to face the others, his expression grim. 'They discovered an underground research facility much like the caverns under Stonehenge where Excalibur was discovered.'

Jenson's heart sank, he didn't like the sound of this at all. It all had a rather familiar and rather disturbing feeling to it. 'I really hope you're not going to tell me that the Dyason have discovered

Excalibur's sister ship and are in the process of making her operational?'

'I'm afraid that's exactly what I'm going to tell you!' Moss replied. 'And to make matters worse, Tychivesk handed over Jennifer and Josh.'

'To Imperial troops?' Sandpiper asked.

'Jennifer said they were all wearing uniforms she'd never seen before.'

'What a balls-up!'

'Balls indeed!' agreed Myrddin dropping himself into a jump-seat opposite Sandpiper.

'And you were planning to put us down next to these caverns and rescue Jennifer and Josh?' Jenson demanded.

'The thought had crossed my mind,' Moss said with a nonchalance he didn't really feel. 'She asked for my help, I can't just leave her in the hands of those bastards!'

'You take us down there now kid and we'll all be walking straight into a trap, ' Jenson stated shaking his head. 'Why do you think they let us get away from that huge tin can so easily? They *want us all* to steam on down there like the seventh cavalry.'

'The boss is right Moss. We're going to have to think this one out very carefully. So far someone has been constantly one step in front of us and we've been led around like a bull by the nose,' added Sandpiper. 'I really sympathise with you, but we can't rush headlong into yet another crisis.'

'Okay, okay!' Moss held up his hands in resignation, 'I'll take us somewhere else, but we can't go back to Colmarrie's hideout. Tychivesk knows where her base is regardless of who he's really working for.'

'That's very true. Han, go and fetch Colmarrie and let's get her advice on where we can put down without falling straight into the Empire's hands,' Jenson ordered. 'In the meantime Moss, can you telepath to Jennifer to hang on in there and get her to pass on any information that may be useful to us?'

'I can, but there's a very real risk that Gulag can tune in to our thoughts,' Moss answered.

'That may well be the case,' Myrddin added, 'but I'm fairly sure if that were to happen, you would feel his presence. Don't forget that his own mind is just as susceptible to telepathic eavesdropping.'

Moss thought this over for a moment then nodded. 'All right, I'll contact Jennifer with the bad news. You find us a place to land, but just remember I'm going after her at the first opportunity.'

'Don't you worry kid. As soon as we've had a chance to figure out just what the hell is going on, we'll *all* go and fetch them out of there!' Jenson stated. 'Some body's been screwing with us ever since we arrived in this bloody star system. I for one have had enough, it's time to fight back!

CHAPTER TWELVE

EMPEROR'S CHAMBERS, IMPERIAL PALACE,
CARANAK

The lighting in the bed-chamber was subdued to the point of being almost non-existent. The few bulbs fitted were red and low-wattage and even these were heavily shrouded. Heavy drapes covered the windows blocking out the murky daylight keeping the bed-chamber in a constant state of semi-darkness. The air was musty and the excessively ornate furniture succeeded in making the room oppressively claustrophobic. Nimue hated her weekly audience with the Emperor of Dyason, but it was a politically necessary chore.

She indicated for the Emperor's private secretary and physician to leave. As always they bowed and scraped their way out of the chambers. Two guards remained in their traditional Imperial uniforms at the huge double doors, but Nimue wasn't concerned about them. She knew for a fact that they had both had their tongues removed many years ago.

It took several minutes for her eyes to adjust to the gloom, during which time she stood quietly by the door going over in her mind affairs of state. When she could finally distinguish objects to the point where she was fairly sure she could navigate without constantly walking into all the clutter, she made her way to the large four-poster bed situated on the far side of the chamber. The Emperor had been feeling weaker than normal lately and his physician had confined him to bed.

A body stirred amongst the pile of bed-clothes. With obvious great effort, the figure pulled itself to an upright position, turned and looked at the Envoy. A pair of albino eyes stared out of a head devoid of all hair, with dried flaky skin that was so pale it was almost translucent. A night-shirt hung loosely on an emaciated body so thin and fragile it looked as if it may crumble into dust at any moment.

'Ah Envoy, it is *so* good to see you!' the Emperor wheezed in a voice that was barely more than a whisper. 'I have not been feeling myself lately, so please excuse me if I do not get up to greet you.'

Nimue bowed low then, with obvious distaste, took the Emperor's thin hand and kissed it. 'The Emperor should excuse me for disturbing him,' she said with an ingratiating voice. 'I realise how much you need to preserve your strength, but there are affairs of state that must be attended to.'

For a moment the Emperor looked confused and lost, his eyes wandered off towards the bed canopy. 'Emperor?' Nimue prodded. 'There are documents for you to sign; affairs of state.'

With obvious great difficulty, the albino Emperor of Dyason tried to focus his eyes and mind on what Nimue was saying.

'Affairs of state?' he whispered. 'Ah, yes, of course. How are the affairs of state Envoy?'

'The Empire is as strong as ever, my lord,' she told him, holding his thin hand in hers. 'The people of Dyason love you more than ever. Not a day goes by without them praying for your long life my lord.'

The Emperor smiled weakly. 'Ah, that is *good* to hear.'

Nimue pulled out several papers from a leather document pouch together with the Emperor's seal. 'Indeed it is,' she crooned. 'Life for the people of Dyason is better than at any time in history. If you would just sign these few documents, you can return to sleep, safe in the knowledge that the Empire is safe.' She placed one of the documents in the albino's thin hands.

'Err, what documents are these?' he whispered unsure of what he was looking at.

'Nothing to concern yourself over my lord,' she told him. 'These are simply trade treaties which seal the relationship of the dominions within the Empire.'

The Emperor smiled weakly. 'How nice,' he whispered, spittle dripping off his chin. Nimue place a quill in his hand and the Emperor of Dyason began to scrawl his mark on all the papers she placed in front of him.

When he had signed all the documents Nimue placed them safely back in the document pouch. Then she turned and took the Emperor's hand once more. 'Now that the affairs of state are settled my lord,' she crooned, 'perhaps I can do something to ease the Emperor's pain.'

The albino lay back in the bed and smiled. 'Ah, yes Envoy, that would be *so* appreciated. As I said, I really look forward to your visits. You look after me so well; what would I do without you?'

Nimue leant over the Emperor as he closed his eyes and breathed into his ear, 'Indeed my lord, what would you do without me?'

She placed her palm on his bald plate and drew energy to herself. Steadily she focused her mind and concentrated her thoughts. Then like a blood transfusion she diverted her life force into the now unconscious Emperor. Power surged from her hand into the albino's body and as it did so, the Emperor's skin visibly became less translucent and took on a more healthy pallor. His face visibly relaxed and his breathing became less laboured. However, the same could not be said of Nimue, her breaths soon came in short panting gasps and the colour drained from her cheeks.

After a few minutes Nimue removed her hand from his head and collapsed exhausted in her chair. Now, her face was pale and bloodless, drained of life. She sat unmoving for over an hour breathing in short, shallow breaths. Eventually, she felt strong enough once more to rise to her feet. Unsteadily she made her way to the entrance to the bed-chamber, ignoring the formal salutes of the two guards. With a sigh of relief she left the room and made her way weakly down the corridors of the Imperial palace. Except for a few rare occasions, she had performed this ritual every week of the year, every year of the decade, every decade for the past five centuries. Now Nimue couldn't wait to be shot of the bastard!

ON BOARD THE *REAL* DOMINATOR

Jennifer sat behind a beautiful walnut-finished table in a conference room that was identical to the senior officers' briefing room onboard the Excalibur. In fact both externally and internally she could discern no difference between the Excalibur and this vessel. There could be no doubt about it, she was sitting in a sister ship built by the same unknown race.

She glanced at Josh Brabazon. His initial fear had been replaced with a keen fascination for this Dyason copy of his 'baby'. Ever since they were brought onboard the entombed vessel Josh had constantly been asking questions about the nature of the beast. Of course, nobody answered any of his questions, but then nobody discouraged them either. There was one thing that they had found out, however, and that was the name the Dyason had given their ship. At first the name had confused her, but once Moss had informed her that the Imperial battle-cruiser in orbit was nothing more than an elaborate hoax, it all made sense. They had spent all this time believing that the piece of space garbage in orbit was the first battle-cruiser of a new invasion fleet, when the real threat lay hidden under radioactive wastelands. The name given was the 'Dominator', and this was the *real* Dominator.

Tychivesk sat opposite herself and Josh once more wringing his hands in an agitated fashion. He was very nervous and despite her efforts, Jennifer didn't know why. She had tried to scan his mind without him being aware, but somebody had trained the traitor to know when his privacy was being invaded. Her attention shifted to the two guards standing at the doorway, their Imperial assault rifles cradled at the ready. Here was another mystery, no one onboard the Dominator wore Imperial uniforms and from casually scanning a few thoughts, Jennifer knew that at least as far as they were concerned the Dominator was *not* an Imperial operation. However, they obviously weren't part of the same anti-Imperial faction as Colmarrie and her mutant fighters.

She had resolved to sit tight, observe and learn as much as she could. Moss was right, she was under no immediate threat and it would be foolish for the others to barge into the caverns unprepared. There was no doubt in her mind that now she knew Moss was free and fit, that he would eventually come for her. In the meantime their best course of action was to go along with whatever these people wanted. Not that that was a problem as far as Josh Brabazon was concerned, she could see that he was desperate to find out more about Excalibur's sister ship. Jennifer couldn't blame him, it was an incredible cosmic mystery—two identical ships and two humanoid races with almost identical evolutions. It was too much to be a coincidence; this was all part of some greater cosmic plan.

The doors silently opened and in stepped a well-built Dyason with a handsome face, but cold, cold eyes. Tychivesk leapt out of his seat and gave a crisp salute. 'Reporting for duty with two prisoners as ordered sir!' he snapped. The newcomer ignored him and stood in front of the conference table, arms folded. He looked at Jennifer and Brabazon carefully, before saying, 'I'm honoured to meet you both. You don't know just how long I've been waiting for this moment.'

Jennifer looked the Dyason straight in the eye and said, 'Piss off Gulag. You were scum in your first incarnation and you're still scum now!'

Gulag smiled in a fashion that sent a cold shiver down her spine. He sat down in a chair opposite her and with a casual wave of his hand dismissed Tychivesk. The traitor looked as if he were going to say something, then thought better of it. Silently he turned and left the conference room.

'Doctor Brabazon, this is a real pleasure,' Gulag smiled ingratiatingly, offering the scientist his hand. Brabazon kept his arms firmly crossed and simply stared at him. Gulag shrugged as if it were of no consequence. 'I would like you both to consider yourselves as my guests rather than my prisoners. You may move about this, the real Dominator, as you please, without restriction. My only request is that you do not attempt to leave the ship. Everyone has orders to treat you both with the utmost courtesy and answer any questions you may have.'

'You have a funny way of showing hospitality Gulag,' Josh Brabazon snapped. 'You use lies, deception and cold-blooded murder to get us here, then expect us to behave as if we'd been invited over for dinner!'

'I apologise for the necessary subterfuge it took to bring you all to Dyason, but I don't believe you would have come of your own free will,' Gulag responded.

'If you want any co-operation from us, you'd better answer a few questions, like how, what and where?' Jennifer demanded.

Gulag cradled his hands on the conference table in a gesture of thoughtful pacification. 'I fully understand your reaction, so I will be perfectly candid with you,' he answered. 'As you are both aware by now, I am a clone, a laboratory generated humanoid as was my predecessor. The genetic process used to create my predecessor was flawed. I think it would be fair to say that the original Gulag was a psychotic genius.'

'I would agree with the psychotic bit,' Josh snapped.

Gulag looked at the scientist with feigned sympathy. 'I'm saddened by what my predecessor did, particularly to one as brilliant as your brother. However, please remember that your brother's thoughts and memories have been passed on to me. In some ways Josh, you and I are brothers.'

Josh Brabazon gagged in horror. 'You're no brother of mine you evil bastard!'

The clone showed no emotion to the outburst, instead he said, 'I hope one day Josh, that you will change your mind about that.'

'Never!' Brabazon snorted.

'So why have you brought us here?' Jennifer intervened, keen to glean as much information as possible.

The clone got up out of his chair and stood by the large panoramic viewing port that showed an army of people working on various parts of the gigantic vessel in the glowing ambient light that emanated from the rock of the massive cavern walls.

'When I was created, I was given the memories of the original Gulag and all those whose minds he raped.'

'When were you created?' Jennifer asked.

'The Emperor's Envoy Nimue escaped from your planet back to Dyason in a stolen fighter-craft. She achieved this by successfully using her paranormal powers to create a fault in the fabric of space. It was and still is, a remarkable achievement.

'Upon her return the Envoy immediately set about creating another Gulag from the DNA of the previous incarnation. I was born and grown in an acceleration chamber in under three months.'

'That's not possible!' Josh blurted.

The clone turned and looked at the slightly built scientist. 'Ah, but it is Josh! It is simply something that is considered ethically and morally wrong on Earth. That is a problem we don't have here on Dyason.'

'I have my doubts, but if what you say is true, what has this got to do with us?' Jennifer probed, keen to keep the clone talking.

'As I amalgamated my predecessor's memories into some sort of order, I couldn't help but be fascinated by similarities between our two races. The chances of two almost identical humanoid races developing in a parallel fashion in the same part of the galaxy is so infinitely small one has to come to the conclusion that it is *not* a cosmic accident. Somebody, some other race, had to be instrumental in both our peoples' development. I know that you have long believed this to be the case Josh.'

Josh leant forward in his seat and became more attentive. Jennifer knew that despite Brabazon's intense hate for the original Gulag, this new cloned version was inevitably arousing his interest. 'Yes, I have written several papers on the common biological and historical background of the human and Dyason races,' the scientist agreed.

'Well, I took your theories one stage further and hypothesised that if the ancients had left a ship like the Excalibur sealed in underground caverns on Earth, then there was a very good chance that such a machine was also buried somewhere on Dyason. I resolved to search for this ship and as you can see, my efforts were eventually rewarded.'

'How did you know where to look?' Josh asked.

'It seemed likely that the caverns would be situated underneath an ancient archaeological site, so I set about examining all the sites on Dyason, paying particular attention to any monoliths.'

'We didn't see any signs of ruins or monoliths on the surface,' interrupted Jennifer.

'That's because the stone circle that sat on the surface directly above us now, was obliterated by a nuclear weapon during the 'great patriotic war'. I had to examine maps from the pre-Empire days to pin-point all the possible sites.'

'Yet you say this is not an Imperial operation. If that *is* the case, who are you working for? Your predecessor was an animal of Nimue, does she yank your strings as well?' Josh demanded.

Jennifer was interested to see a flush rise up Gulag's neck. Josh had struck a soft spot—the clone wasn't devoid of any emotion after all. 'As I have been at pains to make clear to you, although I have access to my predecessor's memories, my mind and soul are my own,' the clone stated. 'I'm sure you can make your own deductions from that. To answer your question about who is running this restoration programme, I can tell you now that everyone here is a member of the Democratic Front.'

The pieces fell into place in Jennifer's mind— how incredible! They'd all been completely fooled, but now it made perfect sense! 'Hang on a minute!' she interrupted excitedly. 'Colmarrie told us that until a couple of years ago the different anti-Imperial factions were disjointed, incapable of working together. Then one person, one *unidentified* person, united the different factions and began to move against the Empire from *within* the Empire. That unidentified person is *you* isn't it Gulag?'

Gulag stood with his back to them and stared out of the view-port. 'I was created and brought into a dying world. We all know that Dyason is drowning in its own excrement—shit created by a corrupt and chaotic regime that laughingly calls itself an Empire. I resolved from the first day of my consciousness to bring sanity and order to this decaying world, after all who wants to inherit a dead planet? I knew that if I could discover the secrets of the ancients I would have the power to achieve my aims.

The reason I brought you all here to Dyason is to help me unlock the hidden secrets of the ancients. Both of our world's would benefit from shared knowledge. Together we can overthrow the Empire, heal Dyason's ecology and return order to the galaxy, as it was intended!

Jennifer and Brabazon sat looking at the clone, their mouths wide in surprise. Gulag turned to face them and smiled when he saw the shock on their faces. 'Now,' he continued with a smile, 'let me tell you about Point Zero.'

SOMEWHERE IN THE SOUTHERN WASTELANDS

Sandpiper handed the last crate to Jenson, who placed it in the pile with the others. Then they both sat on the back of the flat-bed vehicle and wiped the sweat from their foreheads. 'This is the second time we've had to shift this lot,' Sandpiper said referring to the equipment salvaged from the *Observer*. 'I don't know about you but I hope this is the last time. I'm sick of feeling like we're a flock of bleeting sheep being rounded up. This is worse than being in the resistance. At least then we knew who the enemy was and where they were. This planet is so screwed up it's impossible to figure out who're are the good guys and who're are the bad guys.'

Jenson pulled out a hip flask and sipped at the precious water it contained. 'Yeah, I know what you mean Han,' he answered. 'The original mission has completely turned to shit and all we seem to be doing is reacting to events as they occur. This certainly, isn't what I signed up for.'

'Well, at least Colmarrie and her mutants seem to be pretty organised. They arranged a complete evacuation from that last hide out in only a matter of hours. I for one, was impressed,' Sandpiper continued. 'At least her lot appear to be genuine enough.'

'They've been running from the Empire for nearly a century, I should imagine that they've had plenty of practice by now,' Jenson noted, passing the water to his friend. 'In a lot of respects they *are* the same as ourselves; fighting on regardless of the odds. You know Han, as time goes by I feel less and less in control of my own destiny. We were ordered to take on this mission, now we find that we've been given the run-around by a person or person's unknown. I don't know mate—I just feel so bloody useless half the time. Don't you ever feel like that?'

Sandpiper drank some of the offered water then wiped his mouth with the back of his hand. 'Not really boss, I've always known I was bloody useless, so it comes as no surprise to me.'

Jenson laughed, 'You've got a point there Han.'

'Besides, the way I see it is that whatever's going to happen is going to go ahead regardless of what we do. So we might as well stop worrying about it. This show is being run by a few key figures like Moss, Myrddin, Gulag and that bitch Nimue. They're the main players in this game. But come on boss, you knew all those years ago when we first bumped into those weird dudes that the day would come when we would have to let go of the reins. The situation here is more than my brain can fathom. I'm happy to let them sort it out. It'll work out okay in the end boss. They may be weird but I've got every faith in Moss, Myrddin and Jennifer.'

Jenson grinned at his friend and slapped him on the back, 'That's what I like about you Han, you're an eternal optimist!'

'Yeah... I guess,' Sandpiper replied dubiously.

Colmarrie appeared from between the piles of crates and strode over. She gave her new friends a wide grin. 'So what do you think of our new home?' she asked them.

Jenson and Sandpiper looked around them at the cavern they sat in. 'Err...yes, it's very nice Colmarrie,' Sandpiper answered a little uncertainly, 'but it does bear a remarkable resemblance to where we've just come from.'

'Exactly!' Colmarrie beamed. 'Over the years we've excavated numerous bases throughout the wastelands, all to exactly the same design.'

'So you can move bases with the minimum of fuss?' Jenson ventured.

'That is exactly so, friend Jenson. Over the years it has been necessary to move at very short notice innumerable times. So far we have always managed to keep one step ahead of the Empire.'

'I must say I'm very impressed Colmarrie. You have a very efficient and effective fighting force.'

'Ah, you flatter me. However, there is a reason for me coming to find you. Now that the moving operation has been completed, the meeting is ready to start. Your presence is required my friends.'

'What? Us dumb sheep?' Sandpiper asked.

'Sheep? What is a sheep?'

'It's a woolly animal on Earth,' Jenson began to explain. 'Ignore him, Sandpiper was just attempting to be humorous.'

'Baaaah! Baaaah!' Sandpiper bleated.

Colmarrie looked at Sandpiper very strangely, 'I am very sorry, but I do not understand your humour friend Sandpiper,' she said with a frown. 'However, have I ever told you the joke about the Emperor, the whore and the mutant? No? Ah, then I must tell you! Now this *is* a funny joke!'

Jenson and Sandpiper clambered off the vehicle and each took one of the giantess's arms. 'We'd be glad to hear it on the way to the meeting Colmarrie,' said Jenson guiding the mutant toward the stairs. 'God knows we could do with a good laugh.'

Colmarrie beamed and the three of them ambled off with the mutant woman explaining her joke to the two bemused humans.

The briefing room was carved out of solid rock, just as it had been at the previous mutant base, and there was a basic metal table around which they all sat.

The main difference between this meeting and the last time they all sat down together was that the seats occupied by Jennifer and Josh Brabazon were taken by the maverick Hillmead and Shalok. The past weeks hadn't been easy for Moss, like the others he felt that ever since the *Observer* had entered the Dyason system, they'd been part of somebody else's grand plan. It was a feeling he hated, this feeling that they were all being used. This couldn't and wouldn't continue, it was time to regain the initiative. It was time to return Jennifer to his side. There was a new strength and determination to Moss that he'd never felt before and the others instinctively felt it too. Without even thinking about it he took control of the meeting.

'Okay everyone,' he began. 'We've been running around like headless chickens for quite long enough. Now's the time for decisive action.'

'What's a chicken?' Colmarrie whispered to Sandpiper.

'It's a bit like a sheep, but I'll explain properly later,' Sandpiper promised.

'Let's take it from the top,' Moss continued. 'This is what we know so far. Since the remnants of the Dyason fleet returned from Earth four local years ago the anti-Imperial movement known as the Democratic Front has been steadily growing in strength. Separate factions have been united under the leadership of one person and the DF is gradually eroding the power of the Empire. Okay so far?' Moss looked pointedly at Hillmead and Shalok who looked tired and uncomfortable at being in the presence of people they would have considered their enemies only a few days previously. However, they knew more about the current state of Imperial power and politics than any of them, which was the reason Moss had insisted that they be present at the meeting. Hillmead nodded in agreement.

'The decline in Imperial power coincides with the terminal decline of the Dyason biosphere. There is now no doubt that the planet will become uninhabitable in five to ten years' time, unless drastic action is taken.

'The next fact is that what we thought was the prototype battle-cruiser of a new invasion fleet is, in fact, nothing more than an armed space station incapable of interstellar travel. In fact it's incapable of moving from its orbital position.

'During our time onboard the space station Jennifer and Josh Brabazon were led to a secret experimental site by the ex-Imperial officer Tychivesk. There they discovered an entombed vessel now believed to be a sister ship to the Excalibur. This craft is the real Dominator, not the orbital battle-station. In her latest message Jennifer told me that the cloned Gulag is the mysterious leader of the Democratic Front and he's attempting to restore the ancient vessel to operational status in the same manner we did with the Excalibur.'

Colmarrie snorted at the mention of Gulag's name. 'The bastard's no leader of ours,' she stated bluntly.

'I'm glad to hear that Colmarrie,' Moss said diplomatically. 'There is one other thing that I think you should all be aware of. Gulag spoke to me on the battle-station about a project he is desperately pursuing, called Point Zero. If you look at the notes in front of you, there is a detailed description of what Point Zero is. Basically, it is the ability to turn water into its constituent parts of hydrogen and oxygen on a massive scale. Until now it has always been believed that water, H2O, is completely stable. You use it to put fires out, not start them. However, as you know broken into it's constituent parts of hydrogen and oxygen water becomes a very powerful fuel source. The problem is that the total energey need to turn water into hydrogen and oxygen has always been greater than the energey released when the two parts combust.

'This is not the case with 'Point-Zero'. The point about this elctro-chemical reaction is that vastly more power is released than is needed to start the reaction in the first place. As the waste product of the combustion of oxygen and hydrogen is water, the acquisition of 'Point-zero' would provide limitless, clean fuel.

'However, this same chemical reaction could be used as a terrifying weapon. The same process applied to the atmosphere of a water-based planet like Dyason or Earth would rapidly devour everything in an uncontrollable chain-reaction affecting every water molecule on the planet. In an unctrolled reaction every water molecule on the planet would split into it's constituent parts of oxygen and hydrogen. Combustion would then inevitably ocur. Life would be completely extinguished as waves of intense heat and flame swept through the atmosphere devouring everything in its path. But once the reaction had finally exhausted itself the end result would be water once more. The seas and rivers and continents would return, albeit devoid of life. There would no radiation fallout, nothing—just a virgin planet waiting to be repopulated with plants, animals and people. A frightening concept.'

'So,' Moss finished, 'can anybody see a link between all these different elements?'

'We've known for quite some time that the Democratic Front has been permeating into all elements of the Empire,' said Hillmead. 'Shalok and I were ordered to investigate apparent acts of sabotage believed to have been perpetuated by the DF. However, our orders came from the Envoy Nimue and we were meant to report directly to either her or Gulag. Which is why we were so surprised by Gulag's claim to be behind the anti-Imperial elements.'

'What did your investigations reveal?' Myrddin asked.

'Basically we discovered what you already know. There is an environmentalist faction within the military who want all resources to be diverted in a last ditch attempt to save the planet. There is another faction who want to build another invasion fleet with the aim of colonising other planets, starting with the Earth. They believe that this planet is beyond redemption,' Shalok told them holding Hillmead's hand under the table. Since the incident onboard the hoax battle-cruiser, her self confidence, along with her world had been shattered. It took all her courage to just sit at this table with people she still thought of as enemies of the Empire.

'We never suspected that the battle-cruiser was an elaborate hoax and never in our wildest dreams would we have believed that there is ancient starship buried in caverns somewhere in the wastelands,' Hillmead continued. 'There *have* been rumours of prototype weapons and aircraft being tested in the desert regions, but nothing of this scale. Since the invasion of your world there has been a rapid influx of new technology, which we attributed to the spoils of war.'

'Do you think Nimue knows about the entombed starship?' Sandpiper asked them.

'I don't think there can be any doubt about it,' said Shalok. 'Despite anything that he may have said to the contrary, Gulag was essentially created by Nimue. I find it hard to believe that she doesn't know about everything that's happening to him and the Empire.'

'It took us a lot of effort to get Excalibur to an operational state. I would have thought Gulag would equally need a lot of manpower and resources. He would need the assistance of someone as powerful as Nimue to run such an operation,' Jenson added.

'Okay, let's presume, at least for the time being, that Nimue *does* know about the real Dominator and that she *is* part of the conspiracy,' Moss said decisively. 'The question now is, what exactly are their intentions? What's the game-plan?'

Myrddin tugged at his beard thoughtfully. Moss knew he'd been thinking long and hard about matters. 'I have a hypothesis,' he began. 'The Imperial Navy must have known for some time that the long-term effects of prolonged war and heavy industry have resulted in a environment in terminal decline. At some stage, some new technology became available to them from an as yet unknown resource, and the militarists decided to make the most of a worm-hole that appeared in their star system. They dispatched a fleet of Domes through the worm-hole and hit lucky at the other end. The grand scheme was then to turn Earth into a world in their own image and move the privileged few to the new colony before Dyason became incapable of supporting life.

'However, the plan all turned to shit when the resistance movement on Earth gathered momentum and the worm-hole became unstable. The remnants of the fleet were forced to return to Dyason in disgrace. The military became split between those who wished to build another invasion fleet and those who wanted to save the planet's ecology in the final hour.'

'I would say that you have a very good grasp of events so far, friend Myrddin,' Colmarrie encouraged. 'It is good that a third party such as you can make sense of this chaos. Our first contact with the anti-Imperial Democratic Front came soon after the return of the fleet from your planet. In the light of what we know now, I can see that the timing of this is suspicious.'

'Thank you Colmarrie,' Myrddin acknowledged. 'It's good to see that I am on track so far. Now, Nimue managed somehow to find her way back to Dyason soon after the final battle, but the world she returned to was by now factionalised and almost openly hostile to the military. Something obviously had to be done to respond to the growing crisis.

'Somewhere in her warped mind were, and possibly still are, the memories of the original cloned Gulag and all the minds he raped. So Nimue turned to the genetic engineers and told them to perfect another Gulag, this time grown at an accelerated rate. By breaking every rule in the book they were successful and the latest model Gulag emerged ready to do her bidding. Nimue then downloaded all the information into this new receptacle and sent her toy on a crusade to find a starship.

'However, she could *not* be sure that Gulag would succeed in his quest, so she became active in the plan to build a new fleet of battle-cruisers using technology stolen from Earth. She made information gleaned from the mind of Josh Brabazon's now dead brother Luke, available to Imperial scientists. The scientists then began work on a new invasion fleet, with the battle-cruiser that's in orbit being the planned prototype.'

Jenson looked thoughtfully at Myrddin then said, 'So when Gulag eventually did find the entombed starship, the battle-cruiser became superfluous?'

'Not quite,' added Moss. 'Why throw your cards in at that stage of the game? So far as Nimue was concerned, she could afford to hedge her bets *and* continue to support the construction of a new fleet.'

'I understand all that so far,' interrupted Sandpiper, 'but what I don't understand is why we've been dragged into all this? We all but got a guided tour around that piece of space junk whilst Josh and

Jennifer were practically invited aboard the real Dominator. Why the games? Why the big charade?'

'I reckon they hit a major snag that none of the Dyason scientists could find an answer to. Do you remember Neehmad reported seeing several machines of unknown design explode either on the ground or soon after take-off?' Moss asked.

'Yes, I believe that your scientist Brabazon said that there was probably a harmonisation fault in the status fields that was causing these problems,' Colmarrie answered. 'I do not know what this means—does it have some significance?'

'We believe so,' answered Myrddin. 'We suspect that Nimue and Gulag, either independently or together, orchestrated an elaborate ruse to get us all to come here to Dyason, knowing that Josh Brabazon would be a member of our team.'

'Once here, Josh's expertise would be invaluable in getting all their toys to work,' Jenson added, following the plot carefully. 'However, Nimue could not reveal to anybody else the existence of the real Dominator, for fear of compromising her position. Hence the elaborate subterfuge.'

'That would tie in with what we know,' Hillmead interrupted. 'Certainly that would explain why Gulag is doing all the leg-work. She could also divert resources from building the battle-cruiser to the entombed craft by giving them the same name. So far as the rest of the military would be concerned operation Dominator would be legitimate. The real question is whose side will she eventually take? If she can get this ancient machine operational, she will have the ability to roam the galaxy at will. She won't need the help of the Imperial forces or anybody else.

'However, if this Dominator now proves to be a non-runner, then she is going to either have to get off the planet, or pray to the gods that the environmentalists succeed at the last minute. No wonder she's got a foot in each camp.'

'What about this Point Zero business? Where does all this fit in?' asked Sandpiper.

'I know that Gulag found a reference to Point-zero somewhere in his collection of memories and he is pursuing it as a private venture, without Nimue's knowledge. This new cloned version of Gulag resents being created as a slave on a dying world, and like any good monster, he particularly resents his creator for bringing him into a cruel world,' Moss answered.

'But what good will this knowledge do him?' Hillmead wondered aloud. 'How will it change his status?'

'It will give him the powers of a god,' Myrddin stated. 'The acquisition of Point Zero will give him the ability to cure Dyason's environmental problems with a limitless clean power source. Alternatively, he will have the power to start a chain reaction in the atmosphere and start afresh with a new, virgin Dyason repopulated with perfect clones.'

'And of course, he will be able to do this to any planet in the galaxy that has a plentiful source of water,' Moss added.

'By the god's!' Shalok exclaimed in horror. 'That's a horrendous thought! How could anybody be so evil?'

'To be fair to the bastard, he's only as evil as those who created him,' Sandpiper stated.

'This is all fascinating my friends, but it does not answer the question, what exactly are we going to do to stop this madness?' Colmarrie told them. 'We must have a plan of action and soon. Whilst these people play god, the planet and all her life is dying!'

'Our first priority must be to stop the real Dominator from becoming operational.' said Jenson.

'I agree that we must do that boss,' Moss agreed with Jenson, 'but that won't affect Gulag's search for Point Zero and I'm concerned that he's very close to making a break-through. Now that he's got his hands on Josh, he could fit the last few pieces of the jigsaw together at any time.'

'Why's that?' Sandpiper asked.

'Gulag hinted to me that half the formula was buried in the data-banks of the Dominator and the other half was in Excalibur's memory. Josh has devoured an awful lot of Excalibur's data over the years—if he knows the other half of the formula it won't take Gulag long to get his hands on it.'

'That's a seriously worrying thought. It makes an attack on these underground caverns even more important. We must get Josh and Jennifer back before Gulag gets a chance to delve into their minds. Thank God they're both accomplished telepaths. At least it will give them some protection from Gulag's mind probes,' Jenson voiced his concern.

'I'm afraid that our priority must be somewhat different from yours,' Hillmead told them. 'Shalok and I must make our way back to Caranak as soon as possible.'

'What the hell for? They'll be looking for you guys everywhere and I wouldn't like to be in your shoes when they find you,' Sandpiper exclaimed in surprise.

'The people deserve to know what's been going on behind their backs. The military have caused the suffering of millions for over a hundred years. Now the planet is dying because of the greed of the militarists. The least we can do is to let people know why they can't breathe the air anymore, or why the food they eat is slowly poisoning them,' Shalok answered.

'I'm in agreement,' added Hillmead. 'I've seen what it's like for the poor bastards on the street in Caranak. We're all going to die soon anyway, so I think we owe it to those poor sods to tell them why they're dying.'

'I admire your sentiment, but we're not dead yet, so let's not chuck in the towel. The problem at the moment is that even if you did manage to make it back to Caranak there's no way you could get your message across to the masses. As you know, the media is completely state controlled and anything else you tried would just be dismissed as malicious rumour,' said Myrddin.

'Maybe the Democratic Front could help,' Sandpiper suggested. 'They would certainly benefit from the scandal. Who knows? Perhaps your information would be sufficient to start the revolution.'

'The problem with that approach Han, is that if Gulag really is behind the anti-Imperial movement, with or without Nimue's knowledge, he's hardly going to allow anybody to let his little secret out the bag. No, I think we need to approach this problem from another angle,' said Myrddin. 'Hillmead, tell me about the Emperor.'

'What do you want to know?' Hillmead asked.

'What's he like? Does he ever appear in public? Is he popular with the people?'

'Well,' Hillmead answered thoughtfully, 'the Emperor is basically regarded as a God by the subjects of the Empire. From the day they are born, children are told that the Emperor is to be obeyed and worshipped. The reason that the Imperial forces are traditionally so powerful is because of the allegiance everyone swears to the Emperor.'

'Have you guys sworn an allegiance to the Emperor?' Sandpiper asked Hillmead and Shalok.

'Yes we both swore an oath during our childhood and once again when we entered Imperial service,' Shalok replied. 'Despite everything that has happened I'm still loyal to the Emperor. My oath remains unbroken. It is a conspiracy of traitors that I wish to expose.'

'It reminds me of the Japanese Emperor during the 1930s. Japanese Imperial forces swept across the

Pacific and committed all sorts of atrocities in the name of the Emperor. Even when the war was going against them they were prepared to die to the last man and woman to protect a man they regarded as a god,' commented Jenson.

'When was the last time anyone saw the Emperor?' Myrddin asked Shalok.

'He hasn't been seen in public for a number of years. He's now ill and bed-bound—or so we've been told. Why do you ask?'

'Do you believe that the Emperor is a part of the militarist conspiracy?'

Shalok shook her head vehemently, 'I refuse to believe that he would have anything to do with such a scheme, but I still don't understand where these questions are leading.'

'Just bear with me a moment,' Myrddin urged, 'I assure you there is a reason behind all my questions. Now, would the good citizens of Caranak and the Empire do what he bade them to do, regardless of what the military might say or how they might act?'

'There's no doubt about it, the people would follow the Emperor,' she answered.

'In that case our course of action is clear young lady,' Myrddin told her holding her attention with one of his penetrating stares. 'I will accompany the two of you to Caranak where we will attempt to get an audience with the Emperor. If we could persuade him to go on television and radio to denounce the activities of the military, then their days will be very much numbered.'

'Do you really think that's possible?' Hillmead asked somewhat sceptically.

'Nothing ventured, nothing gained, ' he answered. 'I fail to see how any other plan can succeed. Certainly, if what you two have just told me is correct, then yes, I do think that an announcement made by the Emperor would be enough to start a revolution. Whether we can get him to agree to this action is another matter entirely, but I think it's worth a try.'

'That's quite an undertaking Myrddin,' Jenson said shaking his head, 'are you sure you want to attempt this? Remember that Nimue is in Caranak probably waiting for you to show up. Wouldn't it be easier simply to disable or destroy this entombed starship? I'm really sorry that the planet is in such a state, but our mission is to remove any threat to Earth, not get involved in Dyason politics.'

'Myrddin and Nimue are going to have to face each other again at some stage,' Moss intervened, 'and there's no guarantee that a mission to destroy the real Dominator will succeed. Better to attack on two fronts than put all our eggs in one basket, don't you think?'

Jenson sat and thought for a moment. It was obvious that Moss and Myrddin had talked through this whole affair before the conference began. Of course, they were right, Myrddin should go with Hillmead and Shalok to Caranak. The possibility of overturning the military dictatorship was too good an opportunity to miss, but it meant splitting the team up once again. However, Jenson also knew that once Myrddin got an idea into his head there was no stopping him. His earlier conversation with Sandpiper came back to him; it was time to hand over the reins of leadership and he would do it gracefully.

'Okay Moss,' he nodded, 'we'll play it your way. Myrddin will go with Hillmead and Shalok to Caranak. They'll attempt to start the political ball rolling against Nimue and the clone. The rest of us will mount an operation against the entombed Dominator. The priority for that mission will be to rescue Jennifer and Brabazon.'

Moss knew that an important moment had passed and Jenson was giving him the leadership of the operation. His stomach knotted, he just hoped he was up to it—Jennifer was relying on him. 'Thanks for that boss,' he said. 'Now to work out the details. Colmarrie, is there some way you can get these guys to Caranak undetected?'

'It is difficult but not impossible friend Moss. I shall see what can be done.' Colmarrie turned to Hillmead and Shalok. 'I do not agree with much of what you said, but I admire you both for your desire to expose the truth. I have not come across such honour from a member of the Imperial services before. I *will* ensure that you all reach Caranak safely so that you may carry out your mission.'

For the first time Hillmead was at a loss for words; the blessing of a mutant fighter was the last thing he would have ever expected. He nodded solemnly in acknowledgement.

'Okay people,' Moss said decisively, 'let's discuss details. I've already given the mission some thought and this is what I suggest.'

CHAPTER THIRTEEN

EXCALIBUR, EARTH ORBIT.
14.50 HOURS AUGUST 5TH 2031

The formation of Flyship fighters swept past the Excalibur for one last mock attack before peeling away to start a docking circuit. Commander Black watched the exercise on the main bridge viewer with barely feigned interest. The Excalibur and her three new squadrons of the latest Flyship fighters had been on constant alert status ever since the *Observer* had left for Dyason. The WDF command had placed all of Earth's defence forces on a high alert status in reaction to fears over the possibility of a new Dyason invasion fleet. Black had pleaded to be allowed to go with Jenson, Sandpiper, Moss and the others to Dyason, but had been refused. It had been decided that somebody experienced should be left in charge of Excalibur and her fleet of Flyships. That somebody happened to be him and the frustration was eating him up!

'Eagle squadron report all Flyships safely docked and hangared commander,' the operations officer told him.

'Okay,' he sighed. 'Send everyone my thanks, that was another exercise well done. Tell the flight leader, I'll join him for the de-brief in ten minutes.' Black picked up his electronic notebook and headed for the turbo-lift. He always did his best to attend the de-briefing sessions despite the fact that there had been very little for him to say in the past couple of weeks. Excalibur and her defence fleet were now at the peak of their operational capability; the crew of several thousand men and women had never been so prepared for war. If it were up to him, Black would take the Excalibur to Dyason and finish what they had started four years ago. However, he had his orders, regardless of how much he disagreed with them.

He got halfway to the lift when he got a call from the science officer. 'Commander, sir, I think you should take a look at this.'

Black sighed once more then strode over to the science officer's work-station. 'What is it Lieutenant?' he asked. The lieutenant pointed to a pattern of colours pulsating on a display screen in front of her. 'It's this sir,' she said.

Black looked at the display blankly. 'I'm sorry Lieutenant, but it means absolutely nothing to me. What am I looking at exactly?' he asked.

'What you're looking at sir, is a space-time anomaly that is rapidly expanding,' she told him. 'I've been watching it for a few hours now and the rate of its expansion is increasing all the time.'

'Where is this anomaly exactly?' Black asked.

'It's appearing in a sector of space close to the orbit of Jupiter.'

'Jupiter? Isn't that where the worm-hole to Dyason was situated?' Black now alarmed, asked her.

'That's right sir,' she replied uneasily, pointing to another display on her work station. 'This is a computer simulation of the early growth of the worm-hole that appeared before the Dyason invasion, and this is what's happening now!'

Black didn't need a degree in astro-physics to understand that the simulation from the previous worm-hole and the display of the new anomaly were exactly the same. 'Have your observations been corroborated with Earth-side observatories?' he demanded.

'Not yet. The Excalibur's sensors are far more powerful than those of ground-based observatories. However, space telescopes are just now beginning to detect the same anomaly,' the lieutenant replied cautiously.

'So what you're telling me, is that another worm-hole is developing in our system?'

'It would appear that way Commander,' she answered.

'Shit! That's bad news!' he exclaimed. 'Is there any way of knowing where the worm-hole leads to. I mean, does it lead to or from Dyason?'

The science officer shook her head. 'I'm sorry sir, but there's no way of knowing. We can't even be sure that we're actually looking at the formation of a worm-hole yet. If it does prove to be a worm-hole, the only real way of knowing where it will lead is to enter the anomaly itself.'

This wasn't the news that Black wanted to hear. If the worm-hole did fully develop as it had prior to the invasion, then there was a good chance that any new Dyason fleet would make use of it. 'Inform WDF command of what you've discovered,' he told the lieutenant, 'and keep me posted. I want to be informed the moment that anomaly develops into a full-blown worm-hole.'

'Yes Commander.'

Black turned and called over the operations officer. 'Did you catch any of that Jefferson?' he asked.

'I got the general drift, yes sir,' the captain replied.

'Good. Get Pauline here to give you a complete briefing on the situation. Then I want you to work out a mission scenario that includes the emergence of a new Dyason fleet through a new worm-hole,' Black ordered, tapping the display with his finger to stress his point. 'As soon as you've worked out a scenario I want the wargame simulators to play through the possible connotations. If the worst happens I want us to be prepared. Is that clear?'

'Very clear sir,' the operations officer replied. 'We'll get right on with it now commander.'

'Good, keep me informed.' Black headed towards the turbo-lift once more. This was a development that he'd like to talk through with the Flyship pilots. If a fleet did emerge through a new worm-hole, they would be the first to engage the Dyason in combat. However, he never got to the lift as once more he was called over by one of the bridge officers. This time it was the engineering officer.

'Commander, I'm reading a power surge in the status fields of both main engines,' the engineering officer told him with a frown. 'We've tried to contain it but for some reason, were getting no response.'

Black scanned the monitors on the engineering work station. 'What do you mean you're getting no response?'

'I mean sir, that somebody has locked all the engine control systems. The main engines are powering up and we're not able to stop it!' the engineering office told him in alarm. 'I don't know what's going on sir, but we've got no control!'

'What? This is ridiculous!' Black felt the increased vibration though the deck plates, and knew that the Excalibur was underway. 'Helm! What the hell is going on. I haven't ordered us to move from orbit. What do you think you're doing?'

The helmsman sitting at his controls in the centre of the bridge raised his hands in the air and said, 'This has got nothing to do with me sir! I was locked out of the systems a few moments ago. A course has been set and we're underway, but I swear it's nothing to do with me.'

Black leapt over to the helm and punched the emergency stop button. Nothing happened, Excalibur continued to slowly accelerate. 'Where the hell are we heading?' he demanded.

'A course has been set for Jupiter, but we never set it!' the navigation officer cried out in alarm. 'We've been locked out of the system.'

A glimmer of realisation entered Black's mind—it was unprecedented, but it *could* happen onboard a ship such as the Excalibur. As far as he could recall it had *never* happened before, but there was always a first time.

'Sir we're being hailed by space-station Orion; they want to know why we are leaving orbit!' called the communications officer.

Black turned to the comms officer and snapped. 'Tell them we're experiencing some difficulty but don't require assistance. Tell them that we're working on it and we'll get back to them.' He collapsed into the captain's chair in the centre of the bridge and faced the main viewer which was showing a slowly disappearing Earth. 'Excalibur,' he called out to the ship's sentient computer. 'Would you like to explain just what the hell is going on?'

Everyone on the bridge stopped what they were doing and watched the commander apparently talking into empty space. 'Come on Excalibur, if you're going to take us for a ride, you might at least have the courtesy of telling us where we're going,' Black asked once more.

There was a silent pause, then the pleasant female tones of Excalibur's main computer said, 'I apologise for any inconvenience Commander Black, but it is important that we arrive at the rendezvous on time.'

'Are you responsible for locking all the controls?' Black demanded.

'Yes I am Commander. It is necessary,' the computer answered.

'Why is it necessary Excalibur? Where are you planning on taking us?'

'We must enter the worm-hole at the allotted time Commander,' came the reply. 'As I have said, it is important that we arrive at the rendezvous on time.'

'The worm-hole? Rendezvous? What the hell are you talking about Excalibur,' Black called out in frustration.

'The worm-hole leads to the Dyason star system commander. It has emerged so that we can arrive in orbit around Dyason in time for the event,' the computer told him in a reasonable, reassuring voice.

Black was having none of it. He wasn't reassured at all, in fact quite the opposite, he was afraid he had a runaway computer on his hands. 'Excalibur, we've been ordered to stay in Earth orbit as defence against a new Dyason fleet. We can't just disappear on a joyride to God knows where! You'll get me court-martialled!'

'Commander, the Imperial fleet is still in orbit around Dyason. I am sorry that I cannot tell you more, but we must enter the worm-hole at the correct moment,' the computer explained.

Black turned to the engineering officer. 'Can you bypass the computer's command system and return us to orbit?' he snapped.

The engineering officer scanned her console worriedly before answering, 'Yes...well..., possibly sir! It will take a few hours to bypass the main control systems and it will be hazardous. The main computer controls the environmental systems as well as propulsion and navigation. If we're not careful we could end up adrift without power or air.'

'Bloody great! Do it anyway. Make a start, but for Christ's sake be careful!' he ordered.

'Commander!' the comm's officer called out. 'I'm being hailed by the President.'

Black turned in alarm. 'The President of the UN?' he asked. The comms officer nodded. Black's heart sank. The situation was rapidly getting out of control. 'That's all we bloody need! Talk about shit hitting the fan! Okay, put him on the viewer.'

The holographic image of President Gafton appeared on the main bridge viewer. 'President, this is a great honour,' Black began dubiously. The President stood in what looked like the main WDF operations room in New Zealand and Black feared he already knew that the Excalibur's main computer was running amok.

'I think we can dispense with the pleasantries Commander,' Gafton began. 'Our observatories are reading the appearance of a space-time anomaly near the orbit of Jupiter. The astro-physicists reckon it's the prelude to another worm-hole. Do Excalibur's sensors read the same anomaly?'

Black glanced at the science officer who nodded her head, before answering, 'My science officer has been observing the development of the anomaly since its appearance a few hours ago.'

'Good!' Gafton said. 'Next question—are all the Flyships onboard?'

'Yes sir. The last fighter was delivered to us a few hours ago. We have three squadrons with forty-five Flyships onboard the Excalibur.'

'Excellent!' Gafton replied then paused. Black could just see someone out of view hand the

President a note. 'Commander, I'm informed that the Excalibur has left orbit and is heading for the position of the anomaly. Is that correct?' the President demanded.

Black coughed and looked at his boots before answering. 'Err... that's right sir. It um... seemed sensible to investigate the event.'

To Black's surprise the President smiled broadly. 'Well done Commander, that's showing real initiative. Now listen carefully, our scientists down here believe that this worm-hole will once again lead directly to the Dyason system. Therefore, we've had an emergency meeting and decided to change your orders. I know how much you've been pushing for a pre-emptive strike on the Dyason home world. Well, now's your opportunity! Your new orders are to enter the worm-hole and strike at the Imperial Navy's new fleet before it has a chance to leave orbit!'

Black was gob-smacked, how did Excalibur know that their orders would be changed? Had the sentient computer intercepted radio traffic and decided to implement the orders before the rest of them even knew the orders were being changed? Or was that simply coincidence? Either way, he was delighted that they were going to take the initiative, however a problem did occur to him.

'That's wonderful news Mr President, but how do you intend to protect the Earth in our absence? I was under the impression that you believed the Excalibur to be too valuable to risk on such an operation.'

Gafton nodded at Black's question. 'I'm glad you asked Commander. We have another twelve squadrons of Flyships going into operational service in the next few days. We believe that this fighter coverage plus our new orbital weapon platforms should give us some measure of protection in the event of another attack. However, I have every faith that the *Observer* team will have found some way to delay any invasion fleet and I have every faith in you and your crew. There is a risk but we believe this is too good a military opportunity to miss. Your written orders will be transmitted to you in a few minutes. Good luck Commander! Our hopes and prayers go with you! Gafton out.'

The holographic image of the President disappeared and the bridge immediately buzzed with excited talk. 'Quiet!' Black ordered. 'Okay people, we've now officially had a change of orders. Ops?'

'Yes sir!'

'Get moving on those combat simulations. Science officer, let me know the second that worm-hole develops fully!

'Yes sir!'

'Comms I want a full copy of the orders in my office as soon as they arrive. Excalibur!'

'Yes Commander Black?' the main computer asked politely.

'I would appreciate control of the ship returned to the bridge, if you would be so kind. Then perhaps we could have a private chat, if you're not too busy,' he asked sarcastically.

'It would be a pleasure commander,' the computer replied without any hint of emotion.

'Thank you *so* much.' Black leapt out of his seat and headed for the third time towards the turbo-lift. 'We've got a job to do ladies and gentlemen, so let's get on with it! Ops, send my apologies to the flight leader, I won't be able to make the de-brief. However, tell him I want to see his whole squadron and all the other Flyship pilots in the main briefing room at 17.00 hours.'

The doors to the turbo-lift closed before him and he allowed himself the luxury of a deep sigh. 'Well...well...well...,' he muttered to himself. 'Just what the *hell* is going on?'

04.25 HOURS. THE 'GUTTERSWEEP', THIEVES' QUARTER, CARANAK

Myrddin was glad for the well-worn environment suit; not only did it protect him from the corrosive acid rain of Caranak, it was the perfect disguise. The patched and stained suit looked much the same as those worn by all the other citizens of Caranak and when on the street he had to wear the face mask with its built in charcoal filters, which of course meant that his face was hidden.

Hillmead and Shalok had disposed of their Imperial uniforms and were also kitted out with battered environment suits. Shalok had cut off her long mane of red hair and now had a crew-cut as was the street fashion. When she'd cut her hair, Myrddin had seen her shed a quiet tear. He'd felt sorry for her then, in fact he couldn't dislike the poor kid, it wasn't her fault she'd been born and brought up as an Imperial servant.

The journey from the southern wastelands to the Imperial capital had taken just over seventeen days. True to her word Colmarrie had arranged their passage through different cells of the underground movement that she knew could still be trusted. Once outside the boundary of the wastelands they'd travelled mainly at night, usually in the back of lorries carrying foodstuffs or materials. A couple of times they'd been smuggled aboard supply aircraft. The last part of the trip to Caranak had been done in a secret compartment built into a large petrol tanker supplying fuel to the few wealthy citizens who could still afford to run a vehicle. The fumes and poor ventilation in the secret compartment had made all three of them feel faint and sick, but they'd eventually reached the capital safely.

As they'd travelled across desert, plain and mountain, Myrddin had been appalled at the environmental devastation he'd seen. Thousands of square kilometres of once fertile farmland had become arid dust-bowls. Everywhere they went, they saw villages, towns and cities that had been abandoned as the area around them became incapable of supporting life. In the northern lands the arid conditions changed to violent storms and persistent rain that washed the top-soil away. What few crops they saw were withered and disease ridden. Occasionally they saw the Dyason equivalent of cattle standing forlorn in flooded fields, their bones showing through thin flesh.

Myrddin reckoned the total environmental collapse of the planet would happen in less than five years. Most of the population would be lucky to survive another twelve months. It made him furious—how could a few military fanatics squander a whole planet's resources? How could they live with themselves knowing that they were responsible for genocide on such a horrific scale? It made him more determined than ever to bring those responsible to justice and at the top of his hit list was Nimue, his sister.

Hillmead brought three chipped mugs of something that bore a vague resemblance to coffee from the grubby counter of the street bar. Myrddin lifted his face mask took one sip, made a face and put his mug down. 'Eaargh...' he spat, 'how can you drink this crap? It's disgusting!'

Hillmead took a swig from his own mug and also made a face. 'Yeah I know, but it's the only thing that's available except for an ale that's gone green from the shit that grows in it,' he said.

'What's it made of? The brew that is, not the ale.'

'Dried Moosag droppings,' Hillmead answered. Myrddin raised an eyebrow, but said nothing. 'Only kidding,' the Dyason policeman responded with a grin.

Despite the fact that the local time was three in the morning, the bar was packed full of the citizens of Caranak. Shalok had already explained to him that because the habitable part of the city was so massively overpopulated, the majority of people lived in small rooms with anything up to twenty other people. Shift-work was the norm with those getting up for work giving their beds to those who had just finished. Consequently, Caranak was a twenty-four-hour city. There was no real difference in activity between day and night. The weather was so consistently wet and stormy you could never judge the time of day by looking at the sky anyway. For the millions of Caranak citizens it was a *very* miserable existence.

A small wiry figure forced its way through the crowd and evicted a grumbling woman from the stool next to the one Shalok sat on. The figure placed a hand on her leg and gave her thigh a good squeeze through the material of the environment suit. 'Hello gorgeous! Have you missed me? Heh, I like the new haircut—very stylish.'

Shalok turned in alarm to look at the stranger who lifted his face mask and grinned at her. 'Oh, it's you!' she said in surprise.

'Who were you expecting gorgeous?' Pollowzki asked. 'The Emperor?'

Hillmead turned and looked at his one time assistant. 'Where the bloody hell have you been you little weasel? We've been stuck in this shit-hole for hours waiting for you!'

Pollowzki took a swig of the green ale, wiped the fungi froth off his upper lip and grinned at his old boss. 'Piss off! You've just arrived, I'm the one who's been stuck in here for hours looking out for you bastards.' Hillmead grunted and pretended not to be pleased to see his old friend. 'The old git sitting next to you,' Pollowzki whispered looking at Myrddin, 'I take it he's the mythological human?'

Myrddin took hold of the weasel-faced policeman's hand and squeezed it hard enough for the little Dyason's face to contort with pain. 'It's a pleasure I'm sure,' said Myrddin with a cold smile, 'but a little less of the *old* sonny. At least until we're a little better acquainted my friend.'

'Yeah...right...my mistake,' Pollowzki replied through gritted teeth.

'Well that's the introductions out the way,' Hillmead intervened before the situation got out of hand. 'Poll, stop messing around and brief us as to the situation.'

Pollowzki managed to release his hand from Myrddin's grip and shook it in an attempt to get his circulation back. Myrddin continued to sip his brew as if nothing had happened.

'Well, you've certainly started something! Every bloody trooper in the Empire is on the lookout for you guys. Your descriptions are posted everywhere and there's a reward on your heads!' Poll told them.

'How much?' Hillmead asked.

'What do you mean how much?'

'How much is the reward?'

'Thirty five thousand credits for you and the girl. Seventy thousand credits for the old gi... sorry, I mean the human gentleman,' Poll informed him.

'Thirty five thousand? That's disgusting! I'm worth far more than that,' exclaimed Shalok with feigned disgust. 'Still, they must really want you,' she said to Myrddin.

'Honoured I'm sure,' Myrddin responded dryly.

'Basically, the official line is that the two of you were involved in acts of sabotage onboard that space-hulk and you aided the humans in their escape. Therefore, you're wanted for treason.' Poll continued to tell Hillmead.

'That sounds about right,' the ex-police inspector said. 'We know the military is up to all sorts of mischief, but what about the guys at the police precincts? Can we rely on their help?'

'Life on the streets has got a lot worse in the short few weeks you've been away. It's virtual anarchy out there. Food is getting more and more scarce and when you *can* find food, it's barely edible. It's obvious to even the most ardent supporter of the Empire that it's all turning to shit.

'Stories about what you found in orbit are spreading like wildfire. There are a few who believe they're nothing but anti-Imperial rumours, but I think it would be fair to say that the majority of cops are on your side.'

'What about you Pollowzki?' Shalok asked. 'Whose side are you on?'

Poll looked her straight in the eye and answered. 'Remember, I read the reports that started all this. I *know* the truth and I'm on the side of that truth.'

Myrddin looked at the weasel-faced Dyason and tapped on the bar counter thoughtfully. 'What's the plan then? How are we going to get to see the Emperor?' he asked.

Poll took a long draught of his ale and looked around to check that nobody was obviously watching. A couple of nasty looking scum were involved in agitated negotiations nearby, other than that his practised police eye noticed nothing out of the ordinary. They'd chosen this particular bar because it was a well-known rendezvous site for Caranak's underworld. It was the sort of place where you minded your own business because your life expectancy shortened dramatically if you didn't. If anybody here did recognise them, they weren't about to let on. 'That's going to be a tricky one,' he answered with a sigh. 'Our esteemed Emperor hasn't shown his face in public in years. The last time he did, he appeared to be stoned out of his head. I don't know what he's on, but it must be heavy shit. Rumour has it that the Envoy Nimue is the·only member of the government to still have a regular audience with him.'

'Nimue you say?' Myrddin interrupted. 'How long has the Envoy been having private audiences with the Emperor?'

A frown creased Poll's forehead. 'I don't really know to be honest,' he replied. 'Certainly for as long as I can remember. Does it matter?'

'Maybe...maybe not.'

'Anyway, I've arranged a meeting with an officer of the Emperor's private guard,' Poll told them passing a small piece of paper to Hillmead, who slipped it into the inside pocket of his environment suit. 'The time and place are on that paper. This guy's vouched for by the same organisation that got you here. It's a long shot, but it's the best suggestion I have.'

'It sounds very dangerous,' commented Shalok. 'We could be walking straight into a trap.'

'We've been treading dangerously ever since your little discovery dear,' Hillmead said to her. 'I'm not sure now's the time to start worrying about the risks...'

There was a commotion from the other end of the bar and Hillmead turned to look. To his horror, a squad of Imperial troopers were ploughing their way through the crowd towards them, swinging the butts of their assault rifles into the face of anybody who stood in their way. 'Shit! I thought you said this place was still off-limits to Imperial goons!' he yelled in alarm.

'It was until you three turned up!' Poll replied. 'Well don't just stand there, let's get the hell out of here!' The weasel-faced policeman scrambled over the bar and the others followed him. The bar owner saw them and beckoned for them to hurry, holding up a trap door that led to the cellars below. 'This way, quickly!' the barman called. There was a shout from the crowd and the sound of gunfire. Incensed by an intrusion into their own private domain, members of the underworld turned on the troopers, pushing and shoving back at them. One of the squad fired a shot over the crowd's head, but got a bullet from an illegal pistol in the back of his neck for his efforts. More Imperial troops forced their way through the main entrance and yet more came through the soup kitchen. The squad now caught in the middle of the bar unable to reach their quarry found themselves under increasing pressure and brought their guns to bear. From the folds of worn overcoats and ancient environment suits appeared a host of illegal firearms. As Hillmead followed the others down into the cellar the bar dissolved into a full-blown fire-fight. The barman brusquely pushed him out of the way as soon as he entered the cellar and sealed the trap-door with a large iron bar.

'You'd better be bloody worth it Hillmead,' the overweight bar owner snarled at him, his lips curled back over blackened, rotten teeth. 'There's a lot of good customers up there who are bleeding to death just to save your arse!' Hillmead looked at him blankly. He didn't know what he was talking about.

'It's all right Caliskon you'll all get your money,' Pollowzki said, helping the bar owner to secure the entrance.

'Screw the sodding money you little weasel. None of us are interested in that! We just want to be sure the stories are true and if they are, we want to see the bastards responsible splayed out with a hot poker up the arse!' the barman told them. He turned and prodded a grubby finger into Hillmead's chest. 'My little girl died six months ago from throat cancer. She was eight years old and in her short life never had anything to drink or eat that wasn't full of radioactive shit! You make sure that she and all the thousands like her haven't died in vain! Yer' hear!'

Surprised, Hillmead could only nod as the fat barman forced his way past him and made his way toward a series of large ale kegs. Myrddin looked on with keen interest. Caliskon went to the very left of the kegs and released a hidden catch. The round wooden front of the keg opened revealing a series of steps leading down to an old brick tunnel. There was a pounding on the cellar doors and the barman looked up in alarm. 'There's no time to waste, ' he hissed urgently pushing them toward the secret entrance. 'The cellar door will only last for so long!'

'Where are we going?' Shalok asked.

'These stairs lead to the sewers,' Caliskon told them. 'Poll knows the way. He'll guide you. Come-on quick! There's no time to lose!'

'What about you? Are you coming with us?' Hillmead asked.

'Don't worry about me! I can look after myself. Now bloody *move*!'

Pollowzki ushered them into the keg and Caliskon sealed it after them. Then using the light from a torch hidden in his environment suit, he led the rest of them down the steps and into the sewers. An eerie glow emanated from a strange slime that hung from the ancient brick-work of the main sewer they soon found themselves in.

'Urgh! This is disgusting!' Shalok exclaimed. 'It smells like vomit down here and what causes that weird glow?'

Pollowzki pulled down his face mask and peered at her through the thick plastic lenses. 'You'll have to keep your suits and masks sealed whilst we're down here,' he told them. 'Barely treated waste from the nuke power stations has been flowing through these tunnels for decades. The slime on the walls is some weird sort of fungus that glows from the radioactive isotopes it absorbs. The whole sewer system is radioactive which is why the Imperial goons won't follow us down here.'

'I don't blame them,' Myrddin commented dryly. 'How long do we have to be down here ourselves before we start to glow like the walls?'

'Your environment suit should give you some protection. So long as we're out of here in a few hours' time we shouldn't suffer any long-term effects,' Poll replied.

'You hope!'

'Look human, I didn't cause this shit, it was done by a military dictatorship over a long period of time. I'm just as keen as you are to see that the bastards responsible are brought to justice! I'm not helping official enemies of the state for a laugh you know!' Pollowzki answered indignantly hissing through his respirator.

Hillmead placed a hand on his old friend's shoulder. 'Nobody's accusing you of anything Poll. Why don't you show us the way? Where are we going?' he said, his voice distorted through his face mask.

Pollowzki stepped into the sludge that flowed along the bottom of the sewer and started wading through it. Somewhat reluctantly the others followed him. 'You can get to just about every part of the city from these sewers. The underworld has been using them for years. The Imperial palace grounds are about an hour's walk from here. The contact I told you about is stationed there. The meeting is set for tomorrow evening, so we'll have to hide up somewhere until then.'

'You're planning on coming with us?' Hillmead asked.

'I haven't got much choice now, have I boss? Those goons were looking for the three of you and they saw us together. Now they'll have orders to find the four of us,' he answered.

'I'm sorry to have dragged you into this mate,' Hillmead told him.

'Don't worry about it boss. The lieutenant's old bunch, the MDC, have been sniffing around me for ages. It was inevitable I would have to do a runner eventually, it simply happened a bit quicker than expected.'

Shalok made a face and kicked some flotsam out of her way. 'Nice to see you're in the same shit as the rest of us,' she told him in a strained voice.

Pollowzki turned around and did his best to appear as if he were leering at her through the lenses of his mask. 'I wouldn't have it any other way gorgeous!' he hissed through the respirator.

Shalok ignored the little Dyason and concentrated on not stepping on any particularly nasty pieces of slime. For some reason the thought came to her that shit *always* floats.

DOMINATOR, SOUTHERN WASTELANDS.

Jennifer wandered around the bridge of the entombed Dominator, watching Josh Brabazon as he worked on the various work stations that were exact duplicates of those fitted onboard the Excalibur. The monitor and displays were the same, although the graphic outputs were in Dyason rather than the standard English used on the Excalibur. Brabazon was in deep discussion with one of the Dyason technicians, going over the harmonisation graphs for the main engine status fields. Although Jennifer knew enough to be of great help, she preferred to watch the proceedings. She was shadowed by a female guard who although always present, kept a discreet distance. True to his words Gulag had given them the run of the ship and they'd found the crew, although busily restoring the ship to space-worthiness, to be polite and helpful. Certainly these Dyason appeared to be a very different lot from the normal Imperial troopers. Gulag himself had been cold but polite and despite being a clone of the hated original Gulag, Jennifer now accepted that he was a completely different individual. Dangerous, yes—psychotic, no.

Her mind kept on repeating the recent telepathic conversation she'd had with Moss. She found it hard to play along with his suggestions, despite the fact that once she'd analysed what he'd said, she realised the sense in his plans. She'd been wandering around the garden deck examining the mass of native Dyason flora when she'd felt the familiar presence of her lover in her mind.

'Hi, how are they treating you?' he'd asked her first.

'Hi yourself,' she'd thought back at him, her heart lifting at the familiar presence in her mind. *'We're okay. To be fair to these people, they're not like your usual Imperial squaddies. They appear to be more intelligent for a start. We're both being well treated.'*

'That's good to know,' he'd responded. *'I still hate the thought of you being held prisoner though.'*

'We've been through that already Moss. It was my own stupidity that got us caught in the first place. You can't be at my side all the time, there are times when I have to make my own decisions and live by them.'

'I know Jennifer, I know...' Moss had replied with a mental sigh. *'How is Josh getting on, has he found out anything new?'*

Jennifer then sat down beside a pool of fish the like of which she'd never seen before. Their beautiful striped skins flashed in the refracting light of the simulated sun. The sight of them made her sad— like most of the plants and animals on the garden deck, they were extinct on the surface of Dyason. Her ever present guard had sat down at a discreet distance also and Jennifer then concentrated her mind on Moss.

'Gulag has given Josh complete access to the ship's main computer and data-banks. As Gulag must have predicted Josh has been devouring as much information as possible. One thing that quickly became apparent is the fact that although extremely advanced, the main computer isn't sentient like Excalibur,' she'd told him.

'What not at all? That's interesting.'

'Josh says that although the computer is capable of self-education it shows no sign of being self-aware as is the case with Excalibur. Of course, it may be possible that it may simply choose not to advertise its self-awareness, but Josh doubts it,' she'd informed him.

'Perhaps reaching a state of self-awareness is something that is unique to Excalibur, although it does seem strange that the vessels should appear to be exactly the same in all respects except for that one important difference. What about the problem with the harmonisation of the status fields? Does Josh think he can sort them out on that front? Moss had asked.

Jennifer had then told Moss that Josh Brabazon had worked out that Gulag and his team of technicians had basically misunderstood the information supplied by the Dominator's computer and had consistently failed to harmonise the status fields. As the main computer wasn't sentient, it wasn't able to respond to the Dyason technicians' lack of understanding. That had also been the reason for the failure of the experimental fighters that the mutant Neehmad had seen.

'So Josh feels he can get the real Dominator operational?' he probed her.

'There's no doubt about it,' she'd responded. *'Josh reckons the solution is actually fairly straightforward. Obviously he's kept this information from Gulag and he makes sure his mental shields keep the knowledge from slipping into the clone's head.'*

It had been then that Moss had dropped his bombshell on her. She remembered that she'd been so surprised she'd cried out in alarm, immediately attracting curious stares from her escort.

'You can't be serious!' she'd mentally exclaimed. *'You want Josh to give them all the help they need to get this beast into space again? For God's sake, why?'*

'Jennifer,' Moss had answered, *'think about it! Dyason is a dying planet, the Empire doesn't represent a threat to Earth anymore. The military is spent, their resources exhausted, they're incapable of launching another fleet. That piece of junk in orbit was bait designed to attract us here—why? So that Josh could help bring the Excalibur's sister ship to life.'*

'You're forgetting Gulag's search for Point Zero.' she'd reminded him.

Moss had then gone on to explain that he hadn't forgotten about Point Zero at all. Far from it, Moss believed they needed to find the secret to limitless power from water just as much as Gulag did. Which was why he wanted Josh to give Gulag all the help he could. Then Moss would mount a take-over operation for the Dominator to snatch the ship from under Nimue's nose.

'That's a big risk to take Moss,' Jennifer had said to him. *'What if you fail to take over the Dominator and Gulag manages to get the ship into space? He'll be in a position to threaten us once more.'*

'I'm not sure that Gulag is really a threat to us. He has plans all of his own, but invading Earth again

isn't one of them,' he had replied. *'By your own admission, this Gulag is a very different animal from his predecessor. Besides, the Dominator and Point Zero are this planet's only hope of salvation at the moment. I hate the Imperial forces, but I don't hate the entire planet's population sufficiently to want to see them all die slowly.'*

'You've changed,' she told him gently. *'Not so long ago you would have been overjoyed to hear that the planet's dying.'*

'Be nice,' he chided her, *'that was before I met Colmarrie and her fighters—they're an admirable bunch. I even quite like Hillmead and Shalok. The point is, if they and Myrddin succeed in their mission the militarists are going to find they've got a revolution on their hands. In which case the Empire as such, is finished. That gives us the perfect opportunity to form an alliance with the new government and what better way to start a new alliance than to hand over the technology they need to save the planet's ecology?'*

Jennifer had had to sit down and think about that one. It was a very dangerous game Moss was playing. If she were honest with herself she would probably admit that she was more afraid of the rapid changes in Moss, than the risk of the mission failing. It was easy, simple to concentrate the mind when the enemy was so clear, so black and white. Now everything had changed, the enemy was no longer faceless, no longer pure evil. She'd sat beside the pool deep in thought for a very long time, but eventually she had to admit to herself that Moss was right, they would have to risk aiding Gulag. Just as

Moss was growing rapidly, so was Jennifer. She just hoped she could keep up with him.

Her thoughts returned to the present. Once she'd explained the matter to Josh, he agreed to help bring the Dominator to life. Jennifer actually suspected that the diminutive scientist knew more about Point Zero than he was willing to divulge, even to her. After all, he had spent more time examining the Excalibur's data-banks than anybody.

Gulag stepped out of the turbo-lift and onto the bridge. He wore a simple black flight suit bare of insignia and Jennifer had to admit that he looked very striking, albeit in a cold almost clinical fashion. His dark eyes swept across the bridge, paused briefly on Brabazon and one of the technicians before meeting her eyes. He nodded to her in acknowledgement then stepped toward her.

'How's it going?' he asked her politely.

'Okay I guess,' she responded shrugging her shoulders. 'Josh seems to have the situation under control. He's telling your people how to harmonise the status fields as we speak. More than that I'm afraid you'll have to ask him yourself.'

Gulag shook his head, 'No I'd prefer not to interfere. I'm sure he knows what he's doing. I'm glad that you've decided to give us your assistance. It means a great deal to me and the Democratic Front.'

Jennifer chose not to reply, avoided his look and kept her arms folded protectively across her chest.

'To show you how much I appreciate your help, I have some information concerning your friends' mission in Caranak. You would be wise to listen to what I have to say,' he told her, ignoring her rudeness. Jennifer turned toward him, her interest evident on her face.

'How do you know about that?' she demanded.

'That's what I have to tell you,' he replied his face remaining expressionless. 'I know about their mission because there is a traitor amongst them who is in the pay of the military.'

'Who told you this? Nimue? Is it one of her moles?' Jennifer was genuinely alarmed. Their mission had already been compromised by Tychivesk, another mole in their midst would put all of Moss's plans at risk. She was also worried for Myrddin's safety. He was a resourceful survivor, but the odds were mounting up against him especially if Nimue were preparing a trap for him.

'I'm afraid that I can't say anymore than that, except that it's in my interests as well as yours that their mission succeeds. I want Moss to know that— he'll understand,' he answered.

'God, you must really hate her!' she exclaimed, realising the depth of his hatred for his laboratory mother for the first time. It was Gulag's turn to say nothing. She opened her mouth to ask another question when a deep rumbling male voice reverberated across the bridge, 'I believe you will find the parameters work better if you increase the dipole separation by twelve percent Doctor Brabazon.'

Josh stood upright so quickly he swept his electronic notepad and the technician's tool kit straight onto the deck with a loud clatter. 'Who said that?' he looked around the bridge in alarm. 'Come on, out with it!'

Everyone else on the bridge immediately stopped what they were doing and looked around in surprise. None of them admitted to being behind the strange voice. 'I see that I have startled you Doctor,' the voice continued in a strong no-argument manner. 'I apologise for that, until now there has been no need for me to advertise my presence. However, it would appear that despite your more experienced efforts, if we are to achieve anything here, I must direct operations personally.'

Josh stood up in surprise then stuttered, 'You're this ships main computer? You're sentient after all aren't you?'

'Affirmative to both your questions Doctor Brabazon,' the ancient vessel's computer replied in an almost impatient manner. 'Ah Gulag, about time too. You took your time to get here. You're a few years late you know? By the way I like the name Dominator, most fitting I feel.'

Jennifer watched Gulag collapse into an acceleration couch, a look of complete astonishment on his Dyason face. His cold, calculating demeanour had totally evaporated.

'Well, ladies and gentlemen,' the Dominator's computer continued, 'there's much to do and very little time in which to do it. I suggest we crack on immediately.'

Jennifer sat aghast in the acceleration couch next to Gulag. 'Oh shit!' she whispered to herself, 'Oh shit, oh shit, oh shit...!'

CHAPTER FOURTEEN

IMPERIAL AIR STATION GACCIO

The operator from the orbital reconnaissance team checked the satellite-produced infra-red image displayed on his monitor once more. He tapped a rhythm on the console with his pen—this was strange, it was the last thing he would have expected. He set the computer to enhance the image and checked the results. There was no doubt about it, there were signs of activity at the site of the mutant base.

The infra-red signatures showed that tracked vehicles had crossed the desert and entered the recently abandoned base. The number of tell-tale signatures indicated that at least ten vehicles had left their tracks around the base in the seven hours since the last satellite sweep. Obviously the mutants had fled further into the wastelands after their attack on the air station, then, once they had thought it safe, they'd returned unaware that their base had been compromised.

Flight Officer Karatisk ordered a hard copy of the satellite image and took it from the printer as soon as the ink had become sufficiently dry to avoid smudging. He left the gloom of the bunker and with eyes half closed against the glare of the morning sun he ran for the operations block. The CO would want to see these pictures straightaway. This was their chance to wipe out the mutants once and for all!

A few minutes later he was showing the satellite image to Group Leader Baccia, pointing out the numerous tracks in the desert that had recently appeared. Baccia examined the image in silence for several minutes, peering at the markings through a magnifying viewer. Eventually, he put the viewer down and stood upright with a sigh. 'It would appear that your initial analysis is correct flight officer,' he told Karatisk. 'The arrogance and stupidity of these mutants is astonishing. They believe that they got away with their attack on my base—how wrong they are!'

Baccia turned to the operations officer and ordered, 'I want three attack squads and a squadron of attack helicopters ready to go at dusk. Officer briefing in one hour. We'll go in under cover of dark and take the bastards out. I want every one of those freak, mutant bastards killed. Adults, children, the lot! Then I want their base completely gutted and destroyed. Do I make myself clear?'

'I shall set your orders in motion directly sir!' the operations officer snapped, then turned on his heel and began barking orders to everyone in the operations room. Baccia slapped Karatisk on the back. 'Well done lad, bloody good work,' he congratulated the flight officer. 'Get your kit together and make sure you're at the briefing. You can come along and help clear the mutants out as your reward!' Then Baccia strode out of the operations room, barking orders to his adjutants as he went.

'Err yes... thank you sir,' Karatisk mumbled uncertainly. 'Err where do I get a rifle from?' All of a sudden Karatisk's legs turned to jelly and he had to find a seat. All he really wanted to do was to hide in his nice safe reconnaissance bunker. The idea of actually seeing combat scared him shitless. Karatisk sat shaking for a while, then rose to his feet and shuffled off in despair, ignored by the rest of the operations team.

The assault helicopter sped low over the radioactive wastelands, the sound of its blades reverberating off the desert floor. All the navigation lights were out and the instrument panel lights dimmed low. The pilot wore a pair of recently designed night goggles and used the image enhancement to guide him. Through the goggles he could clearly see the other helicopters of the assault force and the desert floor below. It was a very strange feeling to be flying at such a low level with only the infra-red goggles to see by, it was one big adrenaline buzz. The pilot didn't even consider what would happen if he made a mistake and collided with the desert floor, or another assault ship. For him it was one long carnival ride.

'Drop zone coming up in six minutes,' his co-pilot told him.

'Acknowledged,' he answered. 'You'd better let the Group Leader know.'

The co-pilot informed Baccia on the intercom who with, his usual enthusiastic bluster, began to yell at the assault troops strapped into the main cabin with him. Each one of the specially trained squad knew exactly what they were supposed to do and they mutually began to help each other with their last-minute equipment checks, not that this stopped Baccia from shouting at them anyway.

The pilot pulled on the collective control and the assault helicopter leapt up the front of a steep escarpment. As soon as he crested the ridge he saw his landing zone, a flat area next to some low, well-camouflaged buildings. These he recognised from the briefing notes where they had been marked as vents and entrances to the subterranean mutant base. Rapidly he bled off all the chopper's forward speed and dropped the last few metres to the desert floor. As soon as they made contact with the ground the co-pilot hit the main cabin alert light.

As soon as he saw the light Baccia hauled open the main cabin doors and leapt onto the desert floor his breath rasping through the mask of his all black environment suit. Rapidly he made for the nearest bit of cover, a low mud wall. The rest of the assault squad followed suit and as soon as he was sure that everyone had disembarked, the helicopter pilot lifted off and started a holding circuit some distance from the drop-zone.

All around Baccia assault helicopters were dropping onto the desert floor and emptying their cargoes of troops and equipment. Overhead gunships circled the area, their heavy armament covering the entrance to the mutant base. Baccia opened a channel on his suit radio, 'Gold squad and Blue squad, follow me to the main air vent. Assault squads Green, White and Yellow secure the main entrance. Let's *go* gentlemen!'

The squad leaders didn't reply. They knew better than to advertise their presence by using their radios. They also knew better than to underestimate the mutant fighters. They'd been fighting a long running battle with inhabitants of the waste lands for years. Silently each one cursed the stupidity of Baccia and his insistence that he lead the operation. Some of them were already getting bad vibes about this mission.

Not that any of this worried Baccia. His mind was set on retaliation for the mutant attack on his air station. So long as he got his revenge he didn't much care what his assault troops thought. He ran up to the main air vent that was hidden in a rocky outcrop. As expected he found a small service hatch and ladder that descended into the mutant base. Baccia's plan was very simple. His squad would enter the base here, make their way to the main entrance, open the blast door to allow the rest of the assault force to enter, then they would all systematically sweep through the base, sanitising it as they went. He gestured for the squad leader to enter the service duct first. After all, there was no point in him taking any unnecessary risks.

The assault squads descended first followed by Baccia himself. The ladder descended for maybe fifty metres before exiting into a pumping and filtration room. The pump whined away, pushing purified air through the numerous caverns and galleries of the base, but there was no mutant attendant as might be expected. The assault squad swept the whole room but found nothing. *'By the gods,'* Baccia thought to himself, *'these mutants were a sloppy* bunch. *They deserved to be slaughtered.'* However, from the nervous looks the assault troops were exchanging, it was obvious that they didn't feel the same way.

The pumping room led onto a gallery that ran down at a slope toward the heart of the base. Baccia and his squad headed down the gallery, their assault weapons loosely cradled in their arms. According to plans drawn up by the traitor Tychivesk and passed on to the Group Leader by the Envoy Nimue, the main entrance to the mutant base was controlled from a kiosk in the largest of the underground caverns. This gallery should exit somewhere close to that kiosk, although Baccia was unsure exactly where. He would have to improvise that part when he got to it.

Despite the length of the gallery and the weight of their suits and equipment, they soon reached the large cavern. There they found the large tracked vehicles the mutants had used to bring their equipment and personnel back to the hideout. Baccia smiled, here was evidence that the base had been re-occupied. For a while, he'd been concerned that their quiet reception had meant that the mutants hadn't come back after all, but the proof was before them.

He ordered one of his two squads to sweep through the cavern and check that it was secure. It still bothered him that the mutants hadn't made any attempt to stop them yet. Perhaps the freaks were preoccupied with the rest of the assault force on the desert surface. Blue squad followed him as he looked for the kiosk that operated the main blast doors.

There was a shout from the cavern floor as the troop of Gold squad finally came into contact with some of the mutants. Gunfire reverberated off the sandstone and granite walls. 'Gold squad,' he yelled into his suit mike, 'what is happening down there?'

'We've intercepted a small group of mutants,' the gold squad leader replied. 'They're putting up some resistance, but are lightly armed. They're retreating to a small gallery behind these vehicles. Permission to pursue sir?'

Ah, now this was a bit more like it! At last they were seeing some action! 'Of course you've got bloody permission,' he yelled into the radio. 'What do you think we're here for? Get on with it man!'

Gold leader looked at his sergeant through his face mask and mouthed 'wanker'. The sergeant nodded in agreement. However, orders were orders and they pursued the mutants down a service corridor. The freaks obviously knew what they were doing, because every time the squad got the mutants in the sights of their assault rifles, they rounded a corner in the twisting corridor. After a few minutes of racing down the passageway that descended lower and lower into the base, the squad saw the fugitives run into another cavern.

Foolishly, Gold leader pursued the group straight into the new cavern without pausing for thought. He realised he'd made a fatal mistake when he heard the hiss of two blast doors sealing them into the cavern which was now mysteriously devoid of the group they'd been chasing. In a panic he whirled around and saw that the galleries above them were quite suddenly *filled* with hordes of mutants armed to the teeth. Without thinking he raised his assault rifle—it was the last thing he ever did. His body collapsed like a puppet with the strings cut as his environment suit was shredded by a burst of gunfire. The remainder of Gold squad took one look at their officer and immediately put their weapons down. Within seconds the mutants were swarming all over them, stripping them of their arms and equipment.

Oblivious to the fate of Gold squad, Baccia split the troops of Blue squad, sending half down onto the cavern floor to check for marauding mutants. The remainder followed him along an upper gallery heading for what he believed to be the control kiosk for the main blast doors.

'Group Leader, I'm not getting any response from gold squad leader,' the lieutenant in charge of Blue squad told him. 'They've been gone quite a while now.'

Baccia swore and tried calling the Gold squad leader on his radio. The only response he got was an earful of static. Well, he wasn't going to worry about it too much, he was sure that a bunch of poorly armed, undisciplined freaks were no match for Imperial assault troops. 'I'm sure there's nothing to be worried about lieutenant. It's these underground caverns, they shield radio waves.'

The lieutenant looked at Baccia through his face mask with disgust. The idiot was going to get them all killed! His desire for revenge against the mutants blinded him from even basic military procedure. For a moment he considered shooting the arrogant bastard in the back; it was very tempting but his training took over and he gamely followed the Group

Leader to the control kiosk. As they moved along the gallery the lieutenant's heightened senses registered a movement between a pile of storage crates. Immediately he pulled his rifle to his shoulder and dropped to his haunches. The remaining five of his squad followed suit, their weapons covering the crates. Baccia marched on, unaware of what was happening behind him. The lieutenant shook his head in disbelief—the frigging idiot was in a world of his own. Then everything happened at once. The pile of crates fell down onto the remnants of Blue squad with a crash and Baccia whirled round in alarm but got hit twice in the head. By the time the lieutenant had managed to extricate himself from underneath two heavy crates he found himself staring at a lot of heavily armed, very annoyed mutants. With a sigh he let go of his weapon and motioned for those of his troops still moving, to do the same. The last thing to go through his mind before he was clubbed on the head was that at least Baccia had got what he deserved.

Jenson looked at the dead body of Group Leader Baccia and swore. 'Ah shit! I thought we made it clear that he wasn't to be harmed. We needed him to order the rest of the assault force to move into the cavern!'

Sandpiper raised his hands and shrugged apologetically. 'Heh, boss,' he said, 'it wasn't us! I was there, none of the mutants discharged a weapon. He was shot by one of his own troops!'

'One of his own men? What the hell for?' Jenson asked.

'Apparently the squad leader was completely pissed off that Baccia had led them straight into a trap,' Sandpiper answered kicking the dead Dyason's body with his foot. 'I can see his point of view. These guys are veteran troops used to treating Colmarrie's fighters with extreme respect. Baccia being the arrogant tosser he was, threw caution to the wind and steamed in here guns blazing, just as we thought he would.'

'I guess we'll just have to adjust our plans then.' A thought occurred to him, 'I wonder if Moss is any good at impressions? Han, come with me. We need to have a chat with wonder boy.'

Karatisk figured the safest place on this operation was where he was, sitting in the co-pilot's seat of one of the assault helicopters. When he'd learned at the briefing that one of the assault squadron's aircrew had gone sick, Karatisk had explained his predicament to the squadron commander. The guy owed him a few favours so agreed to let him sit in the right-hand seat of one of his choppers.

Once he'd got over his initial fear and controlled his urge to brown the pants of his flight-suit Karatisk had watched the whole operation with interest. As per plan, Group Leader Baccia and two assault squads had secured the main cavern of the mutant base and opened the main blast doors. The remaining assault squads had stormed into the underground complex and cleared out the mutants. He'd been amazed at the speed and smoothness of the whole operation. Karatisk had always considered the Group Leader to be a complete arse-hole, but he'd have to adjust his thinking now.

'Well frig me!' the chopper pilot exclaimed over the intercom. 'Just for once the frigging operation's gone according to plan! It usually ends up as a frigging disaster with us poor idiots having to extract the soldier boys from the usual shit they get themselves into.'

Karatisk felt his stomach rise to his throat as the pilot dropped the helicopter towards the desert floor. Once more he swallowed the rising bile and regretted ever joining the air service.

'Oh yeah, I forgot to tell you,' the pilot said, 'Baccia's ordered us to land and save on fuel. He wants us to help secure the mutants' hovel. Apparently he's got some bizarre idea of turning the place into an Imperial base.'

The assault chopper landed a few metres from the ramp that descended to the entrance of the mutant base. The pilot cut the ignition, secured the cockpit and climbed out of the machine as the rotor blades slowed to a halt. Karatisk remained in his seat for a few minutes until his stomach had settled and the ringing in his ears had disappeared. Once he was sure that he wasn't going to throw up and he could walk without his legs collapsing from fear underneath him, he followed the pilot.

Out on the desert floor Karatisk could see through the perspex of his face mask that all the other helicopters of the squadron, including the gunships were also on the ground and members of the assault force were securing the rotor-blades and tying the machines down. Obviously, Baccia intended for them to remain here for a few hours at least. He helped the pilot secure their machine then followed the other aircrew down the ramp which was now floodlit. Karatisk saw the Group Leader come towards them and for a moment he thought he was going to get a bollocking for not taking part in the initial attack. Instead Baccia put his hand on his shoulder and said, 'Well done men. Good work. Follow the others down into the cavern and you'll get your orders from there. We really showed these freaks who's in charge.'

For a moment it seemed strange to Karatisk that the Group Leader didn't seem to recognise him or care whether he'd been part of the attack or not. He figured Baccia simply had a lot on his mind. Gamely he followed the pilot down the ramp and into the main cavern. Inside there were dozens of assault troops still in their environment suits, moving equipment around. Karatisk felt sorry for some of them, it looked like the suits were at least two sizes too big or too small. The state of Imperial kit these days was appalling. A lieutenant beckoned them into some sort of operations room that was cut out of the rock itself. They followed the officer into the room and pulled off their face masks as he indicated. Karatisk took three lung-fulls of the sweet tasting air, his head swirled, his vision faded and he collapsed unconscious.

Jenson looked at the hoard of arms, equipment and ammunition they'd taken from the duped Imperial assault troops and smiled. The whole plan had worked better than he'd ever believed possible. The shock troops who had first entered the mutant base had been stupid enough to run straight into traps which had taken them out the game. Then, with Moss imitating Baccia, it had been a simple matter of getting the rest of the Imperial assault team to enter the operations room and knock them out with an anaesthetic gas from the medical centre.

'So what's the number of casualties?' he asked Sandpiper.

'Five Imperial assault troops dead—mainly because they tried to resist. One dead Group Leader and lots of sleeping Imperial squaddies who will wake up in a few hours with serious headaches,' Sandpiper replied with a grin.

'What about casualties on our side?' Jenson asked.

'Three gunshot wounds, none of them serious; one broken arm and one sprained ankle. You have to hand it to the kid boss, that was a brilliant piece of planning. Just for once the cards are in our favour,' Sandpiper answered enthusiastically.

Jenson grinned back at his friend. There was still part of him that regretted that the mantle of command had now been firmly passed on to Moss, but

Sandpiper was right; the kid was a brilliant strategist. For the first time since they'd arrived in the Dyason star system they knew exactly what they were doing and Jenson was one hundred percent behind Moss. Where the lad led he would follow.

Colmarrie and Moss walked over from the Imperial equipment they were looking at and joined Jenson and Sandpiper. 'Are you sure that we can't just chop them all up into little pieces and bury them in the desert?' the tall mutant woman was asking Moss.

'No you can't Colmarrie. How many times do I have to tell you?' Moss said to her somewhat impatiently. 'One day in the not too distant future, the Empire is going to collapse and you and your people will have to rejoin society. You're going to have to get used to the fact that it's wrong to kill prisoners. How do you think a new democratic parliament is going to react to you when it finds out you've been butchering unarmed troops, regardless of the fact that they served the Empire.'

Colmarrie shook her head and shrugged expansively. 'Society, democracy, parliament? These are all concepts that I have trouble understanding friend Moss,' she answered.

Moss looked at Jenson and said in frustration, 'You tell her boss. She won't believe me.'

Jenson suppressed a laugh; he couldn't help liking the mutant leader. She had a very straightforward, very blood-thirsty outlook to life that he had to admire, but unfortunately in this instance Moss was right. 'I'm sorry but he's right Colmarrie, you can't butcher them all in their sleep. Strip them of their environment suits and their weapons yes; keep them locked up, yes, but slitting all their throats no. After all they're no threat to us now.'

'All right, if you say so,' she answered dubiously. 'I'll go along with what you say.'

'That would be greatly appreciated,' Jenson responded. 'Now, what's our status?'

'We should be ready to leave in about three hours,' Moss told him. 'We're supplying Colmarrie's fighters with Imperial kit now and refuelling the choppers from the tankers. We'll have one last briefing before we leave and should arrive at the target point just before dawn.'

'Excellent!' Jenson exclaimed. 'Well you've done a brilliant job so far kid so let's go kick some arse!'

The image of the Imperial guard swam into focus in the lenses of the night-vision binoculars. The small figure of Pollowzki was dwarfed by the cloaked member of the Emperor's personal guard. Hillmead had been against Poll going with Myrddin to the palace, but the weasel-faced policeman had insisted that his contact would only give his assistance if he went along. Apparently, the fracas in the bar had spooked the guard and Poll had had a hard time convincing his contact to collaborate. Entering the palace meant that Pollowzki was risking his own neck but after much argument they'd decided that it was a risk that had to be taken.

The Caranak police had set up a safe house overlooking the entrance to the Imperial palace many years ago. The value of keeping a track on those who visited the palace had long been appreciated and it was from the second-storey window of this safe house that Hillmead kept a look-out. The story of recent events had spread like wildfire through the Caranak police force who had always unofficially had an anti-militarist policy. It was the military that had caused the social misery in all the cities of the Empire and it was the police force who were expected to clean the shit up after them. Now that Shalok and Hillmead had exposed just how much the militarists had screwed the planet, anger amongst the hard-pressed police was boiling just below the surface. Hillmead was able to take comfort from the fact that if push came to shove, the chances were his old colleagues would come down on his side—not that he'd like to prove the theory just yet.

'What's happening?' Shalok whispered into his ear.

'They're at the main gates now,' Hillmead answered. 'Poll has handed over his forged orders and the tame guard is using that funny sign language to communicate to his mate. Myrddin is lingering in the shadows close by. Nobody appears to have seen him.'

'Do you believe he can use his magic, paranormal powers, whatever, to get into the palace?' she asked him taking the binoculars from Hillmead and looking for herself.

'I don't really know to be honest. There have been a lot of stories about the paranormal powers of that old man and the boy Moss. How true they are I guess we're about to find out.' Hillmead took the binoculars back off Shalok and looked at the main gate once more. The wide boulevard outside the palace was quiet. Not many citizens came this way anymore and the only vehicles that passed by were armoured patrol cars belonging to the palace guard.

'Hang on,' he said as the gates opened. 'That's it! Poll and his contact are through the main gates and... bugger me, the old sod's done it! Myrddin's slipped by without anyone seeing him! They're in!'

'That's great,' said Shalok pulling a chair to the window and making herself comfortable. 'Now all we have to do is wait and pray.'

Myrddin followed Pollowzki and the Imperial guard through the inner courtyard and into the main palace. The halls and corridors were quiet at this time of night and he had little problem following the pair without being seen himself. He gently scanned the minds of those nearby and with practised ease, encouraging anybody who might have seen him to *forget* what exactly it was they saw.

The palace was opulent to an extent that was almost sickening, particularly in comparison to the squalor and misery outside the walls in the city. The floors were covered in thick carpet, whilst chandeliers dripping with precious gems hung from high ceilings. Paintings by famous Dyason artists and some human artists were hung everywhere. Myrddin recognised a Rembrandt and a Constable hanging in between Dyason landscapes. All the rooms were filled with furniture taken from every corner of the Empire, apparently without too much thought about their presentation or co-ordination. As he slipped from shadow to shadow, Myrddin's heart sank. Did the Emperor have any idea about just how bad life was outside the security of the palace? Did he even care? The decor and furnishings would indicate not.

Pollowzki and the Imperial guard went through several checkpoints and each time the policeman showed his documents to the officer in charge who examined them then briefly spoke to the collaborating guard. Unlike the guards who protected the Emperor's private chambers Poll's contact still had his tongue although he made great use of sign language as well as speech. In fact, as far as Myrddin could make out all the Imperial guards communicated with each other using sign language backed up by the spoken word. He tried to decipher their sign language and managed to pick out a few phrases, but he would need time they didn't have to completely get to grips with the strange signs.

It occurred to Myrddin that the security surrounding the Emperor was far from strict. The light arms carried by the guard appeared to be more for ceremonial use than as actual weapons of war. There were no infra-red scanners, or metal detectors in sight and Pollowzki had only undergone the most cursory body search. The Dyason high command possibly believed that the Emperor was held in such high esteem by the citizens of the Empire that an attempt on his life was regarded as extremely unlikely. It was equally possible that the lack of security was part of some set-up.

Eventually, they reached the outer chambers of the Emperor's private apartment. Myrddin heard the guard explain to Pollowzki that this was as far as he could escort him. One of the mute personal guards would take him into the Emperor's bed-chamber. Once again the officer in charge of the security surrounding the private apartments checked the documents Poll gave him. Without even barely looking at the document the officer beckoned for one of the mutes in their traditional long red cloaks and burnished steel helmets to show Pollowzki into the bed-chamber. Myrddin followed close behind.

The air inside the bed chamber was rank and stale, with that unmistakable aroma of illness. The mute guard nodded to Pollowzki then turned and left, closing the door behind him. They were on their own. Myrddin slipped out of the shadows and into the light cast by a low wattage table lamp.

'Where's the Emperor?' he asked the weasel-faced policeman.

'He's over there,' Pollowzki nodded towards the darkened end of the room with a cold stony face. Myrddin held the policeman's eye for a moment. A change had come over the small Dyason in the past few hours; Pollowzki had become quiet and withdrawn. Myrddin had at first put this down to pre-mission nerves, but he realised now there was more to it. Quickly he scanned the surface of the policeman's mind, but found nothing. Well, whatever it was, it would have to wait.

Myrddin followed Pollowzki toward the large, ornate, four-poster bed standing at the far end of the room. Heavy curtains were drawn and Myrddin could just discern the sound of laboured breathing. While Pollowzki stood by and watched, he gently pulled one of the curtains aside and peered through the gloom at the figure wrapped up in bed clothes. He reached out a hand and gently shook the shoulder of the Emperor. With a groan the figure rolled over and Myrddin looked into the albino eyes of a wasted body more dead than alive. A wave of revulsion swept through Myrddin as he realised he was looking at the body of a creature who should have died centuries ago. He cursed his sister as he realised that she had broken another of the universe's cardinal rules. Nimue had done the unspeakable, created a monster, a creature of the night. By artificially sustaining the life force of this wretched creature, Nimue had created a zombie—one of the living dead! Myrddin was sickened to the very core of his body.

There was a movement from the other side of the room, Myrddin turned and recognised the figure that emerged from the shadows. The creature in the bed grunted and mumbled, 'Ah Envoy, my sweet *kind* Envoy...'

CHAPTER FIFTEEN

SOMEWHERE IN THE SOUTHERN WASTELANDS

There's the ruins of the monument,' Colmarrie told Moss over the helicopter intercom. 'Are you sure that this is the right place? I can't see anything that looks like an entrance to an underground passage. All the night-scope is showing is a pile of irradiated rubble. I fear your plan is flawed friend Moss.'

Moss looked out of the cabin window at the rubble on the desert floor. There still wasn't enough pre-dawn light to see anything but vague shapes, but Moss was almost certain this was the right place. 'Trust me Colmarrie,' he replied, 'the entrance is down there okay. You just get us on the ground and I'll do the rest. Have faith.'

'I'm doing my best, I really am friend Moss,' the mutant leader replied from the pilot's seat of the stolen Imperial assault chopper. She eased off the cyclic control and the helicopter gently sank toward the desert floor. 'But tell me, what makes you believe that there is another entrance to the caverns containing the ancient starship, here?'

'Jennifer told me that Gulag found one entrance to the caverns containing Dominator by examining most of Dyason's ancient and prehistoric monuments. We found Excalibur on Earth, under a ring of stone monoliths known as Stonehenge. Gulag found the Dominator under the foundations of an ancient temple. So it seems sensible to suppose that some ancient sites were built on top of the entrances to these underground caverns,' Moss explained quickly. 'I believe the chambers that contain the Dominator are very similar in design to those that entombed Excalibur, in which case there will be more than one entrance into the caverns. This is the only site of ancient ruins near enough to the main entrance to fit the criteria. Therefore the second entrance is down there somewhere.'

'I understand that,' Colmarrie responded as the rotor-blades of the helicopter wound down. 'What I don't understand is how you intend to open an entrance that has been sealed from the world since the dawn of time.'

'Wait and see Colmarrie, wait and see,' Moss replied mysteriously.

Sandpiper opened the main cabin door and jumped out onto the desert floor. Jenson and Moss passed their back-packs and weapons down to Sandpiper then climbed out themselves. Colmarrie clambered out of the cockpit and helped the others don their equipment and seal their environment suits. The mutant leader, having a natural tolerance to the background radiation and polluted air strolled around in her loose desert clothing, distracting Sandpiper who had decided that a short stocky human male and a giant mutant Dyason woman could have a lot of fun together.

'Behave Han,' Jenson admonished, noting the look on his friend's face. 'Try and concentrate on the job at hand.'

Sandpiper tore his eyes away from Colmarrie's fit figure. 'Hum...What? Oh, yeah, sorry boss,' he mumbled.

Moss strode over to the few remaining stones that marked the site of the ancient ruin, took his glove off and touched one of the ancient blocks of stone. Images from the past swam into his mind like clips from a film. The day the once fertile lands of the area were nuked by the Empire flashed past his inner eye, as did many other important events in the history of the ancient site. However, Moss wasn't interested in the recent past, he was only interested in the distant, prehistoric past. The images flashed through his mind faster and faster until they were a blur, passing too fast for him to consciously recall what he was seeing. He mentally promised himself that one day when his life was a little less hectic, he would spend some time analysing the history being imprinted on his mind.

Gradually the speed at which the stone's history flooded into his head eased, indicating that Moss had neared the day the ancient site came into existence. In his mind's eye he saw an ancient, noble civilisation erecting a beautiful temple on the site they believed to be sacred. One by one he saw the huge stones being hauled by man and beast from a quarry many kilometres from the site. Then as the history rewound he saw nomads watching bright lights in the sky—lights that emanated from a magical orifice in the ground. Back even further, back at the beginning of time, Moss saw a huge starship descend from the heavens and sink slowly into the ground where it had remained entombed ever since. With a sigh Moss stood upright. This was the place all right. All he needed to do was to open the ancient passageway for the first time in several millennia. Moss gathered his will and extended his mind, searching for the hidden entrance.

Colmarrie stood with Jenson and Sandpiper watching carefully as Moss caressed one of the ancient stones. She could feel the telepathic contact Moss had with the ancient ruin, but despite her own telepathic talent she couldn't read what he was receiving. She felt Moss gather, then release his mental power at the ruins. To her amazement the ruins began to pulse with a light that became more and more intense until it was too bright to look at. When the light finally faded an area several metres square became translucent, then disappeared completely. Where only a moment ago had been solid rock, there was now an entrance and ramp descending down into the desert floor. Colmarrie couldn't believe what she'd just seen. Like everyone she'd heard the stories about these mythical humans who had defeated the might of the Imperial Navy, now for the first time she knew that all the rumours and stories were true!

Moss turned and looked at the others with a triumphant grin. 'Ye of little faith!' he declared. 'What did I tell you?'

'I'm impressed!' Colmarrie enthused. 'Never would I have believed such a thing was possible!'

Sandpiper blew a raspberry through the respirator of his face mask. 'I've seen him do better,' he declared dryly.

'Me too,' Jenson joined in.

Colmarrie looked at the pair in horror. 'How could you say such a thing!' she demanded. 'It is a *miracle!*'

Jenson and Sandpiper looked at each other, shrugged and ambled off to the newly created entrance. Colmarrie looked at the humans in disbelief.

'It's okay Colmarrie,' Moss told her telepathically, *'they're just taking the piss—it's their way of dealing with the unusual. Anyway, we'd better get moving and you'd better get back to your fighters. Remember, cause as much havoc as you can, but don't hit those bunkers. We don't want to risk damaging the caverns below. We'll keep in touch using mind-link. Good luck my friend!'*

'I will do my best,' Colmarrie responded, *'Good luck to you too.'* She stood long enough to see the humans disappear into the underground passage, then clambered back into the stolen assault helicopter and started the rotors.

Jennifer found Josh Brabazon buried in the depths of some service duct in the powerplant control room of the Dominator. He looked like shit, with several days' stubble on his chin, his flight suit stained and ripped and a wild look in his eyes. He squatted beside a panel of circuit breakers, analysing them with a diagnostic scanner. One of the Dyason technicians sat next to him watching the scanner readout.

'No, no, no! Not that setting you imbecile! That one!' Brabazon yelled at the unfortunate technician. 'Do I have to do everything myself?'

Jennifer was horrified. This wasn't the easy-going Josh Brabazon she knew. Something had happened to the wiry scientist; he was driving himself to an early grave and she couldn't understand why. Even during their darkest hours onboard the Excalibur, Brabazon had never behaved like this.

She clambered into the service duct and approached the scientist. 'Josh,' she called to him, 'take it easy. Why are you pushing yourself so hard?'

Brabazon ignored her and continued to probe the circuit panel. 'Josh!' she tried again. 'For God's sake answer me! What's got into you? Why are you behaving this way?'

He continued to ignore her and kept jabbing his probe at the circuit board mumbling quietly to himself. The Dyason technician didn't understand English but got the drift of what was going on. As quietly as possible he slipped out of the service duct and made himself scarce. Brabazon didn't even notice he'd gone.

Jennifer shook Brabazon by the arm, 'Josh! Snap out of it! Josh!' He shrugged her off and continued his work without even acknowledging her presence. Desperately, Jennifer extended her thoughts and probed the mind of her friend. His mental shields were firmly locked, but she continued to probe, praying for some clue to his bizarre behaviour.

Without warning a blinding pain lanced through her mind and she was thrown against the side of the service duct. Immediately she slammed her own mental shields shut, but the damage had already been done. She lay there in a semi-conscious state.

When she eventually came to her senses and the effects of the mental attack had dissipated, Jennifer found herself alone, still in the service duct. Brabazon had completed his work, closed up the access hatch and left her lying there. Groggily she dragged herself out of the duct and made her way to the nearest turbo-lift. She was intercepted halfway by her female escort.

'By the gods! Jennifer what happened?' the Dyason woman asked with genuine concern. 'I looked away for a moment and you'd gone. I've been looking for you everywhere for the past three-quarters of an hour!'

Jennifer let her escort take some of her weight and help her into the turbo-lift. 'I'm okay,' she said, her head still spinning. 'I must talk to Gulag. It's Josh Brabazon, something strange has happened to him and I think I know what it is!'

Gulag sat in the commander's chair on the bridge of the Dominator reviewing the progress reports on the starship's restoration. The speed of the completion of repairs since the arrival of Josh Brabazon and the awakening of the main computer was incredible. Except for a few secondary systems the ancient vessel was now fully functional. Jobs that were taking months before had been completed in a matter of days. The master plan was nearing fruition.

The doors to the turbo-lift opened and Jennifer staggered onto the bridge, helped by her escort. Gulag leapt out of his chair and went to help her, but before he could touch her she held up her hand to ward him off shouting, 'Keep away from me you cloned bastard! This is your doing!' The bridge suddenly went quiet as everyone stopped to watch the human woman and the clone.

Gulag stopped in mid stride, a look of surprise on his face, 'I don't know what you're talking about Jennifer,' he said in as reasonable a tone as he could muster. Instinctively he realised that whatever was wrong needed to be handled carefully. 'Please have a seat and tell me exactly what's wrong.'

Jennifer ignored the offer of a seat and clung to the support rail that went around the bridge. 'You know exactly what I'm talking about shit-bag!' she spat at him. 'What have you done to Brabazon?'

'Josh?' Gulag shook his head in confusion. 'I've done nothing to him at all. He's taken over the repairs of the Dominator and he's doing a brilliant job. You have to believe me though, it's entirely at his own discretion. I haven't coerced him into it—far from it in fact.'

'Really? So why's he got that glazed look in his eye? Why's he not eating or sleeping? How long can he keep going like that until he dies of exhaustion?' she demanded, jabbing a finger at

Gulag. 'You're telling me you've got nothing to do with that? You haven't invaded his mind?'

Gulag was genuinely concerned. Now that Jennifer had told him, he realised that Josh Brabazon had been behaving a little strangely, but he'd put that down to enthusiasm for the project. 'I swear to you Jennifer that I don't know what you're talking about. I most definitely have *not* made any attempt to control Josh Brabazon's mind. His knowledge and talent is far too valuable to risk in such a manner.'

'Yeah and you're going to tell me next that you had nothing to do with that mental bolt he fired at me only an hour ago?' she retorted her eyes still wide with anger. 'I know Josh's mind and I can tell you he isn't capable of such a strike! It nearly killed me!'

Mental bolt? Now this *was* serious. Gulag knew that he had nothing to do with that. In which case, if Jennifer were right and he had no reason to disbelieve her, then somebody or some*thing* else was controlling the human scientist. The speed at which the repairs to Dominator were being carried out and Brabazon's condition had to be connected and he suspected he knew the cause of the problem. It occurred to him that the main computer of Dominator was more capable than he had given it credit for!

'Look Jennifer I promise this has nothing to do with me! Now, I'll order the medics to take a look at Brabazon and find out if there is anything wrong with him okay? I'm sure he just needs a good...Gulag was cut short by a warning klaxon reverberating through the entire ship. His attention immediately switched to the operations officer. 'What's going on ops?' he demanded.

The ops officer punched at his control panel and an image of the desert floor appeared on the main viewer. Clearly glinting in the early morning sunshine was a squadron of Imperial assault choppers strafing the bunkers and hangars of the experimental launch site.

'The site of the main entrance is under attack from a force of Imperial assault troops sir!' the ops officer told him, his voice registering surprise.

'What do you mean we're under attack from Imperial troops. Don't be ridiculous!' he shouted, running to the operations desk. Quickly he scanned the video images from security cameras mounted on the desert floor. There was no doubt about it the main entrance was under attack! They'd been betrayed! Somebody in the military hierarchy had got to hear about the Dominator and was mounting a bid to take the ship. The chaos had begun!

'Execute the defence plan!' he ordered. 'I want troops on the desert floor and I want those bunkers kept secure at all costs. We can't risk damage to the cavern structure.' The operations officer began to quick-fire orders into his headset and the rest of the bridge team snapped into action. Gulag turned to Jennifer and said, 'Jennifer, scan my mind and you'll find that I'm telling the truth when I say that I had nothing to do with the attack against you. I promise we *will* find out what's going on—later though, I have to deal with this crisis first.'

For a brief moment Gulag's mind was open and Jennifer realised he was indeed telling the truth. She also saw his fear that perhaps the sentient computer of the Dominator wasn't as benign as he'd believed. She sat down at the spare console and watched the proceedings. She'd just learned two very important facts. Firstly, that Gulag wasn't in total control of the situation and secondly, Moss was on his way to fetch her.

EMPEROR'S PRIVATE APARTMENT, IMPERIAL PALACE, CARANAK

'Ah, dearest brother! What a *pleasure* it is to see you again,' Nimue crooned as she stepped into the pool of light shed by a small lamp.

Myrddin looked at his sister. She wore a long velvet-hooded cloak over her Imperial uniform and her long leather jack-boots gleamed despite the dim light. 'I wish I could say the same Nimue, I really do,' he replied with regret, 'but it would appear that once more I arrive to find that you have broken the most fundamental laws of the universe. Do you remember *nothing* of your teachings?'

'I remember that the "*meek shall inherit the Earth*", but I've learnt that the *strong* shall inherit the universe. Besides, this is tiresome; we've had this conversation before brother. It achieved nothing then and it shall achieve nothing now.' Nimue strode over to the bed and looked down at the feeble body of the Emperor of Dyason who reached out to her with a skeletal hand murmuring, 'My Envoy, my *sweet* Envoy.' Nimue ignored him.

'So tell me,' Myrddin asked looking into the dark eyes of his sister. 'How long has he been like this. How long has he been drinking your life-force?

Nimue kept looking into the albino eyes of the Emperor, her mind lost in the past. 'Three hundred and forty seven years,' she replied. 'Once he was the king of a small country here on the continent of Claxocia. I was his mistress and advisor.'

'Then he grew old while you stayed young?' Myrddin asked guessing how events unfolded.

'Yes,' Nimue answered. 'As always happens when you fall in love with a mortal. He grew old, became weak and senile, whilst I kept my youth and beauty. It's strange,' she went on with a sincerity Myrddin had never heard in her voice before, 'but I really *did* love him when he was young. The foundations of the Empire we built together was a wonderful achievement that I couldn't bear to see collapse. As he grew older, he became incapable of holding the kingdom together let alone an embryonic empire.'

'So you decided to break all the laws of nature and keep him alive albeit in a permanent state of half-death? That was a foolish thing to do sister.'

'Pah!' Nimue spat at her brother. 'What would you know about love and ambition? *You* who have led such a barren life?'

Myrddin chose to ignore the jibe and said, 'So you became the secret Empress, deciding the fate of millions but keeping your zombie for those state occasions? You kept him just sufficiently alive so that he could put his mark on official documents and give you access to the Imperial seal. Over the centuries it's been *you* behind the events that have shaped this planet. In fact you've been manipulating the Dyason ever since you arrived here—haven't you?'

'And whose fault is that?' she snarled at him, her voice dripping venom. 'After you forced me through the space-time continuum I was lost for aeons, floating between dimensions and worlds. What did you expect me to do once I made my way back to my own universe? Did you really expect me to keep my talents hidden? Did you expect me to spend eternity ignoring my destiny? If you thought that then you're a bigger fool than I took you for Myrddin.'

'Congratulations my sister,' Myrddin commented dryly. 'You've managed to create a world-wide Empire. It's just a shame that you committed genocide and destroyed the planet's biosphere in the process—that must have taken some doing. Tell me, what are you going to do now? Now that this planet you completely screwed up is going to die?'

Nimue whirled on Myrddin and for a moment anger contorted the coldly beautiful features of her face. 'How *pitiful* you are brother. Your complete inability to perceive the grander scheme never ceases to amaze me. Can't you see that this is just one of *millions* of planets? That the races that occupy Dyason are but a drop in the ocean compared to the number of civilisations that exist across this and all the other countless galaxies? My job is done here, I have achieved what I set out to do and you helped me achieve it. My inheritance, my prize the Dominator, will be ready to journey to the stars any day now. On board will be the finest minds, those with the strongest wills, the cream that Dyason has to offer. Together we will set out to create an Empire that covers not just continents, but whole star systems!'

'I presume you consider creatures like Gulag to be the finest that Dyason has to offer? Doe's he know that he's a clone of the pitiful creature that lies here; that he is, in fact, a perfect copy of the Emperor? Does he know that he's been created so that you need never again be without your young lover?' Myrddin taunted, his face set like granite. 'Do you have any idea just how much he hates *you!*'

Nimue tilted her head back and laughed, 'Come on Myrddin, you can do better than that! You don't really think I'd fall for such a pathetic lie?'

Myrddin shook his head; her arrogance blinded her to truth just as much now as it did in their childhood all those aeons ago. 'Well you've made a huge effort to get us all here to Dyason. Your clever scheming has brought me before you, now the inevitable question is why? You've got the Dominator, what do you want with the rest of us?' he asked.

Nimue stood up, paced across the chamber and turned on him, a look of glee on her face, 'Even *now* you don't get it, do you brother? You've been led by the nose and you don't know why!'

'Why don't you explain it to me then?' Myrddin asked, knowing that Nimue could never resist the urge to show her brother just how clever she was. It had always been one of her weaknesses.

'I hate loose ends Myrddin,' she began. 'Of course we needed the expertise of Josh Brabazon to restore Dominator to space-worthiness and I knew that any scheme to bring him here would inevitably include the rest of you, which gave me the perfect opportunity to complete unfinished business. When we finally leave in the Dominator I would prefer not to have Excalibur chasing us across the galaxy, so I came up with a simple plan.

'That piece of space junk you believed was the original Dominator is in fact a fully operational battle-station now equipped with several squadrons of brand new X34 Snub-fighters. What you *don't* know Myrddin is that as we speak the Excalibur is travelling through a worm-hole to Dyason.' Myrddin did his best not to show his surprise. Nimue was right, he didn't know that the Excalibur was on its way to Dyason. He wasn't even aware that a new worm-hole had opened. The question was *who* had opened it?

'As soon as the Excalibur enters the star system she will be attacked by the X34 fighters,' Nimue merrily continued to explain her master plan to her captive audience. 'Then of course the battle-station will bring her massive weapons to bear. Their awesome combined fire-power is more than adequate to obliterate the Excalibur. Of course, all this activity will keep the militarists occupied and probably lead to the demise of quite a few of the Imperial Navy's new toys, but that can't be helped.

'Then of course, you will be caught having assassinated the Emperor here in these chambers. That action and all the stories spread by your new friends Shalok and Hillmead will split the already strained political factions. Civil war instigated by the Democratic Front will ensue and in all the chaos, I and a chosen few will launch the Dominator and leave for the new frontier. The biosphere will collapse and the planet will die in a matter of weeks from now, along with any of you who happen to survive the final civil war. As I said Myrddin, I *hate* loose ends!'

Myrddin turned and looked at the weasel faced policeman who covered him with an automatic pistol. He could see that Pollowzki's face was troubled; obviously some or all of what Nimue had said was news to him. 'What did she offer you Poll?' he demanded. 'What did she offer that was worth selling out your friends? How many pieces of gold!'

Pollowzki waved the muzzle of the pistol in Myrddin's face and snarled, 'Shut it you old git! You took me for a fool from the moment we met, you arrogant bastard! Well, I'm no fool! I know that all the gold in the world will be worthless in a few weeks' time. What's the point in having riches when there's nothing to spend them on? Whilst the other fools have been running around fighting their *oh, so noble* cause, I've been working my passage. I'm guaranteed a place on that starship—isn't that right Envoy?'

Nimue pretended not to hear what the treacherous Dyason said; instead she absently stroked the wrinkled, bald pate of the Emperor.

Pollowzki kept the pistol aimed at Myrddin but looked over his shoulder at the Envoy, 'I said, I'm guaranteed a place on that starship—isn't that *right* Nimue?'

She looked up and waved dismissively with her hand saying, 'Yes, yes, whatever. This is getting very boring. Kill the Emperor now, then call the guards. I want them to find Myrddin with a smoking gun still in his hands. It's been nice talking dearest brother, but you must excuse me now. I have pressing matters to attend...'

Myrddin saw the uncertainty on the traitor's face. Nimue had failed to convince him that she was going to keep to her side of the bargain. Too late the weasel had realised that he had sold his soul to the devil without getting a guarantee. This would be the only opportunity Myrddin would have to save both himself and the pitiful wretch that was the Emperor. He flung himself onto the bed, covering the frail Emperor's body with his own. As he jumped, he gathered his will about himself like armour and projected his mind. He saw where he wanted to be, gripped the Emperor as hard as he dared and pushed toward the vision.

Pollowzki was taken completely by surprise by the ancient human's apparently illogical action. Nimue screamed and gathered her will to counteract her brother's spell, but she was too late. There was a rushing sound and the still air in the bed-chamber instantly became a maelstrom of swirling air fighting to fill a vacuum. Flashes of lightning arced across the room. The figures of Myrddin and the Emperor faded, became insubstantial then disappeared.

Pollowzki belatedly pulled the trigger of his automatic and emptied a clip at the translucent images but by the time the room returned to normal their bodies had gone and the empty bed was shredded by gunfire.

CHAPTER SIXTEEN

THE CAVERNS OF THE ENTOMBED DOMINATOR

Moss estimated that they'd covered at least several kilometres. The tunnel had descended gently for all that time never deviating from course. Although they carried torches in their back packs there was sufficient light available not to need them. As they travelled through the passage the strange crystalline structure of the rock glowed gently, showing them the way. As far as Moss could tell it was the same material that lined the caverns and passages that had surrounded the Excalibur when she was entombed below Stonehenge.

They said nothing as they moved quickly and quietly, weapons at the ready. Judging by the undisturbed dust on the tunnel floor, nobody but themselves had travelled the route for at least several millennia. However, that didn't mean they wouldn't encounter a squad of Gulag's troops at any time. Eventually the tunnel levelled out and finally ended at what could only be described as an ornate piece of rock. A huge piece of what appeared to be solid granite completely blocked the tunnel. Chiselled onto its face were numerous hieroglyphics, some depicting scenes from a long-lost civilisation, others completely indecipherable.

'What do you reckon Moss?' Jenson whispered as they examined the rock carefully. 'Looks like this passage has been blocked off. Maybe that's why this tunnel's never been used.'

Moss examined the material of the obstacle carefully. 'I don't think so,' he finally replied. 'The material of this stone is the same as that used at Stonehenge back on Earth. It has a similar unusual property. It's here to stop unauthorised entry to whatever is beyond. I think the civilisation that built the temple on the surface, discovered this tunnel and that rock. Looks to me like they used it as an object of worship, but never managed to get past it.'

Sandpiper pointed to what looked like chisel marks at the edges of the monolith. 'See here?' he asked. 'Looks to me like someone tried to get a lever in here, maybe a spear or sword, and attempted to move the rock. Obviously without any joy, it's far too large.'

'The question is; are we going to have any joy?' Jenson asked looking pointedly at Moss.

Moss shrugged his shoulders and placed a palm on the rock. 'It's a question of authority. I'm hoping that the authority that gives me access to Excalibur, also gives me authority to gain access to Dominator. It's worth a try anyway.' He motioned for Jenson and Sandpiper to move back to a safe distance, then he gathered his will and extended his mind to probe the monolith. There was a small rushing noise, a whisper of a breeze in the tunnel and the monolith became translucent then apparently disappeared. 'Looks like I *have* got the authority,' Moss said with a shrug, looking at his friends. 'Well don't just stand there. What are you waiting for; an invitation? Let's go!'

Jenson and Sandpiper looked at each other, shook their heads then followed Moss into the chamber beyond. As soon as they stepped over the threshold into the chamber the rock reappeared as solid as before. 'Oh well, I wasn't planning on going back that way anyhow,' Sandpiper quipped with only a hint of nervousness.

'Where are we?' Jenson asked looking around. He noted the marble floor and recesses cut into the rock walls that looked like they were shaped for parking your rear on. 'It looks like some sort of reception area or entrance hall.'

Moss walked over to a cluster of crystals set into a podium at the centre of the chamber. He played his hands over the crystals and fresh water began to tumble into a basin cut into the strange rock structure. 'That's exactly what this is,' Moss told them. 'If you remember when we first encountered Myrddin in the caverns that surrounded Excalibur, his personal quarters were laid out like this. It would seem logical that these chambers are for the same purpose.'

'Does that mean we're about to meet another old boy with some strange ideas?' Sandpiper asked removing his face mask and splashing water over his sweaty face.

Moss pulled his own face mask off and joined Sandpiper by the basin. 'I don't think so, Han,' he answered wetting a rag from his suit and wiping his face. 'So far as I can tell, on this planet Nimue and Gulag play the same role as Myrddin and myself. If everything had gone according to the master plan, Nimue would be down here dispensing wisdom to a fresh faced Gulag.'

'So what went wrong?' Jenson asked filling his canteen and drinking some of the sweet tasting water.

'God knows?' Moss shrugged. 'For whatever reason, the plan all went to pot. Gulag blasted his way into the caverns from another direction, Nimue's a head case, and everything's turning to shit.'

Jenson picked his weapon up once more and packed his face mask away. The sensors built into his watch declared the air being circulated throughout the chambers to be pure. 'Well, idle speculation isn't going to get us anywhere boys,' he told them. 'If these chambers follow the same ground plan as those on Earth, then we shouldn't have any trouble finding the main cavern containing the Dominator. Colmarrie's diversion isn't going to last forever, so we'd better get a move on.'

Moss and Sandpiper nodded and picked up their weapons. Then with Moss leading they set off down another passageway heading for the Dominator.

Colmarrie fired another burst at the troops dug in around a bunker then swooped down to strafe a row of buildings. So far, everything had gone according to plan. Kitted out in Imperial environment suits and carrying Imperial weapons, the mutant fighters had dropped from the stolen attack helicopters and struck at the experimental launch site at first light. Once on the ground the fighters had dug in around the perimeter of the site and as ordered by Moss, they'd avoided using any weapons heavier than mortars in an attempt to keep collateral damage to a minimum.

Within minutes of starting the attack, troops wearing environment suits of a style never seen before began to vigorously defend the site which only a few minutes previously had appeared to be deserted. Colmarrie as one of the few experienced pilots amongst her people had remained airborne orchestrating the attack from the air. She was glad that her fighters had dug positions around the perimeter of the site before they had begun the attack—the clone's troops were well trained and disciplined. Their covering fire was accurate and her people were taking casualties. However, the diversion was at least having the effect they had hoped for, drawing attention away from Moss, Jenson and Sandpiper.

She was just about to start another strafing run when she heard a call from one of the other gunship pilots. 'We have company Colmarrie,' the pilot told her, 'there are six attack helicopters moving rapidly on our position. Three klicks and closing.'

Colmarrie's pulse quickened and adrenaline surged through her veins. Although she'd taken every opportunity in the past to practise her flying skills in the helicopters used for communications among the various mutant bases, she had never flown in aerial combat before. However, true to her nature she would rise to the challenge! She tightened her straps, hauled the assault chopper around and headed for the six specks just visible low on the horizon heading toward them. 'Okay I see them Davish!' she called. 'Beta flight follow me and engage those gunships.

Don't let them get near the ground units—they'll decimate them! Alpha flight keep strafing those bunkers; keep the pressure up.'

The flight leaders acknowledged and before Colmarrie had time to say anything more, they were engaging the gunships. Colmarrie went head on to the lead gunship waiting for the last second before she opened fire. For a moment she feared they were going to collide, but the gunship bottled out and hauled on the collective. It nosed up exposing its belly to Colmarrie's chain-gun. Cannon shells ripped into the gunship's underside as her bigger assault chopper dived underneath. As soon as she'd passed her opponent she kicked on the rudder pedals and the tail shot round aided by the torque of the rotor heads. The chopper turned through one hundred and eighty degrees, just in time for her to see her target sink to the desert floor, smoke and flames pouring from its turbine. She grinned to herself triumphantly—scratch one bogey!'

'Colmarrie, we've located the Dominator,' Moss's thought entered her mind. *'We should be onboard soon. How's the diversion going?'*

'We had been doing well until a few minutes ago my friend,' she thought back at him. *'We've got the clone's troops pinned down by those bunkers as per our plan, but there has been a small complication...'*

'What kind of complication?' Moss demanded in alarm.

'We've been engaged by gunships. Presumably they're part of the clone's forces,' she responded tracking another gunship that was attempting to

engage one of Beta flight. *'My pilots have not been trained in aerial combat, but we are doing our best.'*

'Damn! I hadn't considered that eventuality,' Moss told her. *'Stick with it Colmarrie we just need another few minutes.'*

'We shall do our best friend Moss,' Colmarrie answered then severed the mental link. The next gunship was sitting slap in her sights. She closed in on the second bogey as it peppered Beta four with gunfire. Carefully she lowered the collective and her chopper dropped below the gunship; then just as her new target was closing in for the kill on Beta four she opened up with the chain-gun. Once more her cannon shells ripped into her opponent. The results this time were quite different—the shells shredded the gunship's tail unit. The blades of the tail rotor flew off in all directions as the mechanism disintegrated and the gunship began to spin around its own axis, completely out of control. In a matter of seconds it side-slipped toward the desert, spinning all the time until it struck the side of a small canyon and exploded in a fireball.

'Thanks for that Colmarrie!' Beta-four called over the radio, 'I thought my time had come then!

'Your time will be when I say it is Taligshi!' she responded with a laugh. This was a *fine* way to engage combat!

However, the celebration of her second victory was cut short when she felt the impact of cannon fire somewhere behind her in the main cabin of the helicopter. Instinctively she let the machine plummet toward the ground then hauled on the collective before she was turned into scrap metal. Unfortunately the smaller, lighter gunship on her tail was prepared for her move and followed her down, firing all the time. Colmarrie felt more impacts somewhere in the bowels of her machine, which began to vibrate alarmingly. She pushed the nose down and followed the line of the cavern a scant few metres above the desert floor. The gunship followed close behind following her every move, peppering her machine at each opportunity. The vibration in the airframe increased until she could barely hang on to the controls they were shaking so much. She knew that the chopper was fatally damaged and her remaining time in the air could now be measured as only a matter of minutes.

The bunkers of the launch site came into view and in a last ditch attempt to get rid of the gunship she flew low over her own positions. As if reading her mind, a blow-pipe missile streaked away from a dug-out and struck the attacking gunship amidships. Colmarrie saw her opponent disintegrate in a blaze of pyrotechnics at the same moment that the turbine of her machine finally threw a blade and ground to a screaming halt. This was the moment she'd dreaded, the moment where she had to time her movements to the split second. Without power, the main rotors were wind-milling. The helicopter fell out of the sky dropping like a stone, but as the machine fell the rotors were accelerating in speed. Colmarrie saw the ground rushing toward her and just as it seemed certain she was going to be smashed to pieces she hauled on the collective pitch. The acceleration of the main rotor was turned into lift as the angle of the blades changed, biting into the air.

The descent of the helicopter was arrested and it hit the desert floor with enough speed to collapse the undercarriage, but not enough to destroy the machine.

Colmarrie didn't hang around waiting for the shot-up chopper to catch fire. She released her straps and clambered out of the cockpit. Members of a mutant fighting unit reached her before her feet touched the ground. They dragged her to a dug-out just as fuel from a punctured tank ignited sending flames leaping up into the desert air. Colmarrie stood and watched the helicopter burn and crackle. By the gods that had been a rush she would *never* forget!

Shalok was peering out of the window, watching the Imperial palace when she noticed what appeared to be small flashes of lightning dancing across the window frame. At first she had presumed the spectacular light display was caused by some sort of storm outside, but after watching the flashes for a few seconds she realised with a shock that the dancing light was actually on the inside of the window. Hillmead noticed the flashes of light and heard the rumbling noise that sounded like a approaching thunder. 'What the...' he murmured putting the binoculars down and turning around.

The air in the room came alive like a tornado picking up old bits of newspaper, rubbish and fast-food cartons and hurling them around. There was a blinding flash of light that made them jump into each other's arms and Shalok gave a small scream. Then as quickly as it began the room returned to normal, except for the body holding what looked like a bundle of rags huddled in a corner.

'God, how I *hate* doing that!' Myrddin mumbled, then gave out a loud groan. Sweat poured from his flushed face and he struggled to rise from the floor.

Hillmead and Shalok rushed over and helped him get to his feet. 'By the gods, where the hell did you turn up from Myrddin? ' Hillmead asked completely stunned by the human's dramatic arrival, 'and what's that bundle of rags you're carry...?' His jaw dropped when he saw the emancipated figure. Shalok put a fist in her mouth and gagged. 'Oh *god*!' she whispered.

Still breathing hard, as if he'd just completed a marathon Myrddin placed the weakly moving skeletal figure on the floor and gripped it's feeble hand. He looked up at Hillmead and Shalok and with a voice of steel said, 'There's no time to explain. There are events in motion that you will find hard to grasp, but that zombie before you is the Emperor!'

'That's the Emperor!' Hillmead stuttered in horror and surprise. 'I hope you're joking!'

'I wish I was,' Myrddin replied kneeling over the rambling Emperor. 'Now listen the pair of you! There isn't much time; I'm about to do something that will possibly change your view on the universe forever. If you don't want that to happen then look away now!'

Hillmead and Shalok looked at each other then back at Myrddin. 'I think it's a bit late for that!' Shalok told him. 'What the hell's going on? How did you get here? What do you intend to do?

Myrddin sighed wearily. 'You'll have to trust me when I say there's no time for explanations. Turn away or watch, the choice is yours,' he told them. He leant over the Emperor, looked into his albino eyes and said, 'I wish I didn't have to do this, but I can't see any other option.'

Then he raised his face to the ceiling and lifted his arms outstretched, palms raised. Myrddin began a chant that began as no more than a whisper but gradually increased in volume. Once again the air in the room felt charged, full of static. There was a rumble and another flash of lightning, but this time the source was outside the room, not inside it. Shalok looked out of the window and saw a mass of broiling clouds gathering above the city. Lightning flashed constantly through the mass, creating strange colours that changed and moved like a living, moving creature. The wind picked up, rapidly becoming a howling gale that battered at the ancient window panes. Myrddin's chant became louder and more intense until he was shouting for all his worth to be heard above the sound of the horrendous storm that had come from nowhere and was battering the city.

Shalok's head began to spin and whirl as if the storm were also inside her head. She collapsed to her knees and placed her hands against her temples fearing that her head would explode any minute. She felt as if she were being drained, as if the storm were somehow sapping her energy. Hillmead also collapsed to his knees and began to groan in pain.

Myrddin's chant reached a crescendo and he screamed at the storm that seemed to be both inside the room as well as in the skies above. He brought his hands together in a crash and the skeletal body of the Emperor was surrounded in a blue-green nimbus that shimmered, ebbed and flowed. The nimbus increased in strength until Shalok had to turn away, the light too bright for her to look directly at. Her head felt as if it was about to explode and she heard herself screaming at the top of her lungs...

The nimbus faded and died; the storm clouds that had gathered so quickly over the city, just as quickly dispersed and a strange silence befell Caranak.

Shalok slowly opened her eyes, waiting for them to become accustomed to the dark once more. Her head still hurt, but the feeling of sapping energy had disappeared. When her eyes finally became accustomed to the gloom once more, she saw Myrddin collapsed spent on the floorboards. She clambered over to the human and lifted his head onto her knee. His eyes flickered open and he smiled weakly smiled. 'It's okay Shalok,' he said hoarsely, 'I'll be fine in a couple of minutes. What about the Emperor?'

Hillmead got to his feet and staggered over. He took one look at the figure of the Emperor and whispered, 'I don't believe it!'

Shalok followed his gaze and looked into the face of Alorne the third, Emperor of Dyason. She looked into the firm face of a well-muscled man in his late fifties, she looked into the face of the Emperor that had always smiled down benevolently from the pictures hung from her bedroom wall. The horrific, skeletal zombie, with its flaky skin and wheezing voice had gone. She raised a hand to her mouth and tears ran down her cheek. Instinctively she knew what Myrddin had done; he had drawn upon the energy of the citizens that still loved their Emperor and let *them* create a leader of their own image.

Hillmead knelt beside the revitalised body and as it opened its eyes and sat up with a groan he said in an awed whisper, 'You're right Myrddin, you *have* changed my view of the universe forever. May the gods preserve us!'

CHAPTER SEVENTEEN

What's the situation?' Gulag demanded of the operations officer on the bridge.

'We're holding the bunkers, but the Imperial troops have dug in around the perimeter of the launch site,' the ops officer told him from his control station. 'I ordered the launch of our six gunships to intercept and engage their assault helicopters which they're now doing. The situation would appear to be a stalemate for now, or at least until the Imperial troops get reinforcements.'

Gulag sat in the captain's chair and tapped on the arm thoughtfully, 'Why didn't they press forward their attack in the first few minutes when our defences were vulnerable?' Gulag asked. 'These assault troops aren't acting like normal Imperial troops. I can understand why they haven't been using heavy weapons. They'll be just as keen to avoid damaging the caverns as we are, but I'm amazed that they haven't tried to storm the main entrance.'

'Perhaps they underestimated the strength of our defences sir?' the op's officer asked.

'If we've been betrayed, then they would surely have some idea as to the size and strength of our forces,' Gulag answered, 'so why did they arrive with such a relatively small assault group? What about tanks and fixed-wing aircover? Unless...?' Gulag turned to where Jennifer had been sitting only moments ago. Of *course*, how could he have been so stupid? He leapt out of his chair and made for the turbo-lift. 'Ops keep those assault troops pinned down and try to get a couple of prisoners for questioning. I think you'll find out our Imperial troops are in fact mutant fighters wearing stolen uniforms,' he yelled as the lift doors opened. To the ops officer's credit he showed only a little bit of surprise before he started snapping orders into his communications unit.

Gulag ordered the turbo-lift to head for the engineering decks. If he were Moss that's where he'd be heading. He was now sure that the surface attack was no more than a ruse, a distraction, designed to keep him occupied whilst Moss and his team disabled the Dominator. The plan had almost worked.

'Dominator,' Gulag addressed the main computer, 'are you aware of the human being named Moss?'

'Indeed I am,' the strong male voice of the computer replied through the grille of the lift's wall-mounted comm unit. 'There were plenty of references concerning that person in the mind of the scientist, Josh Brabazon.'

Gulag raised an eyebrow, so his presumption had been correct—the Dominator's sentient computer was interfering with the mind of Brabazon. That was very worrying; Gulag knew that the scientist's telepathic powers were limited in comparison to his own, which might explain his susceptibility to the mind of the computer. But that wasn't the real problem; Gulag's real concern was that the computer might destroy the human's mind before he had had a chance to extract the information about Point Zero that he was sure was locked somewhere in Brabazon's head.

'So you *have* been tampering with the human's mind. That's a very dangerous thing to do Dominator. I would remind you that *I* command this ship and without the help of my people, you *will* undoubtedly remain locked in these caverns for eternity,' Gulag told the computer in no uncertain terms. He shook his head in bewilderment; how could the character of the mind that ran this starship be so different to Excalibur? He could see that there would be many battles of will between himself and the Dominator's computer. It was something that he would have to resolve before too long. The thought occurred to him that he should look into replacing the sentient main computer with a more standard mainframe machine. It wouldn't have the same power or ability, but at least it wouldn't go around making its own decisions and frying unsuspecting minds. The computer remained quiet, obviously thinking over what Gulag had said to it— strike one for the home team.

'Is there anyone onboard who fits the description of the human called Moss?' Gulag demanded of the computer. He got no reply. 'Dominator I asked you a question—is there anybody onboard who fits the description of Moss?' The computer remained silent. Gulag cursed and thumped the comm unit; if he didn't know better he would say that the bloody machine was sulking.

The turbo-lift stopped and the doors opened. He stepped out and marched down the corridor toward the powerplant control room. That was the where Brabazon had been when he'd struck out at Jennifer. Gulag was gambling that Jennifer had gone to fetch Brabazon and wait for Moss to arrive. If they were to disable the Dominator, that's where they'd try to do it from. He expanded his mind and searched for the tell-tale signature of Moss. He found nothing, which might mean Gulag was worrying about nothing, or it might mean Moss had learnt to hide his trail. Bearing in mind that he was a clever lad, the latter was the quiet possible. However, he *could* locate Brabazon's mind. It was garbled and confused, which indicated that the computer was still manipulating his mind, but he was definitely still in the powerplant control room.

Three members of the security section pounded down the corridor toward him, short-barrelled machine pistols wedged under their arms. 'Operations ordered us to come and find you sir,' the combat sergeant said to him. 'They said you might need our help.'

'Good thinking sergeant,' Gulag responded taking a spare weapon off one of the other members of the squad. 'I have reason to believe we have intruders somewhere onboard. They're human and I suspect they *will* attempt to sabotage the Dominator's powerplants. Stick close by.'

The combat sergeant acknowledged and together they made for the entrance to the control room. Gulag expanded his mind and located the position of Brabazon. It looked like he was back in the service duct, probably carrying out some errand for the computer.

Silently the doors opened and they cautiously entered the control room. It appeared empty, maybe Moss had decided to rescue just his girlfriend and leave Brabazon behind, although it seemed unlikely. The security team began a sweep of the deck and one of them soon called out, 'Over here!'

Gulag ran over and saw four technicians bound and gagged, hidden behind a console. There, also gagged and bound with insulation tape was Jennifer's escort. So they had been here! He ordered for them to be untied, then made his way to the service duct. Carefully he peered in, machine pistol at the ready. There was Brabazon, just inside the duct, mumbling to himself, working away at a circuit panel. There was something wrong here; Gulag found it hard to believe that Moss would just abandon one of his team. It just didn't seem like him.

'Easy does it Gulag,' a cold voice said from behind him. 'You should have known that I wouldn't leave one of my team behind. Unlike some people.'

Gulag felt the muzzle of an assault rifle in the small of his back. With a sigh he slowly turned around and faced Moss, his hands in the air. 'I'm sorry sir,' the combat sergeant spoke up from where he was being disarmed and bound up like the technicians. His eyes were slightly wild. 'They appeared from nowhere! They just came out of the wall sir!'

Gulag cursed realising he'd been fooled. He'd forgotten that Moss was adept at concealing himself from view in the same manner as a chameleon. Obviously he had extended this talent to include others as well.

'Hello Moss. What a pleasant surprise,' he said dryly. He looked around the control room and took in the situation—nearly the whole team was there. Jennifer held one of the machine pistols covering the security team with Han Sandpiper at her side. Paul Jenson stood beside Moss. That meant the mutant leader was on the surface leading the diversionary attack and Myrddin was in Caranak facing Nimue. Well, he thought to himself, they were all in the right place as per the grand scheme, but the ball was in their court—at least for the moment.

'Jennifer has been telling me a lot of interesting stories Gulag,' Moss began, his face not showing any obvious hostility, despite the situation. 'It would appear that we have a situation here that needs to be discussed.'

Gulag pretended not to know what Moss was talking about. 'What situation is that?' he replied innocently.

'Oh, nothing very important,' Moss replied mildly, but with a dangerous undercurrent to his voice. 'Just little things like a sentient computer that takes control of people's minds. A starship that's ready to launch with the same said computer in control. Things haven't quite worked out as you planned them, have they Gulag?'

For a moment Gulag thought about telling Moss to go screw himself, but he thought better of it. Despite what had happened in the past with his predecessor, the two of them at least, weren't enemies. Gulag didn't really have an axe to grind with Moss. It was only the circumstances they found themselves in that made them opponents. 'Okay,

I'll admit it,' he said with a sigh. 'I was as surprised as you when we discovered that Dominator was sentient, albeit with a megalomaniac ego. I promise you that I had nothing to do with the state of Josh Brabazon. I don't even know how the computer is controlling him. The best course of action that I can think of is to shut the computer down and replace it with a standard mainframe computer or an abacus.'

Moss thought about this for a moment and tried to figure out if Gulag was actually being humorous. 'That might be easier said than done,' he responded. 'If Dominator is the same as Excalibur, then the main computer is spread like an animal's nervous system— damage the central brain and half the bodily functions pack up. It's a very dangerous thing to do.'

'Unfortunately,' Moss continued, 'time is not on our side. Have you had any contact with Nimue recently?'

A frown crossed Gulag's brow. Now that Moss mentioned it, he realised that he hadn't had any contact with the bitch in a long time. She usually contacted him at least once a day. Gulag got a feeling of foreboding. 'No I haven't, why? What's happened?'

'Nimue has put her grand plan into action,' Moss told him, then proceeded to fill the clone in on events in Caranak as reported by Myrddin to Moss a short while ago. 'So as you can see Gulag, the planet is rapidly dissolving into total civil war. Excalibur is flying into a trap and there are only a few weeks left before the biosphere collapses completely. To put it mildly, thing's ain't looking good!'

'So? What do you want me to do about it?' Gulag asked, knowing the answer before he'd even asked the question.

Moss smiled and winked, 'Circumstances makes for strange bedfellows don't you think?'

'What do you suggest?' Gulag asked cautiously. 'Do you have some sort of alliance in mind?'

'That's exactly what I have in mind Gulag,' Moss answered. 'We'll help you get the Dominator into space and share the information about Point Zero that's stored on Excalibur's data-banks. In return you keep the Dominator out of the militarists' hands, and get us to Excalibur before Nimue's trap is sprung. If we can achieve all that together there's a chance we can save Dyason's ecology using the combined technology of Excalibur and Dominator. You once said "What's the point in inheriting a dead planet?" Well I'm giving you the chance to change all that. What do you say?'

Before Gulag could answer he was shoved hard from behind, sending him sprawling to the deck floor. He rolled as he fell and saw Brabazon leap out of the service duct he'd been standing in front of.

'Josh, stop! Wait!' Moss called out, but the wiry scientist ignored him and dashed for the main work station. As soon as he reached the controls, Brabazon maniacally tapped away at the keys. Jenson and Sandpiper dashed over and tried to drag him off the controls, but it was too late. Dominator's main computer intoned, 'Launch sequence initiated. Launch in seventeen minutes and counting.'

Brabazon grinned like an idiot, then collapsed into the arms of Sandpiper. Gulag scrambled up off the deck and yelled at the computer, 'Dominator, *ignore* that command! Terminate that launch sequence!'

'Launch sequence cannot be halted once it has been initiated. Launch in sixteen minutes and counting. I recommend you evacuate the cavern areas Group Leader,' the main computer answered, in what Gulag swore was a smug voice. Damn it! How had he lost control of the situation so rapidly?

Gulag turned to Moss and stated, 'It would appear that we have *no* choice in the matter. You've got yourself a deal!'

Hillmead stood in the shadow of the doorway and watched the armoured personnel carrier that had halted in the middle of the street. The crew had climbed out to look at the bizarre storm that had swept across Caranak only minutes before. The three troopers were now grouped behind the APC talking in hushed reverent tones. Myrddin's little pyrotechnic display had been seen by just about every citizen of the city, which for the time being at least gave Hillmead just the opportunity he needed.

He ran for the cover of the APC, keeping the tracks and the bulk of the machine between him and the troopers. He then motioned for Shalok to follow and she ran to his side. Then with their small automatics drawn they crept around the side of the APC one in each direction. The troopers didn't have a chance to even realise what was happening; there were three silenced gunshots and three dead bodies.

Hillmead opened the rear of the personnel carrier and Shalok ran back to fetch Myrddin and the Emperor. Myrddin had recovered sufficiently for him to clamber onboard under his own steam, but Shalok had to lead the Emperor. Although he now appeared to have the body of a much younger man, his mind was still confused and he needed to be lead by the hand. Shalok quickly stripped a uniform, the least blood stained, off one of the dead troops and threw it into the back of the APC. The Emperor couldn't go on television in his nightgown.

Hillmead jumped into the driver's seat, took one look at the controls and jumped out again. Shalok looked at him and said, 'What *are* you doing? Let's get out of here!'

'I don't know how to drive this thing,' he stated flatly. 'The controls look nothing like those on a ground vehicle!'

Shalok swore at him and pushed him out the way. 'Here,' she said, 'let me drive. I learnt how to control these beasts in the academy.' Hillmead sheepishly got out of the way and climbed into the gun turret. There was a roar as the huge diesel engine fired up, Shalok engaged the gears and the armoured personnel carrier lurched forward. 'Give it full bore!' Hillmead yelled. 'The palace guards are waking up!'

The rear of the APC was peppered by gunfire from a horde of guards that emerged from the palace compound. Hillmead rotated the turret and loosed off a few rounds of cannon fire. He smiled with satisfaction when he saw the guards dive for cover in all directions. There was a headset hanging in front of him which Hillmead put on and dialled the police frequency.

'Police control,' he called into the mike, 'this is Inspector Hillmead, do you read?' He got no response so he called again, 'Control this is Inspector Hillmead recently of the first Caranak precinct. Do you read?'

This time Hillmead got an immediate response, 'Hillmead is that really you? We heard you were on the run for discovering a military scam.'

Hillmead grinned in relief—he recognised the voice on the radio, it belonged to a policewoman he'd worked with many times in past.

'Jaloke listen, there's no time to explain,' he transmitted urgently. 'I'm in an armoured personnel carrier with Shalok from the MDC, a human called Myrddin and the Emperor.'

'You're what?' Jaloke exclaimed.

'As I say,' Hillmead told her, 'there's no time to explain. Just listen! We're heading for the television studios. The Emperor wants to make a broadcast to all the citizens of the Empire. We've exposed a plot by the Envoy Nimue to kill the Emperor. We desperately need a police escort to the studios. Do you understand? This is the time to move against the militarists!'

There was a stunned pause before the policewoman responded, 'Hillmead, I understand your transmission. Hang on and I'll get a response.'

As the APC roared down the boulevard to the main road that led to the studios at the edge of the city, Hillmead waited impatiently for a reply. Would the Caranak constabulary come to their assistance? If they didn't he wasn't hopeful about the chances of getting to the studio in one piece. Even now Nimue would be mobilising the Caranak regiments to stop them. The radio came alive.

'Okay Hillmead you've got it! All precincts have been alerted as to your position and status. The military are already mobilising every troop barracks in a fifty klick radius of the city. You keep heading for the studios, there's a police vehicle escort on its way to you now,' Jaloke told him. 'By the gods, I hope you're not pulling a fast one Hillmead! This has all the makings of the start of civil war!'

'Don't I know it!' Hillmead responded.

Inside the main compartment of the APC Myrddin fought to change the Emperor out of his night shirt and into the uniform. It was a struggle Myrddin could have done without. He had hoped that the rejuvenating energy that the Emperor had received would restore his mind as well as his body, but that didn't seem to be the case—the bloody fool just kept talking gibberish. Eventually he got the Emperor into the uniform, but Myrddin decided that he would have to do something about the Dyason's confusion.

Once more Myrddin extended his mind, this time concentrating on the Emperor's muddled thoughts. There was no whirlwind this time, no storms and lightening, just a gentle breeze not even noticed by Shalok and Hillmead. Myrddin entered the confused mind and supplied the information, the history and the story of events that the near dead Emperor had been starved of for centuries. When he had finished the Emperor blinked and looked at him through clear, focused eyes for the first time.

'Have I been dreaming?' the Emperor asked, finally aware of his surroundings.

'In a manner of speaking my Lord,' Myrddin told the Dyason. 'However, the dreams are over forever now.'

'What you showed me, what you have told me—Nimue, the Empire, the lies, the deaths—is it all true?' the Emperor asked grasping Myrddin's arm tightly, looking deeply into his eyes.

Myrddin returned the Dyason Emperor's stare and said, 'Look in your *own mind*, your own memories for the truth. I have given you the knowledge you require and access to your own memories of the past four centuries. Don't ask me, ask yourself whether your planet and your people are dying because of the actions of *your* lover.' The Emperor collapsed back against the side of the APC a look of anguish on his face. Myrddin almost felt sorry for him.

'How's it going back there?' Shalok asked from the driver's compartment.

Myrddin clambered into the co-driver's seat and said, 'Well, he's got his mind as well as his body back now, so you make sure you get us to the television studio. We'll do the rest.'

Shalok glanced at Myrddin then concentrated on ploughing along the highway. 'He's not going to stay like that is he?' she asked. 'I mean, his appearance now is an illusion isn't it?'

'Yes, I'm afraid so Shalok,' Myrddin answered sadly. 'He's being kept artificially alive by the life-force of the people of Caranak that still believe in him, but he can't stay that way forever. '

'How long has he got?'

'I don't know Shalok. A few hours, a few days at the most. Nimue kept him on a level just short of death. The state he's in now isn't sustainable. The truth is he should have died centuries ago,' he told her. Shalok didn't reply, she just kept concentrating on the road ahead. Myrddin realised that during the past few weeks she'd undergone a total crisis of faith, her world had been completely destroyed and discovering the truth behind the focus of her faith had been the last nail in the coffin. He dreaded to think what the reaction of the rest of the population would be when they realised the truth behind the Emperor.

The highway in front of the APC was suddenly bathed in light and Myrddin could just hear the sound of rotor blades over the noise of the diesel. The tarmac erupted all around the APC and the armour plating rattled with the impact of machine gun fire.

'We've got company!' Hillmead called over the intercom. Shalok immediately began to swerve across the highway in an attempt to throw off the light attack helicopter. Hillmead rotated the gun turret and loosed off short bursts of cannon fire. The attack helicopter pulled up and away from the arc of tracer rounds, moved out of range then turned for another attack run. Hillmead followed the helicopter's movements and fired short bursts every time it approached. It occurred to him that the chopper couldn't have any missiles on its weapons racks. They were probably scrambled to slow the APC down and had to fly with what they'd got, which was just the light machine guns.

The pilot of the helicopter turned back once more and made a track for the APC. This time it looked like he meant to press home his attack. Once more Hillmead lined the chopper up in his sights, but before he could squeeze the trigger there was a flash of flame in the distance and the attack chopper disintegrated in a fire-ball that crashed into a crumbling tenement block, setting it alight.

'Wow! Those babies sure do the job,' an excited voice called over the radio. 'Inspector Hillmead, this is police helicopter one-nine-five. I believe you called for assistance!'

Shalok gave a whoop of joy and even Myrddin couldn't resist a small cheer. 'Police helicopter one-nine-five it's good to see you! We were worried that we'd have to fight this battle on our own for a while there.'

'No chance Hillmead,' came the reply, 'we've been waiting for the opportunity to get our own back on the military for years. If what you say is true, then we're with you all the way mate.'

Shalok called up on the intercom and told Hillmead to look ahead on the highway. There in front of them the whole carriageway was blocked by police ground vehicles, their red and green lights flashing. Shalok eased off the power and rolled to a stop just in front of the lead vehicle. Police officers stood beside the cover of their ground cars, assault rifles at the ready.

'Myrddin!' Hillmead called. 'Get up here and take over this gun turret. I'm going out the back to talk to them. If it looks like it's turning to shit, open fire. Shalok keep the engine running.'

Myrddin clambered into the turret and Hillmead opened the rear doors of the APC. The Emperor looked up and moved to follow Hillmead. 'Hang on there my Lord!' he said to the Emperor holding up a hand to restrain him. 'Where do you think you're going?'

Emperor Alorne looked at him with a deadly serious face and replied, 'They want to see me. They won't give you any assistance otherwise. I've been a worthless vegetable for too long. It's time to lead my people again...*please*!'

Hillmead gave the Emperor a long stare then finally said, 'Perhaps you're right my Lord, this *is* the time to make up for all those years. Let's go.'

Together they stepped out of the rear of the APC into the howling wind and rain of yet another storm. As they rounded the rear of the vehicle they faced the stony stares of nearly a hundred of Caranak's finest police each one with an assault rifle aimed at them. An officer stepped forward and met them just in front of the APC. Hillmead recognised him as Commissioner Koerst, head of the central Caranak precincts and a Dyason with a ferocious reputation.

'So what the *flying frig* is going on Hillmead?' the commissioner began, then saw the Emperor. 'Ah...is this *really* the Emperor?'

Hillmead didn't say anything, instead the Emperor Alorne raised his left arm and showed the commissioner the Imperial seal. Everyone in the Empire knew about the seal; it was unique. Cut from a single diamond centuries ago, before even the start of Alorne's reign it had a strange and individual property—it pulsed and glowed with an internal energy, but only if it were worn by the Emperor of Dyason; or at least that's what legend stated. Barely a handful of people had actually seen the seal.

Knowing that Commissioner Koerst would need to be convinced, Alorne took the ring off and gave it to him. The light immediately faded and died. Koerst looked at the seal carefully, then reverently gave it back to Alorne. The Emperor put the ring back on and it began to glow once more with an angry red light that pulsed with intensity. Koerst had seen enough.

'We've long suspected what Hillmead here has proved to be true my lord,' he said bowing low from the waist. 'The police force remain your loyal servants. What are your orders?'

Alorne took the commissioner's arm and bade him to stand up straight. 'Please,' he said, 'don't bow to me; I don't deserve it. It has been my weakness and stupidity that has brought ruin upon this planet. I should be the one to pay my homage to you for remaining loyal to me during these terrible times.'

'Err...excuse me, my Lord,' Hillmead interrupted, 'but time is pressing.'

'Yes, yes of course. Thank you for reminding me,' Alorne said remembering the purpose of their mission. 'Commissioner, it is vital that the people know about the treachery of the Envoy Nimue and the military leaders. They have been raping this planet for decades and even now intend to flee whilst the ecology chokes to death. I *must* get to the television studio and make a broadcast to the people.'

Koerst nodded. 'We'll get you there my Lord, you can be sure of that,' he said to the Emperor, then turned to Hillmead. 'The studio is being surrounded by Imperial goons with tanks and chain-guns. It's gonna mean a full-scale battle to get in there by the front door.'

'What else do you suggest?' Hillmead asked.

'There's a power sub-station some distance to the rear of the studio. I'm told there's a service tunnel that leads from the sub-station directly into the television centre. I think that's our best bet for getting you into the studio.'

'That sounds as good a plan as any,' Hillmead agreed.

'It's still going to be a real battle to get there. So, you take the Emperor in the APC and hang back. We'll go in with our squad vehicles and keep the goons busy. When I give you the signal, you make a break for the sub-station. Got that?'

'Yep I've got that,' Hillmead acknowledged.

Koerst turned to the line of police vehicles and waved his arm over his head. 'Okay people he's for real,' he called over his helmet radio. 'Crank those engines up and let's do it! We've got a score to settle with those bastards!'

Hillmead took the Emperor by the elbow and turned to lead him back to the APC. Koerst stopped him by calling, 'Hillmead! I always knew you were a good officer! I never doubted you. Well done!'

Hillmead nodded then climbed back into the APC. Now the fire-works were really about to begin!

CHAPTER EIGHTEEN

DOMINATOR

*C*olmarrie!' Moss called out in his mind, *'Listen carefully! We have a situation here!'*

'Gulag's troops have left their positions and retreated back into the caverns, friend Moss,' Colmarrie responded. *'I presume you know the reason why?'*

'I do Colmarrie,' he answered. *'This may sound strange but the computer that runs the Dominator is not responding to the crew's commands. It's started a countdown and is going to launch in less that fifteen minutes. We're stuck onboard and have, for the time being, agreed with Gulag to help him sort the situation out.'*

'You've done what?'

'I know it's hard to believe, but it's vital that you listen to what I've got to tell you!' Moss urged her. *'When the Dominator launches it's going to blast the whole area. It's vital that you move your people out of danger... Wait a minute!'* A thought occurred to him—he turned to Gulag and asked, 'Colmarrie's fighters are in the danger area. There's very little time for them to get away. If we're going to bury the hatchet let's do it properly; bring them onboard Gulag. They're on the same side as you really.'

Gulag looked at Moss and thought about what he'd said. Colmarrie and her mutant fighters had been a constant thorn in his side and had killed some of his best troops in the past few hours. However, he also knew what exceptional fighters her people were. Better to have the mutants on his side than against. Eventually, almost reluctantly, he nodded his head.

Moss grinned at him. 'There may be hope for you yet you bastard,' he told him then returned his thoughts to the mutant leader. *'Okay Colmarrie, listen to me very carefully,'* he thought at her in the strongest manner, *'Gulag's given his agreement to bring you onboard the Dominator. There's not enough time for you all to get away from the launch area, so tell your people to make their way through the caverns. Gulag will send one of his people to guide you.'*

'You are surely jesting Moss?' Colmarrie responded in disbelief.

'I've never been more serious in my life Colmarrie,' he urged. *'Besides I need you here.'*

'Well... if you say so, then we shall do as you ask,' she agreed dubiously, *'but this is very strange.'*

'I'll send Sandpiper to come and meet you and for God's sake, tell your people not to shoot anybody!' Moss told her then signed off. After a brief discussion Sandpiper headed off with the combat sergeant and Gulag's security team to fetch the mutant fighters.

'Can you take the helmsman's position?' Gulag asked Moss once they'd arrived on the bridge of the Dominator as the countdown wound down to zero.

'I can, but I don't know what you expect me to do,' Moss replied with a shrug. 'Dominator has taken control of all systems. All we can really do is sit, watch, and hope everything works.'

'I know that, but you have more experience in guiding a starship than anyone else,' Gulag responded leading Moss to the helmsman's position whilst he took the captain's chair. Jenson and Jennifer volunteered to take other positions on the bridge. Gulag opened a hailing channel to everyone on the ship and informed them of what was going on. Moss saw this as further proof that the cloned Gulag was very different from his earlier incarnation. The original Gulag in this situation would have been obsessively paranoid and secretive.

Six minutes before final countdown Sandpiper called the bridge to tell them that Colmarrie's people were all onboard. 'I had a hard time convincing them not to go on a killing rampage and shoot everyone onboard,' he told them.

'I can imagine,' Jenson said, taking the message. 'You'd better stay down there Han. Make sure they're all strapped in and keep twitchy hands off weapons.'

'Will do boss,' came the reply. 'Some of Colmarrie's people have been injured. Can I take them to the sick bay?'

Jenson checked with the bridge operations officer who was actually doing a magnificent job under bizarre circumstances. Gulag had chosen his crew well, Jenson thought. Not only had he found people in the Imperial Navy who were willing to rebel against the service, he had found *good* people. It was some indication of the huge splits within the Dyason ranks.

'Go ahead Han,' he told his friend, 'I'm informed the medics have been warned and will do everything they can for them. While you're there find out how Josh Brabazon's getting on.'

'I'm on my way skipper,' Sandpiper confirmed, then added, 'this is one weird situation though boss. Do you really think this computer will get this beast into space without any assistance?'

'I don't think it'll have any problems doing that Han. The real worry is what it's going to do once we get there!' Jenson answered then cut the channel.

Moss hooked himself into the interactive flight system connected to the helmsman's couch. The system itself was identical to the one onboard the Excalibur but when he linked himself to the computer the response he got was completely different. The sentient computer that was Excalibur melded and worked with him so that they operated as one. When Moss flew the Excalibur he felt as if he *were* the starship, it responded to his thoughts and actions in the same way his limbs responded to his will.

This certainly wasn't the case with the Dominator. The computer felt hostile, almost begrudging his presence. The machine was going through the count-down sequence to a launch that Moss was familiar with but it was doing it without any interference from the crew. Moss could watch but he couldn't intervene, at least not without forcing his will on it. He really couldn't figure out why this computer was so hostile, so different, from Excalibur. Maybe the years spent in isolation watching the civilisation on the surface slowly murder its own people had made it bitter. It was a problem that needed a solution sooner than later.

'It's as I thought Gulag,' he announced. 'Dominator has locked me out of the flight system and is operating on automatic. However, I *can* monitor all systems and so far as I can judge the count-down is going ahead without incident. Everything appears to be fully operational.'

'Sir, the cavern structure is beginning to change,' one of the Dyason officers told Gulag. 'The cavern roof is disappearing.'

Gulag ordered an image of the cavern to be shown on the main viewer. As they watched, the roof of the cavern began to melt and change. Like a huge expanding iris, a hole appeared in the cavern roof immediately above the Dominator. For the first time in many millennia sunlight fell on the hull of the ancient starship. The pinpoint of light became larger as the iris continued to expand.

'By the god's I would never have believed it was possible unless I had seen it with my own eyes,' Gulag whispered in awe.

'You've seen nothing yet,' Jennifer told him.

'Singularities are on line. Main powerplants are powering up. Launch in two minutes and counting,' Moss declared monitoring the Dominator's innumerable operations. 'All systems functioning normally.'

'What's normal?' one of the Dyason bridge crew murmured to another. 'There's nothing normal about any of this.'

Jennifer sat at the astro-navigator's position which was identical to the one onboard the Excalibur. The Dominator's various sensors had just come on line and for the first time since the crash of the *Observer*, she was able to make an in-depth analysis of the Dyason star system.

'All sensors are now operative,' she declared. 'I'm making a preliminary sweep of the star system and I've pin-pointed the new worm-hole. It's situated close to the moon Alphebus, not far from the point where we left hyperspace in the *Observer*.'

'Is there any clue as to what course has been set?' Gulag asked Jennifer impatiently. 'Do we have any idea where the Dominator is planning on taking us?'

Jennifer checked her sensors once more and tried to access the navigation console. She wasn't surprised when she found herself locked out from the astro-positioning system. She would just have to take a guess.

'Dominator has locked me out from the navigation systems. I can watch our progress but we're obviously not allowed to know where exactly it is we're going.'

'There's no indication that the computer intends to carry out a hyperspace jump,' Jenson added from the engineering console. 'My guess is that our destination is the worm-hole.'

'But why?' Gulag asked. 'What's at the other end of the worm-hole?'

'There's no way of knowing,' Jennifer told him.

'Well it's too late to worry about it now,' Moss told them. 'Launch in thirty seconds and counting. Hang on to whatever you can, the ride is about to start.'

Gulag looked at the image on the viewer of the now open sky above the cavern that had entombed the Dominator for so long and mentally steeled himself. The moment he'd been working towards for so long had finally arrived, but the feeling of triumph wasn't there. Control of the situation had been taken from him by the most unlikely of candidates, but in those seconds before launch, Gulag resolved that one way or another he *would* regain control.

'Five...four...three..two...one. Launch!'

For some reason Gulag was half expecting the thunderous sound of engines and acceleration that forced them into their seats. Instead, there was a gentle vibration felt through the deck of the ship and the main viewer showed the Dominator slowly rising out of its tomb and into the harsh desert sunlight. The massive vessel continued to rise vertically until it hovered above the ground at an altitude of two thousand metres, then after a short pause it gently raised its nose toward the sky and accelerated towards the stars. Gulag sat in the captain's chair amazed that there was no sense of movement onboard the ship. Without the slight vibration and the viewer showing the passage of mountainous clouds he would have sworn that the Dominator hadn't moved at all.

'Altitude ten thousand klicks and increasing,' Moss intoned from the helm. 'All systems operational. We'll be leaving the atmosphere in a few seconds. Speed twenty-five thousand klicks and still accelerating. The Dominator flies once more Gulag!'

Stars appeared and became brighter and brighter until the poisoned atmosphere of Dyason was left behind and the Dominator was finally free of its tomb, once more flying in its natural element. Moss attempted to access the flight system, hoping that now they were in orbit the computer would relinquish control of the ship, but he found the controls still locked.

'We're in orbit, but the flight controls are still locked. Dominator is still very much in control,' he told Gulag.

'Do we have any indication of where we're going?' Gulag asked Jennifer showing signs of agitation.

Jennifer looked at the data once more then answered, 'It's as I feared, we're heading for the worm-hole. We'll be in the gravitational influence of the anomaly in seven minutes and thirty-eight seconds. It would appear that the Dominator intends to take us in there.'

Gulag pounded on the arm of the captain's chair in frustration. Once they entered the worm-hole they could be lost forever. The worm-hole may be the same one that lead to Earth or it may lead to somewhere else entirely. He *had* to regain control of the ship. 'Is there no way we can shut down the main computer and use other computers to run the various systems?' he demanded of Moss.

'Not in the next seven minutes there isn't!' Moss told him. 'It would take days, maybe weeks to complete such a task with the Dyason computers you have Gulag. It's simply not a viable option.'

Gulag drummed a beat on the chair arm then said in a loud, authoritative voice, 'Dominator, even if it means killing us all, I *will* disconnect you if you take us into that worm-hole. Do you hear? I will do it!'

'We must be at the rendezvous at the correct time,' the computer boomed in response.

'What bloody rendezvous?' Gulag demanded. 'What exactly are you talking about Dominator? What's going on? Where are you taking us?' This time the computer didn't respond.

Jennifer looked at her monitors and checked the sensors once more. The worm-hole was expanding, she was sure of it. It was pulsating, opening and that meant just one thing—a ship was coming through the worm-hole!

'Hang-on,' she called excitedly, 'there's a ship leaving the worm-hole! I'm just picking it up on the sensors now...It's...yes... it is definitely...it's Excalibur!'

The escort of police ground cars moved in a line ahead of the APC their red and green lights flashing like beacons in the rain and wind. The rusting, fuel-guzzling hulks that the finance-starved Caranak police were forced to use were no match for the latest tanks and armour that equipped the Imperial shock troops. However, that didn't stop the procession of battered vehicles moving down the highway. Years of pent-up anger and frustration had finally found a focus, a worthwhile cause. The story of Hillmead and Shalok and the truths they'd unearthed had spread amongst the police ranks even before the emergence of the Emperor Alorne. With the appearance of the Imperial figurehead the gutter cops, so long down-trodden by the military, had a focus for their anger. The military government would finally be made answerable for its actions and regardless of the odds the police *would* get their Emperor to the television studio.

Hillmead's attention was grabbed by what looked like a blaze of approaching light from the direction of the centre of the city. He turned the turret and trained the gun on the approaching mass of light then called up the police helicopter on the radio, 'Chopper one-nine-five, this is Hillmead. Can you make out what that blaze of light is heading toward us?'

'Roger APC,' came the reply. 'We've made contact with the light source, but you're not going to believe this.'

'Believe what?' Hillmead demanded in alarm. If an Imperial unit was closing in on them from their rear, they were about to be caught in a vicious pincer movement.

'Well there are three thousand plus vehicles of all shapes and sizes heading toward you at speed,' the police chopper responded. 'However, I can definitely state that they are *not* hostile. They'll be joining your convoy at any time now Hillmead. I tell you I wouldn't have believed it if I hadn't seen it with my own eyes!'

'Three thousand vehicles? Where the hell have they come from?' Shalok called on the intercom. Myrddin clambered up to the gun turret and squeezed in next to Hillmead to take a look.

'Looks like we're about to find out,' Myrddin answered, then addressed the Emperor, 'It would appear, my Lord, that you still have a lot of loyal supporters.'

As the blaze of light came closer Hillmead realised that what he was looking at was a mass of headlights from just about every vehicle in Caranak that was still able to move. Like an approaching tidal wave the bizarre convoy roared toward them, headlights flashing, horns blaring. It was an incredible sight; just about every conceivable type of vehicle was there from huge alcohol burning trucks to taxies, buses, and clapped-out family cars running on petrol hidden at a time when it was still generally available. Every vehicle was overflowing with the citizens of Caranak brandishing various lethal looking weapons, some obviously dating back to the time of the great patriotic war.

The citizens of Caranak surrounded the APC shouting and cheering for a glimpse of their Emperor, the face masks of their dirty, stained environment suits lifted in wild abandon.

'It looks like you've got yourselves an army,' Myrddin said to Hillmead shaking his head in disbelief. 'I've badly underestimated the people of Dyason. Never in my wildest dreams would I have believed such a thing was possible.'

Hillmead turned, looked at Myrddin and said, 'That's because you've never had to live on the street and try to scavenge foods for your kids, knowing that even if you *do* find them something it's going to be completely full of lethal toxins. A lot of those Dyason out there are 'Lobos' who live in the gutter. They've got nothing to lose, they're dying anyway. Better to die in a civil war than to choke on their own poisoned guts.'

Myrddin said nothing for there really was nothing to say. He looked at the thousands of battered vehicles surrounding the APC and the police escort at the front, their lights still flashing red and green in the gloom. For a moment he was almost overwhelmed with guilt. If he'd had the courage to kill his sister all those centuries ago, the Dyason wouldn't have suffered as they had. He vowed that before the night was out he would finish the job once and for all.

'Hillmead this is Koerst,' the police commissioner called on the radio.

'Go ahead Commissioner,' Hillmead responded.

'It's good to have our numbers swelled. The rumour network is obviously working as well as ever. What this mob lack in weaponry and discipline they make up in numbers and enthusiasm. However, they'd be even more enthusiastic if they saw a glimpse of the Emperor.'

'Roger that,' Hillmead answered. 'I'll see what we can do.'

The Emperor didn't need any encouragement. He heard the radio message, immediately opened a hatch in the hull of the APC and stood up. There was a tumultuous roar as the citizens of Caranak saw the face of their Emperor for the first time in living memory. Alorne the third lapped up the adulation, his presence, his confidence seemed to swell with each roar of the crowd as the love of his people filled him with life.

Eventually Hillmead had to physically haul him back into the APC as the convoy approached the television studios. 'Time to baton down the hatches my Lord,' Hillmead said to the glowing face of the Emperor. 'It's going to get very hot out there any time now.'

Hillmead got back in the gun turret of the APC and watched their escort slowly moving along the highway. Pride swelled his chest, all his doubts of the past few weeks, months, years even, were swept away in the infectious mood of the moment. The Emperor Alorne was sitting back in the co-drivers seat next to Shalok a determined look on his face. Shalok, who had been on the verge of despondency for weeks kept looking at Alorne's face as if memorising every detail. Her faith had been restored, at least for the moment. She knew that the face she saw was an illusion, temporary at best, but it didn't matter. Right there, right now, she had a reason for living once more. Only Myrddin remained stone faced, his expression unreadable.

The orange floodlights of the television centre and the yellow searchlights of the shock troops reflected angrily off the low clouds as the massed mob of Caranak's citizens and police approached the entrenched Imperial troops. The convoy moved slowly up the approach road then came to a standstill less than a hundred metres from the front row of massive Imperial battle-tanks. A silence descended upon the convoy as they waited to see what the reaction of the Imperial troops would be.

The radio crackled into life and Hillmead heard the voice of the Envoy Nimue. 'Commissioner Koerst,' she said with a steely voice, 'we have reason to believe that you are protecting those responsible for kidnapping the Emperor. They are enemies of the state and must be handed over to the military.'

'I'm sorry Envoy, but I can't do that,' Koerst replied coolly, 'we're investigating a matter of corruption and fraud in the highest ranks of the government. The Emperor and those who uncovered a plot to end his life are assisting in that investigation. They come under police jurisdiction.' Like the quiet before the storm, everyone was silent as they waited for Nimue's response.

'I'm afraid that I must insist you hand over the Emperor and those responsible for his kidnap,' the Envoy demanded once more. 'If you do not comply I *will* consider you and your rabble to be traitors of the Empire and treat you all as such. Do I make myself clear?'

Koerst responded immediately in a cold clear voice, 'On the contrary Envoy, you and your military henchmen are the traitors. The Emperor wishes to make a broadcast to his people. I insist that *you* move your troops aside and let *us* through.'

'I see that further dialogue is worthless. It would appear that a lesson in force is needed here Koerst. If you wish to be treated as the traitorous scum you are, then so be it!' Nimue stated then cut the connection.

A white phosphorus flare shot into the sky and the air filled with tracer and shrapnel. With a roar the police vehicles hurtled through the gaps between the battle-tanks and engaged the troops at the rear. The citizens of Caranak surged forward and began to swarm all over the Imperial armour shouting and screaming. The Dyason civil war had begun.

Excalibur emerged from the worm-hole in a state of full battle readiness. As soon as the ship had moved sufficiently away from the gravitational effects of the worm-hole, squadrons of Flyships launched. Like aggressive wasps they left the launch bays of the massive vessel and protectively spread out forming a shield of defence around the capital ship. Soon after, three smaller corvettes attached to the exterior hull released their docking bolts and surged ahead, their prototype beam weapons and gatling guns at the ready.

'Status report!' Black ordered the bridge operations officer.

'Planet Dyason directly ahead sir!' she replied rapidly scanning the information sweeping across her work station. 'We have exited the worm-hole near to the moon Alphebus. All Flyships have been launched as have the three corvettes.'

'Are there any ships in the immediate vicinity?' Black demanded.

The navigation officer scanned his sensor readings then snapped, 'There is one unidentified vessel off the port bow at a range of four thousand kilometres and closing rapidly. Displacement, size and configuration of the ship is...' The navigation officer's voiced trailed off in disbelief.

Black caught the look of the navigator's face and said, 'What is it navigator? Come on, I want a positive identification of that vessel!'

The navigator shook his head, swallowed hard and said, 'I'm afraid that the identity of that vessel is a little hard to believe sir. I'm putting a magnified image of the ship on the viewer now.'

Black looked up at the viewer and leapt out of the captain's chair in shock. The ship on the viewer had a delta-shaped prow that bled into an elongated boom. This swept into a wedge shaped body with huge intakes on the underside. It was a beautiful, efficient design reminiscent of a swan in flight. 'Holy shit!' he exclaimed. 'Is this some sort of Dyason trick?'

'I can't confirm that sir,' the navigation officer responded carefully, 'but I can say for sure that the size, configuration and displacement of that vessel is the same as Excalibur!'

Before that information could even set in the comms officer called out, 'We're being hailed by the unidentified vessel sir!'

Black leapt over to the communications console and ordered a channel to be opened up. The main monitor cleared then the familiar face of Jenson and Jennifer appeared on the screen. 'Excalibur, this is the Dominator, are you reading us?' Jennifer asked.

Black stepped into the transmission camera's field of view and asked incredulously, 'Jennifer, Paul? Is it really you? What the hell's going on here? That ship you're on looks like an exact replica of Excalibur!'

'That's because it is Peter!' Jenson responded. 'Now listen up mate, there isn't much time for explanations but here's a quick low-down of the situation. The vessel we're on is the sister ship to Excalibur and it's called the Dominator. The space construction WDF intelligence called the Dominator is in fact a heavily armed battle-station. You've been led into an Imperial trap, but this ship we're on is being crewed by anti-Imperialists. I know it all sounds confusing but I'll explain the rest later. We need you to get us off here and send some of our technicians over to sort out a major malfunction of the comp....'

The screen went blank. 'Get them back! Get them back!' Black demanded. The communications officer tried valiantly to regain the connection but failed.

'I'm sorry sir,' he told Black, 'but it's no use. The connection was cut at the source. They're not responding to my hail.'

Black slammed his fist on the console. Damn! Just what the hell was going on? Was this all an elaborate hoax? He had to have some sort of confirmation before he acted. 'Excalibur,' he addressed the computer. 'Can you confirm that the vessel off our port bow is indeed a sister ship built by the same race to the same configuration as yourself?'

'I can indeed confirm that vessel is a sister ship and the same configuration as me,' the calm female tones of the computer responded.

'And are any of our people onboard that vessel?' Black probed.

'I am registering the brain patterns of Moss, Jennifer, Paul Jenson, Han Sandpiper and Josh Brabazon on that vessel,' came the response.

That was good enough for Black. He wasn't sure what was going on, but the rendezvous that Excalibur had been talking about before they entered the worm-hole, obviously had something to do with that identical starship. Somehow Moss, Jenson and the others had become involved in the game plan and the sooner they were back onboard Excalibur the sooner he would know what the hell was happening.

'Helm!' he commanded. 'Pull up alongside that vessel and hold us in formation at a distance of two hundred kilometres.'

'Yes sir!' the helmsman responded, adjusting the Excalibur's flight path.

Black then turned to the operations officer and told her, 'Order the corvette *Elgin* to return to docking bay one. Then I want a marine squad and a technical team to board her. As soon as they've done that, the *Elgin* is to make for that starship. Make sure that the Flyships escort her in and are prepared for hostile fire. If that machine really is an identical copy of Excalibur there will be a compatible docking bay available. The *Elgin* is to dock and await orders from Group Captain Jenson or Flight Lieutenant Moss. Have you got all that Corbett?'

'Yes sir!' the ops officer confirmed.

'And keep scanning for any other ships. Jenson said something about this being a trap, so I want everyone to keep on their toes. We could come under attack at any time!' As everyone on the bridge leapt to meet his commands Black sat back down shaking his head, the whole situation made him very unhappy. There was something *very* weird going on here and he wanted to know what it was.

'Did they get the message?' Jenson asked Jennifer when the comm link with Excalibur went down.

Jennifer tried to regain contact but she was locked out of the communications network. 'It's that bloody computer interfering again,' she told him, clearly frustrated. 'It purposely cut the link as soon as you made a reference to it.'

'Shit!' Jenson swore, 'I just hope that Black understood enough of what I told him to send a ship over to pick us up. '

'There's a frigate-sized vessel with an escort of fighters leaving the Excalibur and heading toward us sir!' the Dyason operations officer told Gulag.

Gulag looked at Moss who had disconnected himself from the flight control system. 'That'll be the corvette come to pick you up. You'd better go and meet them, there's nothing more you can do here,' he said gesturing for the three of them to leave.

Moss nodded in agreement and made for the turbo-lift. 'I think that's for the best Gulag,' he said. 'So long as the Dominator's computer remains unco operative you can't control the ship. So we're going to need to use the Excalibur to defend both ships from that battle-station. We can't do that from here.'

'Go do it Moss,' Gulag responded. 'We can sort out this bloody computer *and* our differences later.'

Jennifer was about to join Moss in the turbo-lift when she saw the Dominator's sensors register new contacts. Quickly she scanned the console and said, 'We've got multiple contacts heading toward us from the battle-station. Holy shit Gulag! You didn't tell us the Imperial Navy had developed its own version of the Flyship! Christ! There's swarms of them!'

Gulag's face paled. 'I didn't know they had! Are you sure that's what the contacts are?'

'I know how to use these bloody work stations Gulag! Dominator hasn't locked us out of the sensors. I'll put it on the main view. Look for yourself!' Jennifer tapped at the panel and the magnified image of squadrons of needle-nosed fighters filled the screen. Although about the same size as the Excalibur's Flyships their design was slightly different. Engine pods sat on the end of swept forward winglets and various heavy ordinance hung from racks on the fuselage underside. They looked small, powerful and vicious.

'It looks like Nimue hasn't been entirely open with you either Gulag,' Moss noted.

'How long until they intercept us?' Jenson asked.

'Eight minutes, twelve seconds at their current velocity,' Jennifer told him.

'Definitely time to leave!' he replied. 'Gulag, the Imperial Navy may try to board you. If they do you'll need all the help you can get. This may be the time to ask Colmarrie and her mutants to help. They'll certainly boost your own forces.'

'You're right. I'll get on with it,' Gulag answered. 'Having struggled this far, I'm buggered if I'm going to let Nimue's henchmen take the Dominator from under my nose. Go! Go! Keep those little bastards away from us!' He waved his hands at them gesturing for them to leave.

The doors to the turbo-lift closed and the three of them headed as quickly as possible to the main docking bay. The corvette *Elgin* was just docking when they got there and Sandpiper was already over seeing the docking operation from bay control room.

'Where's Josh?' Jenson asked looking around the control room for the wiry scientist.

Sandpiper glanced up from watching the corvette and sighed, 'He's done a runner.'

'He's what?'

'I went to fetch him from the infirmary but his bed was empty. None of the medics had seen him leave. I searched the medi-lab for him but there was no sign,' Sandpiper said apologetically. 'His brain must still be confused by that bloody computer.'

'Shit!' Moss swore. 'Well there's no time to look for him now; he could be anywhere. We'll have to come back for him once we've sorted out those fighters.'

The corvette finished docking and the airlock equalised. The four of them ran down to the bay and were there when the boarding ramp lowered. A squad of marines were the first to leave the *Elgin* and they rapidly formed a defensive perimeter around the corvette. A marine officer ran up to Jenson and said, 'Group Leader Jenson, we have orders to take you back to the Excalibur. If you're ready we can leave now.'

There was a commotion at the end of the bay and Colmarrie appeared. Moss held up his hand and yelled for the marines to hold their fire. The mutant leader made her way past the defensive perimeter and stopped in front of Moss. 'I could not let you leave without saying farewell my friends,' she grinned. 'Who knows what will happen in the battle ahead? I want you all to know it has been my pleasure to fight alongside you.'

Moss took the amazonian woman's hand in his and shook it hard. 'It's not over yet Colmarrie,' he told her, 'we'll be back as soon as we've dealt with that battle-station and those Snub ships. Has Gulag briefed you of the situation?'

'Yes my friend. My people think it is very strange that we should be asked to help those we attacked only this morning, but everything about this situation is most bizarre. We shall simply have to adapt,' she told him, a frown creasing her brow.

'I understand what you're saying, but think of it this way, the Dominator belongs to you and all the people of Dyason. It's your inheritance and that's what you're protecting, not Gulag,' he told her then a thought came to him. 'Listen, we have a problem you can help us with.'

'If there's anything I can do to help I will,' she immediately responded.

Moss turned to the marine captain and said, 'Josh Brabazon is lost somewhere on this ship and there's no time left for us to find him. Can your marines stay on the Dominator and work with Colmarrie to find him?'

The marine captain looked at Jenson for confirmation. Jenson nodded and added, 'You can also protect those technicians you brought with you.'

'Err... yes sir,' the marine captain answered hesitantly looking dubiously at the massive mutant leader.

Jenson saw his concerned expression. 'It's okay captain, Colmarrie doesn't bite. You and your men will be quite safe with her.'

'She only rips the arms off those who *really* annoy her,' Sandpiper added amicably.

The captain gazed up at the mutant leader with a certain amount of apprehension then nodded. Colmarrie beamed down at the marine officer put her arm around his shoulder and led him away. The captain glanced back once, a worried expression on his face, then left the bay, his marines and the technicians following close behind. Moss, Jenson, Sandpiper and Jennifer climbed aboard the *Elgin* and the corvette prepared to head back to the Excalibur as fast as possible.

As soon as the corvette cleared the massive bulk of the Dominator, Jenson called Black and gave him a very brief resume of events since the *Observer* had left Earth. For the first time Black could make some sense of everything that was happening. 'Well that explains why the Imperial Navy is throwing all its new toys into the arena. They'll be desperate to get their hands on the Dominator, but are you sure that we can trust Gulag? How do we know that he's not going to turn that ship on us?' he asked.

'We don't,' Jenson answered from the bridge of the corvette. 'The situation keeps changing from minute to minute. The reality is, we're caught in the middle of a civil war and there's no guarantee who will win. All we can do at the moment is react to each situation as it happens, which at the moment means that battle-station and those Snub fighters.

'We'll be onboard the Excalibur in a couple of minutes. When we get there I want two Flyships ready for Han and myself. We'll launch and lead the Flyship squadrons. Then I want Moss to join you on bridge and take his position at the helm. Jennifer has agreed to stay on the bridge of the *Elgin*. Our priority is to protect the Excalibur first and the Dominator second. Then, if we get the opportunity we'll take out the battle-station. Got that?'

'Yep I've got that,' Black confirmed. 'There'll be two Flyships in the tubes ready to launch as soon as you arrive. Make it as fast as you can Paul, the lead Flyships are about to engage those Imperial Snub fighters any second now.'

Squadron Leader Jameson of number eleven squadron WDF aimed his Flyship at the lead Snub fighter as they closed head to head with a combined speed of over a thousand kilometres per hour. The needle nose and wing mounted power pods of the Imperial fighter were in his sights barely long enough for him to track and fire his lasers before it had swept past him. Using the interactive flight system built into the Flyship he urged his fighter around in a high-g turn and chased after the bogey. As he willed the Flyship around he used the fighter's sensors to check on the progress of the rest of his squadron who had followed him in the head-on attack. They too were wheeling their Flyships around and re-engaging the Imperial machines. There was a flash off his starboard wing and he just caught sight of an expanding fire ball as one of the Imperial Snub fighters exploded. Well, at least the damn machines weren't invincible he thought to himself as the space around him became a confusing mass of machines, laser fire and bright tracer rounds.

'Red two stick to me like glue,' Jameson called as he closed in on a Snub fighter which was lining up for an attack on the corvette *Repulse.*

'I'm right with you Red one,' his wingman answered.

Jameson flexed his muscles and willed the Flyship around behind and below the Imperial Snub ship which was unaware it was being stalked. He waited until he was within a few hundred metres before firing a laser salvo. He watched in fascination as strikes walked across the starboard wing which broke away from the fuselage. The Snub fighter began to spin away out of control, but not before Jameson loosed off another burst of laser fire which finished the Imperial fighter off. It disintegrated into hundreds of pieces which span away into space. 'Scratch one bogey!' Jameson called out to his wingman.

'Good shooting Red one,' his wingman answered. Jameson interacted with the Flyship's sensors and looked for other bogeys.

'Red two look out,' he cried out in alarm as a Snub fighter screamed down on his wingman. Red two heard the warning and broke hard to starboard in a maximum g-turn but the Imperial pilot was just as quick and followed the turn proving that the Dyason fighters were as manoeuvrable in close quarters as the Flyships.

Jameson desperately fought to get a line on the Snub fighter but the Imperial pilot and his wingman were locked in a mad, constantly changing battle that was impossible to track. There was a small flash of flame from the weapons rack of the Snub fighter and a missile leapt toward the Flyship hitting it just behind the rear stabiliser. Jameson shielded his eyes as the released singularity dissolved in a flash of light. When he looked again Red two was no more.

Jameson's heart sank. He pulled the Flyship around and set off in pursuit of the Imperial Snub ship knowing that the squadrons protecting Excalibur were out numbered by fighters equal to their machines in a dog-fight. It wasn't looking good.

CHAPTER NINETEEN

The scene was a state of utter confusion. The citizens of Caranak swarmed over the Imperial troopers engaging them in hand-to-hand combat. The tanks blasted away at the police vehicles and convoy of battered hulks, but for every moving wreck they destroyed there was another one behind it. It was the same for the ground troops, for every Lobo they mowed down there was another behind. Every time an Imperial trooper fell his weapon and ammunition were grabbed by one of the mob and turned on the cause of the people's suffering. It was utter chaos, a fight to the death with the people's army mindless of their casualties.

The APC was surrounded by madness unable to move forward or backwards due to the mass of blazing vehicles around it. It was the end of the line and Hillmead knew it. He clambered out of the gun turret and yelled, 'This is as far as we can go. We'll have to fight our way to the sub-station on foot.'

Myrddin grabbed assault rifles from racks attached to the side of the APC and passed them round. Even Emperor Alorne took one with a grim but determined face; Myrddin briefly wandered if Alorne actually knew how to use a gun. Hillmead opened the rear doors to the personnel carrier and they clambered out. A small group forced its way through the advancing mob toward them—it was Koerst and some of his cops.

'The sub-station is that way!' he pointed, panting heavily when he reached them. 'It's about half a klick away. These men know the way and will escort you there. Go now while the Imperial goons are off-balance. When Nimue's reinforcements arrive the battle will swing their way. Now go!'

Emperor Alorne stepped forward and faced Koerst. 'What about you Commissioner? Aren't you coming with us?'

Koerst shook his head and said, 'This mob needs a general and I'm the only available candidate. Now please, my Lord go now whilst there's still time!'

Alorne looked at the police commissioner and briefly grasped his hand. 'I wish I had known you better Commissioner Koerst, you are a very brave man. I will not fail you or my people again!'

Koerst looked at his Emperor with sadness and regret, turned and headed back into the battle. Hillmead knew that they would never see him alive again. 'Let's go my lord,' he said then turned and followed the squad of cops.

'What do you mean the Dominator has launched?' Nimue raged at an unfortunate Pollowzki. 'That's ridiculous it can't have! Gulag had specific orders not to do anything until I arrived there!'

Pollowzki looked at the studio floor avoiding the Envoy's wild stare. He knew what happened to those who were the focus of her anger and it usually meant a painful death. He desperately wished he was anywhere but standing in front of Nimue. Even fighting the mob outside the television centre was preferable to this.

'I'm sorry Envoy but I'm only passing on the latest information to you,' Poll desperately pleaded, trying to make Nimue realise he was the messenger, not the instigator. 'The Dominator launched twelve minutes ago and is now in orbit. We have *not* been able to make contact with the ship. Because of this the military council has ordered the capture or, if necessary, the destruction of the Dominator.'

Nimue strode across the studio floor her hands raised above her head, 'Just what in God's name is Gulag up to?' she yelled. 'How could he have done this to *me* of all people? He knows that this wretched planet will be dead in a few short weeks. Dominator is our *only chance* to get away to another planet. It's *our* future and he's left without me!'

In her heart she realised that there had been something amiss in the relationship with her clone for some time. The words of Myrddin came back to haunt her, "Do you have any idea just how much he hates you?". No, surely it couldn't be true? Her own flesh and blood turned against her? It wasn't possible!

Yet she'd heard nothing from Gulag for days now. She'd tried several times to contact him both by standard telecommunications and mental thought. But, he'd always been 'unavailable' when she'd contacted the rogue group restoring the ancient vessel. Her mental calls had also gone unanswered. Now she had to face the possibility that the clone she had created in the image of her ancient lover had indeed turned his hand against her.

Pollowzki coughed and mumbled, 'Err...I'm afraid there's more bad news Envoy.'

Nimue turned on him, her anger barely under control. 'What? What did you say?' she shouted at him. 'Speak up you miserable wretch! What news?'

He took a deep breath, looked her in the face and said, 'Rumours about the appearance of the Emperor have spread across Caranak and cities across the Empire. Factions of the Democratic Front have been spreading the stories instigated by Hillmead and Shalok. There is wide spread rioting.'

'What do I care about a few mobs!' she screamed. 'Send the troops out to regain control! Declare a state of emergency! Why hasn't the military council done this already? All I'm concerned about is the Dominator!'

Pollowzki sighed and resigned himself to his fate. The Envoy's plans were falling apart around her and it was beginning to look like he'd backed the wrong side. If Nimue didn't kill him for giving her the bad news, the military council probably would. That is if the police and mob attacking the building didn't get him first.

'I'm afraid that it looks like the military council have decided to sit this one out and see what happens Envoy,' he told her. 'All troops have, for the time being, been confined to barracks. The only military action to be taken is against the Dominator. The council is not openly defying you, but nor will they openly support you.'

Nimue sat down on the corner of the stage suddenly drained of emotion. How could her plans have gone so astray? It was inconceivable! If the Dominator was destroyed, or worse, left without her, she would be stranded on a dying planet. It was all Myrddin's fault—once more he had interfered in matters that had taken her years, decades even centuries to plan.

It was time to finally put an end to his meddling, his interference. Their last confrontation in orbit around Earth had led to a stalemate, one of many over the millennia of their mutual existence. However, she was determined that the final conflict between brother and sister would take place here, in this television centre tonight. Calm spread through her mind and soul. She became cold, calculating once more. The events of that night weren't about Dyason politics, or about the military council and the civil riots taking place throughout the Empire. No, tonight's events were about one thing, the battle between Myrddin and herself. Before the night was out one of them would live, the other would die. The survivor would go on to reap the rewards. Nimue was determined that she *would* be the winner. She *would* defeat Myrddin.

The Imperial Navy would board and take the Dominator and once she had defeated Myrddin she could claim the ancient starship for herself. She would then take great pleasure in slowly killing the traitorous clone with her bare hands.

With a new resolve she turned on the Pollowzki and demanded, 'Is there any sign of the Emperor and the human among that rabble outside?' Nimue referred to the battle raging outside the television centre. The sounds of gunfire and explosions could be heard faintly inside the studio despite the sound proofing.

'No Envoy,' Pollowzki replied. 'We found the stolen armoured personnel carrier they were travelling in. Unfortunately by the time our troops had fought their way to the vehicle it was abandoned.'

Nimue sat and thought about that for a moment. It seemed unlikely that Myrddin and his group would attempt to force their way through the front of the building. There was simply too much fighting going on. Myrddin wouldn't risk the Emperor's life in such a manner. So her brother would attempt to gain access by another route. For a moment it occurred to her that he might try teleportation in the same manner as he had in the Imperial bed chamber. However, she knew from experience just how unpredictable using their talents to physically move themselves through space was. No, Myrddin would be looking for a more conventional route.

'Have you sealed all the entrances to the building,' she snapped at the weasel-faced ex-policeman.

'Yes of course Nimue,' he answered looking at her with a confused expression. The speed at which she changed track in one conversation always left him behind.

Nimue drummed a rhythm on the stage with her finger nails. She thought hard—if all the entrances were sealed Myrddin would have to find another way in. She looked up at the studio spotlights and an idea came to her.

'Where does all the power come from?' she asked.

'I'm sorry Envoy?' Pollowzki stuttered. 'I don't understand the question.'

Nimue stood up and pointed at the studio lighting. 'All this equipment needs large quantities of power. Where does it come from?'

'Well there's an electricity sub-station about half a klick away,' came the reply.

Of course! That's where Myrddin would enter the television centre; along the underground power conduit from the sub-station! She span around and headed for the exit calling after, 'Gather a squad of my personal guard and follow me Pollowzki. I'm expecting visitors and need to arrange a reception.'

Hillmead opened the service hatch and thankfully dropped to the floor of the basement. Quickly he scanned the power junction room and once sure it was deserted he beckoned for the others to join him. The Emperor Alorne clambered out first still holding on to his assault rifle. Hillmead reckoned the old relic was actually enjoying all the excitement. After centuries of being suspended in a state of near death all this action was probably the most exciting thing ever to happen to him.

Shalok and Myrddin followed close behind with the four cops taking up the rear. Shalok stretched and groaned quietly. The tunnel had only been high enough for them to move along if they were bent double. Hillmead opened the door to the power junction room a couple of millimetres and peered up and down the corridor—it was deserted. He pulled the door wide and gestured for the police squad to move out first, followed by the Emperor and Myrddin. Hillmead and Shalok took up the rear.

They moved quickly through the deserted corridors of the television centre. They could hear the battle between Nimue's personal guard and the mob raging outside. Occasionally as they passed a window they saw the orange glow of flames and tracer lighting up the dark sky. The television centre had obviously been evacuated of personnel and the troops were concentrated outside the building, which was fine by him. The only problem they faced now was figuring out how to operate the cameras and transmission equipment.

The cop at the front peered through a set of double doors and beckoned for Hillmead who moved forward. The doors led to the main studio and inside he could see cameras, lights and a transmission control room. This was what they were looking for. Cautiously he slipped through the door into the studio, the others following close behind. The studio looked as deserted as the rest of the building. At one end was a stage set up with the scenery from a popular soap opera; it looked like the place had only just been abandoned. He stepped onto the stage and looked around. With any luck they wouldn't have too many problems getting the lights and cameras back on.

Hillmead turned to Myrddin and the Emperor and was just about to speak when all the lights in the studio were suddenly switched on and the stage was bathed in light. There was the sound of multiple assault rifles being cocked and through the glare Hillmead could just see that the gallery circling the studio was filled with Nimue's shock troops.

'Ah, at last!' said a familiar cold voice. 'I was beginning to think you would never turn up!'

CHAPTER TWENTY

EXCALIBUR. IN THE VICINITY OF ALPHEBUS

The battle was not going well. The Imperial X34 Snub fighters were proving to be an equal match to the Flyships. It was only the superior flying skill of Excalibur's pilots that was keeping the Imperial attack at bay. Moss knew that eventually the Imperial Navy's superior numbers would swamp the defenders and then both Excalibur and the Dominator would be vulnerable. He had to do something about it.

'Gulag,' he called in his mind to the clone.

'What is it Moss?' came the response, 'I'm a little busy here. We're trying to find ways of overriding the computer and getting us the hell out of here.'

'Are you having any joy?' Moss asked.

'Negative. The computer keeps going on about not moving position until the time of the rendezvous, whatever that means.'

'Okay Gulag stick with it,' Moss replied. 'I'm going to move Excalibur. We're sitting ducks here. That battle-station is going to come into range any moment and with the heavy armament that thing packs we're going to be in big trouble.'

'I know that Moss!' Gulag told him. 'But there's not a lot I can do when I can't even move this bloody thing! We've got control of our defensive weaponry so I can take pot-shots at those X34s but that's all I can do.'

'That's why I'm going to move the Excalibur in on that battle-station. It should take the pressure off you and draw their fire away. If I can inflict enough damage they may call off those Snub fighters.'

'Fine. You do that Moss!' Gulag responded. 'We'll keep battling it out with this bloody contraption.'

'Try being nice to it,' Moss suggested.

'Very funny,' came the reply and the connection cut.

Moss explained his plan to Black and the rest of the bridge officers, then willed Excalibur away from the Dominator and toward the Imperial battle-station. However, he got no response. A wave of panic swept over Moss—surely whatever was wrong with the Dominator's computer hadn't infected Excalibur as well? He extended his mind and felt for the familiar presence of the sentient computer that over the years had become his friend.

'Excalibur,' he called, 'what's going on? Why won't you respond to my commands?'

The soft female tones of the computer entered his mind and answered, 'I'm sorry Moss, but to move position now would be a breach of my primary directive. We must remain here until the time of the rendezvous.'

'Excalibur, what rendezvous is this?' Moss asked in frustration. 'Both you and Dominator keep making references to a rendezvous but don't explain what or who it is you're expecting. Please Excalibur, if we don't move, that battle-station is going to blow us to pieces.'

'*I regret not being able to co-operate Moss,*' Excalibur apologised, '*but it is vital that we remain here. I am afraid it is up to you to deal with any hostile action taken against us. However, it may be possible to combine the fire-power of Dominator and myself to protect us from that battle-station.*'

'What's do you mean you can't co-operate? We're at serious risk here! Why link the fire-power of both ships when we can just move out of bloody range!'

'*I'm sorry Moss I can't do that, nor can I say anymore.*' Excalibur apologised once more then cut the mind link.

Moss leapt out of the helmsman's couch and swore, 'Shit, I don't bloody believe it!'

Black turned and saw his face. Something was obviously very wrong. 'What is it Moss?' he asked. 'What's gone wrong?'

'Excalibur's refusing the helm. She won't budge, just like Dominator,' he told Black his face a picture of frustration. 'She keeps going on about some bloody rendezvous just like the Dominator's computer. I'm worried that whatever is infecting Dominator is infecting Excalibur as well.'

'She started doing some strange things just before we left Earth,' Black explained to him. 'Excalibur said something about a rendezvous then. I presumed meeting up with the Dominator *was* the rendezvous.'

'Obviously not,' Moss replied striding across the bridge to the weapons officer. 'I refuse to believe that Excalibur would refuse to respond without good reason. The fact that the Dominator is doing the same thing has to indicate that some event is yet to happen. Though God only knows what!'

'Well I hope whatever it is happens soon. We're under serious pressure from those Snub fighters and once that Imperial battle-station comes into range *we're* in real trouble,' Black stated.

'I realise that, but we'll just have to battle it out. There's nothing more we can do for now.' Moss started to examine the weapons console. 'Excalibur said something about combining the primary weapons of the Dominator and Excalibur to match the fire power of the battle-station,' he said reading the readouts on the console.

'Sir, we don't have access to the primary weapons system. It's had a fault ever since...' the weapons officer looked at her monitor once more with a frown then said, 'Sorry sir, I was wrong. I don't know what happened there, but the primary weapons system is now on line!'

Moss looked up at Black and smiled grimly. 'See, I told you she wouldn't let us down. Excalibur will do just enough to stop us from being blasted to pieces, but she won't allow us to move from this position. She will only give us access to the ship's systems *she* believes we need to operate. Now listen; if I'm right communications will have been restored to the Dominator. Get on to them and explain that we want to feed our targeting system into their primary weapons to combine fire power.'

Black scanned the weapons monitor and got a nod from the communications officer. 'Okay,' he agreed, 'we can do that. It scares the shit out of me to think we only have partial control over our fate, but we'll give your plan a try. What about you? What are you going to do?'

'There's no point in me staying here with the helm inoperative. You can run the bridge better than I can,' he told him. 'Is my Flyship still in the launch tube.'

'Of course it is. Nobody was brave enough to want to fly your personal mount. They were too afraid you might take offence.'

Moss gave a short laugh. 'Just for once my undeserved reputation has done me a service. Well, I'm going to launch and do what I can to put a hole in that battle-station. Paul, Han and the other pilots will need all the help thay can get.'

Black nodded in agreement and began barking orders to the operations officer. Moss headed for the turbo-lift thinking to himself that Black had changed as much as the rest of them in the past few weeks. He was now very much a starship captain.

The dark mass of the battle-station revolved slowly around the planet in geo-stationary orbit. The construction gangs had gone, their work completed. The needle-nosed shape that had first fooled the reconnaissance team on the *Observer* had been buried under a mass of carbuncles each sprouting lethal looking weaponry. The largest of these was nearly half a kilometre across and could have been mistaken for a radio telescope if it weren't for the bright green particle beam that erupted from the epicentre and reached out to the sparkling vessels catching the sunlight in the distance.

The beam swathed a path through two Flyships and a Snub fighter on its way to the Excalibur where it gouged a breach in the outer hull.

'Jesus! Did you see that?' Sandpiper yelled from his position as wingman to Jenson. 'The Imperial Navy must have perfected a particle beam weapon. It just cut a gash in Excalibur like a knife through butter and took out two Flyships in the process.!'

Jenson broke away from his pursuit of a Snub fighter and turned to look at Excalibur. The damage wasn't terminal, but if the battle-station kept up the barrage Excalibur would eventually take a fatal hit.

'I saw it okay Han. We've got to take out that battle-station, or Excalibur and Dominator are finished!' Jenson answered. 'I can't believe the stupidity of the Dyason military. Their planet has only a few weeks left before it becomes uninhabitable and they're putting all their efforts into building a weapon like that! It defies belief!'

'Gold leader this is Moss do you read?' Jenson heard in his head.

'I hear you Moss. Are you piloting your Flyship?' Jenson responded.

'Roger that. Excalibur is refusing to move position, just like the Dominator. She keeps going on about some rendezvous,' Moss explained.

'What? Oh Jesus!' Jenson exclaimed, 'What the hell is going on?'

'I don't know Paul, but I'm more use out here with you boys than on the bridge. Can I make a suggestion?'

'You're right we're under desperate pressure here. It's good to have you with us,' Jenson thought back, 'go ahead.'

'If I lead the corvettes and 53 squadron into an attack on that battle-station can you take the remaining Flyships and keep those X34s off our backs?'

'We can try Moss,' Jenson answered, 'I don't know what else we can do. We have to stop that beast somehow. Let's do it!'

Moss commanded the corvettes and Flyships of 53 squadron to follow him in loose attack formation and they accelerated toward the Imperial battle-station, the X34 fighters snapping at their heels.

Hillmead judged the distance between himself and the cover afforded by the lighting gantries and thought about making a dash for it.

'Don't try it,' Myrddin told him in a voice that broke no argument. 'You'll never make it. Besides it's me she wants, Hillmead, not you.'

He looked at the ancient human, realised he was right and slowly lowered his weapon to the floor. Shalok, the Emperor and the police squad reluctantly followed suit. Pollowzki and three of Nimue's personal guard stepped out from behind the scenery and picked the weapons up off the studio floor. Pollowzki stopped in front of Hillmead and looked him in the eye. Hillmead coughed up some phlegm and spat at the traitor.

'You're beneath contempt you scum!' he snarled at the Dyason he had once considered to be his closest friend.

Pollowzki slammed the butt of a rifle into Hillmead's stomach who collapsed winded, onto the floor. He raised the rifle again ready to strike once more but a series of conflicting emotions raced across his face. Slowly he lowered the rifle and walked away shoulders stooped. Hillmead watched him through narrowed eyes breathing hard.

Myrddin stepped forward and faced Nimue. 'That's enough,' he said to her in a cold menacing voice. 'It's me you really want isn't it? Well I'm here now, why don't we get on with it?'

The Envoy ignored him, her eyes were transfixed by the face of the Emperor. Alorne returned her gaze with clear focused eyes, eyes that were more focused than at any other time in the several centuries of his existence.

'Why?' he asked in a sad voice full of remorse. 'Why are you doing this Nimue? Why are you killing my people? Did you learn nothing from me? All that time and effort we spent unifying the many kingdoms and you turned it into this—a cold, corrupt regime that has poisoned the land and all the people on it. How can you be so twisted, so evil?'

Nimue hissed and tore her gaze away from the face of her one-time lover. 'Shut up you fool! What do you know? You never were anything but a pathetic weakling! You could have had it all; shared with me an Empire that spanned light years, but your mind was too weak, too feeble!'

There was a crash and a commotion from outside the studio. Hillmead realised that Koerst and his rabble army had broken through the cordon of Nimue's personal shock troops and had stormed into the building. Pollowzki shouted at the troops on the gantry and they ran to secure the corridor outside the studio.

'Your time's nearly up Nimue,' Myrddin told her. 'If that mob gets in here they'll rip you and your henchman apart. It's time for the final conflict, you know as well as I do that this is the place and the time. Are you ready?'

'You're right brother dearest, this finally *is* the time. The universe cannot sustain us both; I'm as ready as I will ever be. Prepare to die Myrddin,' she answered in a cold, deadly voice.

Myrddin stepped up onto the stage and faced her on the set of the soap-opera. They stood a few metres apart eyes locked. Imperceptibly at first, then with an ever-increasing intensity an aura of shimmering blue light surrounded each figure like a halo. As the intensity increased so did the size of the aura until the two combined to form one glowing, pulsating mass of light.

Hillmead watched as Nimue raised her hand and pointed one, long finger at Myrddin. The ancient human also raised his hand and pointed at Nimue. To his amazement he saw waves of even more intense blue-green light cascade down their arms to the tips of their fingers then shoot out like bolts of lightning meeting in a blaze of light and pyrotechnics at a spot equidistant from them both. The bolts of energy grew and waned in a battle of wills that sent a shower of sparks flying through the studio and made everyone's hair stand on end.

The four remaining troops of Nimue's guard looked at the battle of wills taking place on the stage, then looked at each other. This wasn't what they'd joined the Envoy's personal guard for. They turned and fled the studio. Hillmead, Shalok, the Emperor and Pollowzki ignored them as they stood transfixed watching the incredible combat.

Up on the stage the battle continued unabated. Myrddin and Nimue stood as still as statues, rooted to the spot, as the aura played about them in a cascading display of pyrotechnics. The ball of flame that was the point at which the bolts of energy met, constantly changed shape and position. One moment it would slip toward Myrddin, the next moment it would drift toward Nimue. But at no time did that lethal ball of pure energy, of cosmic power, really get close to either combatant.

Out of the corner of his eye Hillmead saw the Emperor begin to move toward Nimue, a look of utter sadness on his face. He shuffled up onto the stage his face and body ageing with every step. The life force that had been sustaining his youthful features appeared to be drained by the aura surrounding Myrddin and Nimue. Pollowzki also noticed the Emperor move and raised his assault rifle. Hillmead saw his opportunity and leapt up at the traitor, bowling the weasel-faced Dyason to the floor. Pollowzki released his grip on the rifle, and Hillmead pushed it away with contempt, then drew a blade from the folds of his environment suit. The flashing blue aura reflected in the eyes of the traitor as Hillmead held the knife to his throat.

'No please!' Pollowzki pleaded. 'I didn't have any choice; I had to do what she told me! You don't know what she's like!'

'How many good people died because of your treachery?' Hillmead hissed, pushing the blade hard against Pollowzki's jugular. 'I gave you my trust, my friendship and you abused it! You threw everything away for that bitch—now you'll pay the price!'

Hillmead took one last look at the one person he had considered to be his friend. Then he swept the blade across Pollowzki's throat. The traitor's blood gushed out staining Hillmead's environment suit. Pollowzki gurgled, choking on his own body fluids, hands flailing ineffectually at Hillmead. He continued to struggle weakly for a few moments then stopped moving.

Shalok ran over and knelt beside Hillmead, grabbing his arm and pointing at the mortal combat still raging on the stage. He tore his eyes away from Pollowzki's dead body and looked up at the raging battle of wills and saw the Emperor. Alorne had moved as if in a trance until he stood behind Nimue who appeared to be unaware of his presence, as did Myrddin. They were lost in the blue aura, their bodies and souls locked together.

The Emperor raised his now weak and feeble arms in front of him in a gesture of grotesque embrace. Hillmead and Shalok heard him call out in a tortured voice, 'No more my love! There must be no more killing! My children have suffered enough, it's time to leave this world and we shall leave it together! Let us be one for eternity!'

Emperor Alorne stepped into the aura of shimmering blue light and embraced his ancient lover. Nimue screamed in horror as she realised what was happening. Alorne held her in a death grip as the ball of cascading energy flashed toward them. It hit the bodies of Nimue and the Emperor in a flash of blinding pyrotechnics. It looked and felt as if a star had exploded there in the studio. A tornado of cosmic power raged around the stage vaporising everything it touched streaming showers of pure energy. Myrddin was thrown across the stage as the blue nimbus focused on the entwined bodies of the pair of ancient lovers. Hillmead and Shalok turned their eyes away, but they were sure they could hear the final piercing scream of Nimue as she was devoured by the raging energy storm.

In a final explosion of energy the torrent of cosmic power flashed across the studio then died. The light faded, darkness and a deathly silence befell the studio. Hillmead and Shalok held each other tightly for several minutes amazed to find themselves still alive. Shalok sobbed quietly into the blood-stained shoulder of Hillmead's environment suit. Slow tears of fear, relief, anger and sadness drew tracks across his own face.

The studio lights came back on and they saw Myrddin collapsed on the stage. They ran over and

Shalok bent down to check if the battered human was still breathing.

'Is he alive?' Hillmead whispered urgently looking at his pale, drained face.

'Just about,' Shalok answered lifting Myrddin's head and protectively placing it in her lap. 'He's passed out, his breathing is shallow but even. I think he'll live.'

Hillmead stepped over to where Nimue and the Emperor had stood in their last embrace only moments before. There was nothing there; the stage props had gone, as had the scenery, everything had been sucked into the maelstrom. He bent down and ran one finger through a thick layer of ash that had covered everything including the gantries and cameras.

'It's over,' a voice said from the rear of the studio.

Hillmead looked up and saw the group standing near the entrance transfixed by what they had seen. Commissioner Koerst hobbled forward. He was in a bad way, his uniform stained with blood from a head wound, one arm hanging limp by his side, but he *was* alive. Using an assault rifle as a crutch, Koerst moved to the bottom of the stage.

'We saw everything and so did everyone else in the Empire,' Koerst told him in a tired but triumphant voice.

Hillmead looked confused. 'I don't understand,' he said blankly, unable to focus his mind on the present. The final image of Nimue and the Emperor was still burnt onto his retina.

'The cameras were still on and transmitting when you entered the studio. The television centre was transmitting a live soap opera when Nimue's shock troops arrived. They evacuated the centre so fast the equipment was left running. Everyone in the Empire heard and saw what happened. The images of that horrific scene were broadcast live to the four corners of the globe.' Koerst explained in an exhausted voice.

'I see,' Hillmead said in a dry monotone.

'Nimue's goons have given up the fight, we've taken the television centre! Now that those pictures have been broadcast the military council will be forced to resign. Well done Hillmead. As I said *it's over!'*

Hillmead looked at the unconscious body of Myrddin then stared down at the wounded police commissioner. In a disbelieving voice he said, 'Is it really Koerst? Is it *really?'*

CHAPTER TWENTY ONE

DYASON ORBIT

The Flyship flew low over the surface of the battle-station jinking wildly to avoid the mass of cannon-fire being hurled at it. Moss flew as close to the surface as he dared so that the gun turrets were depressed to their minimum elevation. Most of the tracer rounds flew over the top of the Flyship missing it by scant metres.

He banked hard to port and lined up with the massive structure welded on to the hull of the battle-station. This was the housing for the particle beam generator that was pounding away at Excalibur. He loosed off a burst of laser fire at the beam's aiming mechanism, but he barely scorched the surface. Swearing, he activated one of the JK50 missiles carried in the Flyship's weapons bay; extending his mind he concentrated on the particle beam generator, locked the missile's guidance system and fired. The missile flew away from the Flyship. Moss pulled the nose up and shot away from the surface of the battle-station as the missile found its target and exploded.

'Good shooting!' his wing man called out excitedly. 'It's a direct hit!'

Moss scanned the Flyship's sensors, shook his head and answered, 'It was a direct hit Beta-two, but we barely scratched the armour plating. We'll need a lot more concentrated fire-power before we can take that particle beam out!'

'I'm beginning my attack run now Beta-one.' The wingman rolled toward the battle-station and began his descent but pulled up short. 'Look out leader! Bogey behind you!' Beta-two shouted desperately, seeing a Snub fighter lock onto his tail.

Moss swore and hurled the Flyship into an evasive manoeuvre. He should have seen the Snub fighter follow him up from the surface of the battle-station. Laser fire from the Imperial X34 shot past his starboard wing tip and he broke hard to port piling on the g-forces. Beta-two, tried to close in on the attacking Snub fighter. Moss tried to manoeuvre into a position where his wingman could get in a clear shot at the X34 but just as Beta-two finally got into a good position, lethal gun fire being thrown up from the battle-station's gun emplacements found its mark. The pilot screamed as the Flyship was turned into a fire-ball.

Moss didn't have time to feel remorse at the loss of his wingman; the Snub fighter was still locked onto his tail firing short bursts from his chain gun. Moss dove back toward the surface of the battle-station and flew between the gun emplacements and towering sensor arrays as if they were the canyons and gullies of the training ground back on the Earth's moon. Down here the Imperial pilot would have to be far more careful when firing his guns. Without the effects of gravity and air resistance, the cannon shells of the Snub fighter wouldn't loose any speed or momentum—they just kept going with the same power and kinetic energy until they hit something regardless of distance. Down near the outer hull of the battle-station the X34 pilot was just as likely to hit part of the superstructure as the Flyship. To be sure of a kill the Imperial pilot would have to move in close, very close—which was exactly what Moss wanted.

He let the Snub fighter gradually get closer and closer to him as he flew between the gaps in the battle-station's superstructure, then just as it appeared that the Imperial pilot had a definite kill, Moss flexed his muscles, the nose of the Flyship reared up and he shot away from the surface once more. The Snub fighter immediately attempted to follow his move but Moss was prepared for this. He applied full reverse thrust and the Flyship decelerated rapidly, the g-forces making Moss grunt painfully as the straps dug into his flesh. He nearly blacked out, but not quite. With a grin of satisfaction he saw the bogey flash past his Flyship taken completely unawares. It was a perfect application of the manoeuvre he had practised so many times before. One, two, three, that was it, the perfect firing position. Moss willed the lasers to fire a full salvo and he saw the bogey take multiple impacts and disintegrate. Got the bugger! He flew straight through the debris of the Snub fighter and plied the power. His scorched and battered Flyship flew toward the corvettes holding just out of range of the Battle-station's secondary armament.

'Beta-one, Moss, the is the *Elgin*,' Jennifer called from the bridge of the corvette. 'Was your attack on the power generator successful?'

'Negative *Elgin*,' he replied grimly, 'the particle beam generator is surrounded in armour plating that must be over a metre thick. Both my lasers and missiles caused no discernable damage. I also lost my wing man in the attack. Have Blue and Gold squadron's had any success with the main parabolic dish?'

'Negative Moss. Jenson and Sandpiper both led an attack but their flights were decimated by the Snub fighters and defensive fire. Only one missile from each attack hit the dish and they had no apparent effect on the particle beam. Excalibur is still taking hits—the outer hull has been breached in several places. At this rate it's a battle of attrition that we cannot win!'

Moss swore to himself. He couldn't believe that both Excalibur and Dominator's computers still refused to allow them to move the ships. The way things were going neither vessel would survive long enough to make the rendezvous the computers kept on about.

'Are Paul and Han all right?' he asked Jennifer, worried about his two friends.

'They're both a bit battered but still flying,' she told him. 'They're concentrating on keeping those Snub fighters at bay.'

'Okay,' Moss said decisively, 'I'll join them and keep the X34s away from you and the other corvette's. I want you to then concentrate all your weapons on the power generator of that particle beam. If Excalibur and Dominator can get their shit together and power up their primary weapons the combined fire-power may be enough to punch through that armour plating. Have you got that Jennifer?'

'Roger that Moss. Be careful!' she confirmed. Moss acknowledged and sped off to engage the remaining Snub fighters.

Colmarrie moved silently down the service tunnel, sniffing the air like an animal stalking it's prey—which was exactly what she was doing. As soon as she'd arrived on the Dominator the mutant leader had felt the presence of Tychivesk, a creature she had vowed to kill. She knew now that he had killed Neehmad in cold blood and had been responsible for their capture during the attack on the Imperial air base. Gulag believed Tychivesk worked for him, but Colmarrie reckoned he was and always had been, an Imperial goon.

It was actually the Dyason's thoughts she was following rather than his scent, although in her mind the two were very similar—they both stank of shit. She crawled along the service tunnel on her hands and knees because it wasn't high enough for her to stand upright. After a few hundred metres she came to an opened service hatch which had been labelled by one of the ship's crew as 'Primary weapon power supply controls'.

Colmarrie eased the hatch open and took a look. The area beyond was small, just big enough for two or three people with a single work station and access to a major power junction. The panel was off the junction board and she could just make out somebody buried in the numerous fibre-optic connections. She didn't need to see a face to know it was Tychivesk!

In one fluid movement that belied her size, she leapt out of the service tunnel and grabbed Tychivesk throwing him against the far bulkhead. His eyes widened with fear and he muttered, 'Colmarrie what are you doing here?'

'I was going to ask you the same question,' she retorted.

'There's a problem with the fibre optics...I...well, I was fixing it!' he stuttered unconvincingly.

'What with a wire-cutter?' she said menacingly. 'Come, come my friend—you don't really expect me to believe that do you?'

'I don't know what you're talking about!' Tychivesk continued to stammer, a wild, hunted look in his eyes.

'Ah but you do! Of course you do!' she exclaimed. 'Remember the attack on the airbase and the Imperial goons waiting for us in the yard?'

Tychivesk violently shook his head, 'I had nothing to do with that! I swear!'

Colmarrie smiled at him in the same way a cat smirks at a rodent just before it kills it. 'Of *course* you had something to do with that Tychivesk,' she continued in a purring, deadly voice. 'After all, you *were* the one to tell them that we were going to make the attack. Then there was the little incident with poor Neehmad who you just *had* to kill in cold blood. Then there were all those Imperial Snub fighters just *waiting* to attack and *now* you're attempting to sabotage the primary weapons! I'm sorry my friend, but once an Imperial goon, *always* an Imperial goon!'

Tychivesk look around desperately for somewhere to run to, but there was nowhere to hide in the small junction room. In desperation he threw the wire-cutter at Colmarrie and reached for his hand gun, but she was on top of him before he could raise the muzzle. She dodged the wire cutter and swiped the gun out of his fist. Then she placed her hands around his neck and squeezed. His feet were lifted off the ground and he thrashed around beating at her hands and body with his fists, but to no avail. His face turned red, his eyes bulged and his tongue swelled. She kept the pressure on for several minutes until his struggling stopped, then with a roar of triumph she snapped his neck and threw Tychivesk's carcass against the bulkhead.

The operations officer turned to Gulag and exclaimed, 'That's it sir! We've done it! Communications are back on line and we have a targeting link with Excalibur for the primary weapons!'

Gulag span round in the captain's chair. 'Good! Well done ops. Get on to the Excalibur and tell them that we're ready to fire at their command,' he ordered. 'I don't suppose that the helm is operating as well?'

'I'm afraid not sir!' the helmsman replied. 'The computer still has us locked out of the flight system. We're not going anywhere.'

'Damn,' he cursed. 'Well keep at it.'

The helmsman acknowledged. Gulag saw on the viewer the main laser cannons built into Excalibur and Dominator fire simultaneously. The combined power of both laser cannons cut a path across the hull of the Imperial battle-station. He gave a grunt of satisfaction; well at least they were now returning fire, but he knew from first-hand experience just how heavy the armour plating on the battle-station was. It would take more than a couple of hits to breach the hull and that would take time they simply didn't have. The Excalibur's outer hull had already been breached in a couple of places—a few more hits and she would breakup.

He *had* to move the ship. Although the Dominator hadn't been targeted by the particle beam yet, that would all change if Excalibur was knocked out the battle. There was also the threat of boarding. The Flyships had already intercepted and destroyed three Imperial shuttles filled with assault troops. If the battle-station launched another task force and they managed to reach the Dominator, Gulag knew he didn't have sufficient crew numbers to repel a serious assault.

It was dangerous, it was risky, he knew that, but he was determined that no one was going to take the Dominator away from him and that included the bloody computer! It was time to seriously consider the final resort. As the bridge crew worked and fought around him, Gulag sat in the captain's chair and mentally prepared himself for the final act.

Black stood on the bridge of the Excalibur and grimly watched as the combined force of the two vessels' laser cannons hit back at the Imperial battle-station. It felt good to be finally punching back. Excalibur had taken numerous hits from the particle beam and he had all his damage control teams working on the outer hull, trying to seal up the breaches. It was dangerous work to be outside the ship during a battle and he'd already lost several work teams, hit by further attacks from the battle-station.

He'd asked, pleaded, begged for Excalibur to move away from the Imperial battle-station, but she had flatly refused. Excalibur was still waiting for the mythical rendezvous and until it took place they would remain motionless in space. Black was by now almost certain it never would take place—they would all die waiting for an event that was *never* going to happen.

'Excalibur this is Gold leader,' Black heard Jenson call.

'Go ahead Gold leader,' Black responded.

'The combined fire-power of Excalibur, Dominator and the corvettes is beginning to have an effect on the battle-station. We're beginning to see wisps of vapour indicating that the hull is being breached,' Jenson told them, his voice distorted by g-forces as he continued to dog-fight with the Snub fighters. 'However, you've *got* to concentrate your fire on the particle beam generator. I've got the co-ordinates locked into my targeting computer, I'll send them to you now.'

The weapons officer turned and nodded to Black indicating that they had received the co-ordinates.

'Copy that Gold leader. We're adjusting our target point now,' Black told Jenson. 'Do you have any indication of how many hits it will take to destroy the generator?'

'Negative,' Jenson replied. 'Hang on in there Excalibur!'

'We'll keep praying Gold leader!'

The weapons officer tapped in the new information and the laser cannons fired in harmony once more. Black stood over the weapons console hoping the one hit would be sufficient to take out the generator, but it wasn't. The laser cannons began to cycle through once more. Excalibur juddered as the battle-station's particle beam found its mark again.

'Damage report!' he called.

'Decks thirty-seven through to forty-eight have been breached. Sealing bulkhead doors now!'

Shit! Black knew that there were crew on those decks. He just hoped they had a chance to get out before all the atmosphere escaped and the bulkheads were sealed. They were taking heavy casualties and it made him mad—what was the purpose to it all?

The navigation officer checked the readings of the sensors once more then turned to Black and said in alarm, 'Sir the worm-hole is opening once more. I believe there's a ship coming through!'

Black got out his seat in excitement. Good God! Was this the rendezvous Excalibur had been waiting for? Could he be wrong and there actually was going to be a rendezvous? Were they finally going to get their chance to move? 'What sort of ship?' he demanded.

The navigation officer scanned his console once more and shook his head. 'It's too early to say sir! We'll have to wait until it leaves the worm-hole before we can identify it.'

'Put the worm-hole on the main viewer,' Black ordered his excitement rising. Something told him that this emerging vessel was the reason they were sitting there taking a punishing. It had never occurred to any of them before that the rendezvous included a third machine. He just hoped it was worth it.

The worm-hole was displayed on the main viewer at the far end of the bridge. It looked a lot like a swirling mist of multicoloured vapour rotating around a central point in an anticlockwise direction. Tendrils of gas reached out like the spokes of a wheel from a broiling central mass. If you could set a summer cloud spinning it would look like this. As Black watched the spinning motion increased in speed and a black-hole emerged at the epicentre. For all the world it appeared like some one had pulled the plug and everything was being sucked into the centre. But this was the opposite from what actually happened.

A massive vessel shot out of the centre of the worm-hole like a projectile from a gun and headed directly for the Excalibur. The last tendrils of vapour were sucked in by the black-hole and with a flash the worm-hole closed behind the alien ship. Black looked at the image of the craft as it sped toward them. He didn't need the sensors to scan it to recognise the alien machine. The ship on the viewer had a delta shaped prow that bled into an elongated boom. This swept into a wedge shaped body with huge intakes on the underside. It was a beautiful, efficient design reminiscent of a swan in flight. It was an exact copy of the Dominator *and* Excalibur.

Moss performed a classic Immelman turn and placed himself directly behind the Snub fighter that was part of a flight attacking the *Elgin*. He closed the distance between himself and the Imperial pilot until there was no doubt of a kill. He willed a salvo of laser fire and the Snub fighter turned into a fireball. Moss peeled away from his latest kill and looked for further custom. As was so often the case in a dog-fight, skies that one minute were full of machines battling it out for supremacy were suddenly devoid of anything.

He scanned the battle-zone. The corvettes, Dominator and Excalibur, were still combining fire power and gradually punching holes in the battle-station. The surviving Flyships were finally gaining the upper hand against the poorly trained Imperial pilots, but Excalibur was still taking hits. The battle hung in the balance.

'The time for the rendezvous has arrived,' Moss heard the gentle tones of Excalibur in his mind.

'What?' Moss thought back at the sentient computer. *'Excalibur? You're back! What's going on? The rendezvous is now?'* There was no reply from the computer.

'Moss, Jenson! Get back here!' Black called urgently over the comm unit.

Moss turned the Flyship on it's axis and blasted back toward the Excalibur. He extended his sensor scanning range and was astonished at what he found. Holy shit! Closing rapidly on the Dominator and Excalibur was a third ship, a ship identical to the other two. It was undoubtedly another sister-ship.

'Black! This is Moss,' he responded. 'I'm on my way. I see we've got more visitors. Black, this is the rendezvous the Excalibur and Dominator have been going on about. They've been waiting for their other sister ship!'

'Moss! Our scanners show that the alien vessel is powering up it's primary weapon!' Black told him his voice anxious and strained. 'If we're fired upon we'll break up. Excalibur can't take anymore hits. We're unable to change the targeting co-ordinates of our own weapons. We've been locked out of the system once more!'

'Hang on in their Black! We're on our way! Just hang on...' Moss shouted, willing the Flyship to accelerate even faster until the g-forces were squeezing him to the verge of consciousness.

'It's too late! They're opening fire! They're...'

There was a triple blast as three laser cannons fired simultaneously, but the target wasn't Excalibur. Moss watched as the multiple laser fire struck the Imperial battle-station. There was a flash and the particle beam generator vaporised and the armoured hull of the Imperial Navy's last folly began to collapse. The carbuncles added to the superstructure began to break away, spinning off into the void. One of huge stub wings complete with powerplant broke away from the main body which began to rotate slowly. Gas vented from numerous breaches in the hull exploded in huge sheets of flame. Suddenly, there was the blinding flash of a nuclear explosion followed by shock waves that swept across the corvettes and the remaining Flyships throwing them around like toys.

When his eyesight returned Moss looked back to where the battle-station had been only moments before. There was nothing left of the Militarist's final dream; their foolish greed was now nothing more than an expanding ball of gas and glowing wreckage.

When Gulag saw the arrival of the third sister ship and the destruction of the battle-station he knew it was time to carry out the final act. The threat of Imperial intervention may have disappeared in a cloud of gas, but the threat of alien intervention was even greater. He was as determined as ever that the Dominator would remain his and he was prepared to go to extraordinary measures to secure his claim. Gulag ignored the requests for orders and the activity on the bridge. He ignored the call from the communications officer about a three way message between Dominator, Excalibur and the alien vessel. He was oblivious to the words *Point Zero.*

Gulag sat in the captain's chair, but his mind was elsewhere. He knew of the experiments carried out on other clones. He knew of the theory that the mind alone could open a hole in the space-time continuum and move objects light years in a fraction of a second. He knew of the results and failures of those experiments, but they had been carried out by others not himself. Those failures had been the result of using flawed subjects a problem *he* wouldn't suffer from. After all, wasn't he the *perfect* clone? He extended his mind and probed at the fourth dimension, that place beyond the three dimensional universe they all lived in. The barrier into that dimension was like a solid wall, massive and impenetrable. But Gulag was determined to break through that barrier. He *would* succeed!

To the alarm of everyone on the bridge Gulag began to groan incoherently, his body arching and shaking in spasms that swept through him. As they watched in horror some sort of metamorphosis was taking place. His skin was becoming translucent, as if something were broiling underneath his skin. The crew stopped whatever they were doing and watched with unbelieving eyes as Gulag's skin turned black. But, black was a colour, Gulag's skin had no colour. It was as if the very light was being absorbed from around the bridge of the Dominator and was being sucked into Gulag's writhing body. Console lights dimmed and died and small pinpoints of light flashed across the clone's skin. The flashes became more and more numerous, as if a star cluster were being formed inside his distorted body.

The flashing lights became more and more intense and began to whirl round and round like a vortex. The vortex grew until it spread throughout Gulag's body and then to the crew's disbelief it sprang out of the body and onto the deck of the Dominator. It swept through the bridge absorbing everything and everybody. Then it stormed through the rest of the ship swallowing everything in its path. Within seconds the whole massive bulk of the Dominator was swept up in a vortex. The shape of the ancient vessel became distorted, translucent. A galaxy of stars swam across it becoming more and more intense until it was completely swamped. Then the swirling mass expanded in an explosion of light and energy that lasted for a fraction of a second then vanished. Dominator and everyone onboard was gone.

SO ENDS BOOK TWO OF THE DYASON. THE STORY CONTINUES IN BOOK THREE.

OTHER RIPPING TITLES

THE BATTLE OF BRITAIN MEMORIAL FLIGHT

It all started on September 15th 1945 when a Royal Air Force Spitfire and Hurricane flew over a battered but victorious London in the first ever Battle of Britain flypast. The summer of 1940 when a few pilots and their fighter aircraft held off an aerial Armada had already passed into legend, so it was only fitting that on the anniversary of the Battle of Britain's fiercest fighting, there should be a flypast of a Hurricane and Spitfire to commemorate the Royal Air Force's 'finest hour'.

However, by 1957 nearly all of the thousands of wartime Spitfires and Hurricanes had been reduced to scrap metal. A 'few' dedicated pilots and groundcrew set about the task of keeping at least one example of each of the Royal Air Force's most famous aircraft flying and so was born the Battle of Britain Memorial Flight.

In 1995, fifty years after the end of the Second World War, the Battle of Britain Memorial Flight, attended over 200 events both here in the UK and on the continent. Warren James Palmer and Neil Lawson were there to witness the triumphs and frustrations of the modern day 'few' who maintain and fly the 'jewels of the sky' that are the Lancaster, Hurricane and Spitfires of the BBMF. Given access to archive material never seen before, plus glorious photographs shot by the members of the Flight, Warren and Neil tell the true story of how a handful of dedicated people maintain a living memorial to all those that flew and perished in the skies of a world at war.

With almost two hundred colour photographs the story of the Battle of Britain Memorial Flight shows that it is as much the characters of the pilots and ground crew that bring these classic aircraft to life, as well oiled machinery and aviation fuel.

ISBN 1899884-01-7   £19.95

MINDS OF THE EMPIRE

By the year 2020 the United Nations World Defence Force can finally guarantee the security of every nation on the planet through the use of orbital laser battle stations.

That is until the day the Dyason arrived. The Dyason are humanoid, but not from our star system. In a blitzkrieg attack they wipe out the World Defence Force and within days, force worldwide capitulation, except for a few renegades, mankind is enslaved.

Out of the prison ghettos of London a new hero emerges, a youth with exceptional mental powers. Minds of the Empire follows Moss as he struggles to escape the rubble of London and flee from both the Dyason and the Resistance.

The first book in the Dyason series spans space, time and legend in a fast moving adventure that keeps the adrenaline pumping.

ISBN 1899884-00-9   £4.99

BOTH TITLES ARE AVAILABLE FROM ALL GOOD BOOKSHOPS OR BY DIRECT MAIL FROM MACMILLAN DIRECT ON

01256 302699 (CODE 160)

Cheques should be made payable to Macmillan Direct, Houndmills, Basingstoke, Hampshire, RG21 6XS